To Kenneth Gay
in gratitude for twenty-five years
of patient critical help.

PENGUIN CLASSICS

THE ANGER OF ACHILLES

The Greeks attributed both the *Iliad* and the *Odyssey* to a single poet whom they named Homer. Nothing is known of his life, though the main ancient tradition made him a native of the island of Chios in the east Aegean. His date too is uncertain: most modern scholars place the composition of the *Iliad* in the second half of the eight century BC.

ROBERT GRAVES was born in 1895 in Wimbledon, son of Alfred Perceval Graves, the Irish writer, and Amalia Von Ranke. He went from school to the First World War, where he became a captain in the Royal Welch Fusiliers. His principal calling was poetry, and both his *Selected Poems* and his *Complete Poems* have been published in Penguin. Apart from a year as Professor of English Literature at Cairo University in 1926 he earned his living by writing, mostly historical novels which include: *I, Claudius*; *Claudius the God*; *Count Belisarius*; *Wife to Mr Milton*; *Sergeant Lamb of the Ninth*; *Proceed, Sergeant Lamb*; *The Golden Fleece*; *They Hanged My Saintly Billy* and *The Isles of Unwisdom*. Throughout his writing life he also published over fifty short stories, many of which originally appeared in magazines on both sides of the Atlantic. They have all been brought together in his *Complete Short Stories*. He wrote his autobiography, *Goodbye to All That*, in 1929 and it rapidly established itself as a modern classic. He translated Apuleius, Lucan and Suetonius for the Penguin Classic series and compiled the first modern dictionary of Greek Mythology, *The Greek Myths*. He was elected Professor of Poetry at Oxford in 1961, and made an Honorary Fellow of St John's College, Oxford, in 1971. Robert Graves died on 7 December 1985 in Majorca, his home since 1929. On his death *The Times* wrote of him, 'He will be remembered for his achievements as a prose stylist, historical novelist and memoirist, but above all as the great paradigm of the dedicated poet, "the greatest love poet in English since Donne".'

The Anger of Achilles

HOMER'S *ILIAD*

Translated by ROBERT GRAVES

PENGUIN BOOKS

PENGUIN CLASSICS

Published by the Penguin Group
Penguin Books Ltd, 80 Strand, London WC2R ORL, England
Penguin Group (USA) Inc., 375 Hudson Street, New York, New York 10014, USA
Penguin Group (Canada), 90 Eglinton Avenue East, Suite 700, Toronto, Ontario, Canada M4P 2Y3
(a division of Pearson Penguin Canada Inc.)
Penguin Ireland, 25 St Stephen's Green, Dublin 2, Ireland (a division of Penguin Books Ltd)
Penguin Group (Australia), 250 Camberwell Road, Camberwell, Victoria 3124, Australia
(a division of Pearson Australia Group Pty Ltd)
Penguin Books India Pvt Ltd, 11 Community Centre, Panchsheel Park, New Delhi – 110 017, India
Penguin Group (NZ), 67 Apollo Drive, Rosedale, North Shore 0632, New Zealand
(a division of Pearson New Zealand Ltd)
Penguin Books (South Africa) (Pty) Ltd, 24 Sturdee Avenue,
Rosebank, Johannesburg 2196, South Africa

Penguin Books Ltd, Registered Offices: 80 Strand, London WC2R ORL, England

www.penguin.com

First published in the United States of America by Doubleday & Company, Inc. 1959
Published in Penguin Classics 2008

4

978-0-140-45560-1

www.greenpenguin.co.uk

Contents

CONTENTS

Introduction

The *Homeridae* ('Sons of Homer'), a family guild of Ionian bards based on Chios, enlarged their ancestor's first short draft of the *Iliad* to twenty-four books, and became comprehensively known as 'Homer'. They earned their livelihood by providing good popular entertainment for such festivals as the All-Ionian at Mount Mycale in Lydia, the All-Athenian at Athens, and the four-yearly homage to their patron Apollo at Delos; also, it seems, by going on circuit to various small royal courts where Greek was spoken, from Asia Minor to Sicily, and perhaps even visiting Spain and Western Morocco.

If modern scholars overlook the entertainment motive, dominant in the *Iliad*, and treat Homer as a Virgil, Dante, or Milton, rather than as a Shakespeare or Cervantes, they are doing him a great disservice. The *Iliad*, *Don Quixote* and Shakespeare's later plays are life—tragedy salted with humour; the *Aeneid*, the *Inferno* and *Paradise Lost* are literary works of almost superhuman eloquence, written for fame not profit, and seldom read except as a solemn intellectual task. The *Iliad*, and its later companion-piece, the *Odyssey*, deserve to be rescued from the classroom curse which has lain heavily on them throughout the past twenty-six centuries, and become entertainment once more; which is what I have attempted here. How this curse fell on them can be simply explained.

Other professional story-tellers must have been active in Homer's day, but since not a line of their original work, nor any tradition of it, has survived, we are justified in assuming that, like their ancient Irish, Welsh and Gaelic counterparts, they used prose; reserving verse for incidental passages of religious or dramatic importance only, when they took up their lyres and sang what are still called 'lyrics'. It is probable, however, that court poems had been recited in the glorious Mycenaean civilization of Greece, destroyed by the Dorian invasion not long after the fall of Troy; that they had much in common with those of Ugarit, Accadia, Sumeria and the Hittite kingdom; but that, on the destruction of the Greek royal courts at Mycenae, Pylus, Thebes and elsewhere, prose versions of the tales, adorned with numerous poetic tags, passed into the hands of popular story-tellers.

Such story-tellers survived in Ionia until the Christian era, when Apuleius borrowed their 'Milesian tales' for his *Golden Ass*. Others, called *sgéali*, still practise in Western Ireland, direct successors of the ancient court bards of Munster and Connaught. One characteristic common to them all is an emphasis on departed glories, power and riches, and a love of magnificent, repetitive, old-fashioned language; thus Homer's Greek idioms were no more contemporary in the mid-eighth century B.C., than is the 'fine, hard Old Irish' of the modern Galway *sgéali*. But when a renascence of civilization among the Ionic settlers on the coast of Asia Minor finally closed the Dark Ages, which had lasted from about 1050 B.C. to about 750 B.C., Homer put one of these traditional tales back into verse. What is more, he used the new alphabetic script borrowed from the Phoenicians, to record it in writing. Verse made *The Anger of Achilles* so easily learned by heart, and also exercised so compulsive a charm on his audience (relaxing with wine at their elbows in some royal courtyard), that it became a valuable legacy to Homer's story-telling sons. Their additions are nearly all composed in the spirit of their father, though certain stylistic differences tempt experts to date the various books, or parts of books, from internal evidence.

The dactylic measure which Homer chose may have been an ancient one, since the formal epithets, attributable to Mycenaean days, fit it well; but is less likely to have been used for court epics than for dance-songs around altars. Many of the pastoral, agricultural, and hunting similes which strew the later books and seldom quite suit their contexts, seem authentic festival songs—but of Ionian provenience, because those ruthless lions constantly mentioned in them as preying on flocks and herds were not a feature of Mycenaean Greece, except as *motifs* in Palace art. The *caesuras* that break hexameter lines suggest brief pauses for a stamp or clap; and the final spondee, a longer pause announcing a new forward movement.

The *Iliad* presupposes an earlier story cycle about the events leading up to *The Anger of Achilles*. These were the birth of Helen from Leda's famous swan-egg; the wedding of Peleus and Thetis; the Apple of Discord, thrown by the Goddess Strife, which provoked the Trojan War by causing the Judgement of Paris and his elopement with Helen; the unsuccessful Greek embassy sent to Troy demanding the surrender of Helen and her treasures—we gather that King Priam refused, on the ground that his aunt Hesione, carried off by Heracles from an earlier Sack of Troy, was still a captive in Greece—the recruitment of heroes for the punitive expedition, their landing at Troy, and the first nine years of desultory warfare. The cycle was versified by Stasinus of Cyprus (whom tradition makes Homer's son-in-law) in the nine books of his *Cypria*, composed soon after the *Iliad*. But the *Iliad* assumes popular knowledge of these legends, as also of *The Seven Against Thebes*, *The Labours of Heracles*, and other cycles unconnected with the Trojan War.

Later poets continued the Trojan story, using the same Homeric hexameters: Arctinus of Miletus (Homer's pupil) began his *Aethiopis* where the *Iliad* ended, and closed it with Great Ajax's suicide; Lesches of Lesbos, in his *Little Iliad*, then described the death of Achilles and the departure of the Greeks from Troy. Next came Arctinus' *Sack of Troy*, and Agias of Troezen's *Return of the Greek Heroes*. The *Odyssey* is apparently a rewriting of one such *Return*. That the Homeridae ascribed its authorship to Homer means only that it formed part of their stock-in-trade, and was written by a poet who, for some reason, preferred to be anonymous.

The traditional corpus of prose tales meanwhile remained in being. Though an authorized edition of the *Iliad* and *Odyssey*, published by leading Homeric bards under the patronage of Peisistratus, tyrant of Athens (mid-sixth century B.C.) had given the Homeridae immense prestige, their version of a dramatic event was often rejected by later mythographers in favour of a more popular, and usually more archaic, one. Peisistratus, whose chief adviser Solon travelled widely through the Middle East, saw the advantage of giving his official welcome to a reconstituted Mycenaean epic which recorded a strong Greek confederacy and could be treated as a holy scripture of the Oriental sort. Since Homer claimed to have been inspired by the Muse; since he glorified Nestor, Peisistratus' ancestor; and since the Homeridae ranked as honorary Athenians—Homer having reputedly been born at Smyrna, a colony of Athens—these revised texts of the *Iliad* and *Odyssey* would serve his purpose well enough. The Athenian Theseus cycle survived only in prose; otherwise he might have used that.

Yet though the original Mycenaean court epics must have had much in common with the Accadian Creation epic, the Hittite *Song of Ullikummi*, the Ugaritic *Baal*, and similar works, a great gulf separated all of them from the *Iliad*. Their authors had been endowed Temple priests who set themselves to exalt their gods and praise their rulers, and did not need to think in terms of popular entertainment. Homer, on the other hand, instead of praising his rulers, satirized Agamemnon, High King of Greece and Commander-in-Chief of the Allied Forces before Troy, as a weak, truculent, greedy, lying, murderous, boastful, irresolute busybody who almost always did the wrong thing.

Now, the original High King of the Achaeans was a living god; his palace, a temple; his courtyards, holy ground. He corresponded on equal terms with the High King of the Hittites, a fellow-god. But by Homer's time this religious High Kingship had perished, all the great cities had fallen, and the semi-barbarous princelings who camped on their ruins were ennobled by no spark of divinity. It is clearly these iron-age princes—descendants of the Dorian invaders who drove his own ancestors overseas—whom Homer satirizes in Mycenaean disguise as Agamemnon, Nestor, Achilles and Odysseus; and of whom Hesiod, a late contemporary of Homer's, was thinking when he wrote, in a lugubrious vein, that the divine race of men had been destroyed at ancient Thebes and Troy.

The Homeridae, being sacrosanct servants of Apollo, could risk satire, so long as they remained serene and unsmiling throughout their performances, pointed no finger, cocked no eye, tipped no wink.

Homer's wit is at its most merciless in *Book 2*, when Agamemnon calls a popular Assembly and tests his troops' morale by offering to abandon the siege of Troy. Members of the Privy Council have been warned to shout protests and demand a vigorous assault; but Agamemnon so over-acts his defeatist part that he convinces even himself, and the war-weary soldiers at once rush cheering down to the ships. A fiasco! The Goddess Athene is obliged to intervene. Homer makes Agamemnon superbly ridiculous again in *Book 4*, when the armistice has been broken and he addresses his wounded brother Menelaus:

'Alas, my poor brother! I fear that the oath which pledged you to single combat in no-man's-land has proved your ruin: the Trojans have broken the armistice and transfixed you with an arrow . . . I am more than ever assured that Troy's doom is sealed, also that of King Priam the Spearman and his subjects. Zeus, Son of Cronus, indignant at this outrage, will shake his shield threateningly at them from the Olympian throne; thus the armistice will not have been concluded in vain. Nevertheless, I should be most unhappy, brother, if you succumbed to your wound.'

Agamemnon does not send for a surgeon at this point, but continues self-pityingly and once more in a defeatist strain:

'Your death, by removing the cause of war, might set my men clamouring for home—how ashamed I should be to find myself back on the thirsty plains of Argos, having allowed Priam's people to make good their old boast of keeping Helen. Your bones would rot in Trojan soil, and the proud Trojans capering on your tomb would scoff: "I pray the gods that ill-tempered Agamemnon will have no greater success in his other ventures than in this! He has sailed away empty-handed, and noble Menelaus lies here beneath our feet, his mission unaccomplished." Rather let the earth swallow me alive than that they should say such things!'

Menelaus has, however, only been scratched. Battle is resumed, and Agamemnon stalks from contingent to contingent of his army, encouraging the commanders; but merely succeeds in setting their backs up by his ill-chosen phrases. Idomeneus is barely civil; Diomedes preserves a resentful silence; Odysseus and Sthenelus are downright rude to their High King.

In *Book 9*, Agamemnon's flood of tears and thunderous groans, after a severe defeat due to his own stupidity, introduce further comic scenes. He wakes Nestor, with the odd excuse that he must no doubt be suffering from insomnia. Nestor, courteous though sarcastic, revenges himself by waking everyone else of importance. But for what? He has no idea. Nor has Agamemnon. They solemnly call a Council, and decide to send out a small patrol. Diomedes leads this, and when asked to choose a partner, picks Odysseus as the bravest present; yet he remembers Odysseus' cowardly desertion of him in battle, and Odysseus knows that, unless he redeems his good name, a spear will be driven between his shoulders. He offers Diomedes a half-apology.

Homer is utterly cynical about the Olympian gods. Zeus rules them by fear and cunning, not love, and must keep on constant guard against a palace revolution. In most myth-making societies, what is alleged to happen in the courts of Heaven reflects what happens in the royal palace below; but Homer lets his gods behave far worse than the one royal family to whom he introduces us, namely the Trojan. Priam, in *Book 24*, may rage at his surviving nine sons as malingerers and playboys who have dared outlive their forty-one heroic brothers; but his curses are doubtless intended to avert Nemesis, and so protect them. On all other occasions the domestic atmosphere in the Trojan palace is irreproachable, despite the presence of Helen, prime cause of their continued sufferings.

Zeus, on the other hand, hurls horrible threats at his wife Hera and the rest of the Olympian family, too well aware of their jealousies, grudges, deceptions, lies, outrages, and adulteries. Hera is a termagant, so cruel and sly that she manages to convert her only virtues, marital chastity and an avoidance of direct lies, into defects. She would like to eat the Trojans raw—and all because, long ago, Paris rejected the bribe she offered for a verdict in her favour, and instead gave Aphrodite the prize of beauty. We are left wishing that Hera would commit adultery with some River-god or Titan, to be taken in the act, and thus compel Zeus to chain her down for ever in the Pit of Hell. Zeus' spoilt daughter Athene shares Hera's grudge against Paris—she also entered for the beauty prize—and Homer does not ask us to approve of her mean behaviour when the lovable Hector at last faces Achilles, a far stronger champion than himself, and she robs him of his advantage. Athene shines in comparison only with the foolish and brutal Ares. Of the three Olympians who come pretty well out of the tale, Apollo the Archer was the Homeridae's patron; Hephaestus the Smith ruled Lemnos, one of the Ionian Islands; and Hermes the Helper had invented the lyre and protected travellers. Then there is Poseidon, whom Homer clearly despises for not standing up to Zeus, and for being so touchy about his reputation as a master-mason; but abstains from ridiculing him because the Pan-Ionian Festival falls under his patronage.

Homer's audiences burned sacrifices to the gods, and celebrated annual festivals; yet they felt, it seems, no more and no less religiously sincere than most cradle-Catholics and cradle-Protestants do today—though supporting their Churches for the sake of marriage and funerals, keeping Christmas and Easter holidays, and swearing oaths on the Bible. Libations and sacrifices, the Ionians agreed, might be useful means of placating angry gods—a splash of wine and the thighbones of the victims on which one feasted cost little—and in the interests of law and order one should never swear false oaths, nor break the sacred bonds of hospitality. But they appear to have lacked any spiritual sense, except such few of them as had been admitted to the Eleusinian, Samothracian, Orphic, or other soul-stirring Mysteries. That Demeter and Persephone and Iacchus, the main figures in these Mysteries, are kept out of Homer's Divine Harlequinade, suggests that he, and his sons after him, were adepts —hence their poor view of official religion.

Perhaps it was the very cynicism of the *Iliad* and *Odyssey* that made them acceptable Holy Writ in Peisistratus' day, when the Greeks were already practising free philosophic speculation—Thales was an old man by 560 B.C. Homer soon became the basis of all Classical Greek culture, and when Rome conquered Greece, of all Roman culture too. Nobody could be thought educated who had not studied him under a 'grammarian', and many bright youths knew both his epics by heart. The grammarians (which meant professors of language and literature) discussed Homeric texts with as much zest and minuteness as the third-century rabbis devoted to commentaries on the *Pentateuch*. Homer was quoted in season and out: an apt reference, however irrelevant to the context, might win a

doubtful case at law—where again the rabbinical parallel is tempt-
ing. Peisistratus, who claimed prime historical importance for the
Iliad, managed to interpolate a line in the 'Catalogue of Ships' by
which Great Ajax the Salaminian was credited with beaching his
small flotilla at Troy next to the larger Athenian one. This he offered
as evidence in a court action against Megara. Athens was laying
claim to the Island of Salamis—and managed to fool the Spartan
judges.

Athenian participation in the Trojan War, by the way, seems it-
self spurious. That the material contained in the 'Catalogue of
Ships' cannot be reconciled with the main body of the work was once
thought a proof of its lateness; but scholars now make it a survival
of the earliest tradition. Still, the praise there given to the Athenian
contingent and their King Menestheus, 'ablest commander alive,
save for old Nestor,' is suspiciously fulsome. (Perhaps it records the
gratitude of Ionian refugees from the Dorian terror, who crowded
into Athens before sailing to their new homes in Asia Minor, and
felt that an Athenian contingent must have fought at Troy.) Thus
King Menestheus never figures in Agamemnon's Council meetings,
though he has brought fifty ships, and is hardly mentioned outside
the 'Catalogue'. In *Book 12*, he shows little military skill and has to
summon Great Ajax. Here his name may have been substituted for
that of Idomeneus of Crete; since we learn from a passage in *Book 10*
that Ajax and Idomeneus' flotillas lay close together at one end of
the camp.

The *Iliad*, though popular throughout Greater Greece in the sixth
century, as vase paintings and other works of art prove, earned little
reverence until jurists and grammarians treated it as a Bible: for
instance, Xenophanes of Colophon (about 500 B.C.) complained
of Homer's 'imputing to the gods all that among men is shameful
and blameworthy'. But Thucydides, writing about 420 B.C., already
discusses Homer as a reputable theologian, if sometimes inclined
to figurative language; and it is odd to find the later grammarians of
Rhodes, Athens and Alexandria commenting ponderously on pas-
sages which were no less satirical, in their tragic way, than Mark
Twain's *Huckleberry Finn*.

When I 'did' *Book 23* at my public school, the ancient classroom curse forbade me to catch any of the concealed comedy in the account of Patroclus' funeral games, which distinguishes them from Anchises' tedious funeral games in Virgil's *Aeneid*. Thus: Nestor, too old to compete in the chariot-race, gives his son Antilochus advice before he drives the Pylian team, confessing that the horses are slow and hinting that the race can be won by gamesmanship alone. Antilochus dutifully spurts to overtake Menelaus in a bad part of the track which, as they both know, will soon become a bottle-neck, and declines to slacken his pace. Menelaus, rather than be involved in a crash, lets Antilochus drive ahead, and cannot afterwards retrieve the lost ground. When Menelaus complains of a deliberate foul, Antilochus voluntarily forfeits his prize, though he has recently saved Menelaus' life in battle. Achilles, as President of the Games, thereupon awards Nestor a consolation prize. Nestor, in a gracious speech of acceptance, tells a long story of how, when young, he won all the events at King Oedipus' funeral games—or all except the chariot-race, in which Actor's sons scandalously jockeyed him. Homer leaves his audience to grasp that Achilles symphathizes with Antilochus, and that Nestor means: 'Yes, we cannot blame my son for boldly putting Menelaus to a test of nerves. It was a different matter at Thebes, long ago, when a rival chariot deliberately crossed my lane and headed me off. Yet my rivals were the Moliones who, though putative sons of Actor, claimed Poseidon, God of Charioteers, as their real father; so, of course, I could make no protest.'

In the subsequent foot-race Antilochus, the fastest runner of his age-group—the early 'twenties—is out-distanced by Odysseus, a man old enough to be his father, but makes a polite comment on the athletic pre-eminence of veterans. In fact, Antilochus purposely lost, to rehabilitate himself as a true sportsman—and this becomes clearer when Achilles shows gratitude by doubling the value of his third prize. Agamemnon then sees an opportunity of winning a prize himself: he enters for the javelin-throw, confident that Meriones, his sole opponent, will have the politeness to scratch. Achilles does not even give Meriones the chance, but sarcastically announces that Agamemnon, the best warrior in the world, may as well take both first and second prizes—a contest would be sheer waste of time!

Nestor, Homer's favourite butt after Agamemnon, can never refrain from boasting of his youthful prowess and, though rated the sagest Councillor among the Greeks—as Polydamas is among the Trojans—consistently gives bad advice which Agamemnon always adopts; whereas Polydamas consistently gives good advice, which Hector always rejects. Thus the Greeks would never have suffered such a heavy defeat on the plain if Nestor, instead of encouraging Agamemnon to act upon the false dream sent by Zeus, had done as Priam later did—tested its truth by demanding a sure augury. Again, the Trojans would never have been allowed to break into the Greek camp, if Nestor had not advised Agamemnon to build a grandiose defence system of rampart and fosse—without also suggesting a sacrifice to placate Poseidon's jealousy. Nor would Patroclus have been killed, had Nestor not advised him to borrow Achilles' armour and fight in it.

When a Trojan arrow wounds Machaon, and Nestor agrees to drive him out of danger, Homer's humour is at its dryest. Once back at the Greek camp, they settle down to a refreshing beverage of onion juice, honey and barley-water in a great golden beaker, or tureen, to which the slave-girls add wine flavoured with cheese; and Nestor embarks on a long story of his own youthful adventures at Pylus. He makes no attempt to remove the arrow still protruding from Machaon's shoulder, though after fifty years of warfare he can hardly have avoided picking up a little simple surgery; nor does he send for Patroclus, a competent surgeon who, we know, was not busy at the time; nor does he even return to the battlefield and encourage his hard-pressed troops. He is still droning on when the Trojans swarm over the rampart. Then he hurriedly excuses himself: 'Pray continue drinking, and one of my slave-girls will wash the blood off your shoulder.' Nestor later dishonestly explains his absence from the field as due to a wound; and the *Iliad* ends with no further mention of Machaon who, for all Nestor cared, may have succumbed.

Menelaus, although despised by his brother Agamemnon, comes well out of the story. Conscious that this bloody war is being fought to avenge the wrong which Paris did him, he shows common sense and dignity, keeping up a steady average of kills in various battles, and has even on one occasion decided to spare a suppliant prince—

when Agamemnon, bustling up, officiously murders him. Moreover, Menelaus does not protest against Achilles' usurpation of the army command which, when Agamemnon gets wounded, should be his. Nevertheless, (*Book* 13) Homer jokingly makes him rage against the Trojans as insatiable in their love of war—as though he had not himself been attacking them for the past ten years—and then plunge back into battle.

Homer treats Achilles with irony rather than humour. Though we are enlisted at the start as this ill-used hero's partisans, Achilles is soon discovered to be the real villain of the piece, who heartlessly watches the massacre of his comrades, just to spite Agamemnon. We believe his assurance to the Assembly that whenever he sacks cities and adds their treasures to the common stock, Agamemnon awards him only a trifle and takes the lion's share himself; later, we find Achilles' hut chock-full of loot—he has been selling captured prisoners as a side-line and pocketing the proceeds. We also believe his assurance to the Assembly that he was sincerely enamoured of Briseis; but when Agamemnon at last repents and offers to surrender her, untouched, together with an enormous compensation for his insults, Achilles tells the envoys that he does not really want the girl —she means nothing to him—and that he despises treasure. (Of course, Agamemnon also lied by pretending to have done no better out of the war than Achilles.)

Achilles' famous love of Patroclus, the kindest-hearted and most unselfish soldier in the Greek camp, proves to be pure self-love which grudges his comrade pre-eminence in battle. Patroclus dies, and Achilles, leaving his body unburied, announces that when he can get a new suit of armour, he will kill Hector and collect twelve Trojan prisoners for a human sacrifice at the pyre. Homer emphasizes Achilles' real object—which is to show that he can outshine Patroclus—when the miserable ghost appears in a dream, altogether uninterested in these barbarous works of vengeance, and complains of the delay. Until his body is duly burned, the Infernal Spirits are refusing him entry to Hades' kingdom, and he must wander from gate to gate, a homeless exile. Achilles answers brusquely that he is doing everything possible to make the funeral a success, and resents having his elbow jogged. Eventually Achilles gets Briseis back, accepts Agamemnon's heavy compensation—though not destined, he knows, to enjoy it—and also insists on Priam's paying a tremendous ransom for Hector's corpse: a transaction which he dishonestly hides from the Privy Council. Nor does he respect Patroclus' wishes by honourably marrying Briseis, but continues to treat her as a convenient bed-fellow and chattel.

∗

Homer the satirist is walking on a razor's edge and must constantly affirm his adherence both to the ruling aristocracy, however stupid, cruel or hysterical, and his belief in auguries and other supernatural signs. The most sensible and telling speech at Agamemnon's Assembly, in *Book 3*, is made by the anti-monarchical commoner Thersites, whom Odysseus thereupon flogs. To dissociate himself from Thersites' sentiments, Homer presents him as bow-legged, bald, hump-backed, horrible-looking, and a general nuisance; but the speech and Odysseus' brutal action stay on record. And Homer's real feelings on the subject of auguries are put into Achilles' mouth— he thinks birds are simply birds and fly about on their own lawful business without divine instruction—for Achilles is angry and despairing and can therefore be pardoned. An inveterate hatred of war appears throughout the *Iliad*; and Homer smuggles into *Book 23* a bitter comment on the monstrous slavery it entails, by awarding the winner of the wrestling match a copper cauldron worth twelve oxen, and the loser a captive Trojan noblewoman valued as highly as four, because she is skilled at the loom.

He feels entitled to modernize elements of the out-of-date tradition which he has inherited—very much as Malory's *Morte d'Arthur* puts the pre-Christian legends of the Welsh *awenyddion* (strolling minstrels) into courtly mediaeval dress. Homer distorts his material less than Malory, because he is not working from a foreign language and knows the physical geography of Troy; but can be caught out in frequent inconsistencies. His account of immense earthworks built around the Greek camp adds entertainingly to the legend—it has been suggested that, since the *Iliad* omitted any Greek assault on Troy, a Trojan assault on these defences was invented to supply the lack—but sometimes he forgets that they are there, and allows free passage between camp and plain. However, for listeners who knew the site of Troy well, he remarks how as soon as the war ended, Poseidon angrily washed away all trace of the earth-works.

Numerous other mistakes occur. At one point a parenthesis explains that, since the beach could not accommodate every Greek ship, the latest flotillas to arrive were hauled up the strand in three rows. Very well: yet when Hector attacks the hindmost row, he sets Protesilaus' flagship on fire—the first vessel, as we have been told, to be beached.

Nor do we ever get a clear battle picture. To earn his slices of fat roast mutton and his cup of honey-sweet wine at court, Homer often had to strain his imagination in describing novel varieties of man-slaughter, which he credited to the ancestors of his hosts. Even Aga-memnon, from whom the aristocracy of Lesbos claimed descent, was allowed his day of glory (*Book 11*); though he made as much fuss about a slight wound as though he had been overtaken by the pangs of childbirth. These passages are perfunctory, in the main and, except for the pleasant similes that embellish them, can be skipped without offence to Homer. He is so careless, too, about the names of Trojans killed—Greek sword-fodder—that Erymas, Acamas and Chromius get dispatched twice, and Chromius lives to tell the tale. *Books 16* and *17* are a sad muddle as regards time and weather continuity: first sunset, then bright sun and no cloud, then a rainbow, then a thunderstorm, then a long spell of fighting, then night falls. Hence the Latin tag: 'Our good Homer himself occasionally nods.' Yet some of the major discrepancies are inherent in the prose-tradition; thus the Apple of Discord was flung at the marriage of Peleus and Thetis, just before the Trojan War—which Achilles neverthe-less joined, mysteriously grown to sudden manhood.

Two main reasons prevented Homer from making his battles realistic. One was that the feats or fates of common soldiers did not interest his patrons, who cared to hear only of duels between noble-men. No man-at-arms ever kills a nobleman, even by mistake; which seems odd, since they are all clad in full armour, with corslets, greaves, helmets and shields. The second reason was that, while light-chariot races were still in vogue, the heavy-chariot fighting described in the story-cycle had gone out altogether by Homer's day. So, though

chariot combats occur frequently in the *Iliad*—Hector even drives
a quadriga and orders a couple of mass-charges—the relation of char-
iotry to infantry remains obscure. Homer feels most at ease when
his heroes forget their chariots and fight shield to shield in an un-
broken line, so close that their spears almost get entangled. This un-
broken line is a post-Mycenaean development of Greek infantry
tactics, and implies a changed social organization. The chariot-riding
Mycenaean prince—unless he happened to be a Pandarus or Teucrus
and fancied himself as a bowman—used a long thrusting-lance, a
tower-like figure-of-eight body-shield, and a heavy bronze broad-
sword. Thus prepared, he challenged enemy nobles to single com-
bat, and his crowd of leather-jerkined pikemen, standing in the back-
ground, moved forward only if he fell wounded. (Little Ajax and
Amphius wore linen corslets not from sheer foolhardiness, but be-
cause they carried body-shields.) The free citizens of Homer's day,
however, fought in a close line, like the Roman legionaries, and their
weapons were a couple of throwing-spears, an iron stabbing-sword,
and a small, round targe with a pointed boss. Archers, slingers, and
cavalry supported them. Homer omits cavalry but, though Ajax
fights in true Mycenaean style and so at times do Hector and Achil-
les, he feels obliged to modernize most of the fighting in order to
hold his audience; and often cannot decide whether a particular
hero is armed with the single lance and body-shield or with two
throwing-spears and a targe.

The Mycenaeans buried their noble dead without burning their
corpses or their funeral offerings; Homer makes both Greeks and
Trojans practise the modern total cremation. The forging of Achil-
les' bronze shield is described in a way that shows his total ignorance
of Mycenaean metallurgy: Hephaestus goes to work as though he
were a blacksmith. And simple woodmen wield iron axes, though no
iron but the rare and immensely valuable meteoric sort (containing
a high proportion of nickel) was known at Mycenae—ore-smelting
came in later.

Future events are often anticipated by careful pointers of warning
or prophecy. One important pointer is never taken up: Andromache's
pre-occupation, in *Book 5*, with the weakness of the Western curtain,
where the wild fig-tree grew, and where Great and Little Ajax, among

others, had been pressing their attacks. From Dörpfeld's excavations at Troy, we learn that although the Western curtain would first invite attack, its masonry did not match the other walls. Pindar and his scholiast tell us that only this part of Troy had been built by a mortal—Aeacus, as opposed to the Gods Poseidon and Apollo—and that Aeacus' descendants Great and Little Ajax made their final assault exactly here. The 'Trojan Horse'—according to the *Odyssey*, not the *Iliad*, the instrument of Troy's capture—was, Pausanias says, a simple siege engine (perhaps a scaling tower faced with wet horse-hides as a protection against fire?) rather than a secret receptacle for armed Greeks. Which is one of many reasons why I decline to believe that the *Odyssey* and *Iliad* are by the same hand.

Troy itself is no fiction; nor is the burning of the city (which archaeologists call 'Troy VIIA') by an expeditionary force of Greeks in the thirteenth century B.C.—1230, not 1287, is the date now favoured. But, though the occasion of the war was perhaps a Trojan raid on the Peloponnese, the cause will rather have been a decision reached by the Aeacids, and their allies, to re-open the trade-route through the Hellespont from which the Trojans had lately debarred them. Achilles was a leading Aeacid, and the Cretan followers of Prince Scamander are named by Strabo as among the founders of Troy; which would explain their descendants' participation in the war under Idomeneus.

A tradition quoted by Hesiod makes Helen's numerous suitors sacrifice a horse at Sparta, stand on its bloody joints, and swear that they will defend the chosen husband against anyone who resents his good fortune. Thus, he says, Helen's rejected suitors organized the expedition against Troy when Menelaus was wronged by Paris. Yet it has been convincingly shown by Professor T. B. L. Webster, in his admirably up-to-date *From Mycenae to Homer*, that Helen's abduction formed no part of the original Trojan legend; Homer borrowed the tale from some source dependent on the early Ugaritic epic *Keret*. In the opening lines, Prince Keret mourns that 'his lawful wife surely went away, his rightful spouse, whom he had won with a bride gift, indeed did depart.' Thereupon the God El tells him to besiege Udm and demand the King's daughter Huray—apparently this same lawful wife. Keret does so, and in the end the King of Udm surrenders her, after an attempt to buy him off. Homer's Paris likewise offers to restore with interest the treasures which he has carried off, if he may keep Helen; but this does not satisfy Menelaus.

Professor Webster's discovery of an external source for the Helen-Paris relationship strengthens the contention I made in my *Greek Myths*:

This is to suggest that the *mnēstēres tēs Helenēs*, 'suitors of Helen', were really *mnēstēres tou hellēspontou*, 'those who were mindful of the Hellespont', and that the solemn oath which these kings took on the bloody joints of the horse sacred to Poseidon, the chief patron of the expedition, was to support the rights of any member of the confederacy to navigate the Hellespont, despite the Trojans and their Asiatic allies. After all, the Hellespont bore the name of their own goddess Helle.

In the first nine years of war, the Greeks seem to have blockaded but not besieged Troy, limiting themselves to punitive raids on the Trojan allies all along the Asian coast, and doubtless sailing home every autumn. The unbroken ten-year siege is a dramatic fiction often contradicted by internal evidence: thus Sarpedon the Lycian still has an infant son at home, though he came to Troy with the first allied contingent. And, in *Book 11*, Othryoneus from [Cilician?] Cabesus has just heard of the Greek landing. The mythographer Hyginus records an earlier legend: that King Priam's allies arrived in the tenth year. Also, excavation proves that 'Troy VIIA' could house no more than two or three thousand men, as opposed to the many thousands mentioned by Homer as having spent the entire war there.

Greek traditional story-cycles contained elements taken not only from the south-eastern Mediterranean—Corinthian myths, for example, often parallel the *Book of Genesis*—but, like the ancient Irish tales, from Indo-European legend recorded in the Sanscrit epics. Sometimes the similarity of Greek and Irish myths tempts us to reconstruct a lost Indo-European original. Thus the Irish *War of the Bulls* describes the hero Cuchulain's divine chariot-team, named 'The Grey of Macha' and 'Black Sanglain', which correspond to Achilles' horses Xanthus and Balius and, like them, shed tears of grief. Cuchulain and Achilles both have a charmed spear, each mourns for the death of a blood-brother and fights desperately at a ford; but Cuchulain kills his blood-brother, who has been enrolled by fate among the enemy. *The War of the Bulls* being far earlier in sentiment and style than the *Iliad* (though consigned to writing a thousand years later), their common Indo-European original may have been the *Mahabharata*, before it was heavily and clumsily re-written, where Karna, son of the Sun-god, possessed a similar weapon and fought his own brother. I make this suggestion because, on the battlefield, Cuchulain and Achilles share the unusual charac-teristic of shining with a 'hero light' compared to the Sun; and be-cause Cuchulain is held to be a reincarnation of the Sun-god Lugh. When the River-god Xanthus attacks Achilles at the ford, Hephaes-tus, God of the Forge, rescues him by scorching the riverbanks and making the waters boil. Since the Greek Sun Titan Hyperion never intervened in human affairs, and since Hephaestus' use of coals from his furnace has an artificial ring, we may presume an earlier version of the legend in which the Sun-god came to the hero's rescue.

The weeping of Cuchulain's horses reads far more tragically than that of Achilles' team. The Grey of Macha, who matches Xanthus, defends her master with hooves and teeth; whereas Xanthus does nothing except protest, in a human voice, against Achilles' unjust accusations and foretell his death. Achilles, not at all surprised, re-turns a harsh answer, ordering the beast to mind his manners; which introduces a comic element, heightened by the appearance of a Fury who stops Xanthus' mouth before he can defend himself.

Another borrowed element in the *Iliad*, pointed out by Professor Webster, confirms Achilles' close relation with the Sun-god:

In the *Iliad* the relationship of Achilles and Patroklos may be compared with the relationship of Gilgamesh and Enkidu; and the relationship of Achilles and Thetis with the relationship of Gilgamesh and his mother, the goddess Ninsun. The two passages in the *Iliad* which come closest to the Gilgamesh epic are both in the eighteenth book. When Gilgamesh visited Ninsun to tell her of his resolve to seek out Huwawa, Ninsun raised her hands to the sun god Shamash and said: 'Why, having given me Gilgamesh for a son, with a restless heart didst thou endow him? And now thou didst affect him to go on a far journey to the place of Huwawa, to face an uncertain battle, to travel an uncertain road.' This is surely the tone of Thetis in the *Iliad* (18, 54): 'Ah! wretched me, who have born a hero to misery, I bore a son who was blameless and strong . . . as long as he lives and sees the light of the sun, he is grieved.' When Enkidu dies, Gilgamesh lamented him: 'like a lion he raises up his voice, like a lioness deprived of her whelps. He paces back and forth before the couch'; and later, like Achilles, he prepared an elaborate burial for his friend. In the *Iliad* (18, 316) the Achaeans lamented Patroklos all night; Achilles began the lamentation, laying his murderous hands on the breast of his friend, groaning deeply like a bearded lion, whose whelps had been stolen by a hunter. The parallel between the two similes is striking, but the parallel between the double relationships is more striking.'

Now we come to the question of how Homer understood divine intervention in human battle. It is one thing to ascribe natural catastrophes such as earthquakes, pestilence, deaths in childbirth, men or houses struck by lightning, to respectively Poseidon, Apollo, Artemis, and Zeus; or to regard birds as messengers of the gods. It is quite another when these gods adopt human guise—as when Apollo pretends to be Hector's brother Helenus and gives him tactical advice; or when Hermes disguises himself as Achilles' squire and guides Priam safely into the Greek camp. This is a graphic way of saying that the human hero was inspired, though he kept his familiar appearance; the divine kings of Mycenae and the Middle East were constantly represented by epic-writers and on monuments as being so favoured by their deities. When, however, a god stands at the side of a chosen champion, other than a divine king, and helps him to victory—as Athene did for Diomedes and Ajax, or as Apollo did for Paris when he killed Achilles (a deed, by the way, only prophesied, not performed in the *Iliad*), this seems more like divine possession than divine inspiration. Though by Homer's time, such a possession had evidently ceased to be an everyday occurrence, he has preserved occasional details which make it recognizable.

Both divine inspiration and divine possession occur in West African cultures of Libyan origin; and the Libyan element in pre-Hellenic Greek myth is large: Athene herself, whom Herodotus identifies with the Libyan Goddess Neith, was born on the shores of Lake Triton, near Gades. A mortal inspired by a god's or a goddess' *kra* (soul), is unchanged in appearance, though he may be speaking and acting as the deity dictates. Possession by a divine *sunsum* (personality), on the other hand, leads to behaviour peculiar to the god or goddess concerned. Each god has his well-known character and mannerisms. In Dahomey, for instance, the local Hermes is sly, smooth, eloquent, amusing, dishonest, sympathetic, hating personal violence; the local Aphrodite is amorous, coquettish, bountiful, soft-hearted, shrewd, subtle, and unsporting. When at a festival, under the excitement of drums and dancing, some member of the tribe becomes possessed by a divine *sunsum*, he or she loses consciousness, adopts the character of that particular god, and is temporarily granted divine honours. An authoritative account of the same phenomenon, transplanted from Dahomey to Haiti, is given in Maya Daren's *Divine Horseman*.

The *sunsums* of the Olympians had been established by ancient Greek myth; so that, if a hero were possessed, it would be at once apparent which deity was riding him. Ares, the War-god, a great, tough, swaggering warrior, relied on main force, heavy spear-thrusts and crushing sword-swings; perhaps heroes mentioned in the *Iliad* as 'Ares' favourites', or 'descendants of Ares', were susceptible to his possession. Diomedes, in *Book 5*, fears to face Hector because Ares is with him; but on another occasion, Diomedes has been himself possessed by the Goddess Athene, and Hector prudently avoids an encounter. Among the ancient Greeks, as among the pagan West Africans and *loa*-worshipping Haitians, a man could be possessed by a goddess, or a woman by a god. The Pythoness at Delphi, or the Sybil at Cumae, who were possessed, not merely inspired, by the God Apollo, assumed his voice and demeanour. Athene, the Amazonian goddess, evidently had a more and deadly battle technique than Ares because, whenever two warriors met, one inspired by Athene, one by Ares, Athene always won; two combats between these deities—or their chosen incarnations—are given in the *Iliad*. Hector remarks that fighters have their off-days or their days of triumph, according as Heaven wills. Thus Aeneas, possessed by Aphrodite, is easily defeated by Athene's incarnation Diomedes, after apparently suffering the hand wound which Homer attributes to Aphrodite herself; but makes good his escape. Later, the strong God Apollo possesses him, and he lops down his opponents like pines. But the Greek gods never became bisexual, as their West African counterparts did.

The most interesting case of possession in the *Iliad* is that of Paris, Aphrodite's favourite. When he fights Menelaus, then aided by Athene, he only just manages to extricate himself with Aphrodite's adroit help and escape to Troy. Afterwards, Hector visits him at his house and calls him back to fight, saying sarcastically: 'I cannot regard your grudge against Troy as a very decent one; it is for you alone that our people are dying to defend these walls.' Paris, still under Aphrodite's influence, gives a characteristic answer: 'Sharp words, but not unreasonably so. Allow me to explain that I bear no particular grudge against Troy, but feeling a little sad, I wanted to enjoy a good cry on the chair in this bedroom. My wife has just suggested that I should fight again, and I am taking her advice; because one never knows who will win the next round, does one?' That same day, Paris saves the situation, not by some tremendous lunge with a spear, or cast with a boulder, but by an unsporting arrow-shot, from behind cover, that pins Diomedes' foot to the ground and disables him for the rest of the battle. Paris' laugh is the merry laugh of Aphrodite, and Diomedes' answer carries all the venom proper to Athene.

Homer clearly disbelieves the legends of gods taking part in human affairs, but is always ready to extemporize divine machinery. Since a 'tomb of Sarpedon' was shown in Lycia, whereas the Trojan cycle made him fall in battle, Homer obligingly arranges an aerial transfer of the corpse back to Lycia, at Zeus' own orders. It is reasonable to suppose that he has also altered the ancient account of how Paris killed Achilles. Aphrodite, rather than Apollo, will have guided the arrow that pierced the famous heel since, according to most mythographers, Achilles fell not at the Scaean Gate, but in Apollo's temple, where Deiphobus had lured him—after posting Paris behind a pillar. Apollo would hardly have so defiled his own shrine. Aphrodite seems to have been a far more important character in the original story-cycle than in the *Iliad*. The Homeric *Returns of the Heroes*, clearly based on Mycenaean tradition, makes every Greek leader of note

either return home to find his wife unfaithful, or be shipwrecked.*
Before Poseidon, fairly late in religious history, converted his thunderbolt into a trident and exchanged sweet waters for salt, Aphrodite ruled the Sea as well as human passions; and her alternate forms of revenge for the destruction of Troy yield far better sense than Poseidon's idle spite, to which, though he championed the Greek cause at Troy, these disasters are implausibly ascribed.

∗

Students (lamentably few, nowadays) who read Homer in the original have several competent cribs to guide them. Professor Richard Lattimore's *The Iliad of Homer* is the latest; he and Professor Webster make a reliable team. I approve of cribs, but dislike all the *translations* I have yet read. Translations are made for the general, non-Classical public, yet their authors seldom consider what will be immediately intelligible, and therefore readable, and what will not. Homer is a difficult writer. He was breaking new ground, and often failed to express a complex idea adequately in hexameters; he also omitted many vital pieces of information, or inserted them too late. Few translators save Homer's face by remedying these defects, or soften the wearisome formality of phrase which slows down the action:

'So said the White-armed Goddess Hera, and the Owl-eyed Goddess Athene disregarded not. So Hera the Goddess-queen, daughter of Great Cronus, went her way.'

Is it necessary for Hera to be called 'White-Armed, Queen, Daughter of Great Cronus', or Athene 'the Owl-Eyed Virgin Daughter of Zeus' more than once or twice in every book? Surely: 'Athene took Hera's advice' is enough? And what can the uninstructed reader make of 'Alalcomenean Athene'? Should he not be told that Zeus, who gave her this title, was teasing, and that she resented having been put under the charge of a human tutor named Alalcomenes the Boeotian?

* I write this from the island of Majorca which, according to Strabo and Silius Italicus, was first colonized by the Rhodians whom Tlepolemus brought in nine ships to Troy, and who on their return found themselves unable to regain Rhodes. An early Majorcan bull cult and the islanders' remarkable skill as slingers do indeed suggest Rhodian provenience. Here we like to believe that Tlepolemus did not fall at Troy.

Paradoxically the more accurate a rendering, the less justice it does Homer. Here is a typical passage from *Book 6* of Professor Lattimore's version:

Bellerophontes went to Lykia in the blameless convoy
of the gods; when he came to the running stream of Xanthos, and Lykia,
the lord of wide Lykia tendered him full-hearted honour.
Nine days he entertained him with sacrifice of nine oxen,
but afterwards when the rose fingers of the tenth dawn showed, then
he began to question him, and asked to be shown the symbols,
whatever he might be carrying from his son-in-law, Proitos.
Then after he had been given his son-in-law's wicked symbols
first he sent him away with orders to kill the Chimaira . . .

In other words:

The Olympians brought Bellerophon safe to the mouth of the Lycian River Xanthus, where Iobates received him splendidly: the feasting lasted nine days, and every day they slaughtered a fresh ox. At dawn, on the tenth day, the time came for Iobates to inquire: 'My lord, what news do you bring from my esteemed son-in-law Proetus?' Bellerophon innocently produced the sealed package, and Iobates, having read the tablets, ordered him to kill the Chimaera.

*

A few years ago, before translating *The Golden Ass* from Apuleius' over-ornate Latin, I decided to give it a new lease of life by using a staid but simple English prose. I cannot do quite the same here, because Homer wrote in hexameter verse, and though perhaps nine tenths of it is historic narrative, there remain certain dramatic and lyrical occasions. A solemn prayer, a divine message, a dirge, or a country song disguised as a simile—they sound all wrong when turned into English prose: just as wrong as when muster-rolls and long, detailed accounts of cooking a meal or harnessing a mule are kept in verse. Modern audiences are sharp-witted and more easily bored than Homer's; and since the printing press has almost abolished illiteracy in the West, novels or histories need no longer be clothed in regular metre to make them easily memorized; nor do English versions of the *Iliad*. Broken metre, which some recent translators adopt, seems to me an unfortunate compromise between verse and prose. I have therefore followed the example of the ancient Irish and Welsh bards by, as it were, taking up my harp and singing only where prose will not suffice. This, I hope, avoids the pitfalls of either an all-prose or an all-verse translation, and restores something of the *Iliad's* value as mixed entertainment. But so primitive a setting forbids present-day colloquialisms, and I have kept the diction a little old-fashioned. At times, I incorporate footnotes into the text, but only when the sense is deficient without them; and shall now pour a libation of clear red wine to Homer's shade, imploring pardon for the many small liberties I have taken. He will perhaps grant my plea, despite protests from his loyal grammarians.

Deyá,   R.G.
Majorca,
Spain

THE ANGER OF ACHILLES

Book One:

The Quarrel

INVOCATION OF THE MUSE

Sing, MOUNTAIN GODDESS, sing through me
That anger which most ruinously
Inflamed Achilles, Peleus' son,
And which, before the tale was done,
Had glutted Hell with champions—bold,
Stern spirits by the thousandfold;
Ravens and dogs their corpses ate.
For thus did ZEUS, who watched their fate,
See his resolve, first taken when
Proud Agamemnon, King of men,
An insult on Achilles cast,
Achieve accomplishment at last.

You wish to know which of the gods originated the quarrel between these Greek princes, and how this happened? I can tell you: it was Phoebus Apollo, the son of Almighty Zeus and Leto the Fair-Haired, who sent a fearful pestilence among the Greeks, by way of punishing Agamemnon, their High King. The trouble began with Agamemnon's insult of Apollo's priest Chryses, when he came to the Greek camp before Troy, armed with the Archer-god's sacred woollen headband bound on a golden wand. He was offering a remarkably high ransom for his daughter Chryseis, whom the Greeks held as a prisoner of war.

In an address to the entire army, but especially their two leaders, Agamemnon and his brother Menelaus, Chryses said: 'Royal sons of Atreus, and all you other distinguished warriors! I sincerely pray that the Olympians will permit you to sack King Priam's citadel yonder, and to sail safe home: but only if you honour Zeus' son Apollo, whom I serve, by setting my daughter free.'

The men uttered a generous roar of approval, yet Agamemnon sent Chryses about his business. 'Let me catch you here again, old man,' he shouted, 'among these ships of war, either now or later, and no wand nor priestly headband will protect you! Understand this: I shall never release Chryseis. She must spend her life as a royal concubine and weaver of tapestries in my palace at distant Argos. Begone, and not another word, or you can expect the worst!'

The venerable Chryses, scared into obedience, walked silently away beside the rough sea, until he found himself alone. He then offered a prayer to Apollo:

> 'God with the bow of silver,
>   You that take your stand
> At Chryse and holy Cilla,
>   Protector of our land,

> 'Great Lord of Mice, whose sceptre
>   Holds Tenedos in fee:
> Listen to my petition,
>   Consider well my plea!

> 'If ever I built a temple
>   Agreeable to your eyes,
> Or cut from goats or bullocks
>   The fat about their thighs,

> 'To burn as a costly offering
>   At KING APOLLO's shrine:
> Let the Greeks pay with your arrows
>   These burning tears of mine!'

Phoebus Apollo heard Chryses' prayer, and his face grew darker than night. Shouldering the silver bow, he hurried down from

Olympus. The arrows rattled in their quiver, as he alighted at some distance from the ships, and his bow clanged dreadfully when he let fly. His first victims were mules and hounds; next, he shot their masters, whose pyres were presently seen burning everywhere. For nine days his lethal arrows riddled the Greeks, and on the tenth, inspired by the White-Armed Goddess Hera, who felt compassion for her dying wards, Achilles the Swift-Footed called a General Assembly.

As soon as it met, Achilles stood up and addressed Agamemnon: 'Royal son of Atreus, I am convinced that we shall be driven from the camp—those of us who survive—by this combination of pestilence with war, if we do not at once ask some prophet or priest, or even an interpreter of dreams—dreams, too, are sent by Zeus—the reason for Phoebus Apollo's anger. Could we have failed to keep a vow, or omitted a hundred-beast sacrifice due to him? If so, the odour of prime lambs and goats roasting on his altars should placate him, and thus end the pestilence.'

When Achilles sat down, Calchas, son of Thestor, rose: an expert at revealing the past, present and future—in fact, the best prophet alive. It was Calchas who had guided the Greek fleet to Troy with the divinatory knowledge bestowed on him by Apollo, and his answer could not have been a more proper one.

'Achilles, Favourite of Zeus, you ask me to account for the anger of Apollo, the god who kills from afar. But since my revelation must displease our commander-in-chief, I shall withhold it, unless you solemnly swear to protect me afterwards, both in word and deed. A king, as everyone knows, is the more formidable the less powerful his offender: and though he may swallow his anger for one day, resentment will gnaw at him until he has exacted vengeance. So, before I speak, pray decide whether you can protect me.'

Achilles rose again. 'Do not shrink,' he said, 'from making this revelation! I swear by Zeus' son Apollo—your loyalty to whom assures the truth of all prophecies you utter in his name—that, while I yet live and breathe, no member of this expedition will dare lay violent hands on you: not even Agamemnon himself, though he ranks highest among us.'

Thus encouraged, Calchas spoke freely. 'What has caused Apollo's anger is neither the breach of a vow nor the omission of a hundred-beast sacrifice; but the insult offered his priest Chryses by the High King, in declining a ransom for Chryseis. Though Apollo has avenged this insult on us all, our punishment still remains incomplete. He will not rid the camp of pestilence before we have restored the girl to her father, without demanding ransom or other payment, and have also burned a hundred victims at his shrine on Chryse. This way lies our sole hope of placating him.'

Next Agamemnon himself sprang up, in such a rage that fire seemed to flash from his eyes. Throwing Calchas an ugly look, he cried: 'Evil-minded prophet, you love disaster, and never reveal anything pleasant! Your latest act of spite is the most improbable story that Apollo has punished us Greeks because I prefer keeping Chryseis as my bed-fellow to accepting a ransom. Let me be blunt: I consider her far more attractive than my wife Clytaemnestra, alike in face, figure, intelligence and skill. Nevertheless, I am prepared to surrender Chryseis, if needs must, rather than watch the entire army melt away. My one stipulation is that these princes here assembled will immediately compensate me for her loss. It would be disgraceful were I to find myself the sole Greek without a prize of honour—and everyone can see how valuable a one I stand to lose.'

Achilles replied: 'Son of Atreus, you are the greediest man in the Assembly, as well as the noblest-born! Why should these princes give you a prize of honour? They have no common stock of booty upon which to draw. What we took from captured cities has already been distributed; and it would not be decent were a particular award withdrawn and made over to you. Send back the girl, as Apollo demands, and later, if Zeus lets us sack some other Trojan fortress, we will vote you three or four times her value.'

'Do not argue with me, Achilles!' shouted Agamemnon. 'I refuse to be bullied. So I must surrender Chryseis, and expect no compensation—is that it? You, I suppose, are to keep your prize of honour and leave me chafing empty-handed? No, indeed! If the generous Greeks offer me some fair substitute, well and good. If not, I will choose my own prize of honour, and seize it moreover with my own hands, either from you or from Great Ajax, son of Telamon, or from King Odysseus the Crafty; and the man I rob shall have good reason to feel vexed. However, we can settle this in due course. We must now pick a crew for one of our galleys, put aboard a hundred victims and the lovely Chryseis, appoint some Councillor as captain—Great Ajax, or King Idomeneus, or King Odysseus, or yourself, Prince Achilles—who will sail down to Chryse and there placate Apollo the Archer.'

Achilles scowled at Agamemnon. 'Shameless schemer!' he cried. 'How can any Greek patiently obey your orders, whether to go off on a voyage, or to stay and fight? I did not join the expedition because the Trojans harmed me: they never took my cattle or horses, nor foraged through my cornfields in fertile, healthy Phthia, where I live. Ranges of misty mountains and vast stretches of echoing sea separate that land from this. Though no vassal of yours, I brought my men here as a favour, when asked to punish the Trojans for the wrong they did your brother Menelaus. Dog-faced wretch, you not only forget how much gratitude I deserve, but threaten to steal the prize with which the Greeks rewarded my exertions! At what division of booty after the sack of a populous city did I ever get a share even approaching yours in value, though I led the assault in person? I must always return exhausted to my ship, content with some hard-won trifle. Very well; because I have no intention of humiliating myself any longer by this thankless struggle to fill your coffers, I shall sail home to Phthia.'

'Desert us by all means,' answered Agamemnon, 'if that is your pleasure. I shall not ask you to stay. Others will stay who hold me in respect, especially Omniscient Zeus; and of all his royal foster-children, you are the one whom I most detest—you, with your endless pursuit of quarrels, wars, battles! Unusual strength is a gift from Heaven, rather than of man's making. Go, and welcome: launch your flotilla, play the petty king among the Myrmidons of Phthia! Be as angry as you wish; it means nothing to me. Yet, let me inform you that, since Apollo insists on robbing me of Chryseis, my own ship and crew will carry her back; and that I shall then visit your hut and compensate myself with your prize of honour, the beautiful Briseis. That will teach you which of us two is the greater personage and, at the same time, warn your comrades not to dispute with me on equal terms.'

These words struck Achilles to the heart, but he could not decide whether he should snatch the sharp sword from his thigh, burst through the ranks, and kill Agamemnon; or whether it would be wiser to repress his anger. As he stood in doubt, slowly drawing the sword out of its scabbard, Hera, who cared for both contestants, hurriedly sent her step-daughter, Owl-Eyed Athene, to step behind Achilles and catch him by his yellow hair. Turning about in surprise, he recognized the goddess' fierce eyes, though she was invisible to everyone else, and addressed her impatiently: 'What are you doing here, Pallas Athene, daughter of Zeus? Have you come to witness King Agamemnon's insolence? Then understand that, at any moment now, it may cost him his life.'

Athene answered: 'No, I am sent to curb your rage. You should listen to me, as a messenger of Hera the White-Armed, who loves both you and Agamemnon. Leave that sword-hilt alone! By all means, give him a tongue-lashing and tell him what punishment he must expect; but abstain from violence. For I promise that, one day soon, your wounded pride will be solaced with a prize three times more valuable than this slave. Now, prove that you trust Hera and myself by showing decent restraint.'

'Goddess,' said Achilles, 'I am indeed enraged, but it is always wise to listen when you speak, since the gods bless obedience.' So saying, he loosened his grip on the silver-hilted sword; and Athene, having made sure that he thrust it back into its scabbard, at once rejoined her fellow-deities in the Palace of Zeus on Mount Olympus.

Still furious, Achilles continued his tirade. 'Drunkard, with the face of a dog and the heart of a deer! When do you arm for a pitched battle at the head of your men, or join in setting an ambush for Trojans, as other Greek leaders do? You would rather die than make such an attempt, yet are capable of stealing a prize of honour from a brave man who challenges your pretensions. Devourer of your own people! Such grasping tyranny has left them spiritless; else you would never dare insult so many of my comrades. But I, at least, will say my say and confirm it with a solemn vow.'

Then Achilles took the following vow, on the gold-studded wand which gave him the right of uninterrupted speech:

'By this dry wand, no more to sprout
Or put green twigs and foliage out
Since once the hatchet, swinging free,
Cross-chopped it from a mountain tree,
Then trimmed away both leaves and bark—
By this same wand, which men who mark
Ancient traditions praised by ZEUS
Have set to honourable use
In ruling their debates: I vow
That all you Greeks assembled now
Before me—mark these words!—one day
Shall miss Achilles in the fray
And long for him, finding your chief
Incapable (despite all grief)
To save from Hector's murdering sword
Whole regiments; then at last, my lord,
Your anger inwards you shall turn,
Cursing the folly that dared spurn
Him who indignantly here speaks:
The best and bravest of all Greeks!'

So saying, Achilles dashed the wand to the ground, and sat down, while Agamemnon raged furiously in reply.

Nestor rose to his feet, old King Nestor of Pylus; and though he had outlived two whole generations of his subjects, and was ruling over a third, he addressed the Assembly with honeyed eloquence, in clear, pleasant, gentle tones. 'Alas,' he cried, 'Greece is gravely threatened by this dispute! King Priam, his sons, and all Troy would rejoice to hear of a breach between the two champions who always take the lead in planning and fighting our campaign. Pray listen to me, both of you, because your combined ages do not add up to mine, and because, when long ago I harangued men even better than yourselves, they never disregarded my advice. In my long life I have seen none to equal King Peirithous, or Dryas (a true shepherd of his people), or Caeneus, or Exadius, or wonderful Polyphemus.* They were the toughest warriors that ever walked this earth and chose to engage enemies worthy of their mettle—the wild, cave-

* Here some Athenian has patriotically interpolated a line: '*Or Theseus, son of Aegeus, who resembled the Immortals.*'

dwelling mountaineers—whom they destroyed without trace. These princes once summoned me from distant Pylus to fight beside them —nobody now alive could have resisted such heroes—and, what is more, I joined in their councils and they applauded my opinions. I therefore advise you princes to do the same. My lord Agamemnon, despite the grandeur of your rank, I charge you: keep your hands off the girl whom the Greeks awarded Achilles as his prize of honour! And my lord Achilles, I charge you: respect the dignity of a sceptre-bearing High King, Zeus' representative on earth! You are very strong, I know, and your mother was the Silver-Footed Goddess Thetis; but Agamemnon ranks higher than you, since more vassals owe him allegiance . . . Lastly, my lord King, I beg you, as a personal favour: let your anger cool! The entire army sees in Achilles its surest bulwark against the hazards of war.'

Agamemnon answered: 'What you have said is true enough, venerable Nestor. But this fellow wants to be treated as if he were Commander-in-Chief, High King, and President of the Council: an ambition which, I think, few members of this Assembly will support. Granted that the gods made him a fighter, have they also sanctioned him to revile me in such impudent language?'

Achilles interrupted. 'That is exactly what they have done! If I stayed silent, everyone would call me a coward and accuse me of always yielding to your demands. Trample on whom you please, but not on Achilles, son of Peleus, for his engagement is at an end. And pay attention when I declare that, though I will use no violence against you or your servants in the matter of Briseis—the prize of honour awarded me and now taken back—an attempt to impress me with your power by touching any other possession of mine would be dangerous! Visit my ship in that mood, and royal blood will stain my spear!'

The violent debate ended on this note, and the Assembly dispersed. Achilles, accompanied by his friend Patroclus, son of Menoetius, and the rest of his staff, walked towards the line of huts behind his flotilla.

Meanwhile, Agamemnon had a fast galley launched, picked a crew of twenty oarsmen, put aboard the required victims, and sent Chryseis home under the charge of Odysseus, his choice for captain.

As soon as the galley glided away, Agamemnon ordered a general purification. The whole army cleaned out the camp and, after throwing all its filth and rubbish into the sea, sacrificed oxen and goats to Apollo, a hundred at a time, on altars raised beside the salt waves. What a pleasant odour of roast flesh soared billowing up to Heaven on the smoke!

These pious acts did not, however, prevent Agamemnon from remembering his threats. He told the heralds Talthybius and Eurybates: 'Go to Achilles' hut and fetch me the beautiful Briseis! If he offers resistance, I shall go myself with an escort and take her by force, which will hurt his pride even more.'

Agamemnon's instructions being stern and explicit, Talthybius and Eurybates went through the camp, most unwillingly, until they reached the Myrmidons' lines. Prince Achilles, seated in his compound, gave them no sign; so they kept silence, afraid to utter a word. At last, guessing their errand, he said: 'Welcome, heralds! Since your task is to convey messages from Zeus, and from his royal representatives, step forward, and be assured that I do not blame you but only the High King, who has ordered you to steal my slave-girl Briseis.'

To Patroclus he said: 'Son of Menoetius, pray fetch the girl and let these heralds lead her away. Yet the day will come when I am needed to save Agamemnon's army from shameful defeat; and I shall call both of them to witness, before Immortals and mortals alike, but especially before that stubborn king, their master—what patience I have displayed. If Agamemnon expects his army to guard this fleet against a Trojan attack, he must be mad, as well as evil, not to consider the past and foresee the future.'

Patroclus accordingly fetched Briseis, and the heralds led her off towards King Agamemnon's lines, though she was loth enough to go. Presently, Achilles walked along the beach and sank down at some distance from his comrades, gazing in tears across the endless sea. Then he prayed to his goddess-mother, Thetis the Silver-Footed:

> 'Mother, the lifetime of this man
> Is destined to so brief a span
> That ZEUS, who thunders from the skies,
> Owes him at least a worthier prize

> Of glory than is his today!
> See, Agamemnon wrests away
> The captive girl with whom my sword
> Was honoured by the Greeks' award,
> To work his evil will upon her.
> Indeed, ZEUS holds me in small honour.'

Thetis, reclining under the sea beside her aged father Nereus, heard Achilles' voice. She hurriedly rose from the grey waves, and he saw her mistily through his tears, stroking his hand and saying: 'Tell me what ails you, my child! Instead of hiding your sorrow, share it with me.'

Achilles groaned aloud, and asked: 'Why should I tell what you know already? Nothing is hidden from your divine eyes. When we raided Thebe, Eëtion's fortress, and brought the spoils back here to Troy, the Council divided them equitably, reserving lovely young Chryseis for Agamemnon; but Chryses, Apollo's priest, came to ransom his daughter, carrying the sacred headband bound to a golden wand. After he had publicly appealed to Agamemnon, and his brother Menelaus, everyone present shouted: "Accept the ransom, respect the priest!" But Agamemnon dismissed Chryses, using such rough language that the old man went off, feeling outraged; and Apollo, who loves him dearly, listened to his prayer and at once began shooting the Greeks; they fell in droves, and a pestilence spread throughout the camp. Then Calchas the prophet revealed his Master's will, and I was first in advising my fellows to placate the angry god; which so enraged the High King that he threatened to rob me of my prize of honour. And now, though a ship is returning Chryseis to her father at Chryse, with a propitiatory offering for Apollo, Agamemnon's heralds have just visited me and led away Briseis, the girl whom the Greeks awarded me as my own prize!

'Mother, pray use whatever influence you command; go to Olympus and plead my case; reminding Zeus of any word or deed of yours that ever pleased him. At home, I have often heard you tell Peleus how, when the other Blessed Gods—including Hera, Poseidon, and Pallas Athene—wanted to put Zeus, Lord of the Storm, in fetters, you single-handedly saved him from ruin. Did you not summon the hundred-armed giant Aegaeon, or Briareus as the Immortals nick-

name him, to the peak of Olympus, as Zeus' protector? And did
not Aegaeon, a creature even more powerful than his father Uranus,
sit down beside Zeus, rejoicing in his strength, so that the gods were
too frightened to carry out their evil designs? Crouch at the Father's
feet and, clasping his knees in supplication, remind him of these
services. Perhaps he will assist the Trojan cause, and let the Greeks
be crowded back among their ships, ready for massacre. Then they
can test Agamemnon's fighting qualities, and realize that he was
mad to humiliate the best man serving under him.'

'Poor child,' Thetis sobbed, 'why did I ever rear you? I am cursed
in my motherhood! With so luckless a nativity, you deserved to stay
at your post, dry-eyed and content. Yet I find you alone and in
tears, though fated to a briefer span of life than any mortal. Cer-
tainly, I will visit snowy Olympus and approach Zeus of the
Thunderbolt. But you must stay here a little longer, taking no part
at all in the siege. The fact is that Zeus has gone to be entertained
by certain well-behaved Aethiopians, near the Ocean Stream, and
the other gods are with him. He does not return for twelve days;
when these have passed, I will cross the brazen threshold of his
Palace, and pay him homage. I may be able to win his favour.'

Thetis vanished, and left Achilles brooding over the forcible ab-
duction of slim-waisted Briseis.

Odysseus had meanwhile taken Agamemnon's galley to the Isle
of Chryse. On entering the deep harbour, his crew furled and stowed
away their sails, lowered the mast by the forestays, hastily fitted it
into its crotch, and rowed to the anchorage. There, having thrown
out the mooring-stones, they tied their vessel up and disembarked
the victims. Chryseis too went ashore, and Odysseus led her towards
the altar, where Chryses stood.

'Chryses,' he announced, 'Agamemnon the High King has sent
me to restore your daughter and to offer, on behalf of the Greek
army, a hundred-beast sacrifice in placation of Phoebus Apollo, who
has caused them such sorrow and grief.'

So saying, Odysseus gave the girl to Chryses, and he embraced
her joyfully; after which the victims were ranged around a noble
altar. All present washed their hands and each took a fistful of
barley-meal; except Chryses, who raised his arms, praying:

'God with the bow of silver,
　　You that take your stand
At Chryse and holy Cilla,
　　Protector of our land,

'Even as you plagued this people
　　In answer to my plea,
So now abate their torments,
　　And prove your trust in me!'

Apollo listened to this second prayer also. The Greeks now adored
him and, first sprinkling barley-meal on the victims' polls, pulled
up their muzzles and slit their throats. Next, they flayed the car-
cases, stripped the thighbones and wrapped them in double folds of
fat. When a few slices of flesh had been laid over these, Chryses
burned each sacrifice on a wood fire, his acolytes assisting him with
five-pronged forks, and tossed a libation of clear red wine into the
blaze. Thus the thighbones were consumed and, after tasting the
liver and kidneys, they jointed the carcases, spitted the meat, and
roasted it. The banquet being ready, they set to, and when they
could swallow no more, acolytes filled the bowls, from which a ra-
tion of wine was poured into every cup. All that afternoon, much
to Apollo's delight, the Greeks chanted the beautiful Victory Paean
composed in his honour; but at sunset they lay down to sleep beside
the mooring-ropes, and as soon as

DAWN, DAY's daughter bright,
Drew back the curtain of NIGHT
With her fingers of rosy light,

prepared to sail on a following wind provided by Apollo. They
stepped the mast, and the breeze bellied out the ship's white canvas
as they spread it. Off she sprang across the sea, and dark water
slapped against her bows. Their voyage done, they beached the ves-
sel high on the sand, fetched props to steady her, and then dispersed,
each man to his own hut and ship.

Achilles still idled by the seashore. He appeared neither at the
Council (as his rank demanded), nor on the battlefield; but
brooded miserably, yearning for war-cries and the clash of arms.

Twelve days later, Zeus led the Immortals home; and Thetis, who had not forgotten Achilles' plea, rose through the waves and flew to Olympus. There sat Zeus, Son of Cronus, Lord of the Echoing Thunder, in solitude on the topmost peak of that lofty, many-ridged mountain. Thetis knelt down, clasping his knees with her left hand, and placed the right caressingly beneath his chin.

This was her prayer:

> 'Great Father ZEUS, if ever THETIS
>   Assisted you by word or deed,
> Alone among the Immortal Gods
>   In ministration to your need,

> 'Fulfil, I beg you, this petition:
>   Honour Achilles, her dear son,
> Foredoomed by FATE to end his life
>   Before its prime has well begun.

> 'Now Agamemnon, King of Men,
>   Has roughly robbed him of his prize,
> Lovely Briseis; by this act
>   Dishonouring us in all Greek eyes.

> 'If ZEUS, sage sovereign of Olympus,
>   Rebuking such injustice, lends
> A brief support to Trojan arms,
>   My son may hope for full amends.'

Since Zeus listened but did not reply, Thetis continued, in the same suppliant posture: 'I beg you either to give me a firm promise, sealed with your divine nod, or else dismiss my petition. Why shrink from offending me? I know well that I am the least esteemed of all the Immortals.'

Zeus answered in troubled tones: 'A serious matter, and bound to cause trouble between Queen Hera and myself. She has often accused me of breaking my neutrality and favouring the Trojans. Nevertheless, if she does not surprise us two together, I will grant your plea. Come, take heart, and observe my divine nod: the surest possible sign (as everyone knows) that this is a true, certain, and irrevocable promise.' Zeus nodded his dark, immortal brow, shaking his scented locks, and the whole mountain quaked as he did so.

The two deities thereupon parted: Thetis diving straight into the sea; and Zeus making for his Palace, where the throned Olympians rose in courteous welcome as he entered the hall. But Hera, aware that he had agreed to help Thetis, began her taunts as soon as he was seated: 'Tell me, shifty husband, with what god or goddess have you been plotting? Am I always to be excluded from these secret conferences? Were you ever kind enough to inform me of your plans before they were set in motion?'

Zeus replied: 'Do not hope to be forewarned of all my decisions, Hera! They are sometimes too complex even for my wife to grasp. Whenever I can disclose any particular plan, no Immortal nor mortal will hear of it sooner than yourself; so, if I go apart to meditate, you must not badger me with questions afterwards.'

Hera protested: 'Revered Son of Cronus, what is this? You know that I never badger you with questions; but invariably leave you to reach your decisions in complete solitude. Today, however, I am much afraid that old Nereus' daughter Thetis the Silver-Footed, who was seen crouched, clasping your knees, on the mountain-top at dawn, has persuaded you to retrieve Achilles' honour. Did she not beg you to let the Greeks suffer a severe defeat in their naval camp, and did you not grant her your divine nod?'

'My lady,' cried Zeus, 'you never cease imagining things; but this eternal meddlesomeness, from which I have no means of escape, cannot alter my plans. In fact, the more you meddle, the less I trust you. I always do exactly as I please, so keep silent and learn to obey; for if once I lay my omnipotent hands on your divine frame, no god in Olympus will dare intervene.'

This threat alarmed Hera, who sat silently choking back her anger, amid general embarrassment, until Hephaestus the Smith-god ventured to pacify her. 'It would be disastrous, Mother,' he said, 'if you and my father started wrangling about mortal affairs and drew us into the quarrel. Domestic troubles ruin the taste of our delightful banquets. My advice—though a goddess as learned as yourself can dispense with advice—is to let him be; otherwise he may shout at us again and cause further consternation. The Ruler of gods and men is quite capable of knocking us off our thrones with his thunderbolts; and then where should we be? Come, look pleasant for our sakes, and restore his good humour!'

Hephaestus then rose and offered Hera a two-handled cup full of nectar. 'Mother,' he continued, 'be brave and patient, however vexed you are. I could not bear to watch him man-handle a goddess whom I love so dearly, and without the least hope of saving her. Zeus is far too powerful to be challenged. I will never forget my last attempt at intervention, when he caught me by the foot and hurled me out of the front door. I flew through the air all day, landing on Lemnos only at sunset. The crash half-killed me; but fortunately the Sintian islanders came to my rescue.'

Hera gave him a wan smile and accepted the cup. Then Hephaestus took a wine-bowl and filled every goblet, working from right to left; and what a shout of laughter arose at the sight of this lame god hobbling round and plying his ladle! The feast lasted until dusk. None could complain of the food, the drink, or the entertainment, because Apollo with his lyre, and the Muses with their clear voices, gave alternate performances. At nightfall, the Olympians scattered to their several homes—each cleverly designed for its owner by Hephaestus. Zeus himself retired to his bed-chamber and mounted the couch which he chose when he wished Sweet Sleep to visit him. There he rested awhile—and Hera of the Golden Throne rested at his side.

Book Two:

The False Dream: also 'Catalogue of Ships'

Not only every Greek of chariot-driving rank, but every Olympian too, Zeus alone excepted, slept the whole night through. He lay pondering how best to honour Achilles and arrange for a Greek defeat at their naval camp, until finally it occurred to him: why not send Agamemnon a false dream? Summoning one such to his bedside, he said: 'False Dream, fly down to the Greek ships at Troy, seek out King Agamemnon, son of Atreus—you will find him in his hut—and give him this message, carefully using my exact words:

> 'Know, King, that all Olympus
> Has yielded to the plea
> Brought before ZEUS by HERA
> With importunity.

> 'So rouse your long-haired army
> And march without delay
> In mass against the Trojans—
> Great Troy is yours today!'

The False Dream hurried off as instructed, and found Agamemnon sound asleep. Disguising herself as King Nestor of Pylus, whose advice he valued more than any man's, she cried: 'What, are you asleep, son of Atreus? A commander-in-chief with so many vassals serving under him, and so many preoccupations, has no right to snore the whole night through. Here is an urgent message from Zeus.

Though living far away, he feels a tender concern for your fortunes:

> ' "Know, King, that all Olympus
>   Has yielded to the plea
>   Brought before ZEUS by HERA
>   With importunity.

> ' "So rouse your long-haired army
>   And march without delay
>   In mass against the Trojans—
>   Great Troy is yours today!"

'That was Zeus' personal message; do not forget it on waking from your pleasant sleep!'

Off flew the False Dream. Agamemnon awoke and sat up, the divine words still ringing in his ears. Quite unaware that Zeus planned to cause both armies painful losses, he fondly expected to capture Troy that same day. Rising, he put on a beautiful, soft, bright tunic, and a capacious cloak over it, shod his white feet with elegant sandals, shouldered the baldric supporting his silver-studded sword, took in hand his imperishable sceptre (an ancestral heirloom), and strolled out among the ships.

As soon as Dawn touched high Olympus, notifying the Divine Family of Day's approach, Agamemnon told heralds to summon an immediate Assembly. They did so, and the Greek soldiers hastily gathered in response. Before addressing them, however, Agamemnon called a Privy Council beside Nestor's ship. 'Pay attention, friends,' he said. 'I was sleeping pleasantly last night, when someone resembling you, my lord Nestor, in height, bulk and appearance, invaded my dreams. He stood near me, and I heard him say: "What, are you asleep, Agamemnon, son of wise Atreus the Chariot-Fighter? A commander-in-chief with so many vassals serving under him, and so many preoccupations, has no right to snore the whole night through. Here is an urgent message from Zeus. Though living far away, he feels a tender concern for your fortunes:

> "Know, King, that all Olympus
>   Has yielded to the plea
>   Brought before ZEUS by HERA
>   With importunity.

> "So rouse your long-haired army
> And march without delay
> In mass against the Trojans—
> Great Troy is yours today!

' "This is Zeus' personal message. Do not forget it on waking from your pleasant sleep." So saying, the man in my dream vanished. With your leave, therefore, I shall sound a general call to arms. Yet it might be prudent to test the army's courage first. When I suggest, in Assembly, that we break off the siege and sail home, you must shout protests from all sides and insist on a vigorous offensive.'

Nestor then made a warm speech in support. 'My lord King, Princes and Councillors! Had any other person told us of this vision, we might have either disregarded it or rejected it as false. Agamemnon, however, has every claim to be considered the greatest among us, so we should, I believe, accept the message as authentic, and sanction a general call to arms.' Since nobody said anything else, all the members of the Council followed Nestor out, like sheep; and the men-at-arms came surging around them:

> Flights of bees, a thousand strong,
> From their caverned precipice
> Over flowery meadows throng,
> Some on that side, some on this.

And like bees the various Greek contingents streamed from their ships and huts on the low, sandy shore, urged by the Goddess Rumour, a servant of Zeus; soon setting the Assembly Ground in such an uproar, as they sat down on the benches, that the nine heralds who implored them at least to let the Kings, Zeus' foster-sons, make their voices heard, succeeded only by dint of considerable exertions.

Agamemnon stood up and displayed his sceptre. Lame Hephaestus, the Smith-god, had originally presented this exquisite work of art to Zeus; but Zeus later gave it to Hermes, the swift-flying Helper; who passed it on to Pelops the Charioteer; from whom it went to Atreus, the High King. Atreus bequeathed the sceptre to his brother Thyestes the Sheep-Breeder; and he, in his turn, bequeathed it to Atreus' son Agamemnon. Leaning on this emblem of his sovereignty over the entire Greek mainland, besides numerous adjacent islands, Agamemnon addressed the army:

'Comrades, soldiers of Greece, devotees of the God Ares! Zeus, hard-hearted Son of Cronus, promised me once, in my innocence, even pledging me his famous nod, that I should not return to Argos before sacking yonder great city of Troy. This was a cruel deception, it now appears: he meant us to sail back in disgrace, after suffering severe casualties—or that, at any rate, reflects my present view—and nobody can contend with Zeus, who has humbled many a city and must, in time, humble yet more. It will be a tale to shame our posterity: how such powerful Greek forces fought so long and so useless a war against far weaker opponents. I shall enlarge on this point. Suppose that a solemn armistice were concluded by the two armies; and suppose that the Trojans invited us to enter their gates; and suppose, further, that we Greeks divided into companies of ten, each company engaging a Trojan householder to pour wine for it—why, then, I can assure you, there would not be nearly enough wine-pourers to go round! Such is the disproportion between their strength and ours. Of course, the Trojans possess fighting allies in plenty; and it is these who prevent us from sacking Troy. Nine long years have passed; the ships' timbers are rotten and the tackle is perished; and though wives and children at home still await our return, we seem no nearer to success than we were at the start. Let us therefore do as I suggest: sail back to beloved Greece, in despair of ever forcing a way into the wide streets of Troy.'

Agamemnon's unexpected speech stirred the feelings of every man present, except his Privy Council, much as a tempestuous south-easter suddenly stirs the waters of the Icarian Gulf. Or, as when:

> After long days of summer heat
> A storm blows from the west,
> By which broad ranks of bearded wheat
> Are shaken and oppressed.

The Assembly broke up in such excitement that the soldiers' feet, scampering towards the ships, raised a tall cloud of dust. Down at the shore, men sang out to their comrades: 'Lend a hand with this galley! Clear her launching track, knock away the props, and into the water she goes!'

A confused noise rose to Heaven, and they would have raised the siege then and there, in defiance of Fate, had Hera not exclaimed: 'Athene, you busy daughter of Zeus the Shield-Bearer, what do I hear? Are Agamemnon's men really sailing back across the horizon? And will Priam and his Trojans make good their boast by keeping Queen Helen of Sparta—the woman for whose sake so many Greeks have died far from their native land? It is unthinkable! Hurry off, and prevent the launching of those ships!'

Athene darted straight to where Odysseus, Sacker of Cities, stood lost in grief, not attempting to launch his fine vessel. She confronted him with: 'Son of Laertes, what is this?' Then, using Hera's exact words, she went on: 'Are Agamemnon's men really sailing back across the horizon? And will Priam and his Trojans make good their boast by keeping Queen Helen of Sparta—the woman for whose sake so many Greeks have died far from their native land? It is unthinkable! Hurry off, and prevent the launching of those ships!'

Odysseus knew Athene's voice and, casting away his cloak—which Eurybates, the Ithacan herald, retrieved—ran through the camp, found Agamemnon, borrowed the aforesaid imperishable sceptre and, thus armed, walked around carrying out the goddess' instructions. Whenever he met an officer in command of a ship, he would say politely: 'My lord, it ill becomes you to catch this panic. Sit down, keep calm, and force your crew to do the same. You have entirely missed the drift of Agamemnon's speech: he was just testing the army's courage. And you had better take care that he does not punish you for this morning's rebellion. The foster-sons of Omniscient Zeus are proud of the divine honours bestowed on them; and he jealously protects them from affront.'

But whenever Odysseus met a rowdy man-at-arms, he shook the sceptre at him. 'Sit down,' he would shout, 'and await orders! You count for nothing, either as a soldier or a thinker. All Greeks cannot be kings. It is a bad army in which each soldier claims freedom of action: we need a united command, and our leader is Agamemnon, High King and representative of Zeus, Son of Cronus. Father

Zeus, in his inscrutable wisdom, has conferred this sceptre on him, with the right to exact obedience from you.'

Odysseus made his authority felt everywhere; and the men hurried back to their benches on the Assembly Ground, raising as much noise as when:

> A western wave rolls growling up the reach
> And thunderously breaks on the long beach . . .

There they took their places again and everyone sat quiet—except a certain Thersites, who had no control over his tongue, and poured out an endless stream of abuse against his superiors, saying whatever came into his head that might raise a laugh. Thersites was by far the ugliest man in the Greek army: bandy-legged, lame, hump-backed, crook-necked and almost bald. His main butts were Achilles and Odysseus, who both detested him. On this occasion, careless of the annoyance his words might cause, he taunted Agamemnon. 'Son of Atreus,' he cried, 'what more can you want of us? We have surely by now filled your huts with enough bronze vessels and slave-girls to satisfy your greed? When a city is sacked, you are always voted the pick of the loot. I daresay you hope to do even better soon: by squeezing the father of some Trojan prisoner whom I or my comrades may take, for a gold ransom. Or shall we capture yet another pretty little concubine to warm your bed? No commander-in-chief should treat his men so meanly!'

Then he bellowed at the crowded benches: 'Fools, rascals—women, not men—you should be ashamed of your softness! Go home, as you intended, and let this fellow Agamemnon gorge himself on his prizes of honour! That would soon teach him how much he needs us—especially after putting Achilles, a far finer soldier, to shame by robbing him of his award in that brutal fashion. Of course, Achilles has swallowed the insult; so he can hardly have felt much resentment, else Agamemnon would not still be alive and as presumptuous as ever.'

Odysseus, an impressive personage, walked straight across to Thersites, looked him sternly in the eyes, and said: 'Hold your tongue, you irresponsible windbag! Nobody here is attacking royal prerogatives; and since, in my view at least, you are the meanest member of the whole army landed here under Agamemnon and Menelaus, you had better keep kings out of your nasty talk and show less eagerness to raise the siege. The situation may be obscure—who can tell whether we ought to end this campaign or continue it?— but I will not allow you to taunt the High King with accepting the awards we have voted him. Let me hear any more of your nonsense, and I shall strip off your cloak and tunic, drive you in tears down to the ships, beating your naked buttocks as you run! May this head be taken from my shoulders—may I be denied the title of Telemachus' father—if I fail to make good my threat!'

So saying, he raised the royal sceptre and belaboured Thersites' hump with it. Thersites shrank back, and a big tear coursed down one cheek—for the sceptre had left a bloody weal where it struck— then he subsided in pain and confusion, threw a helpless glance around, and wiped the tear away. His comrades, though regretting the violence, mocked at him, and some exclaimed: 'Odysseus may be an eminent strategist and tactician, but his silencing of this chatterbox is by far the kindest service he has done us. Depend on it, Thersites will never again presume to slander a divine king!'

Odysseus then made an address. Athene, disguised as his herald, called for silence, so effectively that even those seated farthest off could catch every word of the speech. He said earnestly: 'Son of Atreus, these troops intend to make you the most despised mortal alive, by a breach of the oath which they all took on leaving Greece: it was to obey your orders loyally until you had sacked Troy. Now they whimper, like infant children or their widowed mothers, and complain of homesickness! True, this siege is grim enough to sap any man's resolution. When a storm-bound sailor has to stay away from his wife for as little as a month, he grows impatient: and we are already in the ninth year of war. I am not surprised that some men are eating their hearts out; but the longer we remain here, the more shameful will it be to go back empty-handed.

'Take courage, comrades, and have patience yet awhile! We shall soon see whether Calchas was a true prophet. Doubtless you remember that famous scene as though it were yesterday, or the day before. Our fleet had gathered at Aulis, laden with trouble for Priam and his Trojans, and we kings stood beside a spring, offering carefully chosen sacrifices on the altars of the Immortals. The spring ran clear between the roots of a plane-tree. Suddenly we saw a remarkable portent: a snake with blood-red markings appeared from under the altar and darted towards the tree, on the very top branch of which, hidden by leaves, a sparrow had built her nest. Up the trunk glided that ruthless snake, and swallowed each of the nestlings in turn— there were eight of them—while the distressed mother fluttered over- head, cheeping indignantly. Then he coiled his tail about the branch, seized hold of the hen-sparrow's wing, and swallowed her also. Eight and one make nine; and Zeus, Son of Cronus, who always moves in a mysterious way, proved that he had sent this portent himself by miraculously turning the snake into stone. As we stared in amaze- ment at this interruption of our solemn sacrifice, Calchas prophesied:

> ' "Why stand you silent, long-haired Greeks,
>   When ZEUS the Omniscient
>   This late sign, this great sign,
>   This famous sign has sent?
>
> ' "A snake devours a sparrow whole,
>   Likewise her nestlings eight;
>   So shall War swallow nine whole years,
>   And Victory come late:
>   Not till the tenth year shall proud Troy
>   Fall from her high estate!"

'Calchas' prophecy is now approaching fulfilment. So I beg you noble warriors to continue manfully here, until we have sacked King Priam's city.'

Such cheers greeted Odysseus' words that the ships echoed. Old Nestor, however, complained: 'What a disorganized Assembly! You behave like a crowd of foolish boys without any interest in warfare proper. Do covenants and oaths mean nothing to you? Why not throw on a bonfire all the plans, schemes, libation ceremonies, and hand-clasps of friendship on which we rely? So far you have done no more than talk, argue, and waste the entire forenoon in trying to shape a common policy; as though the High King would swerve from his avowed purpose, which is to shepherd us through the hazards of battle! The small party of Greeks who are making a futile attempt to raise the siege before they see whether Zeus keeps his promise, deserve death! As we sailed from Aulis that fateful day, lightning flashed on our starboard bow, his sure pledge that we should be victorious. No one should therefore think of returning until he has avenged Paris the Trojan's theft of Queen Helen, and whatever personal discomfort he may have experienced, by enjoying the wife of some Trojan enemy; but anyone who feels an irresistible desire for home can try launching his ship—and be the first to die!

'My lord Agamemnon, pray consider the following proposal and ask your Privy Council their opinion on it! I move that, when taking the field, you should group your army by tribes and clans: with each clan supporting its fellow-clans, and each tribe supporting its fellow-tribes. If we assume a widespread loyalty to you, we shall thus readily distinguish the brave men from the cowards, and contrive to judge whether the gods themselves oppose your capture of Troy, or whether you must blame the poor fighting qualities of your troops.'

Agamemnon answered: 'Venerable Nestor, as usual you have made the best speech of the session! Ah, if only Father Zeus, and Athene and Apollo would provide ten Councillors as shrewd as yourself, we should soon sack this stubborn city! Zeus has surrounded me with so much fruitless wrangling and quarrelling that my mind is never at ease. Although Achilles provoked that violent dispute about his captive, I confess to having lost my temper before he did. But as soon as we princes reach unanimity on matters of common interest, Troy will no longer avoid her fate—no, not for a single day!

'Now, my men, march off to your dinners, and afterwards we shall take up our battle stations. I want all spears sharpened, all shields tested, all horses fed, and all chariots thoroughly gone over, in readiness for several hours of hard fighting. I cannot promise you the least intermission once the armies are engaged; nightfall alone shall call a halt. By then, baldrics and the necks of your horses will be damp with sweat, and spear-hands numbed. Yet if I catch any soldier skulking among the ships, why, dogs and carrion-birds shall have his corpse!'

Prolonged applause greeted Agamemnon's words—

> As when a south wind forces
>   In never-ending flock
> Tall waves against a headland,
>   A steep and jutting rock;
> This side or that they strike it
>   With loud, continual shock.

Then the troops dispersed hurriedly to their lines, kindled fires on the hearths, cooked and ate their dinners; but each first sacrificed to one of the Olympians, imploring protection from the imminent slaughter. Agamemnon's own victim was a fat five-year-old bull, and he summoned six Councillors to assist at the sacrifice: namely, Nestor of Pylus; Idomeneus of Crete; Great Ajax and Little Ajax, the Locrian; Diomedes of Argos; and cunning Odysseus of Ithaca. Menelaus came uninvited, guessing how busy his brother must be. These seven princes stood around the victim, holding barley-meal; and Agamemnon prayed to Zeus:

> 'O ZEUS, greatest of gods
>   In Heaven residing,
> With unabated power
>   The storm cloud riding:
>
> 'Let not this sun go down,
>   Nor darkness flout me,
> Till I and these seven kings
>   Here grouped about me
>
> 'Have fired the many-doored
>   Dwelling of Priam,
> That not one wall may stand
>   So tall as I am;
>
> 'Till swords have rent the bright
>   Tunic of Hector,
> And ringed him round with dead—
>   Troy's doomed protector.'

Zeus, though accepting the sacrifice, did not grant Agamemnon's plea, but only made matters worse for him. Meanwhile, the princes, having each spoken his prayer, sprinkled their barley-meal on the bull's poll; then one of them drew back its muzzle and slit the throat. Next, they flayed the carcase, stripped the thighbones of flesh, and wrapped these in a double fold of fat. Slabs of flesh having been laid over them, they burned this sacrifice on dry branches; also spitting pieces of liver and kidneys, to be eaten as appetizers. Afterwards they jointed the carcase and roasted slices of beef on the same spits. Their banquet being at last ready, everyone set to, and when they had eaten as much as they could swallow, Nestor spoke again: 'Noble son of Atreus, High King Agamemnon, it is time we ended our meal and, without further delay, undertook the task which Zeus has assigned us. Let the heralds summon all contingents to parade in full armour beside the ships; and then we should review them and foster their fighting spirit.'

Agamemnon accepted Nestor's sensible advice, and the parade formed up at once. The seven princes eagerly marshalled their subjects, and Owl-Eyed Athene stood by. Her indestructible shield, called the Aegis, was fringed with a hundred curiously woven golden tassels, each of them worth one hundred oxen. She dazzled the Greek ranks, giving every man strength and courage to fight all day, and convincing him that battle was much more enjoyable than a long voyage home. The twinkling of bronze arms and armour could have been seen at a great distance—

> As when a mountain-forest burns: the glow
> Visible miles away to men below—

and the soldiers, pouring from their ships and huts into the Scamandrian Plain, recalled:

> Migrating birds of many kinds
> That all together swoop upon
> Asian meadow land where winds
> The Cayster: crane and goose and swan.
>
> No single field contents their eye
> But, with one huge discordant voice,
> Hither and thither on they fly
> And in their splendid plumes rejoice.

The plain menacingly echoed the tread of beasts and men, as the Greeks gathered upon it, eager to pull their enemy in pieces. How numerous they were, too!

> Like leaves and blossoms bursting out
>> From every lusty tree,
> Like flies of spring that buzz about
>> The farmyard busily,
> When milk pours foaming into pails:
> To number them no count avails.

Their leaders controlled them with the easy authority of goatherds, each keeping his flock together on a common pasture. In the centre rode Agamemnon: he had a frown worthy of Zeus, a waist worthy of Ares, a breast worthy of Poseidon! He reminded everyone of a bull, standing nobly prepared to defend his herd; so heroic and grand, by the grace of Heaven, was his appearance.

And now,

> You wise and gentle MUSES,
>> Who on Olympus dwell,
> And truth from idle rumour
>> Can separate and tell:
> MEMORY's daughters, prompt me—
>> Alone, I judge not well.

What I want is the name of every Greek commander and lesser officer who fought against Troy. Any attempt at listing the men-at-arms, too, would be hopeless: for that I should need ten tongues, an unwearied voice, and a heart of bronze, as well as the assistance of these same divine Muses.

∗

Here is THE CATALOGUE OF SHIPS:

The Boeotians sent fifty ships, with a complement of one hundred and fifty men each, under the command of *Peneleos*, *Leïtus*, *Arcesilaus*, *Prothoenor* and *Clonius*. Some of their troops came from the following places: Hyria, the rocky district of Aulis, Schoenus, Scolus, the ridges of Eteonus, Thespeia, Graia, the spreading pastureland of Mycalessus.

Others came from Harma, Eilesion, Erythrae, Eleon, Peteon, Hyle, Ocalea, the fortress of Medeon, Copae, Eutresis and Thisbe (where doves breed).

Still others came from Coronea, the meadows of Haliartus, Plataea, Glisas, the fortress of Lesser Thebes, Onchestus (where Poseidon has a sacred grove), the vineyards of Arne, Mideia, Nisa (sacred to Dionysus), and the frontier town of Anthedon.

*

The Minyans of Boeotia sent thirty ships, under the command of Ascalaphus and *Ialmenus*, twin sons of the God Ares. Their troops came from Aspledon and Orchomenus. Ares had once stolen into the bedroom of these princes' stately mother Astyoche, unknown to her father King Actor, son of Zeus.

*

The Phocians sent forty ships, under the command of *Schedius* and *Epistrophus*, sons of gallant Iphitus, the son of Naubolus. Their troops came from Cyparissus, rocky Delphi and Crysa (both sacred to Apollo), Daulis, Panopeia, Anemoreia, Hyampolis, and the banks of the Cephisus as far as Lilaea, at its source.

Keeping their companies well in control, Schedius and Epistrophus now drew them up on the left flank of the Boeotian contingent.

*

The Locrians from the coast opposite Euboea sent forty ships, under the command of *Little Ajax*, son of Oïleus. Though nothing like so striking a figure as Great Ajax, son of Telamon, this diminutive prince, who always wore a linen corslet, was easily the handiest with a spear in all Greece, Achaea not excepted. His troops came from Cynus, Opus, Calliarus, Bessa, Scarphe, the lovely district of Augeiae; also from Tarphe and Thronion, in the valley of the Boagrius.

*

The Abantes sent forty ships, under the command of *Elephenor*, son of Chalcodon, a descendant of Ares. His troops came from Euboea, Chalcis, Eiretria, and the vinelands of Histaea; also from the seaport of Corinthus, the high fortress of Dios, Carystus and Styra. They wore their hair very long, and would rush forward furiously into battle, eager to rip the enemy's corslets with the blades of their ash-shafted spears.

*

The Athenians sent fifty ships, under *Menestheus*, son of Peteus, the ablest commander then living—if we exclude old Nestor, who had much more experience of warfare.

Athens is the splendid city once ruled by Erechtheus the Courageous, a parthenogenous son of Mother Earth, Giver of Grain. The Goddess Athene, Zeus' daughter, brought up Erechtheus in her own rich temple at Athens, where an annual sacrifice of bulls and rams still honours his memory.

✳

The Salaminians sent twelve ships, under *Great Ajax*, son of Telamon.*

✳

The Achaeans sent two flotillas. The first consisted of eighty ships, under *Diomedes of the Loud War-Cry*; his lieutenants being *Sthenelus*, son of the famous Capaneus, and *Euryalus* the Godlike, son of King Mecisteus, son of Talaus. Their troops came from Argos, the great fortress of Tiryns, Hermione and Asine (seaports on opposite sides of a deep gulf), Troezen, Eionae, the vineyards of Epidaurus, the island of Aegina, and Mases.

The second Achaean flotilla consisted of one hundred ships, the largest of the whole fleet, under the personal command of *Agamemnon*, son of Atreus. His contingent, the most numerous and best equipped in the army, came from the great walled city of Mycenae, wealthy Corinth, the fortress of Cleonae, Orneiae, delightful Araethyrea, and Sicyon, whose first king was Adrestus. Also from Hyperisië, Gonoessa on its crag, the coastal region about Aegion, and the broad lands of Helice. Agamemnon himself, wearing a glorious suit of brightly polished bronze armour, outshone all other princes, and ranked as far the most important.

✳

The Laconians sent sixty ships, under *Menelaus*, deputy commander-in-chief to his brother, King Agamemnon. Menelaus displayed his warlike spirit—sharpened by a desire to avenge himself on the Trojans for the trouble and sorrow their abduction of Queen Helen had caused him—in the zeal with which he fought. His troops came from Lacedaemon (a town cradled in the hills), Pharis, Sparta, Messe (a haunt of doves), Bryseiae, pleasant Augeiae, Amyclae, and the coastal fortress of Helus; also from Laas and Oetylus.

✳

The Messenians sent ninety ships, under the command of *Nestor* the Gerenian. His troops came from Pylus, pleasant Arene, Thryen (where the Alpheius is fordable), the fortress of Aepy, Cyparisseis, Amphigeneia,

---

* In order to strengthen their claims over the island of Salamis, the Athenians here interpolated a line:
                  '*and drew them up at the Athenians' station.*'
Apparently Solon arranged the matter for the tyrant Peisistratus, at whose court the *Iliad* was being edited.

Pteleum, Helus and Dorion. (At Dorion, the Muses waylaid Thamyris the Thracian as he left the palace of Eurytus in Oechalia; vexed by Thamyris' boast that he could outsing them, they not only blinded him but silenced his voice and made him forget how to play the lyre.)

*

The Arcadians, since they lived inland and lacked naval experience, borrowed sixty ships belonging to Agamemnon, and placed them under the command of *Agapenor*, son of Ancaeus. His troops came from the lower slopes of Mount Cyllene, near Aegyptus' tomb, where tough fighting-men abound, the sheep-pastures of Arcadian Orchomenus, Rhipe, pleasant Mantineia, Stymphalus and Parrhasie.

*

The Epeians sent forty ships, under four independent commanders, each in charge of a ten-ship flotilla. These were two of King Actor's descendants: *Amphimachus*, son of Cteatus, and *Thalpius*, son of Eurytus; also *Diores*, the gallant son of Amarynceus, and *Polyxeinus*, son of King Agasthenes and grandson of King Augeias. Their troops came from Buprasion, and from so much of the rich land of Elis as is bounded by Hyrmine, the frontier town of Myrsinus, the Olenian Rock and Aleision.

*

The Western Islanders sent two flotillas. The first consisted of forty ships under *Meges*, son of Phylus, as fine a fighter as Ares himself. His troops came from Dulichium and the Echinean Isles, which lie to the north of Elis. Meges' father Phylus the Horseman, a prince favoured by Zeus, migrated to Dulichium after a quarrel with his father King Augeias, who had cheated Heracles of a reward earned by cleansing out his stables.

The second flotilla consisted of twelve ships with vermilion-painted bows, under the command of *Odysseus* the Crafty. His troops came from the islands of Cephallene, Ithaca, wooded Neriton, Crocyleia, rugged Aegilips, Zacynthos, Samos, and the mainland opposite.

*

The Aetolians sent forty ships, under *Thoas*, son of Andraemon. His troops came from Pleuron, Olenus, Pylene, the coastal town of Chalcis, and rocky Calydon. Thoas was successor to King Meleager the Fair-Haired, who had ruled after the death of bold Oineus and his sons.

*

The Cretans sent eighty ships, under the joint-command of King *Idomeneus* the Warrior and *Meriones*, who rivalled the God Ares himself in battle. Their troops came from all the hundred cities of Crete, including the fortress of Cnossus, Gortys with its huge walls, Lyctus, Miletus, chalky Lycastus, Phaestus and Rhytion.

✳

The Rhodians sent nine ships, under the command of Heracles' son *Tlepolemus*. His troops came from the island's three cities: Lindus, Ialysus, and chalky Cameirus.

Tlepolemus was the son of Astyocheia, whom Heracles had captured at Ephyra beside the River Selleeis, after sacking several cities held by Zeus' royal foster-sons. When Tlepolemus grew to manhood in the fortress of Tiryns, he murdered his father's uncle, old Licymnius, a descendant of Ares. Threatened with death by Heracles' other offspring, he hastily built a fleet, collected a large number of colonists, and sailed away to Rhodes. These immigrants were adopted into the three Rhodian tribes and greatly favoured by Zeus, who made them exceedingly rich.

✳

The Symians sent three ships, under the command of *Nireus*, son of Aglaia and King Charopus. Though the handsomest of all these Greeks, with the sole exception of Achilles, he was a weakling; nor did his contingent amount to much.

✳

The Asian Islanders sent thirty ships, commanded by *Pheidippus* and *Antiphus*, the sons of Thessalus and grandsons of Heracles. Their troops came from Nisyros, Carpathos, Casos and Cos, where Eurypylus reigned; and from the Calydnian group.

✳

The Myrmidons, with their Hellenic and Achaean neighbours, sent fifty ships, under the command of *Achilles*. His troops came from Pelasgian Argos, Alus, Alope, Trachis, Phthia and Hellas (famed for its beautiful women).

This contingent, however, did not join the present parade because their commander, Prince Achilles, was sulking down at the camp—angered by his loss of beautiful Briseis. He had been given her as a reward for sacking Lyrnessus, where she lived, and the walled city of Thebe; also for killing Mynes and Epistrophus, the spearman sons of King Evenus the Selepiad, in a hotly-contested battle. Nevertheless, Achilles was soon to fight once more.

✳

The Thessalians sent seven contingents, led by one of forty ships originally under the command of gallant *Protesilaus*, who was the son of Iphiclus, the grandson of Phylacus, and a descendant of Ares. His troops came from Phylace, fertile Pyrasus (where Demeter has a sanctuary), Itone (famous for its flocks), the coastal town of Antron, and the pastures of Pteleus.

Protesilaus, however, the first Greek to land at Troy, was also the first casualty; a Trojan killed him as he leaped ashore, leaving his widow to disfigure her cheeks in token of grief. Protesilaus had quitted Phylace with their bridal chamber only half-built. The troops missed him greatly because, though a younger brother named *Podarces* took charge of them, Protesilaus had been by far the braver of the two.

The second contingent, of eleven ships, was commanded by *Eumelus*, the son of Alcestis (loveliest of Pelias' daughters), and *Admetus* of Pherae. These troops came from Pherae beside Lake Boebe, the town of Boebe, Glaphyre, and the fortress of Iolcus.

The third contingent, of seven ships, was commanded by *Philoctetes*, the famous archer, and each contained fifty oarsmen expert with the bow. These troops came from Methone, Thaumacia, Meliboea, and rugged Olizon. But Philoctetes himself lay pining away and suffering torments in the pleasant Isle of Lemnos, where the Greeks had marooned him because of his noisome wound caused by the bite of a venomous watersnake. Philoctetes' men, though they missed him, did not stay leaderless; *Medon*, a bastard son of Rene and Oïleus the City-Sacker, took his place. The Greeks were destined, however, to recall Philoctetes before capturing Troy.

The fourth contingent, of thirty ships, was commanded by Asclepius' two sons *Podaleirius* and *Machaon*, both skilled physicians. Their troops came from Tricca, Ithone (with its terraces), and Eurytus' city of Oechalia.

The fifth contingent, of forty ships, was commanded by *Eurypylus*, Euaemon's famous son. His troops came from Ormenius, the spring of Hypereia, Asterion, and the snow-clad peaks of Mount Titanus.

The sixth contingent, of the same size, was jointly commanded by the resolute *Polypoetes*, son of Peirithous and thus grandson of Zeus himself, and his comrade *Leonteus*, son of Coronus and grandson of Caeneus, a descendant of Ares. (Polypoetes' mother conceived him on the day that her husband Peirithous drove the shaggy Centaurs out of their homes on Mount Pelion and forced them to seek refuge with the Aethicans.) These troops came from Argissa, Orthe, Elone, and the white town of Oloosson.

The seventh contingent, of twenty-two ships, was commanded by *Guneus*, King of Cyphus. Among his troops were the Enienians and the tough Peraebians from settlements near wintry Dodona and farms in the delightful valley of the Titaresius. This river, though a tributary of the Peneius, does not mix with its waters, but flows above them like a coat of oil: being itself fed by the dreadful River Styx—on which the Immortals swear oaths that they never break.

✳

The Magnesians, lastly, sent forty ships, commanded by Prothous, son of Teuthredon. His troops came from the banks of the Peneius, and the wooded slopes of Mount Pelion.

✳

> Such were the captains, such the crews.
> Now help me, knowledgeable MUSE,
> To pick the best men and best horses
> From all King Agamemnon's forces!

By far the finest team on parade were two mares bred for Admetus, son of Pheres, by Apollo of the Silver Bow: swift as birds, perfectly matched in colour, age and size—one could lay a rod anywhere across their backs when they stood side by side, and it would always remain level. Harnessed to the chariot of Admetus' son Eumelus, who had brought them overseas, they carried all the terror of battle with them.

In the absence of Achilles, easily the best fighter was Great Ajax, son of Telamon, commanding the Salaminian contingent. Achilles, of course, outshone Great Ajax—as, indeed, his chariot-team outshone that of Eumelus—but while anger against Agamemnon kept him idling in his hut, the men amused themselves along the shore at quoits, javelin-throwing, and archery, or wandered through the camp, heartily wishing that someone would lead them to war. The Myrmidons' horses stood idle too, munching clover and marsh-parsley; and the chariots were stowed away.

Meanwhile Agamemnon had sounded the advance, and—

> The spearmen coursed across Troy's plain
>   As though they trod on coals of fire;
> The broad earth heaved and groaned again
>   As under ZEUS the Thunderer's ire
> When, at Inarimë, he shakes
> Great TYPHON's couch; and the world quakes.

*

At this point, Golden-Winged Iris, the Olympian herald, was entrusted by Zeus with an unwelcome message for the Trojans. She found a meeting in progress near the royal palace—citizens of all ages attended it—and came disguised as the permanent look-out man, Priam's son Polites. He used to perch aloft on the ancient tomb of Aesyetes, and if any considerable force emerged from the Greek camp, he could run fast enough to raise the alarm in good time. Imitating Polites' voice, Iris addressed old Priam: 'Father, though you enjoy listening to eloquent, well-composed speeches suitable for peaceful occasions, the needs of war compel me to brevity. I have done my fair share of fighting; but let me assure you that the largest and most formidable army I ever saw is now advancing across the plain: as numerous as forest leaves or grains of sand on the seashore.'

Iris then turned to Hector and said: 'Brother, pray take my advice! Many allied contingents are serving under you, all speaking different dialects: ask each commander to lead his men out in defence of the city, and post them at his own discretion.'

Hector, recognizing Iris' voice, broke up the meeting. A rush to arms ensued, and soon the Trojan infantry and chariotry poured through the gates, yelling their war-cries.

Between Troy and the Greek camp, a small knoll rises from the Scamandrian Plain; though commonly known as 'The Bateia', its sacred name is 'The Tomb of Leaping Myrine'. This knoll they occupied, and here I give you

THE TROJAN ORDER OF BATTLE:

The Trojans proper, led by *Hector* the Bright-Helmed; easily the biggest and best corps in the army.

The Dardanians, led by Prince *Aeneas*, son of Anchises, with Archelochus and Acamas, Antenor's sons, as his reliable lieutenants. (One night, among the ridges of Mount Ida, Anchises, a mortal, had begotten Aeneas on Laughter-Loving Aphrodite.)

The Zeleians, rich Trojan colonists of the Aesepus Valley, at the very foot of Mount Ida, led by Prince *Pandarus*, son of Lycaon. Pandarus carried a bow which Apollo the Archer himself had given him.

The Adresteians, and their neighbours from Apaesus, Pityeia, and the steep hill of Tereia, led by two brothers: *Adrestus* and *Amphius* of the Linen Corslet. Their father Merops, King of Percote, a prophet of wide repute, had warned them against taking part in this murderous war; but they paid no heed, being lured to their death by the sullen Fates.

The Hellespontians and their neighbours from the Sea of Marmara—men of Percote, Practius, Sestus, Abydus, and pleasant Arisbe beside the Selleeis—whence their commander Prince *Asius,* son of Hyrtacus, drove a chariot-team of tall sorrels.

The Pelasgians of fertile Larissa in the Troad, led by *Hippothous* and *Pylaeus,* twin sons of Teutamus' son Lethus and descendants of Ares.

The Thracians from the farther side of the swift-running Hellespont, led by *Acamas* and the heroic *Peirous.* Included in this contingent were the Ciconian spearmen, led by *Euphemus,* son of King Troezenus of Ceus.

The Paeonians, archers, led by *Pyraechmes,* and men from Cytorus, the neighbourhood of Sesamon, the banks of the River Parthenius, Cromna, Aegialus, and Erytheni high up in the hills. Their country is famous for its breed of wild mules.

The Alizonians from the silver mines of far-off Alybe, led by *Odius* and *Epistrophus.*

The Mysians, led by *Chromis* and *Ennomus* the Augur. Ennomus' auguries did not, however, serve to protect him. When Achilles later caused such havoc among the Trojans and their allies at the Battle of the Scamander, Ennomus died too.

The Phrygians from Ascania, eager fighters, led by *Phorcys* and *Ascanius* the Splendid.

The Maeonians from the slopes of Mount Tmolus, under the command of *Mesthles* and *Antiphus,* sons of the Lake-goddess Gyge by King Talaemenes.

The Carians, with their unintelligible language, men from Miletus, wooded Mount Phthires, the River Maeander, and the abrupt slopes of Mycale, led by *Nastes* and *Amphimachus,* the gallant sons of Nomion. This Amphimachus was vain enough to wear golden armour on the battlefield, as though he were a girl, but would have been wise to choose baser metal. Achilles killed him in the river and very wisely despoiled his corpse of its treasure.

The Lycians from the banks of the other River Xanthus, far to the south, led by *Sarpedon* and *Glaucus* the Victorious.

Book Three:

Paris Duels with Menelaus

> Cranes that flee the wintry storm
>   With trumpetings of doom prepare,
> Flight after flight, to seek those warm
>   Waters of southern Ocean, where
> Black pigmies in undaunted swarm
>   The murderous attack outdare.

It was with a similarly aggressive clamour that the Trojan contingents formed up and marched against the silent, courageous, well-disciplined Greeks. Again:

> Sheep-stealers love the cloud
>   That hangs on every hill
> Better than night's black shroud;
>   They can do what they will:
>
> For they go wandering free
>   (Long may the south wind last!)
> Where shepherds cannot see
>   Beyond a short stone-cast.

Much the same obscurity resulted from great clouds of dust which rose as the Trojan forces advanced at a double across the plain. Before battle could be joined, however, Prince Paris darted out between the two armies and offered to meet any Greek champion in single combat. He carried a bow, a sword, and two bronze-headed spears; and wore a panther-skin mantle.

> A famished lion takes good note
> When arrows wound a stag or goat:
> Greedily on the prey he bounds,
> Reckless of huntsmen or of hounds.

With an equal disregard of danger, Menelaus of the Loud War-Cry leaped from his chariot and ran towards Paris; this seemed a Heaven-sent occasion for avenging the great wrong he had suffered.

Paris at once thought better of his challenge.

> Who meets a serpent in a mountain glade
> Retreats in terror, trembling and dismayed . . .

Having no desire to die, he ceased to brandish his spear and slipped back through the Trojan ranks.

Hector the Bright-Helmed shouted angrily at him: 'Paris, you handsome, deceitful, woman-mad good-for-nothing—I wish you had never been born, or had died too young to disgrace us! These Greeks will sneer at your cowardice, saying that we Trojans chose you as our champion only because of your good looks. Here is a fellow who leads a Trojan embassy to Greece, receives courteous entertainment there, and then brings trouble on father, city, and country by carrying off the beautiful wife of his host, a king of famous military stock! Now our enemies laugh to see him slink away, while we hang our heads. So you feared to face Menelaus the Warrior, brother, and find out what sort of husband you had robbed? That was wise: neither your lyre-playing, nor your pretty curls, nor your exquisite profile will be of much use when he strikes you to the dust. Upon my word, we must be cowards ourselves, not to have stoned you long ago for all the misery that escapade has caused us—we should have wrapped your shoulders in a weightier mantle than a panther-skin!'

'These are sharp words,' Paris answered, 'yet not unreasonably so, coming from a man of your simple courage. They cut like the axe of an expert ship's carpenter: he hacks at a beam, and every stroke tells. But why condemn Aphrodite's lavish kindness to me? Nobody is handsome by his own unaided efforts. Should I show ingratitude for what the gods have freely given? However, if you forbid me to withdraw my challenge, very well: make our men sit down, persuade the

Greeks to follow their example, and I will meet and fight Menelaus between the armies. Let our stakes be Helen and her fortune; the survivor to take both. Since this quarrel is a personal one, the two armies should allow Menelaus and me to settle it ourselves, afterwards swearing an oath of peace. Then you can stay here contentedly, and the Greeks can sail home to their land of thoroughbred horses and lovely women.'

Hector, delighted by Paris' answer, went along the Trojan line, pressing the troops back with his spear held horizontally. 'Stay where you are and sit down!' he shouted. Stones and arrows flew at him until Agamemnon cried: 'Hold your fire, comrades! It looks as if Prince Hector has something to announce.'

They obeyed and, when silence had fallen, Hector spoke as follows: 'Trojans and Greeks, I have a message for you all from my brother, Prince Paris, whose elopement with Queen Helen occasioned this war. He requests you to ground arms, sit down, and watch Menelaus the Warrior and himself fighting it out in the no-man's-land between our front-lines. The stakes will be Helen and her fortune; the survivor to take both. Meanwhile, we should agree on an armistice and ratify it by sacrifice.'

Everyone waited for Menelaus to accept this second challenge. He replied: 'Greeks and Trojans, as the chief sufferer from Paris' misdeeds, I shall now make an announcement, believing that, after all the distress this war has caused our nations, the end is at last in sight. Listen: I say that whichever of us two principals may be doomed, let him die and allow the rest of us to retire without further fighting. But, first, victims are needed: a white lamb for the Sun, a black lamb for Earth. We should also offer Zeus a ram. And King Priam must be summoned to ratify this armistice; we cannot trust his sons to keep their oaths, even if they swear in Zeus' name. Youngsters are often presumptuous and unreliable; old men review a case painstakingly and consider the benefit of all parties involved.'

Menelaus' speech was met with general satisfaction. The noblemen of both armies dismounted from their chariots; the other ranks took off their helmets, grounded arms in the small space available, except their spears, which they planted upright, and sat down, overjoyed at the prospect of final peace.

Hector sent two heralds scurrying across the plain to summon King Priam and fetch the lambs; Agamemnon likewise sent Talthybius to fetch Zeus' ram from the naval camp.

At this point Golden-Winged Iris, disguising herself as Laodice, the loveliest of Priam's daughters, who had married Antenor's son Helicaon, flew from Olympus with a message for Laodice's sister-in-law Helen; and found her weaving battle scenes of the present campaign into a long, double-width, purple tapestry. 'Dear sister,' cried Iris, 'come and see a strange sight! The Trojans and Greeks, hitherto such relentless enemies, are seated quietly in their ranks, facing each other, and every man-at-arms is leaning on his shield, a spear planted beside him. They are arranging an armistice. Imagine: Prince Paris has challenged King Menelaus to single combat! The survivor will keep you as his wife.'

This news made Helen yearn to be home in Sparta with her parents and her former husband. Drawing a white linen veil across her face to hide a sudden shower of tears, she hurried off, accompanied by a couple of ladies-in-waiting: Aethra, daughter of Pittheus, and Clymene the Cow-Eyed. The three women went to a watch-tower covering the Scaean Gate, where they joined King Priam and a group of his Councillors, already posted behind the battlements: Panthous, Thymoetes, Lampus, Clytius, Hicetaon (a descendant of Ares), and the veterans Ucalegon and Antenor the Far-Sighted. Though too old to fight, they were admirable talkers—withered and persistent and shrill as the cicadas that sing all summer-day, perched on the branches of forest-trees.

At Helen's approach, these grey-beards muttered earnestly among themselves. 'How entrancing she is! Like an immortal goddess! Yes, marvellously like one! I cannot blame the Trojans and Greeks for battling over her so bitterly! True, but beautiful though she be, I do wish the Greeks would take her back! I agree, her presence endangers our lives and our children's too!'

Priam hailed Helen: 'Sit next to me, dear child, if you want a clear view of your former husband and your relatives and friends! I am not blaming you for this wretched war; the gods alone are responsible . . . Please tell me: who is the sturdy, fine-looking Greek nobleman yonder? Granted he has comrades a head taller than himself; yet I never saw so regal a bearing—he must be a king?'

'Accept my devoted homage,' Helen cried. 'But, dear Father, I ought to have died before eloping with Prince Paris—imagine, leaving my home, my family, my unmarried daughter, and so many women friends of my own age! But leave them I did, and now I weep for remorse . . .'

When Priam repeated his question, she answered: 'Yes, that sturdy nobleman used to be my brother-in-law. He is the High King Agamemnon himself: a powerful ruler and a brave soldier. Oh, I am a shameless bitch, if ever there was one!'

'A fortunate king,' old Priam exclaimed, gazing at Agamemnon in even greater admiration, 'and evidently well loved by the gods! What a huge number of vassals he can command! I remember many years ago when I had taken some Trojans to reinforce the army of my allies Otreus and Prince Mygdon in Phrygia, a country of vines and horses—their enemies were Amazons, each of them a match for any man at fighting—I came upon the Phrygians encamped by the River Sangarius. A large army indeed, yet small compared with Agamemnon's.'

Then Priam caught sight of Odysseus, and asked again: 'Come, dear child; tell me the name of that nobleman who has just removed his armour! He may be a head shorter than the High King, but his chest and shoulders are even broader. He reminds me of a stocky, thick-fleeced ram ranging among a flock of ewes.'

She answered: 'That is Odysseus, son of Laertes, from the rugged island of Ithaca; he constantly invents cunning new stratagems.'

Antenor agreed: 'Yes, my lady, Odysseus, nicknamed "the Crafty"! He and King Menelaus once came here as ambassadors to demand your surrender. I entertained them both in my palace, and well I recall their appearance and style of speaking. Menelaus towered above our folk while we stood, though when we sat, Odysseus had the more regal appearance. At a council convened to receive them, Menelaus, who was the younger of the two, pleaded his case briefly, clearly, and to the point. As for Odysseus, when he was handed the wand, he rose and held it stiffly before him, without the least gesticulation. We thought: "A fool, a mere rustic," until his deep voice boomed out. Then his words struck a chill in our hearts, like the falling snowflakes of winter, and justified his rigid stance.'

Priam pointed to a third man, and said: 'Helen, tell me the name of yonder giant! He is easily the tallest and strongest in Agamemnon's army.'

She answered: 'You must mean Ajax, son of Telamon, his leading champion. And over there, at the head of the Cretan contingent, stands King Idomeneus. In the old days, he often visited Sparta; Menelaus and I would feast him. I recognize all the other commanders. Only two faces are missing where can my twin-brothers be: Castor the Horse-Breaker and Polydeuces the Boxer? Either they would not enlist in Menelaus' Laconian forces, or else they have absented themselves from today's battle because of the many unkind things said about me.'

The truth was that both her brothers were long since dead and buried in their native country, after they had ambushed a pair of rival twins from Messene: Idas and Lynceus. None of the four survived that fight.

Trojan heralds had meanwhile fetched the lambs, and a goatskin full of wine for the oath-taking ceremony. One of them, Idaeus by name, who carried the necessary golden mixing-bowl and cups, approached Priam. 'Son of Laomedon,' he cried, 'the leaders of the High King's mail-clad Greeks and of your Trojan chariot-fighters join in requesting your presence on the plain for the purpose of ratifying an armistice. It is agreed to settle our differences by a single combat between Prince Paris and King Menelaus the Warrior, the survivor being entitled to keep this lady and her fortune. Afterwards, if you consent, we Trojans will outline a treaty of friendship with the Greeks; they can then sail home to their land of thoroughbred horses and lovely women, leaving us in peace.'

Priam shuddered at the news, but gave orders for his team to be harnessed; and soon he mounted the royal chariot, holding the reins while Antenor stood by him. They drove through the Scaean Gate, and across the Scamandrian Plain until they reached the Bateia. There they dismounted and walked along the Trojan ranks. Agamemnon, sitting near Odysseus, rose to greet them; and presently the sacrosanct heralds, having brought everything needed for a solemn oath-taking, emptied the contents of the goatskin into the bowl, mixed the wine with water, and poured more water over the hands of princes entitled to assist in the rite. Then, drawing the dagger that hung beside his heavy sword, Agamemnon shore a lock from the poll of each lamb. After the heralds had distributed strands of wool among the leaders of both armies, he raised his arms and prayed aloud:

> 'ZEUS, most glorious and great
> On Mount Ida holding state;
> SUN, observant as you go
> Of all oaths taken here below;
> Fertile EARTH, whose sons we are;
> RIVERS, rolling from afar;
> FURIES, in your dismal den,
> That plague the spirits of false men:
> Bear witness, all of you, to this
> Sworn, solemn pact and armistice!'

Agamemnon continued: 'The terms agreed upon are as follows. If Prince Paris kills my brother, King Menelaus the Warrior, he is at liberty to keep Queen Helen with her entire fortune; and we will sail peacefully home to Greece. If, contrariwise, Menelaus kills Paris, you Trojans must restore Queen Helen with her entire fortune, also paying me an indemnity so large that it will become proverbial. Item, should King Priam and his sons, however, fail to pay me the aforesaid indemnity, I shall regard this armistice as no longer in force, and fight the war to a finish.'

Having cut the lambs' throats with a ruthless flourish, Agamemnon laid their carcases, gasping and twitching, on the ground. Wine was ladled from the mixing-bowl into cups, and the princes poured simultaneous libations, inviting the gods to witness their pact. Many Trojans and Greeks used the same form of prayer:

> 'ZEUS, great ruler of the sky,
> And your fellow-gods on high,
> Attend: we Greeks and Trojans both
> Bind ourselves by one strong oath:
> May all evil men who dare

> To forswear the pact they swear,
> Suffer death at your divine
> Rebuke! As this red flow of wine
> Spilling, falls, and falling, stains,
> So may they also spill their brains,
> And may their wives not mourn them dead
> But frolic each in a strange bed!'

Zeus disregarded these supplications too.

Priam now announced: 'I am returning to Troy before my dear son fights King Menelaus the Warrior. Since Zeus and the other Olympians alone know which of the pair is doomed, the anxiety of watching this contest will be more than I can bear.' He took up the dead lambs, placed them in his chariot, and drove off with Antenor.

Hector and Odysseus, having marked out the field of battle, dropped two pebbles into a bronze helmet—one for Paris, one for Menelaus, as lots to decide who should throw the first spear. Prayers were thereupon offered by the Trojan and Greek spectators, many of whom used the same forms:

> 'ZEUS, most glorious and great
> On Mount Ida holding state,
>   Judge these men well:
> And send whichever caused this war—
> Our burden nine long years and more—
>   Hot-foot to Hell!'

And:

> 'Great ZEUS; may this
> Sworn armistice
> Not end amiss!'

Hector, keeping his head averted to ensure fair play, shook the helmet; Paris' pebble leaped out at once. The princes retired and sat down where they had left their chariots and arms. Paris prepared for combat, putting on a pair of greaves fastened at the ankles with silver clasps, and borrowing his brother Lycaon's corslet. Across this stretched a baldric from which hung the scabbard of his silver-

studded bronze sword; and a menacing horsehair crest embellished
his helmet. Then he chose a large, strong shield, and a tough spear
of convenient weight. When Menelaus had also armed himself, a
hush fell on both armies, as the two opponents strode forward simul-
taneously. They approached quite close to each other and stood
brandishing their spears.

Paris made the first cast. His spear struck Menelaus' circular
shield, but the bronze point turned on impact and failed to penetrate
the thick layers of bull's hide. Now came Menelaus' turn; taking
accurate aim, he prayed to Father Zeus:

'Great ZEUS, grant me revenge at last!
Guide well the heavy spear I cast
At Paris, cause of all our woe—
To loathsome HADES let him go!
And let his punishment deter
Each self-confessed adulterer
From what you gods detest the most:
The crime of cuckolding his host!'

His spear tore its way through Paris' shield; but Paris jerked side-
ways, and though his breast-plate and tunic were pierced, he took
no hurt. Menelaus pressed the advantage by rushing at him, sword
in hand, and dealt such a blow on his helmet ridge that the sword
flew into three or four pieces. Gazing reproachfully up to Heaven, he
cried:

'Great ZEUS, most callous god of all,
    You hear but will not grant my plea
For this proud libertine's downfall:
    Look how your spite has injured me!

'Ah, ZEUS, have I not cause for shame?
    My broadsword shatters in my hand,
My only spear has missed its aim;
    Baffled and weaponless I stand!'

So saying, Menelaus sprang forward, took a firm grasp of Paris'
crest, and swung him bodily around with it. Half-strangled by the

embroidered chin-strap, Paris could not help being dragged off towards the Greek front-line. The combat would have ended immediately in Menelaus' triumph and deathless glory, had not Zeus' watchful daughter, Laughter-Loving Aphrodite, reached out an invisible hand and broken the chin-strap, so that Menelaus found himself holding the empty helmet. He tossed this to his comrades, who kept it for him; then picked up Paris' spear and turned again to dispatch him.

But where was Paris? He had completely disappeared, with Aphrodite's timely help.

✳

Aphrodite disguised herself as Helen's favourite slave, an old wool-carder from Sparta. Finding Helen still on the watch-tower by the Scaean Gate, she passed through a crowd of Trojan women, and caught at her perfumed robe. 'My lady,' said Aphrodite, 'Paris has sent me to fetch you! He is home again, stretched on his inlaid bed upstairs, wearing a fine nightshirt, and as handsome as ever he was. Nobody would dream that he had been fighting Menelaus; he looks as though he were off to a dance, or perhaps just returned from one, and enjoying a short rest.'

Helen's heart leaped at the news, but when behind the disguise she made out Aphrodite's lovely neck, white breasts, and sparkling eyes, she exclaimed: 'You demon, how can you deceive me so? Now that Menelaus has killed Paris and I must go back to Sparta, are you luring me to another great city of Phrygia or Maeonia? I believe you have taken a fancy to some new prince—— I believe you want to reward him with my accursed love, as you rewarded Paris! Away now, and court your latest favourite! Avoid Olympus, forget your godhead, listen sympathetically to his troubles, and protect him until he offers you marriage—or enslavement! Myself, I refuse to decorate your chosen lover's couch; all these Trojan women would abominate me if they heard of it, and I have difficulties enough already.'

Aphrodite answered: 'Dare provoke me, hussy, and I shall desert you! My hate is as extravagant as my love. I am capable of still further embittering Graeco-Trojan relations, and arranging a dreadful death for you, whom I have loved so much.'

Helen, in alarm, beckoned to her ladies-in-waiting, and stole from the tower; none of the other women noticed their departure. Aphrodite led the way to Paris' splendid house, where the ladies-in-waiting resumed their work, but Helen hurried upstairs to the spacious bedchamber. Aphrodite fetched a stool with her own hands and took it over to where Paris lay. Helen sat down, scowled, and began reproaching him.

'So here you are! What a disgraceful sight! I almost wish my former husband had put you out of your misery. You used to boast yourself his match as a fighter! Very well, get up from that bed—go back, and challenge him once more . . .'

'Stop being cruel,' he answered. 'This afternoon Athene helped Menelaus to win his round; some other day I may win mine. You and I also have a goddess to assist us.'

'No, no,' Helen sobbed, 'I did not mean what I said! Please keep clear of Menelaus; I could not bear to watch a second single combat. He might kill you.'

'Darling,' Paris coaxed her, 'come here and make love! I never felt so strong a passion for you since I carried you off from Sparta and we spent our first night together on the little island of Cranae. This is going to be no less wonderful for us both.'

He drew Helen towards him. She climbed into bed, and they lay clasped in each other's arms.

*

Meanwhile, Menelaus went prowling through the enemy ranks like a wild beast seeking the prey that has escaped it. But Paris was not to be found, either among the Trojans or among their allies; and, indeed, not a man in the whole of Hector's army would have been charitable enough to conceal him from Menelaus. They all hated Paris, worse than death, for having disgraced them.

At last Agamemnon cried: 'Pray lend me your attention, Trojans, Dardanians, and you other allies! I declare my brother Menelaus victor of the agreed combat, and require you to surrender Queen Helen, with her entire fortune; and further to pay me, as stipulated, an indemnity so large that it will become proverbial.'

The Greeks yelled applause.

Book Four:

Agamemnon Inspects His Army

The Olympians sat in Zeus' presence, discussing mortal affairs and gazing down on the city of Troy, while the pretty Goddess Hebe tripped from throne to throne across Heaven's golden floor and replenished golden goblets with nectar. They drank one another's healths.

Zeus, to tease Hera, said slyly: 'Fortunate Menelaus has a couple of goddesses at his service—Hera, and my friend Alalcomenes' young pupil Athene. Look at them seated close together, watching their champion! Paris, for his part, can count on Laughter-Loving Aphrodite's assistance; just now she rescued him from what seemed certain death. So we should surely decide now which alternative to favour: whether more war, or a reconciliation of the two armies? Everyone, I trust, agrees that the city of Troy must not cease to exist, but that Menelaus should get his wife back.'

Hera and Athene, busy plotting the Trojans' overthrow, muttered their dissent. Athene managed to curb her rage at Zeus' mention of the mortal tutelage under which she had once been placed; but Hera, having less self-control, burst out: 'Revered husband, what are you saying? After I have driven my horses nearly off their feet, and sweated almost as much myself, mustering that immense Greek army and launching it against Priam and his sons, how can you bear to ruin my work? Do as you please, of course; the rest of us are by no means unanimously in favour of your proposal.'

'Heartless, am I?' Zeus echoed gruffly. 'Look at yourself! What great injury have Priam and his sons done you that justifies this furious resolve to sack his splendid fortress? Perhaps the only way of glutting your horrid appetite would be for you to burst through the gates and eat the whole royal family raw—and every Trojan commoner into the bargain? Well, I should let that pass, so long as no fresh trouble arises between us. But here is a serious warning: if some day I feel inclined to destroy a city of which you happen to be fond, I will tolerate no opposition. You must acquiesce, with a loyal pretence of cheerfulness; since of all cities under the sun and stars, holy Troy is the one I most value. Priam and his fighting people have never once failed to honour their altars with the libations and burnt offerings due to my majesty.'

'It is a bargain!' answered Hera. 'If you should feel a sudden dislike for any of the three cities which I most value—Argos, Sparta, and Mycenae of the Broad Streets—I shall certainly not raise a finger in their defence: you may destroy them all. Indeed, it would be foolish to oppose you or bear a grudge afterwards, because your power is far greater than mine. Still, projects at which I have worked so hard should not be baulked. I am as divinely born as you are, and claim the Queendom of Heaven on two counts: being both a daughter of Father Cronus, whose kingdom you usurped, and your wife. Very well then: each of us can humour the other, in a hope that all Immortals will henceforth adopt our common policy. So send Athene down to the Scamandrian Plain where the armies are raising such an outcry over Menelaus' victory; she might well persuade some stupid Trojan to break the armistice.'

Zeus agreed. He called Athene and said briskly: 'Hurry off and do as Hera suggests!'

Pallas Athene darted from Olympus, eager to carry out this plan. Disguised as a meteor of the kind that scatters sparks when it falls, and is greeted with awe by sailors or an army, she plunged down on the no-man's-land between Greeks and Trojans. A cry of astonishment went up, and it was remarked on both sides: 'That meteor must have some deep significance! Either it foreshadows a return of hard fighting, or else it is Zeus' promise of peace.'

Athene next disguised herself as a Trojan—Antenor's sturdy son Laodocus—and ran in search of Pandarus, son of Lycaon. She found him with his Aesepian contingent, and said urgently: 'Take my advice, Pandarus, and shoot King Menelaus! Think of the fame, think of Paris' gratitude! He can be counted upon for a very handsome gift if your arrow flies straight and his rival gets laid on a funeral pyre. Quick! Pick him off while you still may, and vow to Wolfish Apollo, God of Archers, that, once safe home at Zeleia, you will sacrifice a hundred unblemished first-born lambs on his altar.'

Like a fool, Pandarus listened to Athene, and drew his polished oryx-horn bow out of its case: a magnificent weapon. He had once waited long hours in ambush for that oryx to emerge from a rock shelter, toppling it down at last with an arrow through the windpipe; a capable bowyer then secured the beast's four-foot horns together at their bases, polished them well, and added golden tips. Pandarus now lowered the bow to the ground and strung it with bull's sinew; but did so behind a screen of shields in case the Greeks might forestall this treachery by attacking him. Next, he opened his quiver, chose the brand-new shaft which was due to cause so much mischief, fitted it to the bow-string, and uttered the vow that Athene had put into his mouth. This done, he bent the bow back to his chest* until the iron barbs lay level with his bow-hand. A moment later he let fly; horn twanged, string whined, arrow hurtled.

The Immortals did not, however, forget Menelaus the Yellow-Haired: Athene posted herself in front of him and, like a careful mother brushing away a fly from her sleeping child, guided the arrow to where the least damage would be done. It struck Menelaus' golden belt-buckle, piercing belt, inlaid corslet, and the bronze taslet which he wore beneath to deflect arrow shots; and nicked his side.

> Every horseman throughout Greece
> Covets that famous masterpiece—
> An ornamental chafron, stored
> In the treasury of my lord—
> And begs leave, only for a day,
> To fix it on his bay, or grey.
> But no, my lord will not permit
> Any man else to handle it,

---

* Greek archers never learned to draw a bow-string back to the ear.

Any man else from far or near
Save his own royal charioteer—
Whose stallion sports it amid loud
Cries of amazement from the crowd.

This chafron comes from Caria
Or (some say) from Maeonia—
Craftswomen there are taught to stain
White ivory plaques that still retain,
Year after year, their fresh, bold, fine,
Red-purple patches of design.

Another eye-taking contrast of red-purple against ivory-white provoked cries of amazement when the blood from Menelaus' wound trickled down his strong thighs and legs as far as the ankles.

Agamemnon stood aghast. (So did Menelaus himself, until he turned and saw the arrow-head protruding behind his back, barbs, thread and all; then he breathed a sigh of relief.) Clutching his hand, Agamemnon gave vent to a loud groan, echoed by the staff, and exclaimed in ringing tones: 'Alas, my poor brother! I fear that the oath which pledged you to single combat in no-man's-land has proved your ruin: the Trojans have broken the armistice and transfixed you with an arrow. I would never, of course, suggest that oaths sworn over two sacrificial lambs and holy libations, and confirmed by a hand-shake, can be taken in vain! Even if Zeus does not immediately take vengeance on those who forswear themselves, he will do so in his own good time, punishing them with the loss of their lives, their wives, and their little children. I am more than ever assured that Troy's doom is sealed, also that of King Priam the Spearman and his subjects. Zeus, Son of Cronus, indignant at this outrage, will shake his shield threateningly from the Olympian throne; thus the armistice will not have been concluded in vain. Nevertheless, I should be most unhappy, brother, if you succumbed to that arrow. Your death, by removing the cause of war, might set my men clamouring for home—how ashamed I should be to find myself back on the thirsty plains of Argos, having allowed Priam's people to make good their old boast of keeping Helen! Your bones would rot in Trojan soil, and the proud Trojans capering on your tomb would scoff: "I pray the gods that ill-tempered Agamemnon will have no greater success in his other ventures than in this! He has sailed away empty-handed, and noble Menelaus lies here beneath our feet, his mission unaccomplished." Rather let the earth swallow me alive than that they should say such things!'

Menelaus was able to reassure him: 'The arrow has not wounded me in any vital part, though it went through this golden belt-buckle and corslet and metal taslet; so why spread alarm and despondency?'

'Indeed, I hope that you are right, brother,' answered Agamemnon. 'But pray ask a surgeon to examine the wound and apply a healing bandage.' Then, turning to Talthybius, he said: 'Find Asclepius' son Machaon, and inform him, with my compliments, that some Trojan or Lycian archer has unfortunately succeeded in wounding King Menelaus, son of Atreus; will he please attend to him at once?'

Talthybius obediently went down the Greek ranks until he reached the contingent from Tricca, famous for its horses, and delivered the message in Agamemnon's exact words. Machaon accompanied him to the circle of princes that had formed around Menelaus. He examined the arrow, grasped its heel and, first breaking off the barbed head, pulled it free from taslet, corslet, and belt. Having unbuckled these, he sucked out a mouthful of blood from the wound, for fear of poison, and applied a healing herbal bandage, the recipe of which his father Asclepius had been given by Cheiron the Centaur.

Meanwhile, since the Trojans were re-arming, the Greeks followed suit. King Agamemnon rose to the occasion; nobody could accuse him of sloth, fear, or lack of zeal. He left his bronze-panelled chariot and its restive team under the charge of Eurymedon, son of Ptolemaeus and grandson of Peiraeus, with orders to have them ready for him when he grew weary of marshalling the army. Then he strode from contingent to contingent, shouting:

> 'Greeks be eager, Greeks be bold!
> For ZEUS, the God of Law,
> Hates rascals who have failed to hold
> His name in reverent awe.

'Great Troy shall fall, and vultures tear
   The flesh of each proud liar
Whose wife and daughters home we'll bear—
   Rich fruit for our desire!'

If the High King observed any reluctance to fight, he would cry furiously: 'Have you neither honour nor shame? You show about as much courage as fawns that have been chased across the plain to a standstill! I daresay you are waiting until the Trojans drive you back among our ships—where you hope that Almighty Zeus will stretch forth his arm in protection?'

He visited the Cretan contingent and found King Idomeneus the Sagacious, fierce as a wild boar, inspecting the front-line, while Prince Meriones saw that the companies in support armed themselves quickly. Agamemnon smiled and said: 'Idomeneus, I honour you above every one of my allies, not on the battlefield alone, but also when my Council meets to discuss strategic problems over a golden wine-bowl. For though your fellow-princes must content themselves with a single cupful apiece, I make sure that your cup is replenished as often as you drain it. Let me see you fight this afternoon no less staunchly than you have always vowed to do.'

'Son of Atreus,' King Idomeneus answered, 'you need not doubt that I will keep my promise; but pray leave us, and exhort your own troops! There is little time to waste on talk, now that the Trojans have broken the armistice. Yes, I agree: as the first to repudiate their oaths they can expect only sorrow and ruin.'

Agamemnon walked on, well pleased, towards the Salaminian and Locrian contingents, and saw Great Ajax and Little Ajax already advancing, surrounded by a mass of infantry.

Though not forgetful of his flock
   Grazing below the scree,
The goatherd, perched upon a rock,
   Sits watching the wide sea.

A pitch-black cloud whirls into sight
   Across the western wave;
He runs after his goats in fright
   And drives them to a cave.

The cloud provides an apt simile for those dark companies of spearmen marching in close order, shield touching shield. Agamemnon delightedly hailed the two Ajaxes, crying: 'It would be a mistake to give soldiers commanded by such impetuous princes any further encouragement—you have taken care of that yourselves. O Father Zeus, and Athene and Apollo! If only all my Councillors showed the same offensive spirit, we should soon capture and sack Priam's great city!'

Without awaiting a reply, he went on until he found King Nestor haranguing his Pylians—drawn up under their commanders Pelagon, Alastor, Chromius, Prince Haemon, and Bias. In front stood the chariots, supported by his main force of men-at-arms, with less dependable troops placed in the centre, where they had to fight whether it pleased them or not. Nestor was impressing on his charioteers that they must control their teams and avoid the infantry battle.

'I want none of you to presume on his courage or skill as a driver,' he told them, 'by rushing ahead of the rest; neither do I want any dragging at the horses' mouths—that diminishes the shock of a charge. But whoever singles out an enemy chariot, levels his spear, goes for its crew, he is a soldier after my heart! Such, my men, are the spirited, yet not reckless, tactics that used to take fortified cities in the good old days.' For Nestor the Gerenian had a long experience of warfare.

Agamemnon congratulated him. 'Ah, if your limbs were still as young as your heart! We must all grow aged, I suppose. How I wish it had happened to someone other than you!'

'Alas, son of Atreus,' sighed Nestor, 'you should have seen me when I killed Prince Ereuthalion—though the gods never grant a man both youth and wisdom at the same time! I was raw enough then . . . Nevertheless, despite these grey hairs, I intend to keep up with the chariots and exercise my right to direct manoeuvres. Spearfighting can be left to younger and stronger men.'

Agamemnon passed on light-heartedly, and next saw Menestheus the Chariot-Fighter, son of Peteus, standing idly among his Athenians* (famous for their loud war-cry); and with him Odysseus,

---

* An Athenian forgery must be suspected here. The Athenians can hardly have been brigaded with the Western Islanders, nor can Odysseus have spoken before Menestheus did, being far lower in rank. To judge from *Book 5*, Menestheus' name

equally inactive, among his tough Cephallenians. Not having yet received orders, these two princes were waiting until some other Greek contingent made a move. Such caution enraged the High King, who spoke sharply: 'Son of Peteus, Zeus' foster-son; and you, Odysseus the Crafty, inventor of low stratagems, why hang back waiting for others to begin? Noblemen who are always the first to gobble roast meat or swill sweet wine at my Council feasts, and never stop before their bellies are full, should be in the vanguard when serious fighting breaks out! But now, it seems, ten columns of my Achaeans are expected to cut you a passage through the Trojan ranks.'

Odysseus glared at Agamemnon. 'Son of Atreus,' he replied, 'guard your tongue! Do you dare charge us with hanging back? Once the Greek army launches a regular assault on the Trojans, you will see me, Telemachus' father, fighting desperately against the enemy champions—if, that is, you have any stomach for battle yourself. That speech was so much idle wind.'

Realizing that he had hurt Odysseus' pride, Agamemnon smiled and said: 'Illustrious son of Laertes, I did not speak too warmly in the circumstances, nor give you unneeded encouragement. I am, of course, sensible of the respect and loyalty you feel towards me; so, if any expression of mine has sounded offensive, we can settle our differences at some future meeting; but I hope that no harm has been done.'

He hurried away and, rejoining his own Achaeans at last, saw the chariotry still massed, wheel to wheel, but neither bold Diomedes nor Sthenelus making any preparation for combat. 'Of what are you afraid?' he scolded Diomedes. 'Why dally here while the battle takes shape? Your father, Tydeus the Horseman, never behaved in so cowardly a fashion. Everyone who knew him well agrees that he always rushed far ahead of his comrades. Though not having fought beside him myself, nor even had the pleasure of knowing him, I conclude that he was a gallant soldier. Once he visited Mycenae with

---

has been substituted for that of 'Meges, son of Phylus, favoured by Zeus', who distinguished himself in the battle; his troops from Dulichium and the Echinean Isles are bracketed in *Book 2* with their neighbours, Odysseus' Cephallenians, Ithacans, Zacynthans, etc.

King Polyneices, joint-heir to the Theban throne but banished by his brother Eteocles, and appealed for armed help in a war against Thebes. Our people assented, and changed their minds only when they sacrificed to Zeus and found the omens discouraging. The ambassadors went away but, on reaching the rush-beds and grasslands that flank the River Asopus, sent your father ahead to plead Polyneices' case at Thebes. A bold man was King Tydeus! A stranger, and alone, he nonchalantly entered the banqueting hall of King Eteocles and challenged the guests to feats of strength. What is more, with the Goddess Athene's help, he worsted them all in turn. Some aggrieved Thebans ambushed him on his way back—fifty spearmen to one! Maeon, son of Haemon, and Popyphontes, son of Autophonus, were the leaders, both famous warriors. Nevertheless, despite the fearful odds, your father killed the entire Theban force, except Maeon, whom he sent back alive in obedience to a heavenly sign. That same heroic Tydeus of Aetolia has a son now living—who cannot compare with him as a soldier, yet excels him as a talker!'

Diomedes listened to his overlord's reprimand and abstained from comment. But Sthenelus, son of the famous Capaneus (whom Zeus' thunderbolt struck dead a generation before, in the unsuccessful assault on Thebes), answered sharply: 'Why lie, King Agamemnon, when you are capable of telling the truth? Diomedes and I are far better men than our fathers. Although attacking stronger walls with a smaller army, he and I succeeded where they failed: we captured Thebes of the Seven Gates. And how? By not disregarding the omens —by placing ourselves under Zeus' protection; whereas they perished for their foolish pride. So, pray make no invidious comparisons between them and us!'

Diomedes looked sternly at Sthenelus. 'Brother,' he said, 'I forbid you to utter another word! Our High King may exhort the troops in whatever way he pleases. After all, who stands to win the greatest glory if we defeat the Trojans and take their city? And who stands to suffer the worst disgrace if we abandon the siege . . . ? Come, we too must show our fighting spirit!' Then Diomedes leaped from the tail-board of his chariot with a clang of bronze that might have scared even a hero.

The west wind blustering out at sea
  Provokes a wave to lift its head,
To travel shoreward menacingly
  Compact and huge, a sight to dread;
Arching, it breaks with an uproarious boom
Against the headland, scattering clouds of spume.

The Greek army moved forward in the same relentless style, wave
upon wave, bright sunlight glittering on arms and decorated armour.
As soon as the commanders had given their orders, you would have
thought them all dumb, so silently they advanced!

Listen to the ewes complaining
  In our wide courtyard;
They can hear the lambs, I fear,
  From their udders barred.

What loud bleating and entreating!
  Patience, pretty dams:
Half the milk is for my master,
  Half is for your lambs.

Just such a clamour was raised by the Trojan troops, who came from
many distant regions and spoke no common language.

Athene the Owl-Eyed was encouraging the Greeks; Ares, the
Trojans. Moreover:

Some were plagued by ROUT and TERROR,
  Whom EARTH bore to AIR;
Some by STRIFE, dear twin of ARES—
  That collusive pair!

STRIFE at first, flat on her belly,
  Crawls with lowered crest,
Soon she treads the earth in triumph,
  At her hideous best.

Strife, indeed, hurried through the ranks, whipping up angry pas-
sions, and causing much lamentable slaughter.

The two armies met with a clatter of bronze, fighting at spear's length, or shield-boss to shield-boss. A tremendous din arose: cries of agony, shouts of exultation, as men killed or were killed; and blood reddened the earth.

> Two torrents in the green
>   Season of winter rain
>   Met and roared on again
> Down to their deep ravine.

> The shepherd climbed a hill,
>   A mile away he stood;
>   So furious was that flood
> He heard its thunder still!

A shepherd could have heard the roar of this battle at an even greater distance!

The first Greek to kill a Trojan was Nestor's son Antilochus. He struck Echepolus, son of Thalysius, on the helmet-ridge, then jabbed him through the forehead with a spear. Darkness clouded Echepolus' eyes, and he toppled from his chariot like a falling tower. Prince Elephenor, son of Calchodon, commanding the tough Abantes, caught Echepolus' foot in mid-air and dragged the corpse off, coveting the valuable armour; he failed, however, to take his prize very far. Bold Agenor the Trojan, seeing Elephenor's weapon-side exposed, drove a spear deep into him. Elephenor died immediately, and a hot skirmish developed over his dead body: Trojans and Greeks leaped wolfishly at each others' throats, stabbing and hewing.

There followed the death of Simöeisius the Trojan, Anthemion's son, so named because born by the banks of the Simöeis River while his mother was coming home from a visit to her family sheep-range on Mount Ida. Simöeisius did not live long enough to justify the cost of his upbringing: for Great Ajax's spear pierced the lad's right breast, close to the nipple, and emerged behind the shoulder-blade.

> The wainwright with an axe of steel
>   Walks out a tree to find;
> The felloe for some chariot-wheel
>   Engrosses his whole mind.

> Young lakeside poplar, smooth and tall,
>   You catch his ruthless eye!
> He hacks you down, green crown and all,
>   And leaves your trunk to dry.

So fell tall young Simöeisius! Antiphus of the Polished Corslet cast a vengeful javelin at Great Ajax from some distance; but missed his aim and, instead, hit Odysseus' gallant comrade Leucus, who was trying to seize Simöeisius' arms. The javelin caught him in the groin; he dropped the corpse and tumbled dead on top of it. Odysseus, furious at losing Leucus, strode forward in his bright bronze armour, then halted, glanced about him, chose his mark, and let fly a spear. The Trojans shrank back, but the spear was well aimed. It struck Democoon, Priam's bastard son, on the temple and transfixed his skull; Democoon, who had until recently been in charge of his father's racing mares at Abydus, dropped with a rattle of arms.

The Trojan front-line now gave way and, when Hector himself retired, the Greeks, yelling for joy, took possession of the enemy corpses and pressed onward.

Apollo, from his watchpost on the citadel of Troy, shouted furiously: 'Up and at them, men of Troy! Why yield to these invaders? They are human like yourselves, not statues of stone or iron; your weapons will go through them easily! Besides, Achilles, son of Thetis, is absent today—brooding in his hut by the sea.'

The Greeks were being urged to greater efforts by Athene, who exhibited her glory wherever she saw any slackening.

Fate's next victim was Diores the Epeian, son of Amarynceus. Peirous, son of Imbrasus, the Thracian from the River Aenus, threw a jagged boulder which struck his right ankle, smashing bone and sinews. Diores fell to the ground, stretching his arms for help, and gasped in anguish. Peirous completed his victory with a spear-thrust below Diores' navel; out gushed the intestines and he died. Hardly had Peirous stepped back, however, when Thoas the Aetolian's spearpoint pierced his lung. Thoas came in closer, freed the heavy weapon, drew his sword, and drove it into Peirous' belly; yet the Thracian men-at-arms, distinguished by long pikes and peculiar top-knots, defended their leader's corpse. Despite Thoas' rank and courage, they sent him reeling away, without the spoils.

Peirous and Diores lay dead together among the bodies of numerous lesser men. No one could deny that it was a fearful battle—not even if Pallas Athene had taken him by the hand and led him unwounded through the mêlée, warding off spear-lunges, sword-cuts, and random missiles. Hundreds of Trojans and Greeks were already scattered prone in the dust.

Book Five:

Diomedes' Day of Glory

> To Diomedes, Tydeus' son,
>   PALLAS ATHENE lent
> Courage and strength, above all Greeks,
>   To be armipotent.
>
> Glory she kindled on his casque,
>   And glory on his shield,
> From head and side fierce rays she sent
>   Over the battlefield,
>
> That tangled in a blaze of light
>   He like a star should seem:
> The summer evening's star which first
>   Bobs from the Ocean Stream.

Phegeus and Idaeus, sons of a rich Trojan nobleman named Dares, priest of the God Hephaestus, were capable soldiers and shared the same chariot. Together they attacked Diomedes, who was now fighting on foot. Phegeus hurled his spear, but it travelled high over Diomedes' left shoulder. His return cast was more effective; it struck Phegeus full on the chest and sent him flying out of the chariot. Idaeus, not daring to defend the corpse from spoliation, abandoned their beautiful equipage, convinced that he could avoid the same fate by flight alone; and, indeed, Hephaestus cast a veil of invisibility around him, thus sparing old Dares further grief. Diomedes, however, captured the chariot, and some of his men led the team off towards the naval camp.

The Trojans were aghast to see one of Dares' sons fallen stone dead, the other in flight; and Athene grasped brutal Ares by the hand, saying: 'Ares, blood-stained Ares, stormer of fortresses and sworn enemy of humankind, you should leave the armies to fight it out and Father Zeus to choose the winner. He will be vexed unless we break away.'

Though Ares had been keeping the Trojan line steady, he accepted Athene's advice. They sat down together beside the noisy River Scamander. The Greeks being thus free to press the Trojans back, each of their leaders killed his man. For a start, Agamemnon pursued Odius the Great, King of the Halizonians, who had just wheeled his chariot about, and thrust him through between the shoulder-blades. The spear-point emerged from Odius' breast, and he toppled over the rail with a clatter.

Phaestus, son of Borus, a nobleman of fertile Tarne in Maeonia, was mounting his chariot, when Idomeneus surprised him; the spear entered Phaestus' shoulder, and he also fell dead. Idomeneus ordered his squires to strip the corpse of its armour.

Menelaus accounted for Scamandrius the Archer, son of Strophius. Artemis the Huntress had trained him to shoot every variety of wild beast that forests breed; but neither her patronage nor his own marksmanship saved Scamandrius from Menelaus' spear, which caught him in the back as he turned to run. He was thrown lifeless on his face.

Next died Phereclus, son of Tecton, the son of Harmon, on whom Athene had conferred pre-eminent skill in carpentry and smithcraft; yet, having no prophetic foresight, he built the ships which Paris took to Greece—with sad consequences alike for the Trojans and for himself. Meriones chased the fleeing Phereclus and speared his buttock; the blade went in under the bone and burst the bladder. He dropped to his knees and died screaming.

Antenor's wife Theano had given an example of wifely devotion by lavishing as much love on her bastard step-son Pedaeus as on her own children. Pedaeus, however, now succumbed to a thrust from his pursuer Meges, son of Phyleus. It cut the neck-tendon, severed the root of his tongue, and he tumbled headlong, the spear-point clenched between his teeth.

Eurypylus, son of Euaemon, killed Hypsenor, son of noble Dol-
opion, who enjoyed semi-divine honours at Troy as priest to the
River-god Xanthus. He was trying to escape, when Eurypylus' sword
swept down on his right shoulder, hacking off his sword-arm. Death
clouded Hypsenor's eyes.

So much for the feats of the other Greek leaders; but King Diome-
des excelled them all. It seemed doubtful on which side he fought,
so freely did he storm across the battlefield.

> Winter's worst deluge hits the hills,
>   Swelling a torrent
> Which wrecks all that we planned with skill:
>   Fierce and abhorrent,
>
> It bursts the causeys, row on row,
>   Flattening the fences
> That round our well-dug orchards go—
>   Futile expenses!

Against line after line of Trojan troops Diomedes displayed the same
ungovernable violence, and burst through each in turn, despite the
enormous odds.

Pandarus, son of Lycaon, vexed by this magnificent rush, drew
his oryx-horn bow and took careful aim; the arrow pierced Diomedes'
shoulder-plate. Catching a glint of blood, Pandarus shouted: 'Cour-
age, bold Trojans! I have winged their leading champion. If Apollo
the Archer has prospered my journey from Lycia, you may be sure
that the son of Tydeus will not live long with that arrow in him!'

A premature boast! Diomedes merely retired to his chariot which
Sthenelus, son of Capaneus, was driving, and cried: 'Dear friend,
pray dismount and pull out an arrow for me.'

Sthenelus at once did so. Then, though blood dripped from the
wound, Diomedes offered this prayer to Pallas Athene:

> 'Unwearied daughter
> Of the Shield-Bearer,
> You loved my father,
> Tydeus the Strong,

> Steering him featly
> Through battle frenzy—
> Come now, protect me
>   The spears among!
> Let my shaft hurtling
> Transfix that witling,
> That princeling boasting:
>   "He will not live long!" '

Athene granted the plea. She put fresh strength into his legs and arms, whispering: 'Do not fear the Trojans, Diomedes! I have inspired you with the unconquerable spirit of your father Tydeus. I have also dispelled the mist that has hitherto kept your eyes from recognizing gods in human guise. Should any Olympians offer to fight you, decline their challenge! The one exception is Aphrodite: if she enters the battle, use your sharp sword on her!'

Athene vanished, and he resumed the fight, three times the man he had been before.

> There is a lion in the fold;
>   An angry beast is he.
> For why? The shepherd has made bold
>   To wound him cruelly.

> Yet wounds, however deep, will not
>   A lion's rage subdue:
> The foolish man his bolt has shot
>   And no more dares to do.

> The lion, left among those sheep,
>   · Ravens and rends them all,
> Then casts their bodies in a heap,
>   To leap the enclosing wall.

Diomedes ran among the Trojans as furiously as the wounded lion among that terrified flock. He killed Astinous with a spear-thrust; and Hypeiron with a sweep of his heavy sword on the collarbone, that parted shoulderblade from body. Not troubling to despoil the corpses, he attacked Abas and Polyeidus, sons of Eurydamas the

Soothsayer. They never brought home any new dreams for their father's interpretation—bold Diomedes had despoiled them of their lives.

His next victims were the brothers, Xanthus and Thoon; whose father Phaenops mourned broken-heartedly when they did not return. Since he was no longer young enough to beget a new heir, relatives eventually divided his large estate.

> A lion, where fat cows securely graze
> On wooded hills, fixes on one his gaze,
> Then springing at her without more ado,
> Snaps his jaw tight, to bite the neckbone through.

Diomedes displayed the same leonine ferocity. He sprang roaring at two sons of Priam, Prince Echemmon and Prince Chromius, who shared a chariot and, despite their resistance, tumbled them dead to the ground. This time he took both suits of armour, and told his men to lead away the captured teams.

Aeneas, son of Anchises, observing this havoc, went in search of Pandarus, son of Lycaon. He drove across the plain with a fine disregard for the spears that whizzed past, and at length found him. 'Pandarus,' he cried, 'you are by far our best archer, and even in your native Lycia none can claim to outshoot you. Come, invoke Zeus again, and send an arrow into that Greek hero who is dominating the battlefield and has already killed several of our bravest men! I only hope he is not an Immortal in disguise, whom we Trojans have offended by failing to burn the correct sacrifices on his altar! Angry gods often cause mortals a great deal of misery.'

'He looks very much like Diomedes,' Pandarus answered, 'to judge from his shield, his helmet-crest, and the valour of his team. Yet who can be sure that some god has not decided to impersonate him? And even if Diomedes, he must be fighting under a divine spell, with an Olympian standing by, wrapped in a cloak of darkness. I thought just now that I had sent him headlong down to Hell, when my arrow pierced the shoulder-plate of his corslet; but the unknown protector saved his life. Nor have I a chariot from which to shoot over the troops' heads. When leading my men here at Prince Hector's invitation, I foolishly disregarded my father Lycaon's warning; he would have had me bring a chariot. But since fodder promised to be scarce in the large army then converging on Troy, I did not want my horses to eat any worse than at home. So I left eleven teams of them munching spelt and pearl-barley in our Lycian stables, and a beautiful new chariot draped with a cloth waiting beside each team—all the harness was new as well—and set out on foot. My bow would be more serviceable than spears, I thought. Today, however, it has failed me. I have shot at two kings, Menelaus and Diomedes, and drawn blood from both, but merely roused them to greater feats of daring. It was in an evil hour that I took my curved bow-case off its peg! Should I ever see my beloved Lycian countryside again, and my dear wife, and my huge, high palace, may some stranger behead me if I do not instantly snap this bow across my knee, and throw the pieces into a blazing fire! It is as useless as a puff of wind.'

'No more idle talk, pray!' cried Aeneas. 'Until we seek out this Greek, the battle will go still worse for Troy. Look, here is my own team of fast Trojan mares, admirably trained to swing a chariot around in pursuit or retirement. Climb up! Even though Zeus allows Diomedes to push our forces off the field, these nags will carry us back safely. It makes no difference to me whether you drive and I fight, or contrariwise.'

Pandarus replied: 'Very well, Aeneas: take reins and whip! After all, the horses are accustomed to your voice. If we retired in a hurry, they might go wild with fear on hearing mine instead of yours, and baulk, and let Diomedes overtake us. Then neither of us would escape, and he would capture your equipage.'

Aeneas agreed, and they rattled off together. Sthenelus, son of Capaneus, saw them from a distance, and said urgently to Diomedes: 'Dear comrade, a most formidable pair of fighters seem eager to engage you—Pandarus the Archer, son of Lycaon; and Prince Aeneas, who claims to be Aphrodite's son by Anchises. We must avoid their challenge! And I do wish you would not keep rushing into the thick of battle! That is the way to lose your life. Come, remount, I beg you!'

Diomedes quelled Sthenelus with a glance. 'Say no more about avoiding a challenge!' he stormed. 'Am I the man to skulk or withdraw, while my strength still holds? No, I will not remount, but face Pandarus and Aeneas where I stand. Pallas Athene has told me to fear nothing. Though one of the pair may escape, I swear that Aeneas' team will never carry both to safety! So, if Athene grants me victory, you must leave this chariot unattended, first tightening the reins and knotting them to the rail. Then seize Aeneas' equipage and drive it off as our prize. The team is of a divine breed: Zeus the Omniscient gave the original horses—the finest under the sun—to King Tros in compensation for stealing his son Ganymede. After-wards, when Laomedon succeeded to the throne of Troy, King Anchises of Dardanus secretly had some of his own mares covered by those divine stallions, and thus secured six foals. He kept four, and gave Aeneas these two. If we can capture them, that will make us famous.'

Aeneas had approached within spear-cast, and Pandarus cried: 'Ho, Diomedes, son of proud Tydeus! It seems that my arrow did not kill you? Well, rascal, I shall see whether I have better luck with a different sort of weapon.'

He poised his heavy spear and flung: the bronze blade went straight through Diomedes' shield and dinted his breast-plate. Pandarus shouted gleefully: 'A wound in the stomach! You cannot survive that, I think. What a triumph for me!'

But Diomedes answered calmly: 'I am unwounded, and vow that either you or your comrade will now fall a victim to Ares, the stub-born God of War.'

He hurled his spear high in the air, and Athene guided the descent. It struck Pandarus between nose and eye, penetrated his upper jaw, sliced the tongue, and emerged near the crook of his jawbone. Pan-darus fell heavily to the earth, and the horses sprang sideways in alarm.

Aeneas let go his reins, seized spear and shield and, yelling a chal-lenge to all comers, leaped down in defence of Pandarus' corpse. As he straddled it, with the ferocious pride of a lion crouched upon its prey, Diomedes picked up a massive boulder, such as no two men, in these degenerate days, would be strong enough to heave off the ground—and tossed it at Aeneas, crushing the cup-bone where thigh and pelvis join, tearing the flesh, snapping the sinews. Aeneas, now on his knees, gallantly propped himself upright with one hand until he collapsed in a faint. The boulder would have ended his life (which began soon after Aphrodite seduced Prince Anchises on a cattle ranch) had not the goddess dived to her beloved son's rescue. She clasped him in her white arms, wrapped a fold of her shining robe around him as a protection against Greek spears, and began carrying him to safety.

Meanwhile, Sthenelus, son of Capaneus, remembered Diomedes' orders. He got clear of the mêlée, tied his reins securely to the rail, dismounted, vaulted into Aeneas' chariot and drove the sleek mares towards the Achaean lines. There Deipylus, his most intimate friend, took charge of the prize and brought it down to the Greek camp. This done, Sthenelus remounted his own chariot, unknotted the reins, and galloped back.

Diomedes had recognized Aphrodite and, well aware that she was not a fighting Olympian, like Athene or Ares the City-Sacker, chased her across the plain and lunged at one of her hands. His spear-point passed through the beautiful linen tissue woven by the Graces, and cut her palm just above the wrist. This wound did not bleed, because Olympians eat no bread and drink no wine, and therefore have no mortal blood in their veins—which is, of course, why they are known as 'Immortals'—but a colourless liquid called 'ichor' oozed out. Aphrodite screamed and let Aeneas fall; whereupon Phoebus Apollo, catching him up, threw a magical mist over him. Diomedes then surprised and grieved the goddess by shouting: 'Keep clear of this war, Aphrodite, daughter of Zeus, and confine yourself to making fools of weak women! Now that you have experienced a real battle, you will always shudder on hearing the very word spoken, even from afar.'

Iris the Wind-Footed led her away, sobbing for the sting of the wound, and for the ichor staining her lovely skin. Aphrodite found bold Ares still sitting beside his gold-frontleted team, to the left of the battlefield. His spear was resting against a cloud. She fell on her knees and cried: 'Dearest brother, please lend me your chariot! I must return to Olympus without delay. A mortal named Diomedes, son of Tydeus, has severely wounded me; I believe that daredevil would challenge Almighty Zeus himself!'

Ares cheerfully did as she asked; and Iris, assisting her into the chariot, handled reins and whip. The horses scudded to the top of Olympus, where Iris removed the harness and set before them their customary ambrosial forage; but Aphrodite ran off and plumped herself down, blubbering, on the Goddess Dione's lap. Dione fondled her wounded daughter, stroked her hair, and said coaxingly: 'Tell me, darling, which of the Olympians has treated you like a common criminal?'

'It was no Olympian,' Aphrodite wailed, 'it was proud Diomedes, the son of Tydeus! He saw me rescuing your grandson from the battle. I love Aeneas better than anyone in the world! These Greeks no longer merely fight the Trojans; they are at war with Heaven itself!'

'Dry your eyes,' said Dione, 'and try to forget this little gash! Many of us Immortals have received terrible wounds through getting mixed up in human affairs. Those gigantic Aloeids, Otus and Ephialtes, once managed to capture Ares and confine him for thirteen months under the lid of a bronze cauldron. He might have withered away in that prison, had not the Aloeids' beautiful step-mother, Eëriboea, revealed his whereabouts to Hermes, who found the simpleton reduced almost to nothing and let him out. Again, Heracles the Strong, Amphitryon's putative son—but really a love-child of Zeus the Shield-Bearer—shot a three-pronged arrow into Hera's right breast; the pain drove her almost to distraction. Dreadful Hades, too, got hit in the shoulder while fighting Heracles among the corpses at Hell's gate, and ran up here howling for anguish. Since he is, after all, an Immortal, Apollo healed him with an ointment. A head-strong, violent fellow was Heracles! He did not care how much harm he did, and his archery troubled every god on Olympus.

'Now, the same sort of thing has happened. Athene the Owl-Eyed sent Diomedes against you. Poor fool, he fails to understand that no mortal can challenge an Olympian and return from the wars alive; none of his children will ever climb on his knees chattering a welcome! And Diomedes, formidable fighter though he is, must take care not to attack a tougher deity than yourself. Should he do so, the household of Adrastus' clever daughter Aegialeia will soon be

roused by shrieks of lamentation, and learn that her husband Diome-
des, the best soldier in the Peloponnese, has died!'

Dione then grasped Aphrodite's arm with her left hand; with the
right she wiped away the ichor, and made the goddess feel a good
deal more comfortable. But Athene and Hera, who had watched the
scene, commented on it sarcastically. Athene said to Zeus: 'Father,
pray do not frown if I venture a bold guess. It is that Cyprian Aph-
rodite—how wonderfully she loves Troy!—has been persuading some
other Greek woman to get seduced by a Trojan, and scratched her
own delicate palm on a golden brooch-pin while caressing the pretty
creature.'

Zeus laughed at Athene's wit, and called Aphrodite to him. 'My
darling,' he told her, 'you must avoid war! Busy yourself with love
and sensual delights, and leave battles to Athene and Ares!'

Diomedes, though aware of Apollo's presence, tried most irrever-
ently to dispatch Aeneas, and strip him of his splendid armour. Three
times he rushed forward, shield in hand, and each time found him-
self beaten back. At the fourth attempt, Apollo's terrible voice rang
out: 'Son of Tydeus, show proper courtesy, and retire in awe! Why
challenge an Olympian? It is madness to treat me like an earth-
bound mortal.'

Diomedes took his advice, retiring a few steps to avoid Apollo's
displeasure; whereupon the god carried Aeneas away to his large
temple at Troy. There his sister Artemis, and their mother Leto, set
and healed the broken bones, while he created a phantom, exactly
resembling Aeneas and similarly armed, over which Trojans and
Greeks, shield-boss to shield-boss, fought for possession of his
phantom armour.

'Ares,' Apollo cried, 'blood-stained Ares, stormer of fortresses and
sworn enemy of mankind, have the goodness to remove Diomedes!
First he attacked Aphrodite and stabbed her in the palm, just above
the wrist; then he ran at me. Anyone might have mistaken him for
one of ourselves! He will be challenging Father Zeus next.' So, when
Apollo went back to his look-out post on the Citadel, Ares obligingly
joined the Trojan ranks disguised as the Thracian leader Acamas the
Swift. 'Sons of Priam,' he yelled, 'how long must the Greeks massacre
our people? Until they force us back to the city gates? Are you

aware that bold Aeneas, whom we rank with Prince Hector himself, lies dying on the ground? Come, now! To the rescue!'

His rousing words were cheered, and Prince Sarpedon the Lycian, a son of Zeus, began to taunt Hector: 'Where is your courage? You bragged once that Troy could be held by King Priam's sons and sons-in-law alone—no allies nor other troops were needed—but today I can see none of your family on the battlefield. They behave like dogs, cowering in a wide circle around a lion, and let foreigners bear the brunt of the attack. I, for one, came to help you from the faraway banks of the Lycian River Xanthus, where I left my beloved wife, my infant son, and my well-filled treasure-vaults, so much envied by the poor and needy. Yes, I make my Lycians fight hard, and fight hard myself, though we have no houses here for invaders to sack, and no cattle for them to steal; whereas you lounge about idly, not even urging your men to stand fast and defend their homes! Beware now, or the Greeks will, as it were, entangle this army in hunting-nets and destroy us at leisure, after which they will find it easy to storm Troy. A commander-in-chief should never relax his vigilance at any time of the day or night. And unless you set your allies a good example of courage, you can count upon hearing worse reproaches than mine!'

Stung by Sarpedon's words, Hector sprang fully armed from his chariot, and rushed among the ranks, brandishing a pair of sharp spears and urging the Trojans, with his terrible war-cry, to battle for their lives. The forward troops at once rallied and counter-attacked. Hand-to-hand fighting took place all along the front, but the enemy stood firm . . .

> When gusty winnowing time comes round again
> Our golden-haired DEMETER we adore.
> Her wind-fan separates white chaff from grain
> And whirls it thick across the threshing-floor.

The Greeks grew as white with the dust stirred by wheeling chariot-teams, as winnowers do with blown chaff. On came the Trojans, in a mass. At Apollo's request, Ares ranged from front to rear, encouraging them. Apollo also sent Aeneas out on the field again, and his comrades were delighted to find him alive, miraculously whole, and full of spirit. But they asked no questions, being engrossed in the new struggle which Apollo, Ares, and Ares' insatiable sister Strife were busily fomenting . . .

> When ZEUS, peace-making in the sky,
>   Caps every wild hill top
> With cloud that rises thick and high,
>   The obedient breezes drop.
> Even the north wind, who would dare
> The largest cloud in shreds to tear,
>   Conforms, and makes a stop.

The steadfastness of Diomedes, Odysseus, and the two Ajaxes, when they faced the counter-attack, recalled those immobile clouds. King Agamemnon bustled here and there, yelling: 'Quit you like men, be strong! However hard the combat, you have a better chance of survival if you face the enemy, for honour's sake, than if you turn your backs in inglorious retreat!' He emphasized his message by lunging at Aeneas' friend Deicoon, son of Pergasus, who ranked with the Trojan royal princes because of his outstanding gallantry. The spear-point passed through shield, belt, and belly, and sent him sprawling.

Aeneas avenged Deicoon's death on two Greek champions named Crethon and Orsilochus. These twin sons of Diocles, a rich prince from Phere, were also grandsons of King Orsilochus and great-grandsons of the River-god Alpheius, whose broad stream waters the country of the Pylians. They had joined this expedition at the request of Agamemnon and Menelaus as soon as they came of age, but death put a halt to their adventures.

> Two lion cubs, brought up in deep
>   Dark mountain thickets, without fear
> Rove forth to prey on cows and sheep,
>   But die beneath the hunter's spear.

In fact, Aeneas lopped down Crethon and Orsilochus as a forester would treat a couple of tall pines.

Menelaus, grieved at their loss, strode forward, brandishing his spear; he was lured on by Ares, who wanted Aeneas to kill him. How-

ever, Nestor's son Prince Antilochus, foreseeing that Menelaus'
death would give the Greeks an excuse for retiring empty-handed
from Troy, ran to his assistance. Aeneas fell back, not being foolish
enough to engage two such champions simultaneously; so they
dragged off the bodies of Crethon and Orsilochus, left them in charge
of friends in the rear, and continued fighting.

Together they made for Pylaemenes, commander of the tough
Paphlagonian spearmen, who was standing at ease in his chariot.
Menelaus' spear slid under his collarbone, wounding him mortally.
Then Antilochus hurled a stone; it shattered the elbow of Pylae-
menes' driver, Mydon, son of Atymnius, just as he was wheeling the
team around in flight. Mydon's reins, inlaid with ivory, trailed along
the dusty soil, and Antilochus, boarding the chariot, drove a sword
through his temple. Mydon tumbled head-first over the fore-rail into
a pile of sand, and remained wedged upright between the chariot
and the hindquarters of his horses, until they kicked him to the
ground. Antilochus then gathered up the reins, reached for the whip,
and hurried his prize away towards the camp.

Hector advanced, shouting vengefully and followed by a large
Trojan force. Ares, with his ruthless sister, urged them on, brandish-
ing a monstrous lance—now in front of Hector, now behind him . . .

> A shiftless man crossing the plain
> After a season of much rain
> Comes where, most unexpectedly,
> A river rushes towards the sea,
> Foam-flecked and boiling like a pot.
> He backs in terror—who would not?

So Diomedes recoiled from the sudden rush. He exclaimed to his
comrades: 'No wonder Hector earns our admiration! Some invisible
god always protects him; today it is Ares. We must not challenge an
Immortal, but retire in good order.' The Trojans pressed on, and
Hector killed two veteran fighters, Menesthes and Anchialus, who
were sharing a chariot. Great Ajax, to avenge them, made a lunge
at Amphius, son of Selagus, from the rich pastures of Paesus be-
side the Sea of Marmara. The spear struck him on the belt and
pierced his stomach, tumbling him over. Javelins rained at Ajax as he

recklessly bounded forward to possess himself of the armour, several of them lodging in his shoulder. Then, though he planted a heel on the corpse and wrenched his spear free, the enemy were too numerous for even so tough a hero: they drove him off in discomfiture.

Meanwhile, Fate had sent Heracles' tall, brave son Tlepolemus, who could address Zeus as 'Grandfather', against Sarpedon the Lycian, who could address him as 'Father'. Tlepolemus cried: 'Prince Sarpedon, how does a malingerer like yourself happen to stray on the battlefield? I reject your claim to have been begotten by Zeus; his sons of the last generation were far better men than you! It is well known that, when King Laomedon withheld certain divine mares promised to my father Heracles for rescuing the Princess Hesione from a sea-monster, he came here with only six ships, yet sacked and emptied Troy of her citizens. Despite your strength, you are a cowardly fellow, ruler of a moribund race; and not fated to afford your Trojan allies much protection, either, for I am sending your ghost down to Hell!'

'The truth is, Tlepolemus,' replied Sarpedon, 'that Troy fell because of her King's stupidity in breaking a sworn promise. When your father demanded those mares, Laomedon, instead of being grateful for his services, sent him a rude answer. And let me warn you, in return, that yours is the ghost that must visit Hell.'

The champions flung their spears simultaneously. One transfixed Tlepolemus' neck and killed him on the spot. The other struck Sarpedon's left thigh, grazing the bone and lodging in the flesh; yet Zeus preserved his life. A group of Lycians, who hauled him away, were far too excited to think of standing him on his feet and drawing out the heavy spear, but trailed it behind them.

The sight of Tlepolemus' corpse being removed for burial angered Odysseus. He debated with himself whether he should pursue Sarpedon, or vent his rage safely on Lycians of inferior rank. Athene, aware that he was not destined to conquer this son of Zeus, made him attack Coeranus, Alastor, Chromius, Alcandrus, Halius, Noemon, and Prytanis, all of whom he speared. He would have killed many more, but that Hector reinforced the Lycians, and his flashing armour scared Odysseus away. Sarpedon cried in pain: 'Ah, son of Priam, how relieved I am to see you! Pray do not let my enemies kill and strip me; but carry me into your city. If I have no hope of rejoining my dear wife and little son in the land I love, at least give me leave to die at Troy rather than here!'

Since Hector hurried by without an answer, intent on worsting the Greeks and accounting for as many as he could, the Lycians themselves carried Sarpedon clear of the fighting and sat him down near the Scaean Gate beneath an oak-tree sacred to Zeus. There his comrade Pelagon drew out the spear. Sarpedon fainted, as he did so, but presently revived under the fresh gusts of a northerly breeze.

Knowing that Hector enjoyed Ares' protection, the Greeks fell back still farther, yet kept their faces turned towards him. You ask: whom did he kill, how many, and in what order? I will tell you. His first victim was Prince Teuthras; his second, Orestes the Charioteer; his third, Trechus, an Aetolian fighter; his fourth, Helenus, son of Oenops; his fifth, Oresbius of the Bright Taslets, a prudent land-owner from the town of Hyle on Lake Cephisus, in the rich region of Boeotia.

Hera, watching the massacre, cried urgently to Athene: 'What is this, you busy daughter of Zeus the Shield-Bearer? We pledged our word that King Menelaus should not sail home before he had sacked the great fortress of Troy. How can we allow Ares a free hand in its defence? Come, we must do something for the other side!'

Athene agreed, and Hera went off to harness her gold-frontleted chariot-team; Hebe, using lynch-pins, fastened the eight-spoked wheels on the iron axle.

> Those wheels of HERA's chariot,
>   A sight they were to see,
> With spokes of bronze, felloes of gold,
>   And naves of silver free.
> Bronze hoops around the felloes ran;
>   They might not dinted be.
>
> The rails of HERA's chariot
>   Were two, and plaited tight
> With thongs of silver and red gold,
>   Wherein she took delight.

> The pole of HERA's chariot
>   Was silver all unmixed,
> Golden the yoke and poitrels fine
>   Which on that pole she fixed.

Hera thereupon yoked her mettlesome, eager, battle-loving horses, while Athene slipped out of her many-coloured robe (made by herself), letting it fall in a heap on the Palace threshold, and changed into a tunic borrowed from Father Zeus. She next threw about her shoulders the terrible Aegis, a tasseled goatskin crowned with Panic and containing not only the spirits of Discord, Valour and Assault but the marvellous, dreadful, grim, grinning Gorgon's head—also the property of Zeus. Then she donned a double-crested golden helmet, four layers thick, around which was engraved a procession of warriors from a hundred different cities; and finally grasping the long, stout, heavy spear which she uses to destroy mortals who have fallen under Zeus' awesome displeasure, the goddess mounted beside Hera.

Hera's whip cracked, the gates of Heaven groaned open by themselves to admit her exit, and out the chariot shot—past a pair of janitresses named the Seasons, whom Zeus entrusts with the task of parting and drawing the cloud curtain between Heaven and earth. When Hera saw the Thunderer throned in lonely splendour on the summit of Olympus, she pulled up, exclaiming: 'Husband, do you permit Ares' violent behaviour? His reckless and irresponsible slaughter of my poor Greeks can hardly have escaped your notice. Aphrodite and Apollo of the Silver Bow are enjoying the spectacle of this mad fellow's unlawful pranks, which they themselves prompted. Will you be vexed if I attack Ares and chase him wounded and bedraggled from the field?'

Zeus answered: 'Cause your son whatever pain you please; but pray leave the fighting to Athene the Spoil-Winner, who understands it better than any other Olympian.'

Hera nodded agreement and lashed at the horses, which galloped on again, neighing loudly, high above the earth. Each bound took them as far as a man could see from a watch-tower, across the dark gulf of waters, to the misty horizon. Soon they reached Troy, where Hera brought the chariot to a halt at the confluence of the Rivers

Simöeis and Scamander, unharnessed her team and shrouded them in a thick mist. Respectfully, the River-god Simöeis made ambrosial herbage spring up for their pasture. Hera and Athene then flew off together, like a pair of turtle-doves, to rescue their favoured army.

They found a large group of all the boldest Argives gathered around Diomedes.

> Formidable as a wild boar
> And lion-like prepared to roar,
>   Each noble-hearted Greek
> Stood dully waiting for a word—
> Until, above the din, they heard
>   Their white-armed goddess speak.

Hera, disguised as Stentor, the herald, whose brazen voice had a carrying power equal to fifty ordinary ones, shouted: 'Shame on you, rascals! Your bearing is proud enough, yet while Achilles ruled the field no Trojan dared sneak out of Troy, not even by way of the Dardanian Gate in the farther wall. Now that his fearful lance no longer scares them, they have surged forward almost to your camp!' Her words shamed every man present into renewing his courage.

Athene appeared suddenly before Diomedes. He was seated by his chariot, airing the arrow-wound inflicted by Pandarus, and wiping away the blood. He had taken off his broad shield-baldric, which sat heavily on the wounded shoulder and induced a sweat irritating to the raw flesh. Athene, laying one hand on the yoke, sneered: 'You do not resemble your father Tydeus very closely! A little man, but how pugnacious—even when warned against fighting or displaying his strength on that famous visit to Thebes! I had advised him to accept the Cadmeans' hospitality and behave with ambassadorial discretion, yet he challenged his hosts to box or wrestle, and never lost a match. You, however, when I guarantee your life, are either too exhausted or too frightened to face the Trojans! It looks as though Tydeus was not your real father.'

Diomedes answered: 'I recognize your voice, daughter of Zeus the Shield-Bearer, and must tell you in all frankness that I am neither frightened nor exhausted, but only bound by your instructions, which were to fight no Olympian, Aphrodite alone excepted—I was to use my sharp sword on her, you said. This is why, on finding Ares in command of the enemy forces, I have fallen back, and rallied my comrades to me.'

'Diomedes, true son of Tydeus, joy of my heart,' she cried. 'You need not fear Ares or any other Olympian! I shall always be at your elbow. Up with you, and go for that mad, raving fellow—that universal curse, that renegade who recently gave Hera and myself a sworn promise to help the Greeks, but has now seceded to the Trojans and forgotten it!'

Reaching out a hand, the goddess dragged Sthenelus, Diomedes' driver, from the chariot, and climbed in herself. Diomedes did the same, and the oaken axle groaned under their weight. Athene seized whip and reins and guided the team straight at Ares who, bespattered with blood, was busily despoiling the corpse of huge Periphas, son of Ochesius, the bravest man in the entire Aetolian contingent. Since she wore Hades' helmet of invisibility, Ares failed to notice her. He saw only Diomedes and, abandoning his task, lunged murderously at him across the yoke and reins. Athene pushed the spear aside, and Diomedes countered with a swift stab at Ares' taslets. The blade entered his belly close to the groin . . .

> In summer, when the fields are dry
> A west wind, shrieking loud,
> Has overcast the fair blue sky
> With inspissated cloud.

Diomedes was reminded of this pastoral scene as he watched Ares mount to Heaven like a dark mist, and heard him bellow louder than nine or ten thousand men clashing in battle. Both Greeks and Trojans trembled at his voice.

Ares burst into the divine Palace on Olympus and collapsed miserably on a throne beside Zeus the Son of Cronus. 'Father,' he cried, as he displayed the ichor welling from his wound, 'how can you permit Athene's violent behaviour? Whenever we trouble to intervene in human affairs, we seem fated to find ourselves the victims of each other's schemes and, what is worse, to fall foul of you! You should never have created that shrewd, reckless, evil-minded virgin-goddess!

We others obey you loyally, but because she was born out of your own head, you neither say nor do anything to control her pestilential deeds—in fact, you encourage them. Today when she urged the foolhardy Diomedes to challenge us Immortals, he first wounded Aphrodite's palm just above the wrist, and then dared lunge at me, as though he were a god! But for my quick tactics, I might have been left lying in anguish among those grisly heaps of dead, never to recover from some further damage inflicted on my helpless body.'

Zeus scowled at Ares. 'Renegade,' he cried, 'be off, or else stop whining! I dislike you more than all the rest of my family put together—those eternal quarrels, wars, and battles! You are as intolerably stubborn as your mother Hera, whom I find it hard enough to control, even by shouting her down. She must have prompted this disastrous folly. Still, I cannot bear to see you suffer; after all, I am your father. Yet if you had inherited your violent nature from anyone else but Hera, I should long ago have chained you in a deeper Hell than the rebellious Titans themselves.'

Zeus now ordered Apollo to heal Ares' wound. He did so with a soothing ointment that took effect as quickly as when fig-juice curdles the sweet milk into which it is being stirred. Meanwhile, Hebe filled a hot bath and fetched Ares some clean clothes. He was soon comfortably seated at Father Zeus' side, once again rejoicing in his strength.

Hera and Athene also came back to the Palace, pleased that they had prevented him from killing more Greeks.

Book Six:

Hector and Andromache

The Greeks and Trojans were thus left by the gods to their own unaided devices. Spears hummed between the two armies as the tide of battle ebbed and flowed across the plain bounded by the Rivers Simöeis and Scamander. Great Ajax, the Greek champion, saved his Salaminians on one occasion when, single-handed, he broke a Thracian battalion and killed its handsome commander Acamas, son of Eussorus. Swinging his sword against Acamas' helmet-ridge, which was topped by a thick plume, Ajax drove the sharp bronze edge through his brain.

Axylus, son of Teuthranus, died next. This very popular nobleman lived in the town of Arisbe on the road from Troy to the Black Sea, and had kept open house there. Yet none of his former guests ran forward now to protect him and his charioteer Calysius from the onslaught of Diomedes, who dispatched them both. Diomedes' lieutenant, Euryalus, son of Mecisteus, having already killed the Trojans Dresus and Opheltius, went in pursuit of Aesepus and Pedasus, Bucolion's twin sons by the River-nymph Abarbarea—this Bucolion being King Laomedon of Troy's eldest son, a bastard who had been tending the royal flocks when the nymph fell in love with him. Euryalus took Aesepus and Pedasus' lives, and their armour as well.

Stubborn Polypoetes the Thessalian laid Astyalus low; as Odysseus also did Pidytes of Percote; and Teucrus, the magnificent Aretaon. Nestor's son Antilochus speared Ablerus; the High King Agamemnon speared Elatus of Pedasus, a town perched above the

lovely Satniöeis River; Leïtus the Boeotian caught Phylacus as he
fled; and Eurypylus the Thessalian accounted for Melanthius.

Adrestus of Percote, King Merops' son, lost control of his team:
they bolted, stumbled on a low tamarisk-bough, snapping the
chariot-pole at its base, and sent him sprawling beside a wheel; then
off they galloped citywards among the rest of the chariotry. Menelaus
rushed up, brandishing a spear, but Adrestus clasped his knees in
suppliant fashion, pleading: 'Have mercy! My father King Merops
will pay you an enormous ransom as soon as he hears that I am
alive and your prisoner. His palace is crammed with bronze, gold
and valuable iron.'

Menelaus nodded agreement, and would at once have sent Adres-
tus down to the camp under armed escort, had not Agamemnon
come along and protested: 'My dear brother, why this tenderness
towards the enemy? Have they treated you and your relatives well
enough to deserve such compassion? In my view we should not spare
a single male Trojan, not even a child still in his mother's womb; but
make it our duty to extirpate the whole cursed brood, and leave their
dead bodies unwept and unhonoured.'

This righteous argument convinced Menelaus, who thrust Adres-
tus away. Agamemnon murdered him, with a sharp stab in his side,
placed a heel on the prostrate body, and tugged out the spear-blade.

Nestor's shrill voice now echoed across the battlefield. 'Come, my
lads and brothers-in-arms! Press on the rout, and kill as many Tro-
jans as you can. Why compete with one another in collecting loads
of booty? Wait until all is done, and strip the corpses at your leisure.'

The Greeks cheered Nestor, and would have chased the beaten
and dispirited mob of Trojans back into their city, but for Priam's
son Prince Helenus, a most reliable prophet. He approached Hector
and Aeneas, saying: 'My lords, since you are acting as joint com-
manders-in-chief, I beg you to rally your troops in defence of the gate
before they stream through and fall exhausted on the laps of their
wives. This is no time for delay! My lord Hector, while Aeneas
helps us to beat off the Greek attack, weary though we may be you
should briefly visit the city—I see no other alternative—and tell our
mother what to do. She should assemble all the old noblewomen
there in Athene's temple on the Citadel, unlock the holy inner

shrine, cover the knees of the divine image with the largest, grandest robe she possesses—the one she herself prizes most—and vow Athene the Bright-Haired Spoil-Winner a sacrifice of twelve oxen that have never known yoke or goad, if she consents to save the city, its women, and its little children. The goddess will perhaps restrain Diomedes, whose terrible spear has been the main instrument of our defeat. His performances today prove him the best man on the Greek side. Achilles may have a divine mother, but did he ever scare our people so? Nobody can match Diomedes when that divine battle-fury overcomes him.'

Hector took Helenus' advice. He leaped from his chariot in full armour, and ran through the ranks shaking two spears and rallying the disorderly mass of Trojans; until, with a shout of defiance, they turned about. The Greeks, taken aback, discontinued their slaughter and gave ground, believing that some Olympian had darted down from Heaven to check the fugitives. 'Brave Trojans, glorious allies,' Hector yelled, 'fight like the heroes that you are, while I hurriedly return to Troy! I am telling King Priam's Councillors, and our wives too, that they must pray for our safety and offer the gods hundred-beast sacrifices.' As Hector hastened off, the enormous black bull's hide shield drummed against his neck and ankles.

*

Two heroes now advanced towards each other over the no-man's-land which separated the armies. They were Glaucus, son of Hippolochus, and Diomedes, son of Tydeus. Diomedes cried: 'May I inquire your name, sir? We have not met hitherto, and your courage is remarkable. Any Trojan father whose son challenges me to single combat deserves my pity. So pray reassure me that you are not an Olympian in disguise; I am fighting no more Olympians today—warned by the case of proud Lycurgus, son of Dryas, who was King of the Edonians. This Lycurgus, you may remember, armed only with an ox-goad, drove the Maenads of Dionysus' army from the rich land of Nysa. They flung away their ivy-wands in terror, and even Dionysus plunged trembling to the sea bottom, where the Goddess Thetis opened her arms and comforted him. The Blessed Gods, however, enraged by this disrespect to one of their number, blinded Lycurgus and cut short his life. Myself, I want to avoid their hate;

but come forward and fight me, if you are a mortal who eats and drinks just as I do; for then I shall be happy to end your military career.'

Glaucus answered:

> 'Why noble son of Tydeus, why
>   Must you inquire my name?
> All forest leaves are born to die;
>   All mortal men the same.
>
> 'Though Spring's gay branches burgeon out,
>   Their leaves continue not,
> Cold autumn scatters them to rout,
>   And in cold earth they rot.
>
> 'Next year, another host of leaves
>   Is born, grows green and dies;
> Old MOTHER EARTH their fall receives—
>   The fall of man likewise.

'Still,' he said, 'if you insist on it, I will give an account of myself, which many soldiers here will be glad to confirm. In the centre of Greece stands a city called Ephyra, where Sisyphus, son of Aeolus, once reigned. He was the craftiest man of his day, and through his son Glaucus became grandfather to Bellerophon. The gods endowed Bellerophon with such strength and manly beauty, that Anteia, wife of King Proetus the Argive, his powerful overlord, tried to seduce him. When the prudent and honest Bellerophon rejected her advances, she secretly approached Proetus, and said: "If you value your life, husband, kill Bellerophon! He nearly succeeded in raping me." Proetus believed this lie but, despite his anger, could not bring himself to murder a guest. Instead, he sent him across the sea with a sealed package for Iobates the King of Lycia; it contained engraved tablets requesting vengeance on the bearer, who had insulted Iobates' daughter—this same Anteia.

'The Olympians brought Bellerophon safe to the mouth of the Lycian River Xanthus, where Iobates received him splendidly: the feasting lasted nine days, and every day they slaughtered a fresh ox.

At dawn, on the tenth day, the time came for Iobates to inquire: "My lord, what news do you bring from my esteemed son-in-law Proetus?" Bellerophon innocently produced the sealed package, and Iobates, having read the tablets, ordered him to kill the Chimaera. She was no ordinary beast, but a monstrous sister of the Dog Cerberus: her goat's body had the fire-breathing head of a lioness at one end, and the tail of a serpent at the other. Nevertheless, by dutiful obedience to the dictates of Heaven, Bellerophon, with Athene's help, destroyed her. Sent against the Solymians next, Bellerophon defeated them in what he afterwards described as the fiercest combat he remembered. Iobates then told him to crush the Amazons, each of them a match for any man at fighting. Finally, on his homeward journey, the task accomplished, he fell into an ambush laid by Iobates and, though his assailants were the boldest in the wide land of Lycia, killed every one. Iobates realized at last that Bellerophon must be under divine protection, and handed him Proetus' letter, demanding exact particulars of his alleged attempt on Anteia's virtue. Convinced by Bellerophon's frank reply that she had lied, Iobates married him to his other daughter Philonoë, and gave him the co-sovereignty of Lycia. The Lycians further presented Bellerophon with a freehold estate of their best vineyards and cornland. Philonoë bore Bellerophon two sons, named Isander and Hippolochus; also a daughter, named Laodameia, on whom Zeus the Lord of Counsel fathered the famous Sarpedon yonder.

'Bellerophon's life ended dismally. He offended the gods by visiting Olympus uninvited, on the back of his winged horse Pegasus, and they condemned him to wander, a lonely and miserable outcast, over the Aleian Plain, shunning human society. Of his two sons, Isander was killed when Ares the Bloodthirsty came to the aid of the Solymians; and Laodameia while seated at her loom by angry Artemis of the Golden Reins. Hippolochus survives; he is my own father and sent me here under strict orders not to disgrace our family, which combines the noblest blood of Ephyra with the noblest of Lycia, but to outdo all my fellows in skill and courage. This, then, is who I am.'

The delighted Diomedes planted his spear upright in the soil, and returned a most gracious answer: 'Prince Glaucus,' he cried, 'you and I are bound together by inherited ties of friendship; my grand-father, King Oeneus, once entertained your grandfather, Bellero-phon, in his palace for no less than twenty days, and they exchanged gifts at parting. Bellerophon got a belt of Tyrian purple, and Oeneus a two-handled gold goblet, which I still have at home. Unfortunately, I cannot remember my father Tydeus; he died while I was an infant, during the Achaean attack on Thebes; but, the fact is that you in your Lycian, and I in my Peloponnesian city, are guest-cousins and entitled to lavish hospitality whenever we visit each other. It there-fore behoves us to avoid personal combat in future. After all, there are as many Trojans and Trojan allies for me to kill as Heaven per-mits, and there are as many Greeks for you to kill! Let us exchange arms in public acknowledgement of our guest-cousinship.'

Glaucus leaped from his chariot and advanced to meet Diomedes. They shook hands in token of friendship. Yet Zeus, Son of Cronus, must have addled Glaucus' wits: imagine exchanging a golden suit of armour worth at least a hundred cows, against a bronze suit hardly worth nine!

$*$

As Hector the Bright-Helmed reached the oak-tree just outside the Scaean Gate, a crowd of Trojan women ran up, pestering him with inquiries about husbands, brothers, sons and friends. His sole reply, 'Pray to the Gods!', gave them little comfort. He strode on towards the polished stone colonnades of the Royal Palace, and the two rows of bedrooms facing each other across a wide central courtyard—fifty for Priam's sons and their wives, twelve more for his daughters and sons-in-law. The bedrooms were also built of polished stone, and had separate roofs.

Hector's mother, Hecuba the Beautiful, met him, accompanied by Laodice, his loveliest sister. 'My son,' cried Hecuba, seizing him by the hand, 'why have you deserted the battlefield? To invoke Zeus from the Citadel? The accursed Greeks must be pressing us hard if that is your mission! Wait while I fetch you some sweet wine—first for a libation to Zeus and his family, and then for your own refresh-ment. Wine is an excellent restorative when one is as jaded as you look.'

Hector answered: 'I appreciate your kindness, Mother; but wine would cripple my courage and rob me of strength. Besides, I should be ashamed to pour libations with such filthy, blood-stained hands as these—nobody should ever do so before washing himself! Now, please assemble the old noblewomen of Troy in Pallas Athene's temple on the Citadel; then unlock the holy inner shrine, cover the knees of the divine image with the largest, loveliest, grandest robe you possess—the one you prize most—and vow Athene the Bright-Haired Spoil-Winner a sacrifice of twelve oxen which have never known yoke or goad, if she consents to save the city, its women, and its little children. The goddess will perhaps restrain Diomedes, whose terrible spear has been the main instrument of our defeat.

'Do this without delay, while I persuade Paris to resume the battle. O that the earth would open and swallow that brother of mine! The tender protection afforded him by Aphrodite has brought nothing but grief on our noble father and on all his sons and subjects. A glimpse of Paris' ghost descending to the gates of Hell would, I confess, make me happy indeed.'

Hecuba called her maids of honour from the Palace hall, and together they summoned every old noblewoman in Troy. Then she descended to her fragrant store-room, where she kept the embroidered robes which Prince Paris had looted at Sidon on his return voyage from Sparta with Helen—Sidonian women are famous for embroidering. Hecuba chose the largest and most beautiful robe of the whole pile—it lay at the very bottom, twinkling like a star. She took this up to the Citadel, followed by her flock of aged dames.

There Athene's priestess, pretty Theano, who was Cisseus' daughter and Prince Antenor's wife, unlocked the inner shrine, and the company raised their hands in lamentation to Athene; while Theano, taking the robe from Hecuba, spread it on the knees of the divine image, and prayed as follows:

> 'ATHENE, guard this Citadel!
>   ATHENE, fair beyond compare,
> I pray you, guard it well!
>
> 'Snap Diomedes' lance, let Fate
>   Cause him to fall, in sight of all,
> Dead at the Scaean Gate!

'And listen well, for here and now
  A sacrifice of no small price
Most reverently I vow!

'Twelve oxen which have never yet
  Suffered the goad, to you are owed—
Think not we shall forget!

'But when Troy's soldiers call on you,
  Guard well their lives, guard well their wives,
Their tiny children, too!'

Athene, however, stubbornly disregarded Theano's prayer.

Hector stopped at the fine mansion which the best masons and carpenters in Troy had built for Paris, to his own design. It adjoined the Royal Palace and Hector's own house, and consisted of a courtyard, a hall, and a large bedroom above. Hector hurried up the stairs, proceeded by his bronze spear-point with its gold socket-band —the spear measured nearly fourteen feet in length—and entered the bedroom. He found Paris furbishing his handsome breast-plate, arms and shield. Helen sat not far off, superintending her maids as they wove or embroidered linen cloth.

Hector said bitterly: 'I cannot regard your grudge against Troy as being a very decent one. It is for you alone that our people are dying in defence of these walls—their shouts must surely have reached your ears? Yet you often scold a friend who shirks battle.'

Paris, now busily testing his bow, answered: 'Sharp words, though not unreasonably so. Allow me to explain that I bear no particular grudge against Troy; but, feeling a little sad, I wanted to enjoy a good cry on a chair in this bedroom. My wife has just suggested that I should fight again, and I am taking her advice; because one never knows who will win the next round, does one? Wait, while I re-arm; or else go ahead, if you prefer—I will soon overtake you.'

When Hector remained silent, Helen said sweetly: 'Brother-in-law—if a bitch like myself may venture to claim kinship with you—pray listen to my complaint:

'O that a storm had burst
    And carried me away
New-born, so that my first,
    Was also my last, day—

'Had burst and carried me
    To some far, rocky steep,
Or in a grave of sea
    Buried me fathoms deep!

'Ah, if I had never grown to womanhood, none of these dreadful events would have taken place! But, since the gods planned things as they did, I wish at least that I had eloped with a better man—someone sufficiently honourable not to make light of the general contempt which he earns. Paris is, I fear, incorrigibly shameless: all your troubles have been caused through my being a bitch, and Paris being rotten to the marrow! Zeus, of course, will punish us both severely; and long after we are dead, bards will compose derisive songs about our failings. But do sit down and rest on this settle!'

Hector answered: 'I am sorry that I have to decline your friendly invitation, Helen. My heart is set on getting back as soon as possible; the troops miss me. Make your husband hurry, if he will not do so himself, and see whether he can overtake me this side of the Gate. I must first visit my own home for a brief goodbye to my beloved wife and our little son; we three may never meet again.'

Hector left the house, but on reaching his own hall, could not find Andromache. He shouted to the staff: 'Tell me, where has your mistress gone? Visiting one of my sisters or sisters-in-law? Or to the Citadel, where my mother is propitiating Athene? I want the truth, not guesses!' A maid-servant looked up and said: 'My lord Hector, if you want the truth, she has not gone visiting any sister or sister-in-law of yours; nor is she at the temple. She ran out to the Ilian Tower in a fit of distraction, having heard that our men were being severely handled by the Greeks. The nurse-maid took your little boy along, too.'

Hector thereupon retraced his steps, down the well-paved street leading to the Scaean Gate and the plain beyond. Fortunately, Andromache intercepted him before he passed through. (Her father,

the magnanimous King Eëtion of Cilicia, who lived in the city of
Thebe, under the wooded slopes of Mount Placus, had demanded a
large dowry when she married Hector.) Behind Andromache came
the nurse-maid, carrying Scamandrius, Hector's son, a child of star-
like loveliness and universally nicknamed Astyanax—'King of the
City'—because Hector, on whose shoulders rested the defence of
Troy, felt such affection for him. As Hector stood gazing at Scaman-
drius with a quiet smile, Andromache clung to his hand, and sobbed:
'Dear husband, this reckless courage will be your undoing! Have
pity on Scamandrius and on me! What if the Greeks make a con-
certed rush at you? I would rather die than become your widow!
Once you are gone, nothing but sorrow awaits me. It is not as though
I still had parents: Achilles killed my father in the sack of Cilician
Thebe—he showed proper respect, I admit, by burning his corpse
without removing the fine inlaid armour, and raised a royal barrow
over the ashes; after which Zeus' daughters, the Mountain-nymphs
of Placus, planted an elm-grove to mark the site. In the same raid,
however, Achilles had slaughtered all my seven brothers, out in the
fields among their cows and sheep; and captured my mother, the
Queen, whom he brought to the Greek camp with the rest of his
booty. Later he accepted a prodigal ransom for her, and she returned
to my grandfather's palace; but soon died of some disease sent by
Artemis the Archer.

'So, dear Hector, you are now not merely my husband—you are
father, mother, and brother, too! Be merciful, stay here on the
Tower; do not orphan this darling, do not widow me! And, another
thing, I beg you to draw up your men beside the fig-tree over there,
where the wall is weakest and more easily scaled. Three attempts
on it have already been made by Great and Little Ajax, and Idome-
neus of Crete; also by Agamemnon, Menelaus, and Diomedes. I
wonder whether a prophet revealed the weakness of that wall to
them, or whether they noticed it themselves?'

Hector answered: 'Your forebodings weigh heavily on my heart,
yet I should lose my self-respect if the Trojan nobles and their
womenfolk caught me malingering. I could not bring myself to do
so, in any case; I have always fought courageously with the vanguard
for my father's glory and my own. But let me tell you this: it is my

conviction that our holy city must soon fall, and that every man in Troy must die around King Priam. What agony awaits my mother, my father, my brothers, and the many hundreds of brave Trojans doomed to lie in the dust at our enemies' feet! I confess, though, that all this troubles me little when I brood on the agony that awaits you—led weeping into slavery by some mail-clad conqueror! In Greece you will have to work the loom under the eye of a harsh mistress, and draw water at her orders from the spring of Messeis or of Hypereia, suffering ill-treatment and perpetual restraint. As your tears flow, fingers will point, and it will be said: "Look, she was once the wife of Hector, the Trojan Commander-in-Chief during the recent war!" Then fresh grief will stab your heart for the loss of a husband who so long postponed the dreadful hour of your captivity. May I lie deep beneath a barrow before you are rudely carried off —may I be spared the sound of your heart-broken shrieks!'

He stretched out a hand towards little Scamandrius, who shrank away, hugging his pretty nurse-maid; the bronze armour terrified him, and so did the tall horsehair plume that nodded fiercely from his father's helmet-top. Andromache smiled; Hector smiled too. He removed the helmet, laid it shining on the ground, took Scamandrius in his arms, kissing and dandling him, and then prayed:

'O ZEUS, Sole Ruler of the Sky,
And all you other gods on high,
Grant that my infant son may live
To gather fame superlative.
Reserve, I beg you, for this boy
A bold, strong heart to govern Troy
And shine as once his father shone.
May the whole city muse upon
His feats, as often as the car
Brings him spoil-laden home from war
(Spoil reddened with the owner's gore)
To cheer his mother's heart once more;
Then let all say, if say they can:
"His father was the lesser man!"'

The prayer done, he handed Scamandrius to Andromache. As she embraced him, half-laughing, half-crying, Hector stroked her shoulders pityingly. 'Dearest Andromache,' he whispered, 'control your grief! No Greek will kill me, unless Heaven permits him; and what mortal, whether he be courageous or a coward, can evade his destiny? Go home now, attend to your spinning and weaving, keep your women hard at work; but war is a man's task, and especially mine as the Trojans' leader. You must leave it to me!' With that, Hector fell silent, picked up the plumed helmet, set it on his head again, and made for the gate.

As Andromache ascended the hill, glancing frequently over her shoulder, great tears rolled down her cheeks. Arrived at the house, she raised a lament, in anticipation of Hector's death, and all the womenfolk wept with her—none of them expecting him to survive his furious stand against the Greeks.

Paris did not, as it proved, stay much longer in his bedroom. Though fully armed, like a run-away horse he galloped along the streets:

> A stallion on pearl-barley fed,
>   A nimble horse of noble breed,
> Has burst the halter-rope and fled
>   From his full manger at full speed.
>
> He runs in pride with streaming mane,
>   Towards waters that will cool his rage,
> And whinnies at the mares again
>   In their accustomed pasturage . . .

So Paris ran, with exultant laughter, and overtook Hector as he turned from his farewell to Andromache. Paris said grinning: 'I apologize for delaying so busy a man—I should have come directly you ordered me.'

Hector replied: 'Nobody in his senses would under-rate your fighting qualities, brother; you are strong enough. But I find it painful to hear our people complaining of the distress that your wilful irresponsibility and carelessness have brought on us all. Well, we shall put everything right one day perhaps, if Zeus ever lets us chase the Greeks from our country and dedicate a thanks-giving bowl at the Palace to himself and his fellow-Immortals.'

Book
Seven:

Hector Duels with Great Ajax

> Watch the sailors, how they row,
> Bright oars flashing to and fro,
> All day long without complaint
> Hauling, until like to faint—
> Wearied muscles, bodies wet
> With sea-spray and their own sweat!
> None too soon, a Heaven-sent gale
> Bellies out the broad main-sail.

The exhausted Trojans, still fending off Greek attacks, felt a similar relief when Hector the Glorious and his brother Prince Paris emerged at last from the gates of Troy, both of them in fine fettle. Paris at once made for Menesthius of Arne, the son of Thracian King Areithous and his Queen Phylomedusa the Large-Eyed, and struck him dead. Hector then drove a spear into the neck of Eïoneus the Magnesian, below the helmet-rim; he died instantly. Glaucus, too, the Lycian commander, saw Iphinous, son of Dexius, mounting his chariot, and sent him mortally wounded to the ground with a javelin through the shoulder.

None of these incidents evaded Owl-Eyed Athene's watchful gaze. She flew down from the peaks of Olympus to prevent the slaughter of any more Greeks; but, on reaching Troy, found herself confronted by Phoebus Apollo, patron of the Trojans, who rose to greet her beside Zeus' oak-tree.

'To what,' he asked, 'may I attribute your visit, Athene, daughter of Almighty Zeus? A decision to give the Greeks an unfair advantage in today's fight, after refusing the hard-pressed Trojans' plea for mercy? Well, sister, my advice is that we should unite in ending this battle. The war is of course another matter: it may be resumed later, until Hera and yourself have achieved the total destruction of Troy, on which your hearts are set.'

'By all means,' Athene answered, 'let us end the battle, Lord of the Silver Bow! I came here with this very intention, but how do you think we should put it into effect?'

'Suppose,' said Apollo, 'that Hector caused a diversion by challenging any Greek to single combat? Would the Greeks not, for honour's sake, send someone against him?'

Athene agreed, and Prince Helenus, catching the message that they flashed into his mind, hurried towards Hector. 'Listen, brother,' he cried, 'I have received an assurance from the Immortals that your death is not yet due. You should shout a challenge, they suggest, announcing your readiness to meet the best man on the enemy side in single combat—but both armies must be seated and observe a truce.'

This news pleased Hector. He went along the Trojan front-line pressing men back with his spear held horizontally until they sat down and removed their armour; and Agamemnon the High King, when he saw what was happening, followed Hector's example. Athene and Apollo, wearing vulture disguise, perched together on a branch of Zeus' sacred oak: Athene beaming at her Greeks, Apollo beaming at his Trojans, as the closely packed armies crouched opposite each other, their ranks a-bristle with shields, plumes, and spears planted upright.

> The west wind rises, ugly ripples spread
> Across the sea, and clouds race overhead . . .

Such was the scene which the dark waves of men-at-arms, extended across the dusty plain, brought to their minds.

Hector spoke: 'Trojans and Greeks, pray give me your attention! Earlier today, Zeus Son of Cronus, enthroned on high, disrupted our attempt at peace-making; he plans, it seems, a continuous struggle until you Greeks either take Troy or suffer a decisive defeat. Meanwhile, I propose a duel between your bravest champion and myself, Prince Hector. And I will abide by the following terms, which I invoke Father Zeus to witness: that, if your champion overcomes me in fair combat, he may freely possess himself of my arms and armour—on condition, however, that the Trojans may retrieve the body for decent burning and burial. If, contrariwise, Apollo grants me victory, I promise to surrender my opponent's body after dedicating his arms and armour in the god's temple at Troy. Thereupon:

> 'You long-haired Greeks the corpse shall burn,
>   And weep, and give him praise,
> And by the banks of Hellespont
>   A glorious mound shall raise.

> 'Then some bold captain, born too late
>   To know that man or me,
> Long hence will sight it from his ship
>   In sail across the sea.

> 'And, pointing, cry: "That glorious mound
>   Heaped upon yonder shore
> Holds Such-and-such whom Hector's hand
>   Slew in a bygone war."
> Thus shall my name inherit fame
>   When I have gone before.'

Silence ensued. The Greeks, though ashamed to refuse Hector's challenge, were equally loth to accept it. At last, King Menelaus arose, groaning quietly, and upbraided his companions: 'Cowards! Women not men! Despite your persistent threats against Troy, none of you will face Prince Hector. What a disgrace! What wickedness! But, for all I care, you may continue sitting there, scared and inglorious, until you turn to mud on this plain! I accept the challenge myself, aware that the Immortals hold the threads of fate in their fingers, and will bestow victory on whichever champion they favour.'

Menelaus at once buckled on his armour, prepared to fight; which would have been his ruin, Hector being by far the more experienced soldier of the two, had not his fellow-princes leaped up and restrained him. Agamemnon caught at his arm, exclaiming: 'Are you mad, brother? This is no time for one of Zeus' foster-sons to behave so extravagantly. Yes, I know that you will withdraw now only with shame and reluctance, but you should never let mere ill-temper send you against Hector, son of Priam! Many Greeks beside yourself have reason to hate him, and he is more than your match as a duellist. Why, even Prince Achilles, though he delights in battle, has always steered clear of Hector, and you can hardly be compared to Achilles! Sit down again among your comrades—I insist upon it—while we choose some other hero to accept the challenge. And I can tell you that, however fearless and pugnacious our champion, he will be glad enough to rest his legs afterwards—if indeed he survives the combat.'

Dissuaded from persisting in his rash resolve, Menelaus allowed his friends to disarm him. But old Nestor, King of Pylus, sprang up, and shouted indignantly: 'Fie upon you! Were Peleus the Horseman here, he would be scandalized by this disgraceful scene—I am referring to Achilles' father, the eloquent King of the Myrmidons who once entertained me in his palace and questioned me at length about the lineage and family connexions of all our Peloponnesian nobles. He would be so scandalized, I repeat, to see you cowering before Hector, that he would hide his face in horror and pray for instant death! Ah, if only Zeus and Athene and Apollo would restore this aged body of mine, and make me as once I was when my Pylians fought the Arcadians outside the walls of Pheia, near the River Jardanus! I must tell you of the triumph that Athene vouchsafed me. Well, for a start: the God Ares gave Areithous, King of Arne [whose son Menesthius has now been killed] a fine suit of armour; but Lycurgus the Arcadian, knowing that Areithous was nicknamed "the Mace-man" because he always preferred a mace to bow or spear, trapped him in a narrow defile where the mace had no play, and toppled him over with a javelin through the belly. So Lycurgus won the armour, and wore it constantly, until, growing too old for battle, he gave it to his favourite squire, Ereuthalion. Ereuthalion sported the armour that day at Pheia, when he came forward and issued the same sort of challenge as you have just heard from Hector's lips. My Pylian comrades recoiled in fear, and it remained for me, though the youngest among them, to show my courage by facing the Arcadian champion . . . I have never killed a taller or a stronger man! Ereuthalion's corpse, spread-eagled on the ground, looked positively enormous. Ah, if only I were still young and vigorous, Hector would soon find a worthy opponent. But it seems that not a single one of you Greek princes will dare cross swords with him.'

Nestor's reprimand brought nine princes flushing to their feet. First, Agamemnon; next, Diomedes of the Loud War-Cry; then Great and Little Ajax. These were followed by Idomeneus of Crete; his comrade Meriones (a rival of Ares himself); Eurypylus, son of Euaemon the Thracian; Thoas, son of Andraemon the Aetolian; and, lastly, Odysseus of Ithaca.

Nestor spoke again: 'Since nine of you seem eager to fight Prince Hector, lots must be cast for the privilege; and, should the lucky winner escape alive, his salvation will be the salvation of us all.'

Each of the volunteers chose a lot (a potsherd or a twig) which he marked with his sign, and let fall into Agamemnon's helmet. Both armies then prayed to Father Zeus: the Greeks, that Great Ajax might be chosen as their champion or, failing him, Diomedes; the Trojans, on the contrary, that Hector might meet Agamemnon, the rich King of Mycenae.

Nestor shook the helmet; and a herald, picking up the lot that leaped out, carried it sunwise round the circle of contestants, asking each in turn: 'Is this yours, my lord?'

'It is!' cried Great Ajax, amid general satisfaction. When the herald placed the lot in his outstretched palm, he flung it down, shouting: 'Comrades, what joy! That lot was mine; I recognized the mark. Now, although my victory is a foregone conclusion, you should invoke Zeus the Son of Cronus while I re-arm. Ask him to grant me victory—and pray in silence, lest the Trojans overhear you—ah, what am I saying? Pray aloud, by all means, I am not afraid. No man living is strong enough to force me back once I come in close: nor skilful enough, either. I was born on the island of Salamis with my fair share of intelligence, and have been well schooled since then in the profession of arms.'

The Greeks did as Ajax asked, and the prayer which most of them used ran as follows:

'ZEUS, most glorious and great,
On Mount Ida holding state:
Grant Ajax to achieve renown
By hewing noble Hector down—
Yet if, of your esteem and care,
Prince Hector's life you deign to spare,
Grant both the champions equal might
And equal glory in this fight!'

Ajax buckled on his armour and, with a savage grin, strode forward brandishing his spear—like Ares when he leads men out to fight at Zeus' orders.

The Greeks watched their champion delightedly; the Trojans trembled for alarm. Hector's own heart thumped beneath his ribs, but he could neither retract his challenge at this stage, nor shrink away and disappear, as Paris had done. Ajax advanced, under the protection of his enormous shield—Tychius the Hylean currier's master-piece: nine layers of bull-hide, sheathed in bronze.

'Prince Hector!' cried Ajax in menacing tones. 'You shall soon learn what sort of champions we Greeks can still put into the field, though Achilles the Lion-Hearted is absent—a fighter who tears his enemies to pieces! Resentment against Agamemnon, our Commander-in-Chief, keeps Achilles brooding in his hut; yet several more of us dare duel with you. Come, make the first cast!'

Hector replied: 'Ajax, son of Telamon, descendant of Zeus: you should not bait me as if you were a small boy, or an ignorant woman! I have fought many battles; I possess the soldierly arts of manipulating a shield against attacks from either flank, and driving a chariot through the mêlée, and treading the dance of war in close combat. Nevertheless, since you are a brave man, I will not take advantage of any awkwardness betrayed by your defence, but rather destroy you, if possible, in a fairer style of fighting.'

He hurled his heavy spear at Ajax's shield; it pierced the outer layer of bronze and six of the bull-hides underneath, but not the seventh. Ajax's return cast went right through Hector's bright round targe, to penetrate his inlaid corslet and tunic—yet he had twisted aside, so that the blade only grazed his flank. Then both simultaneously grasped the butts of their spears, wrenched them out, and attacked each other like ravening lions or formidable wild boars. When Hector lunged, the point turned on the bronze of Ajax's shield; whereas Ajax's spear again went right through Hector's targe, and not only staggered him with the shock of its impact, but wounded him in the neck, drawing blood.

More than that was needed to dismay Hector, who retired a few paces, chose a rugged boulder from the plain, and let fly. The huge shield clanged as Hector's missile struck its boss. Undeterred, Ajax picked up an even larger boulder, one as big as a mill-stone, and hurled it with such terrific force that his enemy's targe burst inwards and flung him supine.

Apollo at once pulled Hector to his feet again; and the champions drew their swords. They would soon have begun hacking at each other, had not a pair of heralds intervened, most discreet persons: Talthybius from the Greek side and Idaeus from the Trojan. As they thrust their sacrosanct wands between the combatants, Idaeus spoke:

> 'Desist, refrain, sons dear to me,
> 　And to ZEUS throned afar!
> Talthybius and I agree
> 　What warriors you both are;
> Yet darkness comes to close the fight—
> Princes, obey your mother, NIGHT!'

'Idaeus,' Ajax replied, 'you must first ask Hector to call a halt, since the challenge was his. If he consents, I shall cheerfully do the same.'

'Ajax,' said Hector, 'by the grace of Heaven you are not only tall, strong, and the best spearman in the Greek army, but wise; let us therefore break off this fight. Later it can be resumed, until the gods award victory either to you or to me. Meanwhile:

> Since darkness comes to close the fight—
> We will obey our mother, NIGHT!

However, before parting—you, to win congratulations in the camp, especially from your friends and relatives; I, to comfort my people,

especially the women, who will doubtless be at prayer in some temple
—before parting, noble Ajax, let us exchange princely gifts and make
everyone, whether Greek or Trojan, cry out for wonder: "That so
bitter a duel could end in such brotherly affection!" '

Hector gave Ajax his silver-studded sword, complete with scab-
bard and well-cut baldric; whereupon Ajax gave Hector his bright
purple belt. Then they parted and went away.

The Trojans were overcome by joy that their leader had escaped
alive from the irresistible fury of Ajax's attack, not having even
hoped that their city would escape capture that day. The Greeks
similarly welcomed Ajax, exulting in his success and, when they
marched back, escorted him to the hut of King Agamemnon, who at
once sacrificed a five-year-old bull in Zeus' honour. Servants flayed it,
jointed the carcase and distributed the meat, which was then care-
fully sliced for the spits. The slices having been roasted, the banquet
was ready. Agamemnon's guests set to and ate heartily, no one being
stinted of his share; but Ajax had won the hero's portion, consisting
of roast beef from the entire length of chine.

As soon as they had eaten and drunk all that they could swallow,
old Nestor favoured them with more of his famous advice: 'King
Agamemnon, and you other princes of Greece! Since a great many of
our comrades have lost their lives on the Scamandrian Plain, you
should ask the Trojans for a truce, beginning at daybreak. You should
then arrange ox and mule transport to fetch in the corpses, and burn
them just outside the camp. The bones can be collected, and even-
tually returned to each fallen hero's children or near kinsfolk. And
we should heap an extensive barrow on the plain, by way of honour-
ing the dead—but, at the same time, convert it into a defensive ram-
part around the camp. Such a rampart would need towers above, a
deep fosse in front, and a bridge guarded by stout gates as a sally-
port for our own chariots. I consider these necessary precautions
against a surprise attack by Trojan chariots and other arms.'

Agamemnon and his Privy Council agreed.

*

A heated Assembly was being held in the outer court of Priam's Pal-
ace. Antenor the Prudent addressed the fierce, confused crowd.
'Trojans, Dardanians, and honoured Allies,' he cried, 'pray give me

your attention! I have an important resolution to move. It is that we immediately surrender Queen Helen, with her whole fortune, to Agamemnon and Menelaus. Our cause is an impious one, since Paris violated the sacred laws which forbid an ambassador to rob his hosts. Unless we offer such amends, I neither desire nor expect victory to attend us.'

When Antenor sat down again, Paris rose and exclaimed passionately: 'Antenor, you used to be a man of common sense, but what you have now said displeases me greatly. Are you joking, or have the gods addled your brains? Let me make this clear once and for all: I do not, and shall never, consent to give up Helen! I am willing only to restore the treasure that I brought away with her, and pay King Menelaus adequate damages from my own purse.'

The next speaker was Priam himself. 'Trojans, Dardanians, and honoured Allies!' he said. 'Pray give me your attention! I move another resolution: that we disperse to our usual suppers, but keep a double watch until dawn, when Idaeus, our herald, shall lay before King Agamemnon and King Menelaus the offer made by my son Prince Paris, who originated our quarrel with them. Let Idaeus also suggest that both armies abstain from further acts of aggression while the dead are being duly burned. At the end of this truce, if the Greeks reject my son's offer, the war may go on until one side wins.'

Priam's resolution was adopted, the Assembly dispersed to their suppers, and at daybreak Idaeus visited the Greek camp. Finding a Privy Council already gathered behind the stern of Agamemnon's galley, he spoke as follows:

'King Agamemnon, King Menelaus, and you other princes of Greece! My sovereign lord Priam orders me to present an offer, supported by his leading Trojans, which he hopes will cause satisfaction. It comes from Prince Paris, the originator of our quarrel—speaking for myself, I heartily wish he had died first—and is to this effect. He proposes to restore the treasure that he brought away with Queen Helen, and pay her former husband adequate damages from his own private purse. He will not, however, give up Helen—though the Trojans have urged such an act of self-denial. I am further to request a truce, while our dead are collected and burned. As soon as it ends—

unless, of course, you accept Prince Paris' offer—the war may go on
until one side wins.'

After a pause, Diomedes gave his opinion: 'Since every fool knows
that Troy is doomed, I hold that we ought to decline the offer, even
if it included—which it does not—the surrender of Queen Helen.'

Diomedes was cheered to the echo, and Agamemnon addressed
the herald: 'You have heard the Greek answer, noble Idaeus, which
carries my approval. As for the second matter: I shall not grudge
King Priam a truce while his dead, being naturally entitled to purifi-
cation by fire, are collected and burned. Let Zeus the Thunderer,
Husband of Hera, witness my compliance with this request.'

Agamemnon raised his sceptre aloft in sight of all the gods; where-
upon Idaeus took his leave. The Trojan Assembly was waiting for an
answer, and no sooner had he delivered it, than everyone present
hurried off, either to retrieve the dead or to gather fire-wood.

By the time that parties from both armies met peaceably on the
battlefield, the sun had climbed out of the slow, deep Ocean Stream
and was beaming down. Even under his fierce rays, the Trojans found
it difficult to identify some of their despoiled comrades, before wash-
ing away the blood. Hot tears fell as the wagons were loaded; but
Priam forbade any lament. After silently crowning a huge pyre
with corpses and seeing that the flames did their work, the Trojans
went home in dejection.

Long before dawn the Greeks, who had been occupied by the same
melancholy task, gathered around the ashes of their pyre and began
heaping an extensive barrow over them. On Nestor's advice, they
enlarged this into a defensive rampart; adding towers above, and a
broad, deep fosse in front, but left a bridge guarded by a pair of
strong gates, as a sally-port for their own chariots.

*

In Heaven, as the fascinated gods sat watching Agamemnon's men
hard at work, Poseidon the Earth-Shaker asked Zeus an awkward
question: 'Father Zeus, is there no man left on the wide earth who
takes us Immortals into his confidence? You must have noticed that
those Greeks started digging without the customary hundred-beast
sacrifice? Yet, you can depend on it, this rampart will earn praise
as far as Dawn reaches, and make everyone forget a much greater

feat: how speedily Phoebus Apollo and I once built the enormous stone walls of Troy for King Laomedon.'

Zeus answered in vexation: 'What a mean fellow you are, Brother Poseidon! Though a god less powerful than yourself might perhaps feel jealous of these Greek earth-works, surely you know that your own magnificent masonry will continue to earn praise as far as Dawn reaches? Very well: wait until the Greeks have sailed home, and you may wash that rampart away with a strong sea and spread a level beach where it stood, so that no vestige survives.'

By sunset, the rampart was completed. Several Lemnian ships had just arrived from King Euneus, a son of Jason the Argonaut and Queen Hypsipyle, carrying a thousand measures of wine as a free gift to Agamemnon and Menelaus, and many measures more for public sale. This wine found a ready market; the Greeks paid in bronze, iron, hides, cattle and prisoners. Then they slaughtered oxen, ate their suppers, and caroused all night, despite the frequent ominous mutterings of thunder with which Zeus threatened them—though nobody dared drink unless he first honoured Zeus by spilling a cupful of wine on the ground—but finally lay down and relaxed in sleep. The Trojans had also feasted to their hearts' content.

Book Eight:

An Indecisive Battle

As Dawn spread her saffron light over the earth, Omniscient Zeus, Lord of Thunder, called a divine Assembly on the very summit of rocky Olympus, and spoke as follows:

'Give ear, all gods and goddesses
  Who dwell in Heaven apart,
For I shall freely broach to you
  The counsels of this heart,

'And let no god nor goddess think
  Such counsels to gainsay—
Nod your approval, that my word
  Accomplished be this day.

'But if I hear of stealthy aid
  To Greeks or Trojans lent,
At my strong hands that god shall earn
  Egregious punishment.

'I surely shall lay hold of him,
  To whirl him round and round,
And cast him head-long down to Hell,
  The great gulf underground.

'As far below our teeming earth
  As earth below the skies,
With iron gates and brazen floor
  That gloomy kingdom lies.

'Immortals all, I challenge you:
    Take now a golden chain
And strive to drag me down from Heaven
    With your bright arms astrain.

'Such puny strength will never stir
    So huge a lord as me,
Nay, I will haul you up instead,
    And with you, Earth and Sea.

'Then to this peak the chain I'll hitch,
    Being strong beyond compare,
And leave yourselves, and Earth, and Sea
    Suspended in mid-air.'

Zeus' masterful threat commanded a dead silence, finally broken by Athene the Owl-Eyed: 'Father Zeus, Ruler of all the Gods,' she said, 'though we have no delusions about your enormous strength, that does not prevent us from pitying the wretched Greeks, who will be ruined without our help. We promise to abstain from active intervention, since these are your orders; but let us at least advise our wards how they can avoid utter disaster.'

Zeus smiled at her. 'Dear child,' he said, 'you must not take me too seriously: I am very well disposed towards you.'

*

He then gave instructions for the harnessing of his bronze-shod, fleet-footed horses and, dressed all in gold, mounted the chariot. Crack! went his golden whip; the team leaped forward between earth and sky, their fiery manes streaming behind them. Zeus' destination was Gargarus on Mount Ida (home of wild beasts), where he owned a private estate and an altar always fragrant with the odour of sacrifice. There he alighted, unharnessed the horses, threw a thick mist around them, and went for a stroll up the mountain, rejoicing in his glory. He chose as his seat a crag which commanded a clear view of Troy and the Greek camp. The Greeks were eating a hasty breakfast and arming themselves for battle; so were the Trojans. But the Trojans, though numerically far inferior, had resolved to defend their women and children and display a courage that matched the occasion. Out they all streamed, chariotry and infantry, through the wide-open gates of Troy.

With a clash of bronze the two armies met, fighting at spear's length, or shield-boss against shield-boss. A tremendous din arose: shouts of exultation, cries of agony, as men killed or were killed; and blood reddened the earth.

Spears, javelins and arrows took equal toll of both sides that morning; but at high noon Father Zeus, producing his pair of golden scales, laid a fate in each pan (one for the Greeks, the other for the Trojans); then lifted them by their pivot. The Greek fate plummeted down and the Trojan fate soared. Zeus thereupon thundered aloud from Mount Ida and flashed lightning into the invaders' eyes, which caused them dismay and fear.

Idomeneus of Crete, Agamemnon the High King, and the two Ajaxes, seasoned soldiers though they were, all lost heart. Only Nestor, Watch-Dog of the Greeks, stood fast, and even he did not do so deliberately; the fact being that an arrow from Prince Paris' bow had struck one of his four horses on the crown of its head, where the mane starts—a most vulnerable spot. When the arrow entered the horse's brain, it reared agonizedly and the three other beasts became unmanageable. Nestor leaped to the ground and hacked at the traces with his sword, in an attempt to free the wounded horse. Hector the Bright-Helmed, however, was on his track, and that would have been the end of Nestor, had not Diomedes of the Loud War-Cry observed his predicament. He yelled at Odysseus the Crafty: 'Son of Laertes and Aphrodite, are you running away? Beware, or someone will plant a spear between your cowardly shoulders! Halt, man, help me protect this venerable prince from a furious Trojan!'

Odysseus, paying no heed, rushed on. Diomedes, thus deserted, drove his chariot close to Nestor's and said urgently: 'Son of Neleus, these youngsters are pressing you hard, I see. Your body is old and weary, your charioteer is a weakling, and you have a slow team. Come, mount beside me, and watch the performance of my horses— I won them from the gallant Aeneas—the horses of Tros, admirably trained to swing a chariot around at full speed, whether in pursuit or retirement. Leave your own equipage under the care of our two charioteers, while we counter-attack the Trojans. Hector must learn that my spear is as thirsty for blood as his.'

Nestor accepted the invitation. Leaving his horses in charge of the good-natured Eurymedon, he changed places with Sthenelus, Diomedes' charioteer, whose reins and whip he took up, and immediately counter-attacked. As soon as they came into range, Diomedes aimed a javelin at Hector; but it flew wide and caught Hector's charioteer Eniopeus, son of gallant Thebaeus, high on the breast and tumbled him dead over the rails. His horses swerved in alarm.

Though deeply grieved by this loss, Hector left Eniopeus lying and went to find another charioteer. Soon he came upon Archeptolemus, son of Iphitus, a reliable fighter, whom he ordered to climb up and manage the team.

Diomedes and Nestor continued their pursuit of Hector, and this might have caused irremediable disaster—Hector speared, and the Trojans herded into Troy like a flock of lambs—had Zeus not decided on sudden action. His awe-inspiring thunder rolled out, and lightning struck the earth at the feet of Diomedes' team. Fumes of sulphur rose, the horses baulked, cowering, and Nestor dropped the bright reins, muttering fearfully: 'Diomedes, let us turn back! Zeus is warning you that this is Hector's day. Later, perhaps, we will win our share of glory; but no man, however courageous, can close his eyes to so plain a portent. Zeus' strength is immeasurably greater than ours.'

'True enough, venerable Nestor,' answered Diomedes, 'yet what if Hector boasts: "Diomedes fled from me to the shelter of his camp"? Should the Trojans ever hear him say so, may the earth open and swallow me!'

Nestor reproached Diomedes: 'Son of Tydeus the Wise, you ought not to talk in this stupid strain! Even though Hector dared call you a coward, no Trojan nor Dardanian soldier would believe him; still less would the many noblewomen whom you have robbed of their vigorous mates.' He wheeled the chariot about and drove through a mob of excited Trojans who were aiming at him from all sides.

Hector taunted Diomedes: 'Ah, son of Tydeus, the Greeks used to honour you with the highest place at their feasts, and the finest joints of beef, and cups filled to the brim! Now they will say: "After all, he is no better than a woman!" Hurry off home, poor little doll! You shall never scale our walls, nor carry away our women. I should crush you without a qualm if you tried!'

Diomedes hesitated. Three times he nearly paused to face Hector, but each time Zeus gave the Trojans a victory sign, thunder on their right flank from Mount Ida, and he desisted. Hector cried: 'Trojans, Lycians, and hard-fighting Dardanians! Be men, be heroes! Zeus' thunder assures me of his favour: he will grant us the upper hand and bring disaster on the Greeks. What fools they were to raise those miserable fortifications! Why, our horses could clear the fosse in their stride. Once past the rampart, we must set fire to the Greek fleet and destroy their crews in the smoky confusion.'

He yelled at his horses: 'Hey, Chestnut, Bright-Foot, Fire-Eye, Beacon! Earn your feed! Prove your gratitude to Andromache, daughter of Eëtion! The way she has spoiled you by pouring the best wheat into your mangers and mixing wine in your water-troughs! She thinks of you even before she thinks of me and, Heaven knows, I am her husband! Get along with you now! Overtake those horses of Tros! Help me to capture Nestor's celebrated shield—the gods themselves talk of it—solid gold, arm-rods and all! I also covet Diomedes' inlaid breast-plate: a piece made by Hephaestus himself. If I can win both trophies, I should be able to send what remains of the Greeks scurrying off in their ships, this very evening, too.'

Hector's confident words stung the Goddess Hera to the quick. She bounced up and down on her throne until Olympus shook, and cried to Poseidon the Earth-Shaker: 'This is outrageous, brother! You show not the least pity for the defeated Greeks, though they have always heaped splendid offerings on your altars at Helice and Aegae. Why do you deny them victory? If only we friends of Greece could drive the Trojans back in defiance of Zeus, he would regret having left us and gone to sit in lonely state on Mount Ida!'

Poseidon, shocked by his sister's suggestion, answered: 'Hera, you head-strong creature, what do you mean? I certainly have no intention of offending our Brother Zeus. He is altogether too powerful for me.'

Zeus now allowed Hector to pen the Greeks behind their rampart, and soon the camp area enclosed by the sea and the fosse was crowded with their demoralized troops. Hector would have completed his glorious success by destroying the Greek fleet, had not Hera flashed a message to Agamemnon: that he must bestir himself at once and put new heart into his army. So Agamemnon strode past the line of ships and huts, a purple cloak on his arm, until he reached Odysseus' huge black vessel, which was beached exactly halfway down. Standing here and pitching his voice high, he could make himself heard from Great Ajax's flotilla at one end to Achilles' at the other—for each of these two heroes had boldly stationed his command on an exposed flank.

'Fie, oh fie!' Agamemnon yelled. 'You Greeks look fierce enough, but you are mean-spirited rascals. What of our landing on Lemnos? There you bolted good beef and swilled good wine, and bragged that, when it came to battle, one Greek was worth fifty or a hundred Trojans! Today Hector alone has put thousands of you to flight and, unless you display a little more manhood, he will burn our fleet. O Father Zeus, have you ever cursed a great king like myself with such blind faith in his allies, or robbed him of so much glory? Yet what is my error? On our mad voyage to these shores, when did I sail heedlessly past any of your altars? I always landed, and sacrificed bulls' thighbones to you, folded in fat, as a token of my eagerness to sack Troy. Ah, Zeus, at least do not dash my last hopes! Permit us to re-embark without further loss and escape total extinction at our enemies' hands!' Tears bedewed Agamemnon's eyes.

Zeus took compassion and sent the Greeks the most favourable augury: an eagle, grasping a fawn in its talons, swooped and let it fall beside the altar where they habitually sacrificed to him. The army rallied at once and found fresh courage.

No Greek could claim to have forestalled Diomedes by driving a chariot out beyond the fosse and killing a fully-armed Trojan. As Agelaus, the son of Phraedmon, wheeled about in avoidance of Diomedes' charge, a spear struck him between the shoulders and its point emerged under the breastbone; Agelaus fell to the ground with a clang of armour.

Agamemnon and Menelaus followed Diomedes, and after them galloped Great and Little Ajax, Idomeneus of Crete, his joint-commander Meriones, and Eurypylus, son of Euaemon. Teucrus was the ninth of this gallant company; bow in hand, he hid behind the immense shield of his half-brother Great Ajax. Whenever Ajax stealthily shifted it, Teucrus would aim at someone in the throng, shoot him, and take cover again, as a child shelters behind the folds of his mother's skirt.

You ask me who were Teucrus' victims? I will tell you in the order of their deaths. First, Orsilochus, then Ormenus, then Ophelestes, Daetor, Chromius, noble Lycophontes, Amopaon son of Polyaemon, and Melanippus—Teucrus shot them all. Agamemnon, who had watched the havoc, ran up and cried happily: 'Dear Teucrus, if you continue this sharp-shooting, you will save the army and bring glory on your father Telamon, in distant Salamis. I am aware, of course, that you are a bastard; yet Telamon was generous enough to acknowledge the paternity and educate you at his palace. Here is my firm promise: should Zeus the Shield-Bearer and his daughter Athene let me sack the fortress of Troy, I will award you a prize of honour—either a tripod, or a chariot and team, or a beautiful woman for your bed.'

'My lord,' Teucrus replied, 'why spur a willing horse? Naturally I shall continue. Since this sortie began, eight of my long-barbed arrows have sunk into the flesh of sturdy young Trojan noblemen. So far, however, I have always failed to hit that mad dog yonder.'

Teucrus aimed at Prince Hector as he spoke, intent on killing him, but missed once more. The arrow struck Prince Gorgythion, Priam's son; his mother was a divinely beautiful woman from Aesyme named Castianeira.

> Oh, poppy in the garden bed
> Oppressed by summer rain,
> You loll your burdensome bright head
> And powerless you remain
> To lift it up again.

So Gorgythion's bright head also lolled under the weight of his helmet; and he died.

When Teucrus aimed again, Apollo deflected the arrow. It caught Archeptolemus, Hector's new charioteer, high on the breast and tumbled him dead over the rails. His horses swerved in alarm.

Though deeply grieved by this second loss, Hector left Archeptole-
mus lying, and persuaded his own brother Prince Cebriones to take
the reins. Hector then sprang down, shouting terribly, picked up a
jagged stone and ran straight at Teucrus. Teucrus pulled another
arrow from his quiver and fitted it to the string, but before he could
shoot, Hector's stone landed on his collarbone—a most vulnerable
spot—and broke the sinews of his arm, numbing the wrist. Teucrus
dropped his bow and sank to his knees; Ajax, however, straddled him
protectively, shield advanced, until two loyal friends—Mecisteus, son
of Echius, and noble Alastor—stooped and carried Teucrus groaning
away to the camp.

A further roll of thunder from Zeus encouraged the Trojans, and
the Greeks fled again, hotly pursued by the triumphant Hector:

> With nips at flank and haunch, a well-trained hound
> After a lion or wild boar will bound,
> The fleeing monster dares not turn around,
> 　So sharp his teeth!

Hector adopted similar tactics, spearing stragglers and driving the
main body over their fosse, through their gates, and behind their
palisaded rampart. The cornered Greeks began yelling for dismay,
and lifting hands in desperate prayer to Heaven. Hector drove his
chariot here and there, killing heroes by the score; he looked as grim
as a Gorgon, or as Ares, that curse of mankind.

✳

Hera the White-Armed, watching the battle, spoke urgently to
Athene: 'Daughter of Zeus the Shield-Bearer, can we allow any more
of this? Why not intervene, if only for a last time? Our wards are on
the point of massacre; and all because no one dares face the battle
rage of a single man, Hector, son of Priam! He has inflicted fearful
casualties.'

Athene answered: 'Indeed, Goddess, nothing would make me hap-
pier than to watch Hector being overborne and killed. But my father
is a perverse, stubborn, evil-tempered wretch, who continually de-
ranges my plans! He forgets how often I rescued his son Heracles,
when King Eurystheus, acquiescing in your relentless hatred, set him
those Twelve Labours that nearly brought about his death. Heracles

would always invoke Zeus, who then hurried me to his aid. Had I foreseen my father's ingratitude, I should never have troubled to save his bastard from the fearful, high-tumbling waterfall of Styx—Eurystheus, you remember, sent him down to the Palace of Hades, King of Hell, in quest of the Dog Cerberus? As it is, my father has turned against me and grants Thetis whatever she asks, just because she recently kissed his knees and caressed his beard, begging him to honour Achilles the City-Sacker! In time, Zeus will be glad to call me his bright-eyed darling again, but not today. Come, harness your horses, while I visit the Palace and arm myself for battle; I shall be interested to watch Hector's face when we come charging on the scene. Trojan as well as Greek corpses will soon feed the dogs and carrion birds along that waterfront!'

Hera went off to harness her golden-frontleted team, and Athene visited the Palace where she slipped out of a many-coloured robe (which she had made herself) letting it fall in a heap on the threshold. Instead, she borrowed a tunic belonging to Father Zeus, and over it buckled her armour. Then, grasping the heavy, long, stout spear which she used to destroy mortals who have fallen under Zeus' awesome displeasure, Athene mounted beside Hera on the glowing chariot. Hera cracked her whip, the gates of Heaven groaned open by themselves to allow their exit, and they shot through—past a pair of janitresses named the Seasons, whom Zeus entrusts with the task of parting and drawing the cloud curtain between Heaven and Earth.

Zeus, from his seat on Mount Ida, saw what was afoot, and indignantly summoned Iris the Golden-Winged. He told her: 'Fly as fast as you can, intercept those two goddesses, and warn them to keep out of this battle!

> 'For I do solemnly affirm
>   (And so the thing shall be)
> That those who dare adventure there
>   Must take good heed of me,
>
> 'Lest I should hough their horses' legs,
>   And crush their chariot wheels,
> And roughly from their glowing car
>   Toss them, head over heels.

'Ten long years will not cure the wound
   Torn by a thunderbolt,
My bright-eyed girl may learn too late
   The rashness of revolt!

'With HERA I am not so wroth:
   Her nature is, indeed,
To break or thwart, with wifely art,
   All laws by ZEUS decreed.'

Iris flew off, like a whirlwind, and stopped the chariot just as it emerged from the Palace gates. 'Where are you bound in such haste and anger?' she asked. 'You surely know that Zeus the Son of Cronus has banned all aid to the Greek army fighting before Troy? Here is his message: "Keep out of this battle—

"For I do solemnly affirm
   (And so the thing shall be)
That those who dare adventure there
   Must take good heed of me,

"Lest I should hough their horses' legs,
   And crush their chariot wheels,
And roughly from their glowing car
   Toss them, head over heels.

"Ten long years will not cure the wound
   Torn by a thunderbolt,
My bright-eyed girl may learn too late
   The rashness of revolt!

"With HERA I am not so wroth:
   Her nature is, indeed,
To break or thwart, with wifely art,
   All laws by ZEUS decreed."

But you surprise me, Athene! Only a reckless, shameless bitch would dare use so prodigious a spear in defiance of her own father!'

Iris disappeared, and Hera turned to Athene with a shrug. 'Such being the case,' she said, 'I am against opposing him for the sake of mere mortals. Why not let Fortune decide whether So-and-so lives or dies; and Zeus himself whether the Greeks or the Trojans win the war? After all, that is his responsibility!'

She wheeled the chariot about. The Seasons unyoked the long-maned horses, tethered them to their ambrosial mangers, and tilted the chariot beside the golden gates. Hera and Athene, rejoining their fellow-Olympians, sat down on their thrones in profound gloom.

When Zeus presently drove back from Mount Ida to preside at the divine session, it was Poseidon who unharnessed his team, set the chariot on its stand and spread a tarpaulin over it. Zeus thereupon occupied his own golden throne, and great Olympus shook under his weight. Athene and Hera alone ignored Zeus' entry, neither questioning nor greeting him. He took immediate note of their discourtesy, and asked: 'Why so glum, Goddesses? Have you tired yourselves by making mincemeat of the hated Trojan army? No, I am sure that is a bad guess! There is not a god in Heaven who could force me to alter my mind; and you pair of beauties started to tremble before you saw any fighting at all—

> 'For I had solemnly declared,
>   And so it must have been,
> That should you dare adventure there,
>   Bold daughter and false Queen,
>
> 'Then would I snatch my thunderbolts
>   And hurl them monstrous well,
> Nor let you two ride scatheless through
>   To where the Immortals dwell!'

Athene and Hera, still busy plotting the Trojans' overthrow, whispered discontentedly. Athene managed to restrain her mounting fury; but Hera, having less self-control, burst out: 'Revered Husband, what was that you said? Though we have no delusions about your enormous strength, it does not prevent us from pitying the wretched Greeks, who are suffering terrible losses.'

Zeus replied: 'Tomorrow morning, my Queen, if you care to use your beautiful large eyes, you will see me causing even greater havoc in the ranks of that immense Greek army. I shall let Hector press his dauntless assault on the naval camp until the fight rages around the corpse of Achilles' friend Patroclus, and Achilles is provoked to rise up in vengeance. Thus runs my divine decree!

> 'Wife, though you mumble, though you rage,
>   It matters not to me—
> Be off, go brood in furious mood
>   Far beyond land and sea!
>
> 'Deep down at the horizon's verge
>   Where, loathing their sad plight,
> Iapetus and Cronus lurk,
>   Bereft of air or light:
>
> 'Bound on the sunless plain of Hell
>   Most piteously they pant . . .
> Be off! I care not how or where,
>   Perfidious termagant!'

Hera disdained to answer.

✳

Then:

> Swift into Ocean plunged the Sun again
> And Night fell black on Earth, giver of grain . . .

an event which the conquering Trojans found most vexatious, but which the Greeks welcomed as an answer to repeated prayer.

Hector now disengaged his army and occupied a corpse-free open space near the river. He stood, leaning on his fourteen-foot spear with its gold-socketed blade, and signalled for silence. The Trojan noblemen dismounted and crowded up to listen.

'Your attention, pray, Trojans, Dardanians, and honoured Allies!' shouted Hector. 'Though I had hoped to make a shambles of that camp, destroying the Greeks and their entire fleet, Night saved them. There is nothing for it at this hour but to lay off and prepare our suppers. Unharness your teams, my lords, if you please, and feed them well. Cattle and sheep should be fetched from Troy at once, also wine and bread, and enough fire-wood gathered to light up the plain until daybreak; for I fear that the enemy may escape under cover of darkness. If they make the attempt, see that as many of them as possible take an arrow-wound, or a spear-wound, home to nurse as a memento of their flight. That should discourage another Trojan War.

'Now let heralds go through the city warning girls and old men for all-night sentry duty—on those great walls built by Poseidon and Apollo at my grandfather's orders—while mothers of families keep huge fires blazing in their courtyards. The gates, too, should be secured against a surprise attack. Trojans, kindly respect my wishes! At dawn I shall address you once more. And I pray that Zeus and his fellow-gods drive off this noisy pack of hounds which the Fates have set upon us!

'Tonight, we keep watch! At daybreak we renew our assault. Will Diomedes, son of Tydeus, press me back from the ships to the rampart? Or will I kill him and carry off his blood-stained armour? Who knows? We shall see whether he dares face this spear! Yet I trust that the rising Sun may find him fallen in a ring of his henchmen. Could I only feel as sure of remaining youthful and triumphant for the rest of my life—honoured like Athene and Apollo—as I do that Agamemnon's army is doomed to disaster!'

The Trojans, after a burst of applause, unharnessed their sweating teams and tethered them to the chariots. Next, they fetched cattle and sheep from Troy, also wine and bread, and collected kindling-wood in plenty. A wind rose and blew up to Heaven the smoke of their hundred-beast sacrifices. Nevertheless, the gods would not regale themselves with the delicious smell, because of the deep hatred they bore Priam and his people. That night, the Trojans bivouacked on the battlefield, confident of victory.

> About the lovely Moon each separate star
>   Twinkles; remote and windless is the sky;
> Peaks, woods and promontories stretch afar—
>   As clear as day to the glad shepherd's eye . . .

Thus, from the walls of Troy, the sentries' glad eyes saw a thousand little lights illuminating the plain between river and sea; each light

a camp-fire, around which sat fifty Trojans. Their teams were teth-
ered to the chariots, munching pearl-barley mixed with spelt, and
awaiting the regal glory of Dawn.

Book Nine:

A Deputation to Achilles

While the Trojans kept watch that night, utter confusion reigned among the Greeks. It was as when:

> Two furious winds come striving
>   South-easterly from Thrace,
> Brown weed in tangles driving
>   Across the sea's wan face—
> So wild a storm provokes despair
> Among the dumb fish lurking there.

Though dazed by grief, Agamemnon collected a few heralds and sent them off to convene a hurried council-of-war. 'But give each prince a private warning,' he said. 'The Trojans might overhear a public summons.' When he addressed the Council—

> His tears ran down as mournfully as if
> They were some dark stream oozing from a cliff . . .

Agamemnon spoke in a broken voice: 'Comrades, Zeus Son of Cronus must have cursed me with blindness; I never suspected so cruel a trick. Despite his firm promise that I should not quit these shores before sacking Troy, he now expects me to sail home dishonoured by immense losses. Yet, such being Zeus' pleasure, what can we do? He has humbled many a proud city and, since his power is supreme, will often do so again. I propose therefore that we raise this siege and make the best of our way back to Greece; for Heaven denies us victory.'

A long silence greeted this outburst, all the Councillors feeling too glum to venture a reply; but at last Diomedes of the Loud War-Cry rose.

'My lord Agamemnon,' he said, 'I shall exercise the right of free speech and you must not resent any strictures on your incompetence —especially after having called me a coward, as everyone in the camp, whatever his length of service, well remembers. The truth is that Zeus Son of Cronus the Crooked-Dealer has a habit of doing things by halves: he has, for instance, granted you the title of High King and appointed you leader of this expedition, while denying you the supreme gift of steadfastness. My lord, do you really consider us mean-spirited? Your ships lie beached beside the many hundreds that followed you from Greece; yonder stretches the sea . . . But none of us other Greeks will desert the allied cause; or so I trust. Even if I should be mistaken about my fellow-commanders, at least Sthenelus and I, who came here in Zeus' name, are resolved to stay— just the two of us—until Troy falls.'

A burst of cheering rang out, and King Nestor spoke next. 'Diomedes, son of Tydeus,' he cried, 'you are not only a remarkable fighter, but the best public speaker of our generation! Nobody can disregard or contradict what you have said. Though young enough to be a son of my old age, you gave advice that was both sound and honest—so far as it went. Now, as a soldier of much greater experience, I shall carry the argument to its conclusion; for neither the High King himself nor anyone else is likely to treat my words with disdain:

> Only a tribeless, lawless, homeless man
> Discord will meditate, and discord plan!

And which of us could be described as tribeless, lawless, or homeless?

'However, I do not propose to speak on an empty stomach. Since night has fallen, let us prepare supper, while some of the more active men form outposts in the space between the fosse and the rampart. My lord Agamemnon, pray spread a banquet for us Councillors! As High King this is at once your duty and your privilege; and these huts are well stocked with wine ferried across from Thrace. When we have supped, you can review our various suggestions and adopt the wisest. Wisdom we certainly need. To be ringed round by the enemy's numerous camp-fires is no laughing matter. The fate of our expedition must be decided tonight!'

No sooner said than done. Seven companies, each of a hundred spearmen under a captain, acted as outposts, lighting fires and cooking their suppers in the space between fosse and rampart. The captains were: Thrasymedes, son of Nestor; the Minyans Ascalaphus and Ialmenus, sons of Ares; Meriones the Cretan; Aphareus; Deipyrus; and Lycomedes, son of Creion. But Agamemnon feasted the Council in his hut, and when they had all satisfied their hunger and thirst Nestor, whose advice had always been voted the best—in the old days—generously gave them more of it.

He said: 'Most noble son of Atreus, my lord Agamemnon the High King! If I both start and end this speech with your name, I do so because Zeus has entrusted you with the sceptre of sovereignty, and placed you in command over many different contingents; it is therefore your duty, as President of this Council, to guide the debate, and approve the sagest proposal made. You can rely on us to follow in whatever direction you then point. I shall be as helpful as possible —and doubt whether anyone present will hit upon a wiser comment than mine—the thought has been floating in my head ever since the day when you sent heralds to take the captive Briseis from Achilles' hut, not only without our approval but against my express warning —in short, you were a fool to let your proud heart betray you into dishonouring a hero whom the gods themselves honoured—for you robbed Achilles of his prize, and still retain it! Yet it is not too late to think how we may win his renewed support by appeasing him with kind words and friendly gifts.'

'Venerable Nestor,' Agamemnon answered, 'your animadversions are well deserved. I do not deny having acted like a fool. A military commander beloved by Zeus—as Zeus now loves Hector, and allows him to destroy us—is worth many armies. So, repenting of my hasty passions, I shall make amends in the form of a stupendous indemnity herewith offered to Prince Achilles: Seven unused, three-legged bronze kettles; ten gold ingots weighing a talent apiece*; twenty shining copper cauldrons; six pairs of race-winning chariot horses—the man would not be poor, no indeed, my lords, who owned as much wealth as those horses earn me in prizes! To these gifts I add seven craftswomen—marvellously beautiful girls—I chose them for myself from the booty which Achilles won at Lesbos; also the woman of whom I deprived him the other day—namely Briseis, daughter of Briseus—taking an oath that I have had no carnal knowledge of her. All goods and prisoners will be delivered to him at once; and if the gods grant us the good fortune of sacking Troy, then he may claim the further right to select not only a whole shipload of gold and bronze treasures, but the twenty loveliest women in Troy, Queen Helen the Fair-Haired alone excepted. Moreover, if we come safely back to the rich land of Greece, I vow to adopt Achilles and accord him the same rank and honours as my own son Orestes, who is now enjoying a luxurious education at Mycenae. Besides, I have three daughters in that splendid palace of mine: Chrysothemis, Laodice, and Iphianassa. Achilles is free to marry whichever girl he prefers and, when he fetches her away to Phthia, I shall demand no bride-price but, quite the reverse, provide a dowry larger than any king ever settled on a daughter! I will give him lordship, too, over seven towns: Cardamyle, Enope, Hire (where the grazing is excellent), Pherae, sacred to Apollo, Antheia with its lush meadows, lovely Aepeia, and Pedasus, famous for its vines. They lie together near the sea, beyond Sandy Pylos; and the inhabitants, who own enormous flocks of sheep and herds of cattle, will bring him gifts worthy of a god when they swear allegiance. I make these promises on the understanding that Achilles yields to my entreaty and forgets his grudge. Let him not behave like Hades—the most hated of all the gods, because his stern heart is never softened, nor his mind changed, however cogent the appeal! I expect Achilles, in fact, to be ruled by me; since I am far higher in rank and, what is more, considerably his senior.'

Nestor replied: 'Most noble Agamemnon, such gifts cannot be lightly declined; but we must send acceptable delegates to Achilles'

* Some 822 lbs. of gold, if Agamemnon used the earlier Aeginetan standard; 570 lbs., if he used the Attic.

hut . . . See here: if I choose them myself, will anyone raise objections? First, I name the venerable Phoenix, King of the Dolopians, and Achilles' own tutor; second, Great Ajax; third, King Odysseus. The heralds Odius and Eurybates should accompany them. How is that? Now, pray my lord, call for water to wash our hands, and then for holy silence while we address Zeus Son of Cronus in prayer; he may well show us mercy.'

Nestor's suggestion being approved, the heralds poured water over every guest's hands; after which servitors filled the mixing-bowls and ladled out wine. Every guest took his cup, emptied it on the ground by way of libation to Zeus and, when replenished, drank heartily. The banquet thus came to an end and Nestor, with many searching glances at each face, but especially at that of Odysseus, gave the delegates full instructions how best to overcome Achilles' resistance.

Phoenix, Ajax, Odysseus and the two heralds went along the seashore, praying that Zeus, Supreme Ruler of this Earth, might induce Achilles to accept Agamemnon's advances. Arrived at the Myrmidons' lines, they found him singing a lusty ballad about ancient heroes, and accompanying himself on his lyre. This was a resonant, beautifully constructed instrument, with a silver cross-bar, looted from Eëtion's fortress of Thebe. Achilles' intimate friend Patroclus sat listening near and, when the delegation reached the hut, did not interrupt his performance. The five men entered, headed by Odysseus, and Achilles sprang up in surprise, still holding the lyre. Patroclus also rose.

Achilles greeted his guests. 'Well met,' he cried. 'I am glad to see once again the faces of my dearest comrades—I have missed you all sorely, despite my anger.' He offered them seats on settles and bales of purple carpet, then said to Patroclus: 'Son of Menoetius, fetch a larger bowl, mix stronger drink, and produce five more cups for these friends of mine.'

Patroclus complied. He also carried a huge chopping-block into the firelight, and laid on it the chines of three fat carcases—a sheep's, a goat's, and a porker's. Automedon the charioteer held these in place, while Achilles hacked at them, afterwards slicing and spitting the meat. Patroclus made up the fire and, as soon as its flames died down, spread out the embers evenly and rested the spits on racks over their hot glow. When the slices of meat, which had already been salted, were done to a turn, Achilles heaped trenchers with them; at the same time Patroclus took bread and distributed it in neat baskets around the table.

Achilles sat facing Odysseus, and asked Patroclus to offer the gods a sacrifice by tossing pieces of meat into the fire. This done, they ate and drank heartily until, at the close, Ajax nodded to Phoenix. Odysseus, however, intercepted the nod and, before Phoenix could say what he had come to say, filled his own cup crying: 'Your health, Achilles! We can always be sure of a splendid feast not only in Agamemnon's hut, but also, it seems, in this. But where to find good food and drink is by no means our sole preoccupation at the moment; on the contrary, great foster-son of Zeus, after our serious reverse, we are wondering whether, unless you step into the breach, we shall manage to save the fleet. The Trojans and their allies are, as you know, bivouacking behind a long line of fires just outside our defence system, resolved that we shall not survive their next assault. Yesterday Zeus Son of Cronus encouraged them with thunder on the right flank; and Hector, welcoming so favourable a sign, fought like one possessed. He rejoiced in his great strength, charged furiously through our ranks, shouting defiance at gods and men, and dealt death wherever he went. Now, having ordered his men to chop the high stern-ornaments from our ships, set the hulls ablaze, and massacre us in the confusion, he prays that bright Dawn will quickly shine for him. I fear the gods may allow him to fulfil his threats and leave our bones rotting on this alien shore. My lord, here is your last chance to save a demoralized Greek army from the triumphant Trojans. Fail us, and you will always regret it! A disaster on such a scale can never be undone; take my warning and rescue us in the nick of time.'

Odysseus then proceeded: 'My friend, your father Peleus' strict injunctions, when he sent you off to serve under King Agamemnon, still haunt my memory. "Achilles, dear son," he said, "though the Goddesses Athene and Hera give you success in battle, pray try to restrain that proud spirit of yours; gentleness becomes you far better. And keep clear of quarrels, for quiet behaviour is admired by Greeks of all ages!" My lord, even if you have forgotten your father's words, do, pray, let your anger finally cool! King Agamemnon is anxious to conciliate you with gifts that match your achievements. Listen while I enumerate the valuables which he promises from his treasure-hut: Seven unused, three-legged bronze kettles; ten talents of gold; twenty shining copper cauldrons; six pairs of race-winning chariot horses—the man would not be poor, no indeed, who owned as much wealth as those horses earn Agamemnon in prizes! To these gifts he adds seven craftswomen—marvellously beautiful girls—he chose them for himself from the booty which you won at Lesbos; also the woman of whom he deprived you the other day—namely Briseis, daughter of Briseus—taking an oath that he has had no carnal knowledge of her. All goods and prisoners will be delivered to you at once; and if the gods grant us the good fortune of sacking Troy, then you may claim the further right to select not only a whole shipload of gold and bronze treasures, but the twenty loveliest women in Troy, Queen Helen alone excepted. Moreover, if we come safely back to the rich land of Greece, he promises to adopt you and accord you the same rank and honours as his own son Orestes, who is now enjoying a luxurious education at Mycenae. Besides, Agamemnon has three daughters in that splendid palace of his: Chrysothemis, Laodice, and Iphianassa. You are free to marry whichever girl you prefer and, when you fetch her away to Phthia, he will demand no bride-price but, quite the reverse, provide a dowry larger than any king ever settled on a daughter. He will give you lordship, too, over seven towns: Cardamyle, Enope, Hire (where the grazing is excellent), Pherae, sacred to Apollo, Antheia with its lush meadows, lovely Aepeia, and Pedasus, famous for its vines. They lie together near the sea, beyond Sandy Pylos; and the inhabitants, who own enormous flocks of sheep and herds of cattle, will bring you gifts worthy of a god when they swear allegiance.

'All this he offers. But if hatred of Agamemnon prompts you to refuse, at least take pity on your wretched compatriots! Save them and earn semi-divine honours! You might even have the undying glory to kill Hector: if his battle-madness comes upon him he is sure to seek you out as our supreme champion.'

Achilles answered: 'My lord Odysseus, pray waste no more breath in coaxing me to change my heart! I hate a man who conceals his true feelings, as much as I hate the Gates of Hell, and shall therefore make myself plain. Since Agamemnon never showed the smallest gratitude for the countless feats which I performed at his request, neither he nor any Greek alive will persuade me to accept these belated advances! On the ground, I suppose, that death strikes down every mortal irrespective of his service, Agamemnon, when he allotted spoils, would not distinguish between the coward who had elected to stay in his hut and the hero who had borne the brunt of the fighting. What thanks did I get from him, though I hazarded my life time after time?

> "The hen-bird flutters out to find
>   Food for her callow chicks,
> And nobly bears their needs in mind
>   When, from the grass, she picks
> Beetles or grubs with tireless bill;
> But her own maw may never fill."

'That was how I used to work: on watch all night, at war all the bloody day, robbing brave soldiers of their wives and daughters to provide Agamemnon with concubines! I led no less than twelve successful sea-raids on Trojan towns, and eleven successful land attacks. In each case I brought back a huge haul of booty, which the High King shared among his subordinates. He reserved most of it for himself, doling out a few treasures only as prizes of honour. Though my fellow-princes have kept theirs, Agamemnon chose me, Achilles, to rob of my sweetheart! She is still in his power; but now he can do with her what he pleases—Briseis no longer means anything to me.

'Confess, my lords; how did this war come about? Was it not that Agamemnon raised an immense expedition to recover Queen Helen? Then are he and his brother Menelaus the sole husbands who value their wives? Surely all decent, sound-witted men feel alike? I loved Briseis wholeheartedly, even if she was no more than my prisoner. But since the High King has cheated me of my prize, and I have learned to distrust him, he may as well abandon his attempt at flattery. No, my lord Odysseus, if Agamemnon wants his fleet to stay unburned, he should forget my existence, and call on you and the rest of the Council for advice. He has accomplished many things lately without my help: such as raising a rampart and digging a deep, wide, palisaded fosse—not that they will serve to check the death-dealing Hector! Besides, while I still took the field, Hector never ventured far from his walls; he seldom even reached Zeus' oak just outside the Scaean Gate, and waited for me there only once. He was fortunate to escape alive!

'Having, however, no further quarrels with noble Hector, I shall sacrifice to Zeus and his divine family at sunrise tomorrow, before launching and leading the ships; those of you who are interested can watch my Myrmidons pulling lustily at the oars as we sail off across the Hellespont. If Poseidon the Earth-Shaker grants us a prosperous voyage, we should sight Phthia on the third day. I left great possessions behind me when I had the ill-luck to set out for Troy. They will soon be augmented with further gold, bronze, iron and beautiful captives—whatever fell to me by lot, since it was only my prize of honour that Agamemnon spitefully deprived me.

'I count on you to repeat these exact words, in open Assembly, so that my fellow-princes may express their indignation and be on guard against the High King's greed and treachery. He has sent you here as his delegates because the shameless dog would not dare to meet my eyes! Make it plain that, after the wicked trick played on me, I will have no further dealings with him; nor join in any enterprise he sponsors; nor listen to any more of his flattering messages—one is quite sufficient. Zeus has robbed my lord Agamemnon of his wits; so let him go his way in peace, and I will go mine!

'I reject the indemnity. I do not care a straw for him! Though he offered me ten or twenty times his entire present fortune, and all the wealth that may accrue to him in future—though he were to capture Boeotian Orchomenus, or sack the bulging treasure-houses of Egyptian Thebes—Thebes, where two hundred chariotmen stand always ready-armed at each of its hundred gates—though he offered me gifts as numerous as the grains of sand on the seashore, or the specks of dust on yonder plain, he could never soften my rage—without first making full amends for those outrageous insults!

'Tell him that I would not marry any daughter of his, not even if she rivalled Aphrodite the Golden in beauty, and Athene the Owl-Eyed in arts and crafts! Let him match them with bridegrooms of his

own rank, and of better blood than mine . . . If the gods accept my
sacrifice and bring us safely across the sea, my father King Peleus
will himself find me a wife. There are enough girls in Phthia and the
rest of Greece to pick from, daughters of princes who rule fortified
towns. While still at home, I often considered marrying a loyal and
capable wife and settling down to enjoy my inheritance.

'And another thing: I value life far more than I covet wealth—
albeit such wealth as the Trojans amassed during the years of peace,
or Apollo the Archer has heaped in the massive temple he raised at
rocky Delphi. Herds and flocks may be won in forays; tripods and
chestnut horses may be peacefully bought; but neither raiding nor
trading can redeem a man's soul once it has fled from his dying lips.
My goddess-mother, Thetis the Silver-Footed, prophesied as follows:

> "Twin fates dispute your death, heroic son,
>   Of which two fates you must, perforce, choose one:
>   Either to stand fast on the Trojan shore
>   Until you die, renowned for evermore,
>   Or to retreat and from your Phthian town
>   Rule long, nor hope for any high renown."

'You may as well warn Agamemnon to raise his siege. Troy shall
never fall; everyone can see that Zeus protects her walls, nor do their
defenders lack courage. Now, pray go and announce my reply! It will
be the Council's task to discuss some other means of saving the
Greek army and fleet, since I cannot, for rage, accept the compen-
sation offered on their advice. By your leave, I should like King
Phoenix to spend the night here, in readiness for our homeward
voyage. I shall not, of course, take him off against his will.'

Achilles' vehemence so astounded the delegates that it was some
time before any man of the five ventured a word. The venerable
Phoenix said with tears in his eyes: 'Glorious Achilles, if you are
really thinking of departure, and are too angry to care whether or not
the fleet gets burned, what will become of me? How can I remain
here, alone and unprotected, my dearest foster-son? When Peleus
sent you to join Agamemnon's army—do not forget that you were
still a callow youth without battle experience or distinction in debate
—he appointed me your tutor, to teach you the rudiments of warfare

and oratory. So now I could not bear to be deserted by you, even if Zeus himself stripped my years away, making me as young and vigorous again as when I left the country where I was born!

'I must at last reveal what drove me from Thessaly, land of lovely women . . . My father, Amyntor, son of Ormenus, had a beautiful slave named Clytia, whom he admired more than he did my mother. My mother, feeling wronged, ceaselessly implored me to anticipate him by seducing her rival. I yielded; but my father heard of the act, and laid a solemn curse on me, charging the dreadful Furies never to let any child of mine sit on his knees. Since the Lord of Hell and Persephone, his terrifying Queen, approved this curse, I drew sword and would have taken vengeance, had not some god or other restrained me, with a warning that I should be ever afterwards hated and shunned as a parricide by my subjects. None the less, I could not bring myself to stay in the palace, though numerous friends and relatives begged me to change my mind, and determined that I should not escape. Having made ready a great banquet of beef, mutton, fat pork, and wine galore from the royal cellar, they took turns to watch me for nine nights, keeping one fire continuously ablaze in the colonnade of the fenced courtyard, and another in the porch outside my bedroom. On the tenth night, when it was dark, I broke through the strongly barred door, vaulted over the courtyard fence, unseen by any watchmen or servant women, and fled across the green Thessalian meadows to the fertile sheep-lands of Phthia. There your father Peleus welcomed me as if I had been an only son, the young heir to all his riches, and appointed me King of the Dolopians, who live on the Phthian frontier.

'Yes, glorious Achilles, I tutored you with unwavering care and affection. As a little boy, you would not enter the banqueting hall in any company but mine, nor eat and drink there unless I set you on my knee, gave you tit-bits from the trencher, and put the wine-cup to your lips. You were so helpless that often, on rising, I found my tunic was stained by the sputtered wine. Why I lavished such care on your upbringing and treated you as my foster-son, was that the gods had doomed me to impotence; and now, in return, I trust that your filial love will prove my salvation. Prince Achilles, curb your pride; this vindictive spirit does not become you! The Olympians themselves relent sometimes, though ineffably stronger and more majestic than you are. If a mortal has transgressed the divine law, he appeals to Heaven, burns incense, pours libations, sacrifices victims, utters vows, and counts on the gods to forgive him:

> 'Penitential PRAYERS that go
>   Withered, lame, with eyes askance,
> In a long unhappy row
>   Following TRANSGRESSION's dance,

> 'Never hope to overtake
>   Her quick-moving wanton feet:
> Queen TRANSGRESSION still shall make
>   Mischief by her foul deceit.

> 'Yet the man who dares reject
>   Heaven's commandments with abuse,
> In his downfall may expect,
>   By the gracious leave of ZEUS,

> 'This angelic company
>   To come limping up pell-mell;
> Who, if handled reverently,
>   Heal his hurt and use him well
> But, if scorned, ensure that he
>   Suffers for their scorn in Hell!

'Come, Achilles! Just as Zeus listens to the penitential prayers of transgressors, so every right-minded mortal will accept the apologies of whoever has wronged him. Had Agamemnon failed to offer you amends, with promises of additional treasure and honours at a later date, then I should certainly not have joined this delegation, nor begged you to swallow your grudge and save your desperate compatriots from massacre. But since his immediate offer is a very handsome one, and his further offers are even more so; and since his delegates were chosen out of the whole army as the three princes whom you love best, do not put yourself in the wrong by rebuffing us! Tradition teaches that whenever an ancient hero grew angry, he always yielded in the end. A story occurs to me that illustrates this point—

the events happened long before my day—and because we meet here
as friends, I should like to tell it you:

∗

THE TALE OF MELEAGER'S ANGER

A bloody war broke out between Thestias, King of the Curetians and
his brother-in-law, Oeneus, King of the Aetolians; the Curetians trying
to capture Oeneus' fine city of Calydon. What caused this war was that
at one harvest thanks-giving, Oeneus, whether deliberately or by inad-
vertence, failed to give Artemis of the Golden Throne the first-fruits of
his rich demesne. The other eleven Olympians having received their
hundred-beast sacrifices, Oeneus deeply offended her by the omission.
She let loose a divine monster, a huge white-tusked boar, which did se-
rious damage to the Calydonian orchards, even felling large apple-trees
—root, blossom and all. Meleager, Oeneus' son, gathered a great com-
pany of princes from several cities to hunt the boar—this being no task
that two or three only could undertake—and was valiant enough to de-
stroy it himself.

Artemis then provoked a hot argument between the Aetolians and their
Curetian allies when it came to awarding the prize of honour—the boar's
head and shaggy pelt. For, though it was Meleager's spear that dis-
patched the monster, Atalanta, an Arcadian huntress, had already driven
an arrow in behind its ear, thus saving the lives of your own father Peleus
and of Telamon, Great Ajax's father. Meleager flayed the carcase and,
thereupon, waived his award in Atalanta's favour, announcing that the
beast would soon have succumbed to her arrow. Plexippus the Curetian
took exception to such gallantry. Since Meleager declined the prize of
honour, he said, it must not go to Atalanta but to himself, as the most
important personage present. Meleager, now fallen in love with Ata-
lanta, flew into a temper and murdered Plexippus, and another uncle
who supported his contention.

In the ensuing war Meleager, a favourite of Ares, won every battle
he fought—so that after awhile the Curetians, although far outnumber-
ing the Aetolians, kept inside their own city walls. But Althaea, Mel-
eager's mother, mourned for her two brothers; she would kneel weeping
on the ground, belabouring the earth with her palms, as she supplicated
the Rulers of Hell to destroy her son; and the pitiless Fury who walks
in darkness heard this plea from the Pit below. Althaea's curse roused
an anger in Meleager's heart such as other men, however wise, have been
equally unable to subdue. He laid down his arms, and stayed at home,

in the company of his wife Cleopatra . . . Cleopatra's mother, I should mention, was Marpessa the Neat-Ankled, daughter of Evenus; and her father was Idas, the strongest hero alive, who had once even dared catch up a bow and challenge Apollo, his rival for Marpessa's love . . . Everyone knew Cleopatra by her proper name at the time of my story, but later Marpessa and Idas nicknamed her 'Alcyone' because, when Apollo widowed her, she returned to their palace, mourning Meleager as loudly as the halcyon bird mourns her dead mate in the midwinter season.

Meleager now used to lie beside Cleopatra, brooding angrily on his mother's curses, and refusing to defend Calydon. At length, a huge din of battle rose from the gates, and the Curetians began battering at the towers; so the Council of Calydon delegated the leading priests to make Meleager change his mind and save their city. They offered him as much fertile land as it would take a yoke of oxen fifty days to plough—half of it already planted with vines—and he could choose the estate, they said, from whichever part of the plain he wished. Old Oeneus also implored his son to fight and, standing outside his fine bedroom, rattled desperately at the door. Meleager's sisters and a group of his closest friends joined in the plea, and so did Althaea herself—an intrusion that made his refusal even sterner. He continued obdurate, until missiles came hurtling through the bedroom roof; by which time the Curetians had won a lodgement on the fortifications and were setting fire to the houses. Then Cleopatra wept, reminding her husband of the disasters that attend the sack of a city: men killed, buildings aflame, women of whatever rank forced into concubinage. Her tears finally roused Meleager. He sprang from bed, buckled on his glittering armour, and drove off the Curetians. But since he fought of his own free will, after declining the reward offered by the Calydonians, they were under no obligation to pay him. Nevertheless, he had saved Calydon.

*

'Dear son, I can see how angry you are; yet do not withhold your help until the very last moment, as Meleager did; ships, once they catch fire, are more difficult to extinguish than stone houses! If you accept Agamemnon's advances, you will be treated like a god; if you reject them and then fight, as Meleager did, the honour will be far less, however vigorous your intervention.'

Achilles answered: 'Dear foster-father, I want no honour from my enemies. It is enough that Zeus has agreed to justify my stand— a most encouraging sign, while I remain alive and well. But I cannot have you lamenting in my hut on behalf of Agamemnon, your obstinate love for whom must forfeit you mine. It would be more proper to cause him as much trouble as he has caused me. Show a royal independence—let us join forces—and allow your companions to take my message unassisted! Stay here on a soft bed, and by the light of dawn we shall decide whether to sail home.'

Achilles nodded at Patroclus, as a sign that Phoenix should be given his bed; and also as a hint that the other guests should take their leave without further ado.

Great Ajax, son of Telamon, then spoke: 'My lord Odysseus, having clearly failed to fulfil the High King's commission, we ought to be off. The Council awaits Prince Achilles' answer, which must be delivered at once, though a downright unsatisfactory answer it is. I much regret that he has worked himself into such a proud, stubborn, furious rage as to spurn the friendship of comrades who consider him our leading champion. What a merciless fellow you are, Achilles! Any other man accepts blood-money even for the loss of a brother or a son; thus a homicide is able, at enormous cost, to appease the relatives of his victim and avoid exile. You are different, it seems. The gods have planted in you a proud and implacable grudge—and all because of a single girl captive! Now the High King offers seven others, the loveliest and most talented in his possession, with additional gifts of fabulous value. Why deny us the courtesy due from a host to his guests? We have come not only as the Council's chosen delegates, but as your brothers-in-arms, and are hurt to find ourselves received like strangers.'

Achilles answered: 'Ajax, son of Telamon, descendant of Zeus himself, what you say very nearly makes me relent. Yet my blood boils when I think of Agamemnon's abusive arrogance in the Assembly— I might have been some ignoble camp-follower! So here is my message: I will take no further part in the war unless Prince Hector attacks this station, killing my own men and attempting to burn my ships; I believe, however, that he will keep his distance, eager for battle though he may be.'

No more was spoken. Each delegate in turn poured a libation from a two-handled cup; then all except Phoenix went back along the line of ships, led by Odysseus.

At Patroclus' orders, the valets and slave-women made up a comfortable couch, fetching rugs, fleeces, fine linen sheets; and Phoenix stretched out on it, prepared to sleep until sunrise. Achilles' bed stood in a corner of the stoutly-built hut, and beside him now lay pretty Diomede, Phorbas' daughter, one of the prisoners taken by him on Lesbos. Patroclus occupied the opposite corner in company with another captive—slim-waisted Iphis, a gift from Achilles after the sack of Scyrus, Enyeus' city perched on a steep hill.

When the delegates returned to the High King's hut, the entire Assembly rose and drank their healths. Agamemnon was the first to question them. 'Tell me at once, Odysseus, glory of Greece,' he said. 'Is Achilles ready to forget his grudge and save the fleet, or does pride prevent him?'

'Most noble Agamemnon,' Odysseus answered, 'so far from forgetting his grudge, he seems angrier than ever and declines your gifts contemptuously. He recommends that you should call on us princes for advice, if you would save your fleet and your army. Achilles himself launches his flotilla at daybreak, and warns you to raise the siege—on the ground that Troy can never fall while Zeus the Far-Sighted protects her walls and their defenders do not lack courage. This was his message, as Prince Ajax and your two discreet heralds will testify. Old King Phoenix, at Achilles' request, is spending the night in his hut. He has been asked, though not compelled, to sail away when his foster-son gives the word.'

A miserable silence greeted Odysseus' terse speech, for the news stunned everyone present. At last Diomedes spoke: 'Most illustrious Agamemnon, it was a great mistake to offer Achilles bribes. You only flattered his immoderate pride. Nevertheless, let us wait and see whether he really means what he says: my view is that as soon as he feels inspired to fight, fight he will. My lords, I propose an adjournment. This noble banquet must have revived your strength and lent you courage for tomorrow's ordeal, but you need sleep. King Agamemnon, we expect you to marshal us in defence of our fleet at the earliest flush of dawn, and head the counter-attack yourself.'

The Councillors applauded Diomedes, then poured libations, and made off, hoping for a good night's rest.

Book Ten:

The Dolon Incident

All the Greek leaders slept sound, with the sole exception of King Agamemnon and his brother Menelaus; both of whom had far too much on their minds.

> ZEUS, lovely HERA's husband,
>   HERA the Golden-Tressed,
> Lets thunder loose, and lightning,
>   Upon a land of rest.
>
> Portending rain in torrents
>   Or sleet or driving snow
> To blast the joys of harvest—
>   Or war with all its woe.

Agamemnon's thunderous, soul-shaking groans drawn from the very bottom of his heart seemed a storm in miniature; and whenever he glanced southward and saw the sky lit up by Trojan camp-fires, or heard the distant sound of flutes, pipes, and singing voices, further dismay seized him. It was worse when he looked at the huts and the fleet; he tore out his hair in handfuls, and invoked Zeus, Lord of Counsels, with pitiful sobs. At last he decided to rouse the noble-hearted Nestor, son of Neleus. Perhaps he might suggest some stratagem by which disaster could be averted? Rising, Agamemnon put on his tunic, an elegant pair of sandals, and a magnificent tawny-yellow lion-skin that hung right down to his feet. Then, spear in hand, he left the hut.

Menelaus had been kept awake by a premonition that his quarrel with the Trojans might prove the ruin of countless Greeks who were making it their own. He rose too, threw a leopard-skin over his broad shoulders, donned a helmet, grasped a spear, and went off to consult his famous and powerful brother. Agamemnon, busy buckling on armour near the stern of his vessel, was delighted to see him.

'Why are you arming, dear brother?' asked Menelaus. 'To make somebody find out for you what the Trojan intentions are? If so, I doubt whether any man will dare patrol the battlefield alone this beautiful night, and bring back a trustworthy report.'

'Menelaus, foster-son of Zeus,' Agamemnon answered, 'our greatest need is a truly brilliant stratagem for saving the army and fleet, now that Zeus has once more turned against us. Hector's sacrifices must have given him immense pleasure because, until yesterday, I never saw or heard of such terrible havoc made by a single man in the course of one afternoon; and it is not even as though he were the beloved son of a god or a goddess! Yes, we Greeks will have good reason for generations to remember the lesson he taught us! Now, please run quickly to the far end of the camp and wake Great Ajax and King Idomeneus of Crete, while I visit Nestor. He may be persuaded to inspect the outposts and give some sort of orders. They will obey him, if anyone at all; his own son is commanding them, jointly with Meriones the Cretan.'

'You do not make yourself plain,' grumbled Menelaus. 'Am I supposed to stay with Ajax and Idomeneus among the outposts until you arrive, or shall I return and fetch you?'

Agamemnon considered the question. 'You had better await me there, for fear we miss each other in this wilderness of huts. But summon each prince by name, and do not be too proud to add his lineage, patronymic, and titles of honour! We must work hard tonight, as usual; such is the destiny that Zeus laid upon us from birth.'

Menelaus, having got the instructions clear, disappeared, and Agamemnon went towards Nestor's quarters. The veteran lay sleeping in a luxurious bed between his hut and his ship, with an exquisite suit of armour, a shield, two spears, and a polished helmet placed ready to hand; also the gay baldric which he always wore in battle. No, Nestor did not make old age an excuse for shirking his duties as a commanding officer. Raising himself on an elbow, Nestor challenged Agamemnon: 'Who are you, prowling through the darkness, when everyone else is asleep? Has a mule broken loose, or have you lost a comrade? Use your voice, man; don't come creeping up in silence! What do you want?'

The High King disclosed himself. 'Nestor, son of Neleus, Glory of the Greeks,' he said, 'it is I, Agamemnon, son of Atreus, whom Zeus has condemned to undergo perpetual hard labour so long as his breath lasts and his legs move. I am wandering about because fear for the fate of my troops keeps me wide awake. Yes, I am altogether unnerved. I tossed to and fro in bed; my heart pounded; and now, look how my knees are shaking! But you, too, seem unable to sleep; so would you kindly help me inspect the outposts and reassure myself that the sentries are vigilant, despite yesterday's exhausting battle? For all we know, the Trojans may plan a night attack from their position just beyond the fosse.'

Nestor replied: 'Glorious son of Atreus, Agamemnon the High King, of one thing I am certain: that Almighty Zeus will not allow Prince Hector to consummate his grandiose design. In fact, if Achilles only forgets his grudge, Hector's anxieties may soon be even worse than yours! Yes, of course, I will accompany you! Let us also rouse Diomedes and Odysseus, and brisk Little Ajax, and Meges, the son of Phyleus. And why not Great Ajax and King Idomeneus as well? Their flotillas lie next to each other at the farthest end of the camp. But, my lord, much as I love and respect King Menelaus, I must frankly say—whether you like it or not—that he deserves a strong reprimand for sleeping so sound and leaving all the work to you. He should make it his duty, in this desperate situation, to run from hut to hut and wake everyone.'

'You are quite right, venerable Nestor,' Agamemnon agreed. 'My brother often shirks his responsibilities. Though I cannot call him slow-witted or careless, he always expects me to tell him precisely what he should do. Please, however, reserve your abuse for another occasion; because tonight, as it happened, he rose earlier than I did and paid me a visit. I sent him off to wake those very princes whom you mention. Come out by the camp gates, and we should find them beside the fosse, awaiting my arrival.'

'I am glad to hear it,' cried Nestor. 'Such zeal will certainly commend Menelaus to his fellow-Councillors when he offers advice or gives orders.'

Having put on a tunic and sandals, and a wide, pleated, purple cloak with a soft nap, Nestor took a stout, bronze-bladed spear, and strode along the line of ships. First he stopped at Odysseus' quarters, shouting his name. Odysseus emerged and cried in a startled voice: 'Who goes there, prowling through the darkness, this beautiful night? And why am I wanted in such a hurry?'

Nestor revealed himself. 'Odysseus, son of Laertes, scion of Zeus himself,' he said, 'pray do not be vexed! The emergency is great. Come and help me wake a few other princes—it seems that the High King wishes us to decide at once whether we should hold the camp or evacuate it.'

Odysseus slipped back, picked up a shield, and followed Nestor but, still drowsy after his two huge meals, did not think of bringing away a sword or a spear. They found Diomedes stretched on a bull's hide by the entrance to his hut, a bright roll of carpet serving as pillow, and weapons within reach. About him lay his somnolent comrades, every head propped on a shield. The glow of Trojan camp-fires caught the bright blades of spears planted upright and made them twinkle like flashes of lightning. Nestor stirred Diomedes with his toe. 'Wake, son of Tydeus,' he cried. 'Must you snore all night? Have you forgotten that the Trojans are bivouacked on a slope just beyond the fosse?'

Diomedes leaped to his feet: 'It is the indefatigable Nestor!' he exclaimed. 'My lord, are no younger men at hand to raise the alarm?'

Nestor replied: 'A very proper question, King Diomedes! Numerous younger men, including sons of my own, might well perform the task. But this is a crucial hour. We stand as if poised on a razor's edge: on one side disaster, on the other, victory! Therefore, since you pity my feebleness, or so it appears, be good enough to summon Little Ajax, the son of Phyleus.'

Diomedes seized a long, tawny lion-skin, which matched Agamemnon's, and a javelin. Soon he was leading his companions towards the outposts, who proved to be awake and armed:

Hounds at watch on the dark wold
Ringed around their master's fold
Growl a warning. Do they hear
Some huge beast approaching near?
Distant shouts and bayings keep
All alert who else would sleep.

The Greek sentries were no less watchful that wicked night, and
stood peering into the darkness whenever they heard sounds of ac-
tivity from the Trojan bivouacs. Nestor, much relieved, gave them
welcome encouragement: 'Dear children,' he shouted, 'I commend
your sharp look-out! If anyone falls asleep on sentry duty, our ene-
mies will have the laugh on us.'

Then he led the group now reinforced by Menelaus, Idomeneus
and Great Ajax, over the fosse. With them went the two out-
post commanders—Idomeneus' friend Meriones, and Nestor's son
Thrasymedes—both of whom the High King invited to join a council-
of-war. They chose a spot free of corpses, near where the Trojans had
broken off the battle, sat down, and discussed the crisis.

'My friends,' Nestor began, 'which of you dares volunteer for spe-
cial service? We need someone to visit the enemy lines and either
capture a prisoner who can be brought back and interrogated, or at
least overhear some fragment of talk that may give us a hint of Prince
Hector's plans. Will he attack from his new position, or will he rest
on his laurels and withdraw behind the city walls? Anyone able to
supply an answer to this question would win a name for conspicuous
heroism—and a valuable prize into the bargain. I suggest that each of
us should promise him a black ewe and her lamb—I can think of no
more distinguished prize in the way of livestock—and also make him
free of all private feasts and clan-drinkings.'

Diomedes sprang to his feet. 'King Nestor,' he cried, 'I will go!
But I should feel more at ease if I had a companion. Either he or I
would be almost sure to notice something that the other missed; and
even if we were equally observant, two heads are better than one in
times of peril.'

Great and Little Ajax both volunteered, as also did Meriones and
Nestor's son Thrasymedes—he was chafing to be sent—and Mene-
laus, and Odysseus.

Agamemnon gave this ruling: 'Diomedes, son of Tydeus, joy of my heart, you are free to choose your companion from these eager candidates.' Then, fearing that Diomedes would feel obliged to pick Menelaus, he added: 'And, pray show no polite regard for high rank or lineage, but name whoever will be of most service to you on this dangerous mission.'

'Since you grant me a free choice,' said Diomedes, 'I can hardly overlook the claims of Odysseus the Ever-Daring. If he comes, we should have a good chance of returning alive, even though we burn our fingers; because Pallas Athene always protects him, and he is the quickest-witted man alive.'

Odysseus answered: 'Son of Tydeus, pray spare me alike compliments and censure; everyone here knows my record. But the stars warn us that there is not a moment to waste! Two watches of the night are already gone, and dawn will soon be upon us.'

Thrasymedes then lent Diomedes a two-edged sword, a shield— he had left his own behind—and an uncrested skull-cap of bull's hide, such as youths wear. Meriones lent Odysseus a bow, a quiver, and a sword; also a felt-lined leather casque. This casque, ornamented with a fine ring of boar's tusks set close together and lashed tightly about it, had been stolen from Phoenix's father Amyntor, son of Ormenus, by Autolycus, a notorious thief and reputedly Odysseus' real father, when he burgled the palace at Eleon. Autolycus later gave it to Amphidamas the Argonaut. Amphidamas took the casque home to Scandeia, the port of Cythera, where Molus the Cretan won it as a guest-gift; and from Molus it passed to his son Meriones.

As Diomedes and Odysseus set out, well armed, Pallas Athene sent them a favourable augury: a heron flying close by on their right hand. Though darkness made the bird invisible, they both heard its shrill cry. Odysseus at once offered a grateful prayer to his patroness Athene:

> 'Unwearied daughter
> Of ZEUS Shield-Bearer,
> Through toil and danger
> Protecting me,

> Send us victorious,
> Return us glorious!
> To all that war on us
> Let sorrow be!'

Diomedes also prayed:

> 'Swift ATHENE, undefiled
> Maiden-goddess, ZEUS his Child,
> Speed me with your kindly aid
> As when my father Tydeus made
> A valiant embassage, alone,
> To Eteocles the Theban's throne.
> For, having said his threatening say
> With honeyed mouth, and gone his way
> Toward where (beside the Asopus' brim)
> Six valiant peers awaited him,
> He found you watchful by the path
> And, at your side, his righteous wrath
> Glutted—as low in death he laid
> The murderous Theban ambuscade!

> 'Protect me now, record my vow:
> A yearling heifer broad of brow
> To be your sacrificial due—
> And I shall gild her horns for you!'

Athene graciously listened to these prayers, and guided Odysseus and Diomedes, as it might be two lions, across the dark battlefield: between heaps of corpses, over strewn weapons, through blackening pools of blood.

In the meantime Hector, who had been at pains to keep the Trojans alert, summoned his own officers to a council-of-war, and asked them: 'Will any one volunteer for an important service? I am offering the finest chariot and team captured tomorrow as a prize of honour to the man who will now go on reconnaissance, and tell me whether the Greeks have posted sentries around their camp. They may well be demoralized and exhausted, and have taken no precautions against surprise, thinking solely of escape.'

A short silence greeted Hector's speech. But among those present

was a rich, swift-footed, ugly Trojan named Dolon, the son of
Eumedes the famous herald, who otherwise had only daughters—
five of them. Dolon cried: 'I am your man, Prince Hector! But first
raise that sacred staff and swear to award me the team and splendid
bronze chariot of Achilles, son of Peleus. The Greek leaders are cer-
tain to be holding a council-of-war beside Agamemnon's ship, and
deciding whether they should abandon the siege; I shall enter the
camp, steal up close, listen, and return with the information you
need.'

Hector raised his staff and took the required oath:—'I call to wit-
ness Zeus the loud-thundering Husband of Hera, that no other
Trojan but you, Dolon, shall touch those horses, your inalienable
property!'

This vain oath satisfied Dolon. He went off at once, javelin in
hand, a ferret-skin cap on his head, a crooked bow slung on one of
his shoulders, and a grey wolf-skin cloak thrown over both. But
would he ever bring any information back to Hector? It was unlikely.

Odysseus saw Dolon approaching, outlined against the camp-
fires, and whispered to Diomedes: 'Here comes a Trojan! He may be
either a scout or a looter, I cannot say which. Why not let the fellow
pass, then pursue and capture him? If he runs faster than we do and
tries to circle around towards the city, head him off with your javelin,
making sure that he goes in the direction of our camp.'

Diomedes nodded, and they lay down among the corpses. Dolon
hurried by, not suspecting a trap; but when he had gone the length
of a mule-furrow—mules, by the way, are far better plough-beasts
than oxen—Diomedes and Odysseus rose and rushed after him.
Dolon stopped. He thought that they must be messengers from Hec-
tor, countermanding the mission, and allowed them to come within
easy spear-cast. Then he realized his error, and ran away at full
tilt. The Greek heroes followed in pursuit, like—

> Two well-trained hounds that flush
>   A doe from its green lair,
> Or through the woodland rush
>   After a doubling hare
> That screams in its despair.

They headed Dolon off, as agreed, and he was nearing the Greek outposts, when Diomedes, strengthened by Athene, spurted forward to deny anyone else the honour of killing him. 'Halt, or you die!' he cried, and flung his javelin over Dolon's right shoulder, intentionally, so that it quivered in the ground ahead of him. Dolon halted, green with terror; limbs shaking, teeth chattering. Odysseus and Diomedes panted up and seized him by the wrists.

'Spare me!' blubbered Dolon. 'My father Eumedes will pay you an enormous ransom as soon as he hears that I am your prisoner. Bronze, gold, and valuable iron cram our house.'

Odysseus said: 'Courage, friend! Do not fear the worst. But tell us what you are doing here, alone at dead of night! Looting corpses, or spying? Spying, eh? On your own initiative, or did Hector send you?'

Dolon faltered: 'I foolishly listened to Hector . . . He promised me Achilles' horses and beautiful bronze chariot if I would discover whether you Greeks were perhaps too demoralized and exhausted to post sentries. He believed that you might have taken no precautions against surprise, and be thinking solely of escape.'

'You had your eye on a fine prize indeed,' Odysseus remarked with a smile. 'But Achilles' horses are difficult for a mere mortal to control; he is a goddess' son, of course! Now answer me a few more questions. Where did you leave Hector?—had he his arms and chariot handy?—are your bivouacs protected by outposts?—in what order are your allies disposed? And does Hector intend to attack from his new lines, or to rest on his laurels, and withdraw behind the city walls?'

'I will answer your questions truthfully,' said Dolon. 'I left Prince Hector and the allied leaders holding a council-of-war in a secluded spot beside the tomb of his ancestor Ilus. As for outposts, no, my lord! Hector has given instructions neither for outposts nor for standing patrols. The Trojans themselves know it is their duty to keep careful watch around their camp-fires—but our allies are all fast asleep, counting on us to guard them against surprise. Since they come from distant lands, they need not feel so anxious for the safety of their women and children.'

'Be more precise!' Odysseus commanded. 'Tell me whether these various allies are integrated with the Trojans, or whether they occupy separate lines.'

'I will tell you everything,' Dolon answered. 'The Carians and the Paeonian archers are stationed towards the sea; next lie the Lelegians, the Cauconians, and the famous Pelasgians. We Trojans and Dardanians form the centre. On the other flank, towards Thymbre, are stationed the Lycians, the proud Mysians and, beyond them, a force of Phrygian and Maeonian chariotry. But why this questioning? If you are out on a raid, I recommend the Thracian lines as the most vulnerable. The Thracians have just arrived at Troy, under their King Rhesus, son of Eïoneus, and are holding the extreme flank, beyond the Maeonians. Rhesus owns the finest team that ever I saw—tall, whiter than snow, fast as the wind—with a gold and silver chariot; also a suit of golden armour far too magnificent, in my view, for anyone less than a god to wear. Come: take me to your camp, or else tie me up here so securely that escape is impossible, while you satisfy yourselves that I am no liar.'

Diomedes looked coldly at Dolon. 'Once in our power,' he said, 'you must abandon all hope of liberty. Though welcoming your good news, we cannot accept a ransom. You would soon be back to trouble us: either as a spy or as a fighting man. I shall end this matter without further ado.'

Dolon tried to clasp Diomedes' beard in supplication. The sword-blade struck the nape of his neck while he was still stammering an appeal, and his head rolled to the ground.

Having stripped Dolon of ferret-skin cap, wolf-skin cloak, bow, and javelin, Odysseus gratefully lifted them up to Athene the Spoil-Winner, praying briefly:

> 'O let this gift your heart rejoice,
> ATHENE, goddess of our choice
>   And first in our esteem!
> Now guide us, for the night is black,
> To where the Thracians bivouac
>   Around a snow-white team!'

Odysseus hung the spoils on a tamarisk bush, which they marked with a bundle of reeds and green shoots taken from other bushes, so as not to miss it on their return. Then they went forward again, over fallen weapons and through blackening pools of blood, until they came close to the Thracian lines.

The weary Thracians had grounded arms and were sleeping in three orderly ranks, each man's chariot and team standing beside him. Rhesus, whom Odysseus identified by the white horses tied to a chariot's fore-rail, lay in the middle of the second rank. Nudging Diomedes, Odysseus whispered: 'Those must be the horses, and that must be Rhesus! Quick! Cut the horses loose, or leave them to me, if you prefer, and kill a few Thracians.'

Athene gave Diomedes a murderous strength, and he began killing the recumbent Thracians. They groaned hideously in their sleep as his sword flashed down, reddening the earth:

> Ah, what grim slaughter when the lion notes
> An unattended flock of sheep or goats!

Diomedes dispatched twelve men, one after the other, while Odysseus cleared a path for King Rhesus' horses (which, being still new to battle, would baulk if led across dead bodies) by seizing each victim's feet and hauling him out of the way. Diomedes then stole up to Rhesus, who lay breathing heavily, and whom Athene had evidently afflicted with a nightmare about him. Rhesus was the thirteenth Thracian to die. In the meantime Odysseus untied the team, knotted their halters together and, forgetting to borrow the handsome whip from King Rhesus' chariot, used his bow to control them.

He whistled gently as a signal, but Diomedes stood wondering whether to drag the chariot away by the pole; whether to seize the golden suit of armour which he saw inside, and hoist it on his shoulders*; or whether perhaps to kill more Thracians. Athene hurriedly appeared: 'Brave son of Tydeus,' she warned him, 'you should start back at once! Some other Olympian might well raise the alarm, and then you would have to run for your life.'

Obeying the divine voice, Diomedes leaped on one of the horses; Odysseus, already mounted on its team-mate, struck them both with

---

* Some translators read the text as meaning that, in his battle-madness, he thought of carrying the chariot itself away on his shoulders. But this seems too heroic even for Diomedes when under Athene's inspiration.

his bow, and off they galloped, neck and neck, towards the naval camp.

Phoebus Apollo had noticed Athene's covert support of her favourite. He stepped angrily among the Thracians and woke King Rhesus' cousin Hippocoön, a member of the Royal Council. Missing the white horses and hearing the death-rattle of his comrades, Hippocoön groaned aloud and called 'Rhesus, dear Rhesus!' A fearful clamour and clang then spread through the Thracian lines, as everyone crowded around to gaze horror-stricken at the scene of slaughter.

Recognizing the tamarisk bush, Odysseus reined in; whereupon Diomedes dismounted, handed him the bloody spoils taken from Dolon, and soon they were flogging the obedient team on again.

Nestor first became aware of their return. 'My lords,' he said, 'correct me if I am wrong, but do my ears not catch the sound of galloping hooves? May Heaven grant that Odysseus and Diomedes have made a successful raid on the Trojan lines; yet that angry din frightens me—I fear for our two heroes' lives!' The words were not out of his mouth, before Odysseus and Diomedes rode up, to be greeted with general acclamation.

'What marvellous horses!' Nestor cried. 'They remind me of sunbeams. Tell us, Odysseus, Glory of the Greeks: how in the world did you and Diomedes possess yourselves of such a team? They cannot be stolen from the Trojans: I have fought them for years now, and nobody could accuse me of skulking in the camp but, upon my word, I never saw horses like these among their chariotry, or guessed that they could exist! You must surely have met some generous god who gave them you as a keepsake. Zeus the Cloud-Gatherer and his daughter Athene the Owl-Eyed are, I know, fond of you both.'

'No, no, redoubtable Nestor,' answered Odysseus. 'An Olympian who wished to make us a present would have created a far superior breed of horse—one must not under-estimate a god's powers! In point of fact, they belonged to King Rhesus the Thracian, whom Diomedes has just killed, and twelve of his comrades as well. We had already accounted for a fourteenth enemy soldier: a Trojan, sent by Hector to spy on the camp. Diomedes and I caught him not far from here.'

Odysseus grinned as he led those white horses over the fosse, followed by the whole Council, and soon tethered them to the manger where Diomedes' own team stood, champing delicious barley.

When Odysseus had stowed Dolon's poor relics in the hold of his vessel—they would later be formally dedicated at the goddess' altar— he and Diomedes went down to the shore, where they scooped up sea water and rinsed the dried sweat from their shins, necks and thighs. Refreshed, they each took a good warm bath, an olive-oil rub, and afterwards filled their cups from a wine-bowl and shared a substantial meal. Before drinking, however, they poured libations in gratitude to Athene.

Book Eleven:

Agamemnon's Day of Glory

Dawn rose from where she lay beside her mortal lover, proud Tithonus, bringing the gift of light to gods and men. But, at Almighty Zeus' orders, a second goddess, namely Strife, also rose; and she went among the Greeks to raise the banner of war. Standing on the deck of Odysseus' huge black vessel in the middle of the line, Strife could make her voice carry all the way from Great Ajax's station at one end to Achilles' at the other; both these heroes having courageously beached their flotillas on a flank. In loud, shrill tones she convinced the Greeks that to stay and fight would be far more glorious than to sail home.

Agamemnon shouted at his servants: 'Quick, my armour!' When they fetched it, he began buckling the silver ankle-clasps of his handsome bronze greaves, and then put on the corslet, given him by King Cinyras of Cyprus. Cinyras, hearing a rumour that the Greeks planned an expedition against Troy, had sent this master-piece of smithcraft as a complimentary gift. It was inlaid with ten courses of lapis lazuli, twelve of gold, and twenty of pure tin; a design of blue serpents arched up towards the neck, three on either side, none of them less brilliant than the rainbow which Zeus provides for the pleasure of humankind. From Agamemnon's baldric a gold-studded silver sheath hung by golden chains, and held a gold-studded sword. Inlaid on his ample leather shield were ten bronze circles, twenty bosses of pure tin, a central boss of lapis lazuli, and a grim, glaring Gorgon's head flanked by figures of Dread and Terror. The silver baldric bore a lapis lazuli design: a triple-headed serpent. His helmet had four thicknesses of bronze, a double crest, and a menacing horse-hair plume. Sunlight caught the blades of his two sharp spears, and when the flash reached Hera and Athene, high up in Heaven, a thunderclap of salutation welcomed this rich and glorious king.

The Greek princes ran hither and thither in full armour, greeting dawn with irrepressible war-cries, and each told his charioteer to have a team ready for him between the fosse and the rampart; but they all arrived at the rendezvous long before any charioteer. Zeus now created an ill-omened din, and the dew he let fall was dark as blood, portending widespread carnage.

The Trojans, still encamped on the slope, clustered about their leaders: Hector the Bright-Helmed, Prince Polydamas, Aeneas (who received almost divine honours from his Dardanians), also Polybus, Agenor, and splendid young Acamas, Antenor's three sons.

> Among the clouds afar
> We watch in fear
> A single baneful star
> Shine out and disappear.

Equally ominous were Hector's advents and disappearances: the Greek sentries could see that lightning-bright figure with the round shield come forward for a moment and exhort the front companies; after which he would retire to inspect the rear. Battle was presently joined.

> Gather to the rich man's field;
> What a harvest it should yield!
> Draw your sickles, labouring men,
> Grasp the stalks of barley, then
> Slashing hard, advance like foes
> Toward each other in two rows!

Thus also the Greeks and Trojans reaped an equal harvest of death—savage as wolves and scornful of retreat.

The Goddess Strife enjoyed herself hugely; but the other Olympians stayed in their handsome rooms on Mount Olympus, all except Aphrodite and Apollo, complaining that Zeus insisted on favouring the Trojans. Zeus paid not the slightest attention. He sat proudly apart, and gazed at Troy, the Greek camp, and the Scamandrian Plain, where a constant glitter of bronze told of a brutal struggle in which neither side gained the advantage, though the dead came crashing down by the hundred.

> It was high noon, the hour of silence when
> The woodman, having hewn enough tall trees,
> Makes dinner ready in a mountain glen,
> Fierce hunger urging him to take his ease.

Yet nobody broke off for dinner on this battlefield, because the Greeks, having at last forced a gap in the Trojan ranks, were encouraging one another to pour through it.

Agamemnon, who headed the charge, killed Bienor, a Trojan commander. Bienor's charioteer Oïleus at once dismounted and ran at Agamemnon, whose spear, however, pierced the brim of Oïleus' heavy bronze helmet, and the brain behind it, which halted that reckless rush. He stripped both corpses, leaving them bare-breasted on the ground; then turned to attack Antiphus, and his bastard-brother Isus, a charioteer. He recognized these as a couple of Priam's sons, recently captured by Achilles in a raid, while guarding their father's flocks on Mount Ida. Achilles had brought them bound with withies to the naval camp, and later accepted a ransom from King Priam. Now Agamemnon speared Isus high up on the breast, dealt Antiphus a sword-cut just above the ear which knocked him out of his chariot, and hastily took their valuable armour.

> The lion enters a green lair
> And grips the fawns in hiding there
>   Between his fearsome teeth;
> The hind dares not defend her brood
> But bounds in terror through the wood
>   And scuds across the heath.

Nor did the terrified Trojans make any attempt to save the lives of Antiphus and Isus.

The High King's next victims were Peisander and Hippolochus;

their father Antimachus, a member of Priam's Council, had been heavily bribed by Prince Paris to oppose Helen's surrender. Like a beast of prey Agamemnon went at these brothers, whose team had torn the reins from Hippolochus' grasp and stampeded. 'Spare us, great son of Atreus!' cried the unfortunate young men. 'Our father Antimachus will pay you an enormous ransom when he hears that we are your prisoners. His house is rich in bronze, gold, and valuable iron.'

Agamemnon answered mercilessly: 'As sons of Antimachus, the Royal Councillor who urged the assassination of my brother, King Menelaus—he and Odysseus had come to Troy on an embassy—you must die for your father's iniquities!' With that, he lunged at Peisander's corslet and toppled him over the chariot-rail. Seeing Peisander stretched dead, Hippolochus tried to escape. Agamemnon caught him, struck him down, lopped off his head and limbs, and tossed the trunk at the enemy as if he were trundling a stone bowl. He did not add these suits of armour to his large collection, but rushed into the thick of the retreating Trojans.

Men-at-arms speared men-at-arms; and chariot-fighters, chariot-fighters, in a dense cloud of dust raised by their horses' hooves. Agamemnon headed the advance, killing Trojans by the score, and urging on his comrades.

> A fire has seized the forest:
> Flames from the brushwood start,
> They strike the leafy thickets
> And tear them wide apart.

> Winds whirl along destruction,
> A hissing, fiery wall,
> Against the forest giants
> That catch and blaze and fall.

So the proud Trojan noblemen fell before the High King's red-hot progress, and lay lifeless on the ground—of less use now to their wives than to vultures. Numerous empty chariots went careering across the battlefield.

Zeus helped Hector to extricate himself unhurt from the murky, murderous, roaring rout, though the indomitable Agamemnon, his hands stained with blood, followed close behind him. They rattled past the tomb of Ilus, son of Dardanus, which rises in the middle of the plain, and the wild fig-tree, another prominent landmark. It was only on reaching Zeus' oak beside the Scaean Gate that Hector drew rein.

> The lion leaps at dead of night,
> Dispersing a whole herd in flight.
> A single cow, the unlucky one,
> Will never know tomorrow's sun:
> His sharp white teeth her neckbone snaps,
> And greedily he gulps and laps.

Unlike this lion, which claimed a single victim, Agamemnon mauled a great many Trojan fugitives, knocking them out of their chariots and leaving them prone or supine in the dust. He was already approaching the sheer walls of Troy when Zeus, Father of Gods and Mankind, grasped a thunderbolt, came purposefully down from Olympus, and seated himself on a spur of well-watered Ida. He told the golden-winged Goddess Iris: 'Command Prince Hector to rally and encourage the Trojans, but to do nothing violent for a while. As soon, however, as Agamemnon is wounded and quits the field, I shall let Hector drive the Greeks right back to their starting point, and kill without pause until nightfall.'

Iris flew to the Scaean Gate, where she found Hector standing among his chariotry. 'Hector, wise son of Priam,' she said, 'I have orders from Father Zeus. You are to rally and encourage your men, but to do nothing violent for a while! As soon, however, as King Agamemnon is wounded and quits the field, Zeus will let you drive the Greeks right back to their starting point, and kill without pause until nightfall.'

After Iris had vanished, Hector sprang fully armed from his chariot and rallied the Trojan ranks, brandishing a couple of spears. They faced about again, but the Greeks brought up reinforcements and pressed their attack.

You wise and gentle MUSES
Who on Olympus dwell,
Here comes a tale of battle
That you alone can tell!

What I want to know is which Trojan, or Trojan ally, first chal-
lenged Agamemnon at this stage of the battle. Ah, it was bold
Iphidamas, the son of Antenor and beautiful Theano, born and bred
in the fertile meadows of Thrace. Cisses, his maternal grandfather
and guardian, had tried to keep him at home when he came of age,
by marriage with a young aunt; but, hearing of the Greek invasion,
Iphidamas went straight from the bridal chamber to war, in com-
mand of twelve ships; beached them at Percote, and finished his
journey on foot.

The javelin thrown by Agamemnon glanced aside, and Iphidamas'
spear-point caught him below the corslet—only to bend like lead
against the silver girdle-clasp. Agamemnon snatched furiously at the
spear, then a sword-cut across Iphidamas' neck sent him to eternal
rest.

Coön, Antenor's illustrious eldest son, grieved to see his brother
Iphidamas lying there, far from his wife, fallen in defence of Troy.
That marriage had profited him little, though the bride-price was a
hundred cows and he offered Cisses a thousand sheep and goats as
well, having more flocks than anyone could count. Agamemnon
stripped the corpse; but Coön ran up, weeping, and speared him
clean through his upper arm, near the elbow. With a shudder of
agony, Agamemnon attacked Coön, who had called his men-at-arms
to protect him and was dragging Iphidamas away, feet foremost.
Agamemnon thrust at him under the guard of his shield, then drew
his sword, and struck. Coön's severed head tumbled on his brother's
body. Thus died Antenor's two sons, and their ghosts passed into the
possession of Hades.

While warm blood continued to ooze from his shield-arm, Aga-
memnon plied spear and sword busily; sometimes he even threw
large stones. But after a time the bleeding ceased and his wound
grew painful. Hera's divine daughters,

> The Eileithiae, whose task it is
> To watch a woman's pregnancies
>   And ward off doom,
> Give cruel notice of the same
> By shooting arrows, tipped with flame,
>   Into her womb.

Feeling that a similar travail had overtaken him, the High King re-mounted his chariot and headed for camp. The driver lashed at the long-maned horses, which galloped home delightedly, their breasts white with foam, their bellies grey with dust. As they disappeared, Agamemnon's miserable voice shrilled out: 'Friends and Council-lors! Zeus, in his wisdom has cut short my triumph. I trust you to de-fend the fleet!'

Prince Hector, watching Agamemnon's course, shouted: 'Trojans, Lycians, and Dardanians! Show your mettle, fight like heroes! The High King has left the field at last, and Zeus Son of Cronus has promised me undying fame. Prepare for a chariot charge! On to victory!' Hector might have been a huntsman urging hounds to bait a wild boar or a lion; and his soldiers obeyed nobly.

Here is an accurate list of Hector's new victims: Asaeus, Autonous, Opites, Dolops son of Clytius, Opheltius, Agelaus, Aesymnus, Orus, and Hipponous, all of princely rank. Afterwards he vented his rage on Greeks of lesser note.

> The stormy west wind scatters
> White mist that the white south
> Piled on the hills above us—
> How furious is his mouth!
> Huge seas come rolling down the bay;
> Tall cliffs are pelted with sea spray.

Nothing could have staved off an immediate Greek massacre, had Odysseus not cried to Diomedes: 'What ails us, friend? We two must make a stand! It would be shameful to let Hector destroy our fleet.'

'It would, indeed!' Diomedes answered. 'I will fight to the bitter end, though we cannot gain much by smothering this advance, when Zeus clearly intends the Trojans to win.'

Still protesting, Diomedes drove his spear into the left breast of a Trojan named Thymbraeus, and at the same time Odysseus disposed of Molion, Thymbraeus' handsome charioteer. They then counter-attacked noisily and gave their comrades a brief breathing space—

> As when a couple of wild boars break back
> Undauntedly, to charge the yelping pack.

Diomedes killed Adrestus and Amphius, the sons of Merops, King of Percote, who, as I have already said, was the most reliable of prophets and had warned them to keep out of this murderous war; but they would not listen, being lured onwards by the gloomy Fates. Diomedes stripped Adrestus and Amphius of their fine corslets; Odysseus dealt similarly with Hippodamus and Hypeirochus.

Zeus, watching from Ida, delayed the Trojan advance by allowing Diomedes to kill Agastrophus, son of Paeon, with a spear-thrust on the hip-joint. Agastrophus' charioteer had reined in his team some distance away, leaving him to blunder on until he died.

Hector caught sight of Odysseus and Diomedes, and drove shouting at them, followed by a mass of Trojans. Diomedes shivered as he cried: 'Here comes disaster rolling down on us in the person of Hector! Hold fast!' He leaned back and flung his spear, which flew unerringly at the top of Hector's helmet, a gift to him from Phoebus Apollo; the point, however, was turned by three thicknesses of brass and a crest-socket. Hector recoiled several paces. For a moment he lost consciousness and dropped on one knee, supporting himself with his palm. Diomedes hastened to retrieve and use the fallen spear, but Hector somehow struggled aboard his chariot and got away. Diomedes taunted him: 'Once more you have escaped death at my hands, dog; and by what a narrow shave! Doubtless you invoke Phoebus Apollo, and fight under his wing; still, if I can secure some other god's assistance, I will kill you when next our paths cross. Meanwhile, one of your comrades must die instead!'

As Diomedes knelt to remove Agastrophus' bright corslet, shield and helmet, Prince Paris, Helen's husband, hidden behind the pillar which marked Ilus' tomb, fitted an arrow to his bow-string and took aim. It was a neat shot that transfixed the sole of Diomedes' right foot, and pinned him to the ground. Paris came forward, laughing gaily. 'A hit!' he exclaimed. 'But why did you not expose your groin and let me make the shot mortal? That would have been a great favour to my people; you scare them as much as a lion scares goats.'

Diomedes bellowed back: 'You nasty-mouthed, mean, jeering lady-killer, with your bow and your kiss-curl! If we met in single-combat, using proper weapons, what would your chances be? This arrow has grazed my sole, coward! Yet it means less to me than a slap from a woman or a foolish small boy. When I fight, I fight! Once my spear touches the man at whom I hurl, his wife is soon tearing her cheeks, weeping for their fatherless children. The corpse rots; and vultures, not women, attend the funeral.'

Odysseus stood guard while Diomedes sat down and, shudderingly, plucked the arrow from his foot. Then, sick at heart and no longer able to laugh at the injury, he ordered Sthenelus to drive him off in his chariot. Left all alone, Odysseus exclaimed: 'That such a thing should happen to me! Shall I basely run away, or shall I take on the whole Trojan army by myself? I know the answer only too well. A hero's task is to face the enemy, and either kill or be killed!'

The Trojans now poured around noble Odysseus, barring his retreat.

> When hounds give tongue for the wild boar,
>   The young men form a ring;
> From his deep lair with eyes aglare
>   He darts out ravening.
>
> He gnashes between crooked jaws
>   White tush against white tush:
> Yet, man and hound, they stand their ground,
>   Daring the savage rush!

Odysseus made an equally savage rush. First he leaped in the air and drove his spear downwards into Deiopites; next, he accounted for Thoon and Ennomus. After that he lunged at the belly of Chersidamas, who had dismounted, and was holding his shield a trifle too high; Chersidamas collapsed, grabbing a fistful of dust. Odysseus did not attempt to despoil these corpses, but lunged again and mortally wounded Charops, son of Hippasus. Prince Socus, fighting at his brother's side, shouted: 'Why, Odysseus the Crafty, what a glutton you are! Now if you fail to brag of having killed the two redoubtable sons of Hippasus, and taken their armour, it will be because death has ended your braggart's life!' The spear flung by Socus tore a hole in Odysseus' round shield, penetrated the corslet, and scored his flank; yet the Goddess Athene—so Odysseus knew at once—had steered it clear of his guts. He withdrew a pace, growling: 'Poor doomed Socus! Black Fate hovers above you; here I stay, until I have avenged myself and sent your ghost to Hades.'

Socus turned to run, but a spear flew between his shoulders, its point emerging near his breastbone. Odysseus exulted: 'Ah, Socus, son of Hippasus the Horseman, that was the doom I foresaw—no father and mother present to close your sightless eyes; but carrion-birds pecking at them, and shrouding you with their multitudinous wings! I at least have this solace: should Death come for me, I can expect burial by friendly hands.'

He wrenched Socus' spear from his shield and corslet; but the sight of his own blood gushing out alarmed him as much as it en-couraged the Trojans.

He fell back before their charge, and three times yelled: 'To the rescue!' King Menelaus observed to Great Ajax, who stood by him: 'Son of Telamon, surely that was Odysseus' voice? He must be bat-tling for his life single-handed. You and I ought to rescue him! It would be a black day if so hardy a champion were cut off and killed.'

Menelaus hurried in the direction of the cries, followed by the enormous Ajax, and found Odysseus still feebly grasping his spear:

> Away he runs, the wounded stag,
>   With undiminished pride,
> Though soon those gallant leaps will flag—
>   An arrow galls his side.
>
> And hungry jackals scent his blood;
>   Yet where he stands at bay,
> A lion roaring from the wood
>   Turns preyers into prey.

Indeed, these two heroes went roaring to Odysseus' assistance, and the Trojans, recognizing Ajax's immense shield, scattered like jackals. Menelaus guided Odysseus to his chariot, which had just drawn up; but Ajax sprang at the Trojans, killed Doryclus, another of Priam's bastards, and wounded Pandocus, Lysander, Pyrasus, and Pylartes.

> The river, swollen by torrential rain
> Pours down destructively on the wide plain;
> Dead oaks and pine-trunks weapon-wise it wields,
> And stains the sea with earth filched from the fields.

Ajax's charge proved no less destructive.

Hector was meanwhile fighting noisily beside the Scamander, and dispatching numbers of Greek noblemen led by Nestor and Idomeneus the Cretan. Yet these could perhaps have continued to resist, had not Paris driven a triple-barbed arrow into the shoulder of Machaon, son of Asclepius, the heroic Thessalian surgeon. This alarmed Idomeneus: if Machaon were taken prisoner, the whole line might collapse. He shouted: 'Nestor, Glory of the Greeks! You must save Machaon without delay! We can ill afford to lose a comrade so skilled at extracting arrows and healing wounds: one surgeon is worth several spearmen.'

Nestor thereupon helped Machaon into his chariot, and lashed the willing horses towards the camp.

'Hector,' cried Cebriones, his charioteer, 'we Trojans are doing well enough over here, but Great Ajax seems to be holding our centre in check. That is the critical point; let us visit it!'

He swung his whip; the long-maned team bounded forward, trampling on corpses and fallen shields. The axle was soon red with blood kicked up by their hooves; and the car with splashes thrown by the wheel-rims. Hector, eager to break the Greek resistance, used his spear indefatigably, never pausing except to draw his sword, or to dismount and hurl stones; yet he avoided Great Ajax, for fear that Zeus would be angry if he attacked so much stronger a champion than himself.

Father Zeus, however, who sits enthroned high above all other

gods, made Ajax feel a sudden anxiety. He gazed about him, like
a cornered wild beast, then turned and retreated step by step, the
huge shield protecting his rear—

> All night long we countrymen
> Guarding cattle in their pen
> (With the aid of dogs that growl
> Fiercely when marauders prowl),
> At a neighbouring thicket stare.
> Ay, a tawny lion's there
> Mad with hunger, waiting for
> A chance to leap with sudden roar
> On the neck of a plump cow . . .
> 'Look, my lads, he's coming now!'
> In a volley from strong hands
> Spears are cast and burning brands!
> Be his anger what it may,
> We have baulked him of his prey;
> Off he slinks before the day.

The leonine Ajax, though equally loth to retire, did so because he
feared the Trojans would work round on the flank and burn the
fleet. In fact, since he had already done considerable execution, he
may rather be compared to an ass chased from a barley-field by small
boys:

> All unwillingly our ass
>   Up the pathway goes,
> What most irks him is to pass
>   Land where barley grows.
>
> We have splintered many a stick
>   On his tough old hide,
> Oh, that ass knows every trick:
>   Soon he may decide
>
> To break loose and eat his fill
>   By superior strength;
> We are only boys but still,
> When we flog him with a will
>   Out he trots at length.

Numerous spears flung by the Trojans or their allies fell short, and none of those that struck Ajax's renowned shield went through, though they seemed greedy to drink blood. Every now and again he would face about and defend himself, before retiring once more; his stubborn rear-guard action undoubtedly delayed the Trojan offensive.

Eurypylus, Euaemon's gallant son, who had seen Ajax's battle against odds, advanced and fought at his side. He killed an enemy commander named Apisaon, son of Phausius, with a spear-cast in the liver, and leaped forward to take his armour. Paris seized the opportunity: he sent an arrow into Eurypylus' right thigh. The shaft broke off and caused Eurypylus such torment that he withdrew, crying shrilly: 'Help, noblemen of Greece! Unless you rally to Ajax's assistance, he will be overwhelmed.'

His comrades ran up in a body. Ajax met them, and then covered their retreat as they used a cradle of shields, supported by spears resting on their shoulders, to carry Eurypylus away. It was indeed a flaming, fiery battle!

When Nestor's mares bore him and Machaon towards the camp, Achilles the Swift-Footed, watching the Greeks' disorderly rout, summoned his friend Patroclus, son of Menoetius. 'Do you need me, Achilles?' Patroclus shouted, appearing at the entrance to the hut.

Achilles, from his post near the stern of his ship, answered: 'Dear Patroclus, I am sure that the Greeks will soon be falling in supplication at my knees; they can hardly do otherwise. But I want you to ask Nestor who was the wounded man with him . . . From behind he looked like Machaon; the horses went by too quickly for me to distinguish his features.'

Patroclus, not suspecting the evil consequences of this mission, hurried along the line, until he reached Nestor's quarters. Eurymedon the charioteer had already unharnessed his team, while Nestor and Machaon stood disarmed on the seashore, letting the breeze dry their sweaty tunics. They then entered the hut, where fair-haired Hecamede, daughter of the valiant Prince Arsinous, mixed them a delicious beverage. Hecamede, one of the women captured by Achilles on Tenedos, was Nestor's prize of honour: a reward for his sagacious advice.

Nestor and Machaon settled into chairs, and Hecamede drew up a grand, well-polished table, its legs inlaid with lapis lazuli. On it she placed a bronze beaker containing a restorative drink of boiled onion juice, pale yellow honey, and the flour of pearl-barley; also a magnificent four-handled, two-footed, gold-studded bronze goblet, brought from Nestor's own palace. Each handle was formed of two golden doves, which inclined their beaks as if sipping. The goblet, after being filled, was of tremendous weight, though Nestor could still lift it easily; and now held Pramnian wine. Hecamede, beautiful as a goddess, used a bronze grater to flavour this with goat's cheese and added a little barley flour. 'The drink is ready, my lords!' she told them.

Nestor and Machaon quenched their thirst, and were enjoying a pleasant chat, when they noticed the handsome figure of Patroclus at the doorway. Nestor rose and, though seeing that Patroclus did not wish to come in, pulled him forward. 'Pray be seated!' he said.

'I fear I cannot spare the time, venerable Nestor,' replied Patroclus, 'so make no attempt to persuade me! I have been sent by a prince universally feared and honoured—Achilles, in fact—to identify your wounded companion; and since I recognize Machaon, the Thessalian leader, I must be off without delay. King Nestor, you know of Achilles' quick temper. Unless I go straight home, he may get angry and hold me responsible for what is not my fault.'

Nestor launched into a long speech. 'Why should Achilles be so anxious to learn my unfortunate companion's name? He has no conception of the Greek losses. All our leading champions are back wounded: Diomedes by an arrow, Odysseus and Agamemnon by spears; and I have just brought Machaon off the field with another arrow in his shoulder. But what would this bad news mean to Achilles? He has far greater courage than kindliness! Indeed, it looks as though he were waiting for the fleet to go up in flames, and the entire army to be massacred!

'Alas that my youth is gone! I remember well how we Pylians fought against the Epeians of Elis . . . It all began with a raid I led on the cattle of Itymoneus, the son of Hypeirochus. My spear caught and killed him as he was bravely defending a farm at the head of his frightened peasants. We made a tremendous haul of livestock: fifty herds of cattle, fifty droves of pigs, fifty flocks of sheep, fifty of goats, also one hundred and fifty chestnut mares, many of which had foals; and that night we drove them all into Pylus. My father, King Neleus, congratulated me heartily, this being my first experience of active service, and at daybreak his heralds announced that any of our people to whom the Epeians owed debts must come and register these. Numerous Pylians did so, because we were then an insignificant folk, despised and oppressed by our Epeian neighbours ever since the war in which Heracles killed our best men, including my own eleven brothers.

'Some years previously, my father entered a prize-winning team of four horses for the chariot-race at the Olympic Games—the winner was to receive a tripod—but King Augeias of Elis kept them and sent the driver home empty-handed. This angered my father so much that he now distrained upon a large herd of cattle and a flock of three hundred sheep with their attendant shepherds. He allowed his Councillors to divide the remaining spoils equitably among the people.

'Thus the affair was settled in a decent manner, and we sacrificed to the gods around the walls of Pylus. Three days later, the entire Epeian army appeared, a mass of infantry and chariots, led by the two young Moliones, who had not yet won much fame as fighters. They encamped before the Pylian frontier fortress of Thryoessa, perched on a hill overlooking the River Alpheius, and swore to level its walls. While they were still advancing towards it, Athene had flown in by night from Olympus and told us to arm—an order which we eagerly obeyed. My father thought me too inexperienced to handle a chariot, and hid my horses; but Athene took such care of me that, though I began the battle on foot, I ended in a chariot and outshone everyone, too!

'Near Arene, where the River Minyeius joins the sea, our chariots assembled for a dawn advance, and were reinforced by parties of infantry. Next morning we marched off in a compact column, sighted the River Alpheius at noon, and there offered a magnificent sacrifice to Almighty Zeus—also a bull to the River-god, a bull to

Poseidon, and a heifer to Athene the Owl-Eyed—dined without breaking ranks, and went to sleep fully armed beside the stream.

'Finding that the Epeians had not yet stormed Thryoessa, we attacked them at sunrise, after invoking Zeus and Athene. I killed the first Epeian, none other than Augeias' son-in-law Mulius; his wife, the eldest princess, fair-haired Agamede, was the best-known herbalist of her day. As Mulius charged us, my spear sent him flying to the ground; then I leaped into his chariot. The Epeians fled when they saw their leader fall, but I harried them like a black storm, and captured fifty chariots, having speared the owner and charioteer of each! I might have done the same with the twin Moliones, who passed as sons of Augeias' brother Actor; unfortunately for me, their real father, Poseidon the Earth-Shaker, came to their rescue by shrouding them in a thick mist. Zeus gave us Pylians remarkable endurance; our chariotry pursued the Epeians, killing them and stripping them of their armour, until we reached the wheat-fields of Buprasium and the Olenian Crag, where Athene called a halt. I was that sort of man once, believe it or not!

'Achilles, however, thinks only of his own reputation; I fear that he will repent too late, and shed vain tears over our heaped corpses. Patroclus, have you forgotten your father Menoetius' words when he sent you from Phthia to accompany this expedition? Odysseus and I, on a recruiting journey through Greece—land of beautiful women—visited King Peleus' palace, and in the courtyard met Menoetius, Achilles, and yourself . . . I well recall how old Peleus stood burning bulls' thighbones folded in fat, at Zeus the Thunderer's altar, and pouring wine on them from a golden chalice. You and Achilles were busy with the carcase, as we entered. Achilles sprang up in surprise, clasped our hands and courteously asked us to be seated. At the close of our meal, I discussed Agamemnon's coming attack on Troy, and you were both eager to take service under him. Your fathers then laid down what they expected of their sons while on campaign. King Peleus made it clear that Achilles must be the leader in every enterprise, and outdo all his comrades; whereas Menoetius said, as I remember: "Patroclus, my son, Achilles' lineage is superior to yours, and though you are the elder, he is by far the stronger. Yet gently offer him sensible advice on matters of conduct, and he will accept and profit by it." Perhaps these instructions have passed from your mind, but I think that if you now spoke seriously to Achilles, he might be persuaded to listen. Yes, with divine aid you might bring about a salutary change of heart in him; there is no one like a friend for breaking down a stubborn spirit.

'It occurs to me that Achilles may be abstaining from warfare because of some oracle, or because Zeus has given his mother Thetis some dissuasive message . . . Nevertheless, why does he not send you out at the head of his Myrmidons, to encourage the other allies? And even let you borrow his own splendid suit of armour? The Trojans would probably mistake you for Achilles, and withdraw; thus affording our people the rest which they so badly need. Once a battle is joined, who finds any opportunity to relax? Besides, such fresh and vigorous troops as yours should have no trouble in driving Hector's exhausted army behind the walls of Troy.'

This speech excited Patroclus. He took his leave and ran towards Achilles' ship, but paused in an open space by the station of the Western Islanders, where Odysseus always paraded his contingent, did justice, and offered sacrifices. Here he met the undaunted Eurypylus, son of Euaemon, limping painfully along; sweat streamed from his neck, blood oozed from his ugly thigh-wound.

Patroclus cried in deep compassion: 'Alas, poor heroes, sentenced to die on a distant shore, and glut the hunger of Trojan hounds with your plump white bodies! Tell me, Prince Eurypylus, foster-son of Zeus, have the Greeks any hope of repelling Hector's assault, or will he butcher everyone in the camp?'

Eurypylus answered: 'My lord Patroclus, descendant of Zeus, the fleet is doomed! All our best men are wounded, and Trojan attacks are growing more violent than ever. But pray assist me to my hut, remove the arrow, bathe the wound in warm water, and apply soothing ointments! It is said that Cheiron, the virtuous Centaur, taught you the use of vulneraries. We possess only two other skilled surgeons: Machaon, and his brother Podaleirius. Machaon has, I believe, come back wounded to the camp, and needs attention as much as I do. Podaleirius must still be fighting on the plain.'

'You cannot know what you are asking, heroic Eurypylus!' exclaimed Patroclus. 'I am in a dilemma. Nestor has just sent me with an urgent appeal to my friend Achilles. Yet how can I refuse to dress your wound?'

He grasped Eurypylus by the waist and helped him slowly towards his hut. There, Eurypylus' charioteer prepared a couch by spreading hides on the floor. Patroclus borrowed a sharp knife, knelt down, extracted the arrow, washed the wound in warm water; then, taking from his pouch a bitter root, which had both analgesic and styptic properties, crumbled it over the raw flesh. Eurypylus' pain presently ceased; and so did the flow of blood.

Book Twelve:

The Trojans Attack the Greek Camp

So Patroclus, son of Menoetius, successfully treated Eurypylus' wound, and the battle went raging on. It seemed clear that the defence system, built by the Greeks to protect their fleet and treasure, would not long fulfil this purpose, since work on it had begun without the Olympians being offered a large propitiatory sacrifice. True, while Hector lived and Achilles nursed his grudge, the rampart still stood, however irreligious its origin: Poseidon and Phoebus Apollo did not remove every trace of it until Troy and all her bravest defenders had fallen (later in that tenth year) and the surviving Greeks sailed away. Poseidon then ordered a confluence of the eight rivers which rose on Mount Ida—the Rhesus, the Heptaporus, the Caresus, the Rhodius, the Grenicus, the Aesepus, the noble Scamander, and the Simöeis, beside whose banks so many shields, helmets, and semi-divine heroes had lain in the dust. Apollo led their streams into a single channel which he directed at the rampart; Father Zeus provided nine days of continuous rain; and Poseidon, trident in hand, helped the sea to swamp the whole defence system—including laboriously laid revetments of stone and timber. Afterwards, Poseidon turned the Hellespontine currents against the ruins, spread sand over the entire area, and brought those eight rivers back to their proper beds.

Now, the rampart and its towers echoed the din of war as the Greeks were driven behind them by Hector's whirlwind advance and the crack of Zeus' whip.

Lion or boar
With sullen roar
Or angry grunt
Attacks the hunt,
And proud of heart
Displays his art
By ravening
Around our ring.
Hunter and hound
Courage have found
Here to stand fast;
Javelins are cast
From every side,
But are cast wide;
Friends, when he wheels—
Take to your heels!

Though such courage usually proves fatal to a wild beast, Hector routed the Greeks, who had almost cut him off earlier in the day. Yet his chariot-teams baulked, whinnying, when they came to the fosse, terrified by the sheer drop and the formidable palisade of huge, sharp stakes, set close together, which lined the opposite side.

Prince Polydamas approached the allied leaders. 'My lords,' he said, 'you will agree on the folly of bringing our chariots any farther. That palisade makes it impassable, and once down there, we would have no room for manoeuvre. If Zeus the Thunderer really means to destroy these Greeks, nothing would please me more; but let them catch our massed chariots in the fosse and I doubt whether a single Trojan will escape to tell the tale. Why not leave our teams here, while we assault the rampart on foot under Prince Hector's leadership?'

Hector agreed. He sprang from his chariot, and the allied leaders did the same, their charioteers taking charge of the horses. An assault force of five companies was organized. Hector led the largest, boldest and most enterprising company in person; his lieutenants being Polydamas and Cebriones. (Since Cebriones seemed too valuable a soldier to guard Hector's chariot, a weaker man acted as his substitute.)

The remaining companies were officered thus:

SECOND COMPANY
Commander: Paris
Lieutenants: Alcathous (Aeneas' brother-in-law); Agenor.

THIRD COMPANY
Commander: Helenus, son of Priam
Lieutenants: Deiphobus, son of Priam; Asius, son of Hyrtacus, from Arisbe.

FOURTH COMPANY
Commander: Aeneas the Dardanian
Lieutenants: Archelochus and Acamas, the sons of Antenor, both experienced fighters.

FIFTH COMPANY
Commander: Sarpedon the Lycian
Lieutenants: Glaucus the Lycian; Asteropaeus the Paeonian—chosen by Sarpedon as the two leading allied champions, after himself.

✳

One Trojan who would not take part in this enterprise was Prince Asius, son of Hyrtacus. Loth to abandon his chariot, as the others did, he drove towards the sally-port, on the left flank, through which the routed Greeks had been streaming. Here Asius made an error of judgement, because Fate ruled that he would never return from his adventure, but be speared to death by King Idomeneus of Crete, the proud son of Deucalion. When Asius found that the gates were being held open to admit Greek stragglers, he headed for them, across the bridge; his exultant retinue fondly believing that the battle had ended and that they would soon be burning the fleet. The sally-port was, however, defended by two brave Lapiths—Polypoetes, son of Peirithous, and Leonteus, a grandson and rival of Ares.

> On a hill two noble oaks
> Stubbornly resist the strokes
>   Of winter weather;
> Rooted deep and rooted strong,
> They for generations long
>   Stand fast together.

Polypoetes and Leonteus stood equally fast. Asius' people—among them his son Adamas, Iamenus, Orestes, Thoön, and Oenomaus—advanced shouting and flourishing their leather shields. 'Save the fleet!' bawled Polypoetes and Leonteus to their Lapith friends.

> Wild boars that on the mountain
>   Defy our hunting crew,
> From either flank come charging;
>   We raise the view halloo!
>
> Tremendous tushes clatter,
>   Young trees are tumbled flat,
> But hounds and spears and javelins
>   Soon put an end to that!

The din of a boar hunt was nothing compared to the sound of blows raining on the bronze corslets of Polypoetes and Leonteus. They fought in front of the gateway, all the more hopefully because their friends had manned the rampart and were pelting the Trojans from above.

> Wind, how fierce you blow!
>   Clouds look dark as night,
> Heavy flakes of snow
>   Flutter from a height.

Stones flew thick and fast as snowflakes, though by no means so quietly: the hollow boom when they struck Trojan helmets and shields made Asius groan. 'Father Zeus,' he exclaimed, slapping his thighs, 'how you love trickery! You let us believe that the Greeks had already yielded to our unconquerable arms. But now:

> 'Like wasps of nimble body
>   Or angry bumble-bees,
> That nest beside the cart-track
>   All among rocks and trees,
>
> 'Guarding their grubs with fury
>   When hunters pass that way,
> So these two reckless heroes
>   Defend their camp today!'

Zeus the Shield-Bearer paid no heed whatever to Asius' protest; he would soon grant Hector the glory of forcing the gates.

Polypoetes ran at a vigorous Trojan, Damasus by name, who was wearing a bronze helmet with cheek-pieces; pierced it, scattered his brains, and proceeded, further, to fell Pylon and Ormenus. Leontus did no worse: he drew sword and rushed through the mêlée at Antiphates, whom he cut down; then killed Menon, Iamenus, and Orestes, one after the other.

While these two Greek heroes bent to harvest their spoils, Hector's company paused in doubt beside the fosse. They had been on the point of entering it and scaling the palisades, when a portent occurred. They saw an eagle soaring high on their left hand, a large, blood-red serpent clutched in his talons. But the serpent was still unsubdued: writhing, it darted its fangs into the eagle's breast. The bird gave a scream of anguish, released his prey, and sailed away on a current of wind. A cry of horror arose from the Trojans among whom this bright reptile fell, for they recognized it as a sign sent them by Zeus. Prince Polydamas said to Hector: 'You always silence me if I oppose you in debate: on the ground, perhaps, that we who are not members of the Trojan royal house must applaud your views. However, I will risk another rebuke by begging you to call off the attack! This prodigy is a manifest warning to us. An eagle flies high on the left hand, clutching a large, live, blood-red serpent, which he releases before the eaglets in his eyrie can feed on it! What reputable augur could misread the divine message? He would announce: "Even if you force the Greeks to take refuge behind their rampart, the battle must continue. On reaching the fleet, your troops will be driven off with heavy losses, and rolled back across the plain."'

Hector scowled. 'Polydamas,' he said, 'your new proposal displeases me. Unless it is humorously intended, the gods must have turned your wits. Imagine asking me to forget Zeus' promises, which his famous nod has confirmed! So I am expected to study the habits of carrion-birds, am I? Well, they mean nothing to me, whether they fly east towards the dawn, or west towards the mist and darkness. I would rather trust the word of Almighty Zeus, the King both of gods and men. A divine message? The best divine message is: "Defend your country!" Are you scared? One thing stands to reason: that, though all the rest of us die among the enemy ships, you at least need have no fear—cowards always elude danger! Yet hang back from this assault, or try to talk your comrades over, and I will use my spear on you!'

Then Hector signalled the attack, and Zeus sent a great wind from Ida which blew dispiriting clouds of dust into the Greeks' faces. Hector's excited company had soon scaled the rampart, demolished the parapet, and begun to strip a tower of its large supporting buttresses. However, the Greeks made their shields into a new parapet, and went on pelting the Trojans still massed below.

Great and Little Ajax went from tower to tower, urging the troops to fiercer efforts. Some they encouraged with gay shouts, others, who had lost heart and were slinking off, they reprimanded sternly. The gist of their harangue was: 'Friends, despite differences in rank, there is work for everyone—princes, junior officers, and common soldiers—as you know well! Disregard those Trojan boasts! To your posts, and cheer your comrades on! Olympian Zeus may yet send Hector's men scampering behind their city walls.'

> Mercilessly falls the snow!
> Missiles cast on earth below
> From the fist of ZEUS. He stills
> Every breeze, and swaddles hills
> Headlands, ploughlands, grassy plain
> In a glistering counterpane:
> Harbours, bays, and broad sea-strand
> Blanch like death on either hand!
> Yet the sea, our dark grey sea,
> Of this wintry change goes free.

Stones were falling as thick as snowflakes, and the rampart echoed like a cliff struck by heavy waves.

The Trojan allies would never have broken into the naval camp, had not Zeus roused his foster-son Sarpedon to battle-fury. He ran forward under cover of a magnificent round shield—wrought bronze, and several thicknesses of bull's hide secured to the rim by numerous gold rivets—and shook his two spears.

The mountain lion
Has nothing eaten
    These many days,
And thinks to havoc
Inside the paddock
    Where fat sheep graze.

It does not matter
To this proud raider
    That men are there,
Or hounds are watchful;
His need is fearful—
    Why should he care?

No spear appals him
When nature calls him
    To drag down sheep.
A death from hunger
Holds no less danger;
    He leaps his leap!

Sarpedon, with equal disregard of the consequences, had resolved
to gain a lodgement on the rampart, and shouted to his comrade
Glaucus, son of Hippolochus: 'Cousin, why do the Lycians pay us
semi-divine honours? Why do we get the most honourable seats at
banquets, the finest cuts of meat, the fullest goblets, and great es-
tates of orchard and wheat-land beside our River Xanthus? Surely
it is because we lead their forces to war? Let us show ourselves
worthy of such generous confidence! I want to hear the troops ex-
claim: "Our princes feast on fat mutton and sweet wine, but they
are great champions, always in the thick of the fighting . . ." Dear
Glaucus, if only this battle were over, and we could become Im-
mortals—never growing old! I would no longer need to risk my life,
or ask you to risk yours. But ten thousand unavoidable hazards men-
ace us. Up with you! We must either win glory by dealing death, or
fall ourselves and yield the glory to our victors!'

Glaucus shared Sarpedon's sentiments; so they advanced together
at the head of the fifth company.

Menestheus son of Peteus, the Athenian King, aware that his

tower had been chosen for the assault, glanced anxiously along the rampart, in search of Greek champions who might help him; and saw Great and Little Ajax, bellicose as ever, and Teucrus, just approaching them from his hut. Unable to make himself heard above the clash of weapons on armour, and noisy Trojan attempts at battering down the gates, Menestheus beckoned Thoötes, a herald, and said: 'Pray, my lord Thoötes, ask Great Ajax to reinforce us—and Little Ajax, too; their assistance would be a godsend, since utter disaster threatens this command. Two Lycian princes are attacking the tower—these Lycians were always formidable fighters. But should Little Ajax have too much on his hands, at least fetch Great Ajax, and Teucrus the Archer!'

Thoötes darted away and delivered the message in Menestheus' exact words.

Great Ajax said urgently to Little Ajax: 'I wish you and Lycomedes to stay here! I shall help Menestheus, and return as soon as the Lycians are beaten back.'

He and his half-brother Teucrus went off, skirting the rampart; also Pandion, Teucrus' squire. When they reached Menestheus' tower—and very welcome he made them—the Lycians had already arrived. Great Ajax yelled his war-cry, and seizing a jagged stone of a weight that the strongest young man today could not easily lift, he hurled it at Epicles, Sarpedon's stalwart brother-in-arms, who was scaling the parapet. It crushed his four-crested helmet, splintering the skull; Epicles fell as if he were diving from a cliff. At the same time Teucrus—whose broken collarbone had by now knit together again—shot Glaucus, son of Hippolochus, in the right shoulder; which put an end to his pugnacious mood. Glaucus slid down the rampart and quietly disappeared, to forestall any Greek jeers. Sarpedon missed Glaucus, but kept his courage: he lunged at Alcmaon, son of Thestor, drew out the spear, and watched him crash on his face. Then he gripped the parapet and heaved, until a whole length of it collapsed, thus making his comrades' ascent much easier.

Ajax and Teucrus now attacked Sarpedon with spear and bow. Teucrus' arrow glanced off his plated baldric—Zeus saw to that—and Ajax's spear rang ineffectually against his shield. Sarpedon, somewhat sobered though still eager for glory, retired a few paces. 'Lycians,' he shouted, 'where are you? Though I am no weakling, do not expect me to carve my way to the ships single-handed! Forward again! More men spells better work.'

The Lycians spared themselves another reprimand by supporting their prince energetically; but Menestheus brought fresh forces into action, and a desperate struggle ensued on the rampart. It recalled stubborn peasants disputing the ownership of tillage strips on a common:

> The field's not broad, but we contend
>   How much is his, or mine.
> Says he: 'Your frontier, greedy friend,
>   Runs here, along this line.'
>
> So I have brought a measuring-rod
>   And grudge him every inch,
> Scoring my own line in the sod—
>   I'll fight him, at a pinch!

Here the disputed frontier lay between opposing parapets of shields, and spears took the place of measuring-rods. Many men got wounded, whether as a result of turning and exposing a flank, or because some shields were not weapon-proof. Rampart and towers dripped blood, yet neither side could dislodge the other.

> The honest widow spins all day,
>   Her children being small.
> A pound of yarn their food will pay,
>   She rolls it in a ball,
> And lifts the balance, with dismay
>   If either pan should fall.

The fortunes of war remained no less delicately poised until Zeus conferred on Hector the perennial fame of first entering the Greek camp. Shouting 'On, Trojans, on! Breach the defences! Burn the fleet!' he led his company over the bridge of the sally-port. While his Trojans scaled the parapet and swarmed into the towers, Hector grasped a great, rough, conical boulder that lay near the gateway. It was so enormous that the two strongest men living today could only just heave it from the ground into a wagon, but the spirit of Zeus had come upon Hector. He lifted it as easily as a shepherd would a sheepskin, and ran towards the gates, which were tall, massive, and reinforced by cross-bars bolted together. Planting himself a short distance away, advancing one foot in order to lengthen his cast, and aiming at the very middle of the barrier, he let fly.

With a deafening crash the cross-bars flew in pieces, and the gates burst their hinges. Hector's armour glinted, his eyes blazed, yet he looked grimmer than sudden night. No man alive could resist him now; it would need a god for that! 'Follow me!' he yelled at the Trojans on the rampart, and a number of them leaped down; others hurried through the gateway after him. The Greeks fled in panic to their ships amid an indescribable hubbub.

Book Thirteen:

The Greek Defences Are Breached

Having thus brought Hector's Trojans within a short distance of the Greek fleet, Zeus left them to complete their difficult task and, not suspecting that any Olympian would again dare assist either army, turned his attention elsewhere. He gazed beyond the Hellespont at the horse pastures of Thrace and other northern plains, such as those of the fighting Mysians, the lordly Hippomolgians who drink mares' milk, and the exemplary Abians.

However, Poseidon of the Dark Locks watched the battle as attentively as before. Having come out of the sea and chosen a seat on the highest peak of Samothrace, from which Mount Ida, Troy and the naval camp were plainly visible, he was seized with pity for the Greeks, and with rage against Zeus, who had permitted their discomfiture. Three great strides down the rough wooded hillside made the island tremble, and then an enormous leap carried him right across the Aegean Sea to Euboean Aegae, the town off which his famous, imperishable, golden palace glitters at the sea-bottom. There he gave orders for the harnessing of a swift, yellow-maned, bronze-hooved team, put on a golden corslet, seized an elegant gold whip, and drove away eastward over the waves. Sea-beasts frolicked in homage under and around his chariot, the water parted complaisantly, and the wheels went so fast that their bronze axle was still dry by the time he sighted the Trojan coast. Reining in at a huge submarine cave between Tenedos and the rocky island of Imbros, he unharnessed his horses, which he tethered securely with golden chains, strewing ambrosial fodder for them, then visited Agamemnon's camp on foot.

Sworn to capture the Greek fleet and massacre its defenders, Prince Hector and his triumphant Trojans had advanced like a storm, or a forest fire. But Poseidon, whose Ocean Stream girdles the earth, stepped ashore and, disguising himself as the indefatigable Calchas, stiffened Greek resistance. First he approached Great and Little Ajax. They were already eager enough to fight, but he cried: 'Keep up your courage, my lords Ajax son of Telamon and Ajax son of Oïleus, for all will be well! Though the Trojans have broken through in large numbers, we can count on holding their attack. The only point of danger is here, where Hector, who claims to be Zeus' favourite son, is advancing ferociously. I trust that some other god will inspire you to oppose him, and organize the defence; even if Zeus himself backs Hector, you may yet save the fleet!'

Two taps of Poseidon's staff lent the champions such battle-fury, that their hands and feet seemed to weigh nothing.

> Perched on a sheer, tremendous height
>   The hawk, with gaze acute,
> Observes a bird of feebler flight
> Careering almost out of sight,
>   And plummets in pursuit.

Poseidon's departure being equally swift, Little Ajax at once understood its significance. He said to Great Ajax: 'That cannot have been Calchas the Prophet! As he turned away, I noticed his knees and feet. They were superhuman ones, clearly belonging to an Olympian, whose salutation has given me renewed courage: my hands and feet itch for battle!'

'The same has happened to me!' Great Ajax answered. 'I have a sense of invincibility. My breast swells; my hands clutch the spear-shaft furiously; my feet dance . . . Yes, I am ready to confront Hector's terrible rage.'

Poseidon, having put these two in a high good humour, next visited a group of weary, tearful, breathless, demoralized Greeks who had retired to the shelter of their ships, and stood observing the Trojans as they swarmed down the rampart. Still disguised as Calchas, he reprimanded their leaders Teucrus, Leïtus, the usually dashing Peneleos, Thoas, Deipyrus, Meriones and Antilochus. 'For shame, Greeks!' he cried. 'I expected you to behave less irresponsibly than a rabble of boys. Unless you show more spirit, the Trojans will win a complete victory. I never saw anything so disgraceful or so singular! A few days ago, they were timid as hinds scurrying through the woodland in perpetual fear of jackals, leopards, wolves. They dared not emerge from their walls for the briefest of skirmishes; but now, look at them, ensconced in our very camp . . . And all because a grudge against King Agamemnon disinclines you to protect the fleet he commands! My friends, even though he may be a villain, and may have brought this trouble on himself by dishonouring Achilles, son of Peleus, is that a good reason why you should not save your own lives and property? I never blame an unwarlike man whom I see avoiding battle, but it outrages me to see our finest champions doing so! Show a change of heart, and be quick about it, for at bottom you are heroes! Feel shame and indignation at your defeat, and realize that with the gates forced and Hector attacking our ships, defeat may presently become disaster!'

Poseidon's speech roused the fugitives to immediate action. They formed two strong companies, some around Great Ajax, some around Little Ajax. A charge by Ares or Athene in person would hardly have shaken them. Shield to shield, shoulder to shoulder, helmet to helmet, they were wedged so tight together that their plumed crests touched, and their spears, which resembled a close-set fence, could not be brandished without entanglement. When Hector arrived, they would surely yield no ground.

> A winter torrent, savaging
>   The hill's well-wooded shoulder,
> Gravel and clay has gnawed away,
>   Dislodging a vast boulder;
>
> This boulder thunders down the hill,
>   Its course exactly keeping,
> And leaps amain till level plain
>   Prohibits further leaping.

Hector's course had been no less straight and destructive; but the regular line of shields halted him. He reeled back from the spear-thrusts and sword-cuts that greeted him. 'Come on, Trojans, Lycians, sturdy Dardanians!' he yelled. 'The Greeks cannot long resist me, though they stand packed like the stones of a tower. Zeus the Thunderer is behind me; they are bound to fail!'

Hector's light-footed brother Deïphobus ran up in support, and Meriones the Cretan flung at him. Deïphobus, who felt a twinge of fear, kept his shield well advanced; and the spear snapped off at the socket without so much as dinting it. Vexed that he had missed his man and shattered his only weapon, Meriones hurried away to fetch another from his hut.

The fight roared on. Imbrius of Pedaeon, Mentor the Horse-breeder's son, and husband of Priam's bastard daughter Medesicaste, had returned to Troy on the outbreak of war, and been treated by King Priam as if he were a son. But now Teucrus thrust a spear into the base of his skull, below the ear—

> Observe the distant flash
> Of bronze: a mountain-ash
> Topples and heaves
> Earthward its crown of leaves!

So fell Imbrius. Hector cast at Teucrus, who was attempting to strip the body. Teucrus bent aside, and the spear whizzed on, making for the breast of Amphimachus the Epeian, Cteatus' son, who had just entered the fight. He too fell dead. As Hector tried to seize Amphimachus' close-fitting helmet, Great Ajax lunged—not at his breast, which was heavily armoured, but at his shield-boss—and repulsed him by main force. Stichius and King Menestheus, the Athenian leaders, then rescued Amphimachus' corpse, while Great and Little Ajax bore off that of Imbrius for despoilment.

> The hounds have slaughtered a wild goat,
>   Which offers a rare meal
> Until two lions, taking note,
>   The carcase dare to steal.
>
> Together in their mighty jaws
>   They lift that carcase high,
> And through the glade, still unafraid
>   Pad off triumphantly!

Little Ajax avenged the death of Amphimachus: severing Imbrius' head from its delicate neck, he bowled it like a ball among the fighters, to fetch up at Hector's feet.

Grieved by the loss of his grandson Amphimachus, Poseidon disguised himself as Thoas, a prince to whom his subjects gave almost divine honours; he would make still greater efforts to animate the Greek laggards and dishearten the Trojans. Presently he met King Idomeneus, about to enter his hut after fetching surgeons for a Cretan with a wounded knee, whom two comrades had carried from the battlefield on their shoulders. Poseidon challenged him: 'Well, you wise Cretan, why have your loud threats against Troy miscarried?'

Idomeneus answered: 'I cannot blame anyone. We are all good soldiers, and it would be wrong to accuse this man or that of shirking or running away. The sole cause of our reverse seems to be Almighty Zeus' decision that we must die ingloriously on a foreign shore. But, Thoas, you were always famous for your courage in venturing behind a man and urging him to stand fast. Keep it up!'

'Idomeneus,' said Poseidon solemnly, 'I trust that no Greek who evades his duty today will survive the battle—may the dogs make free with his carcase! Quick, arm yourself, and though only two against many, let us show the meaning of true valour! Even cowards derive strength from company—how much more a pair of bold champions, prepared for the worst?'

Poseidon hurried forward, while Idomeneus went into his well-appointed hut, buckled his polished armour on again, grasped two spears, and sallied out like a flash of Zeus' lightning. Meriones, son of Molus, Idomeneus' trusty lieutenant, met him near the entrance. 'Swift-footed Meriones, my dearest friend, what is this?' Idomeneus asked. 'Why are you not fighting? Have you been injured, or do you bring me a message? I am not one to sit idle in my quarters, you know: I fight!'

Meriones said: 'Can you lend me a spear? I splintered mine on the shield of Prince Deïphobus.'

'Of course, I can lend you a spear!' cried Idomeneus. 'At least twenty are decorating the walls of this hut, mementoes of Trojans killed by me. Who dares suggest that I fight from far in the rear?

My large hoard of Trojan spears, shields, helmets, and fine corslets will give him the lie!'

'As to that,' said Meriones, 'I have a similar armoury stored in my hut and my ship, though yours happens to be nearer. So, please, do not imply that I am any less of a champion than yourself, or averse to facing the enemy! You should be the last to slight my battle record.'

Idomeneus soothed him: 'Why then insist on what is ungainsayable? Imagine that an ambush had been set for the Trojans, and we were kneeling under cover . . . An ambush is the supreme test of a brave man. A coward's colour changes frequently as he alternates between hope and despair; he shifts from one knee to the other; his heart pounds, and his teeth chatter at the prospect of death. A hero masters his fear, remains calm, and asks nothing better than the signal to attack. Well, in such a situation, none of us would question your courage. And were you unlucky enough to be wounded, by an arrow fired from a distance, or at close quarters by a spear, I am sure that the wound would not be in the nape of your neck, or between your shoulderblades, but either in breast or belly, as you made for the thick of the struggle. But, no more of this! If we loiter here much longer, arguing like small boys, our comrades may grow impatient. Off to my hut without further delay, and choose the stoutest spear you can find!'

Meriones did as he was invited, then hastened after Idomeneus.

> All men detest the face
> Of ARES, when from Thrace
> Escorted by his son
> TERROR, who makes men run,
> He goes well armed to where
> With proud and martial glare
> The valiant Phrygians
> Confront the Ephyrians
> In stern battle array.
> Our side must win the day:
> The God of War is loth
> Ever to honour both.

Idomeneus and Meriones might now have been mistaken for Ares and Terror. 'Son of Deucalion,' asked Meriones, 'shall we visit the right flank, the left, or the centre? I believe the left flank is weakest.'

'We need have no anxiety about the centre,' Idomeneus answered. 'Great and Little Ajax are there, also Teucrus, a fine spearman and our best archer; they will keep Hector fully occupied, however voracious his appetite for battle. In fact, I think it most improbable that he will contrive to burn our ships, unless Zeus himself hurls a flaming torch at them. Great Ajax, son of Telamon, would certainly yield to no champion whose food was barley-bread, rather than divine ambrosia, and from whose body sword-strokes and boulders did not rebound harmlessly. When it comes to close combat, Ajax could stand even against Achilles; though in a running fight, I admit, Achilles has never met his match. So let us choose the left flank, and learn whether we are destined to win glory by killing Trojans, or whether the glory will be theirs.'

To the left flank they went, shouting assent. The Trojans surged forward, and met them near the sterns of their beached ships.

> Winds in a pack attack
> A much-used wagon-track,
> Flurry its dust and shroud
> The scene with a white cloud.

Similar flurry and confusion reigned throughout the camp, and eyes dazzled at the play of sunshine on helmets, newly-burnished corslets, bright shields, and the two lines bristling with long, sharp-bladed spears. Whoever did not feel his heart stirred by joy and pain at this spectacle must have been a man of remarkable composure.

The rival aims of the brothers Zeus and Poseidon were causing excessive grief and anguish on earth. It will be remembered that Zeus meant Hector's Trojans to gain the victory, short of a Greek massacre, and thus avenge the wounded honour of Achilles, his benefactress Thetis' son; whereas Poseidon had stolen from the grey salt sea to animate the Greeks—disgusted by Zeus' preference for their enemies. These two gods could claim the same parentage and birthplace; but since Zeus was both elder and wiser, Poseidon dared not take an active part in the battle. He merely adopted human guise and encouraged the Greeks to hold fast. Over the opposing armies, therefore, two divine ropes were stretched, knotted together and pulled taut from either end in a tug-of-war. Nobody could break or undo that knot and, while it held, the slaughter went on.

Idomeneus, despite his grizzled beard, entered the battle with an alarming leap and cry. Recently, an adventurer named Othryoneus had heard tell of the Greek expedition, and come to Troy from Cabesus as a suitor for Cassandra, King Priam's daughter; ingenuously undertaking to drive the Greek army out of the Troad, if Priam would accept this service in lieu of a bride-gift! Priam having sworn agreement, Othryoneus was keeping his side of the bargain, and now strode confidently ahead of the Trojan line. Idomeneus, however, hurled a spear with such force and so true an aim that it pierced Othryoneus' bronze corslet and buried itself in his belly. He crashed to the ground, and Idomeneus taunted him: 'Othryoneus, I shall call you the most formidable hero alive, if you can still make good your undertaking to King Priam in that matter of the bride-gift! But why not change sides? We promise you as handsome a reward for the capture of Troy and prompt payment, too, when you bring it off. Agamemnon will have his prettiest daughter sent from Greece, so that you may celebrate the wedding here. Rise, and let us conclude the marriage covenant at once; he seldom drives a hard bargain.'

Idomeneus stooped, caught Othryoneus by the foot, and was dragging him away, when Prince Asius appeared. He had dismounted from his chariot, and the driver kept the horses so close in his rear that their breath warmed his shoulders. Asius tried to kill Idomeneus before he could despoil Othryoneus' corpse, but Idomeneus struck first, spearing him in the throat, just under the chin; the point emerged at the nape of his neck.

> With newly sharpened axes, see,
> Ship's carpenters attack a tree,
> And whether poplar, pine or oak
> No timber stands against their stroke.

Asius fell, like a tall oak, and the driver lost his habitual presence of mind. He should have wheeled the team around and saved them from capture; instead, he gazed in horror at Asius, who lay moaning and clutching the bloody soil. Nestor's son Antilochus thrust him through the belly, despite his stout bronze corslet; he gave one gasp and tumbled over the rail. Antilochus took the chariot.

Deiphobus hoped to avenge Asius by a short spear-cast at Idomeneus. But Idomeneus, watching him intently, ducked behind the brass-bound bull's hide shield, fitted with arm-rods, which he always carried; and the spear clanged as it glanced off the rim. Nevertheless, it had not been thrown for nothing: because Hypsenor, son of Hippasus, the Trachian commander, chanced by; he was struck in the liver, and died at once. Deiphobus exulted: 'Aha, Asius is avenged! Even on his road to Hades' kingdom he will rejoice at the escort I have sent to accompany him.'

This boast disheartened the Greeks, but made Antilochus quit the captured chariot and straddle the body of his dear comrade, plying shield and spear until two friends, Mecisteus, son of Echius, and bold Alastor, groaning for sorrow, bent down, lifted Hypsenor on their shoulders, and bore him to the rear.

Idomeneus fought indefatigably, careless of death so long as he might destroy a few more Trojans. Among them was Prince Alcathous, the son of King Aesyetes; he had married Anchises' eldest daughter Hippodameia, the most beautiful and talented Trojan girl of her age; Aesyetes and his queen doted on Hippodameia, and chose the best man in the whole city for her husband. Poseidon caused Alcathous' death by glazing his eyes and paralyzing his limbs: when attacked by Idomeneus, he could neither step back nor dodge aside, but stood motionless as a pillar or tall, leafy tree and let Idomeneus' blade harshly rip open his bronze corslet. He crashed to the dust, the spear trembling, as if from the pulsations of the heart it had pierced.

In the heat of battle, Idomeneus taunted Prince Deiphobus by shouting: 'And are you quits with us now, despite your boasts? We have killed three men to your one! Come, test the quality of my spearmanship! I am a king of divine stock. For Zeus fathered Minos on Europa, and Minos' son Deucalion was my father; therefore I rule the populous island of Crete . . . My flotilla brought me here to plague Troy, King Priam, and yourself.'

Should Deiphobus persuade some sturdy Trojan to assist him against Idomeneus, or would it be nobler if he fought alone? After a moment of doubt, he called upon Prince Aeneas. Aeneas had hitherto kept out of the battle, feeling resentful because Priam denied him honours worthy of his feats. 'Aeneas!' Deiphobus cried urgently. 'Both as a member of the Royal Council, and as Hippodameia's brother, you should display more family feeling! Her husband Alcathous, whose house you often visited when a little boy, and who showed you every kindness, is dead, and Idomeneus the Cretan has despoiled him; but at least we must rescue the corpse!'

Deiphobus' words spurred Aeneas to take bloody vengeance; yet Idomeneus was no easily scared child:

> The wild boar leaping from his lair
> High on a lonely hill
> Dares to confront the rabid hunt
> That counts upon a kill.
>
> He bristles up his sturdy back
> And, covetous of fame,
> Whets tush on tush, facing the rush
> With eyes as bright as flame.

Though Idomeneus likewise faced Aeneas' rush, he did not disdain to summon Ascalaphus, Aphareus, Deipyrus, Meriones, and Nestor's son Antilochus, all seasoned fighters. 'To the rescue!' he yelled. 'Here comes Aeneas, a fine spearman, at the peak of his powers, too, which gives him a great advantage in single-combat. If I were no older than he, we should be well enough matched for a duel to the death. As it is, I confess myself terrified!'

The five champions advanced to Idomeneus' support. Aeneas similarly summoned the help of Deiphobus, Paris, and Agenor, who hurried towards him, followed by their men-at-arms.

> Have no dread,
> Have no dread,
> Shepherd boy:
> Stride ahead
> Full of joy
> With your crook!
>
> Lead your sheep,
> Lead your sheep,
> Pretty creatures,

> From the steep
> Mountain pastures
> To the brook!

Aeneas was happy as a shepherd boy when he saw his comrades flock up; and savage spear-thrusts were exchanged over Alcathous' body, making armour ring. Aeneas flung at Idomeneus; but he skilfully avoided the spear, and it stuck quivering in the ground. Idomeneus retaliated by a jab at the belly of Oenomaus, who fell clutching the soil as his intestines gushed through the hole torn in his corslet. Idomeneus withdrew the weapon, whereupon so many Trojans made for him that he dared not despoil Oenomaus. Indeed, feeling too winded to challenge any further Trojans, or recover his spear once he had thrown it, or even dodge an attack, he could only shelter behind his shield and slowly retire. Deiphobus hurled at the hated Idomeneus, and again killed the wrong man: this time it was Ascalaphus, son of Ares the Warrior. The spear struck his shoulder, and down he went. (All the Olympians, except Poseidon, were obeying Zeus' instructions and taking no part in the war—reclined at ease on a peak of Olympus, under the golden clouds. Thus terrible, loud-voiced Ares did not know that his descendant Ascalaphus had just died.)

A fierce struggle took place when Deiphobus tried to pull off Ascalaphus' bright helmet. Meriones transfixed his upper arm, made him drop the helmet; then, swooping like a vulture, recovered the spear and disappeared again. Prince Polites clasped his brother Deiphobus' waist and guided him to the waiting chariot. The charioteer took Deiphobus home, groaning and red with blood that spurted from the wound.

Meanwhile, Aeneas rushed at Aphareus, son of Caletor, who happened to expose his throat, and drove a spear into it. Aphareus' head jerked backwards, his helmet and shield dropped, and he died instantly. Nestor's son Antilochus saw that Thoön had turned around, and attacked him, his spear severing the spinal cord that runs from haunch to neck. Thoön fell supine, flinging out both hands in appeal to his comrades. At once Antilochus removed Thoön's armour, keeping a shrewd eye on the Trojans who tried to prevent him. Blows rained against Antilochus' ample shield, and if none so much as grazed his delicate skin, that was because of Poseidon's protection. Nor did he break off the fight: he darted here and there, always on the look-out for a chance to make a long cast or thrust from close quarters. Adamas, son of Asius, who had been watching Antilochus, suddenly lunged at his shield with great force; but Poseidon grudged Adamas this victory. The spear snapped, its forepart remaining embedded in the hide, as if it were a burned tree-stump, the butt falling to earth. Thus disarmed, Adamas would have slipped away, had not Meriones, coming in pursuit, speared him just above the genitals, where wounds are incurable. His hopeless writhings recalled a familiar bucolic scene:

> Bound by green willow wands, the bull
> Wildly resists the herdsmen's pull,
> All his four feet in action till
> They drag him roaring down the hill.

Adamas' struggles ended as soon as Meriones pulled out the spear.

Next, Prince Helenus, son of Priam, dealt Deipyrus a mortal blow on the temple with a Thracian broadsword, which sent his helmet spinning; a Greek picked it up as it rolled between his feet. Menelaus of the Loud War-Cry then resolved to avenge Deipyrus, by attacking Helenus. Helenus, however, shot an arrow at him before he could throw a spear.

> When strong the sea-wind whistles,
>   Our threshing-floor we man,
> Where swarthy beans or chick-peas
>   Await a winnowing-fan.
>
> Into the wind we toss them,
>   From fans both wide and deep;
> For though the chaff goes flying
>   They'll tumble in a heap.

The arrow glanced off Menelaus' corslet, like a chick-pea tossed by a winnowing-fan; but Menelaus' spear drew blood. It pierced Helenus' bow-hand, and he retired, trailing the shaft behind him. Prince Agenor removed it; took some twisted yarn which one of his squires carried for such emergencies, and bound up the wound.

Peisander's attack on Menelaus was not destined to succeed.

When they exchanged thrusts, the blade of his spear broke off in Menelaus' wide shield, whereas Menelaus missed altogether. Undeterred, Peisander grasped the long, polished, olive-wood haft of his battle-axe and swung at his opponent's helmet, but only shore away the plume-socket. In return, he caught a horizontal blow from Menelaus' silver-studded sword across the bridge of the nose, which sliced his skull, and sent both eyes dripping bloodily into the dust.

Menelaus placed a foot on Peisander's prostrate corpse and, after despoiling it, yelled: 'Look, Trojan war-mongers! This is how your adventure must end! And when Ruin overtakes you, dogs, she will heap upon your heads the same shameful insults that you once heaped upon mine, in impudent defiance of Zeus the Thunderer. Zeus avenges the ill-treatment of host by guest, or guest by host, and cannot but destroy the Trojan Citadel before he has done. Your ambassadors, whom I feasted at Sparta, wickedly stole my wife, with a great part of my treasure; and now you threaten to burn this fleet and massacre its crews! No, no, greedy Trojans! Monstrous though your appetite for violence may be, you will soon have a bellyful!'

He then addressed Zeus:

'ZEUS, evermore excelling,
Of wisdom infinite,
Are you yourself compelling
These men to fight their fight
And sin against the light?

'Dances are good, in measure,
Like love and sleep and song,
And yield more certain pleasure
Than to defend the wrong
By battling all day long!'

Having stripped Peisander of his gory armour, and presented it to his comrades, Menelaus plunged into the mêlée again. The ill-fated Harpalion, son of King Pylaemenes of Paphlagonia, rushed to meet him, but failed to pierce his shield; so withdrew, first glancing around lest anyone should throw a spear. He did not see Meriones' drawn bow; the arrow entered his right buttock, tore the bladder, and emerged under the groin. Harpalion sank down, to die like a crushed earth-worm, and his life-blood darkened the soil. Loyal Paphlagonians lifted him on their shoulders and bore him over the fosse to his chariot.

Paris grieved for Harpalion, having been his guest once in Paphlagonia; and, since Pylaemenes had not exacted vengeance before removing the corpse to Troy, did so himself by killing Euchenor, son of Polyidus the Corinthian prophet, with an arrow that struck him below the angle of his jaw. Euchenor had embarked for Troy in full foreknowledge of this fate; because Polyidus often warned him that he must either stay at Corinth and succumb to disease, or sail away and be killed by the Trojans. He chose the second alternative, and thus avoided both a lingering death and the heavy fine which Agamemnon would have made him pay for not volunteering.

Meanwhile Hector, confident of Zeus' favour, attacked the Greeks' right flank, unaware that, encouraged and magically assisted by Poseidon, they were more than holding their own on the left. He fought close to the flotillas of Little Ajax the Locrian, and of Podarces the Thessalian, Phylacus' grandson, who had succeeded his dead brother Protesilaus; here the rampart was lowest, and the battle most furious. The Locrians, the Thessalians, the Boeotians, the Ionians with their long tunics, and the famous Epeians, were all hard pressed and unable to repel Hector. The Ionians included some excellent troops from Athens led by King Menestheus, son of Peteus, and his lieutenants Pheidas, Stichius, and Bias. Meges, son of Phyleus, assisted by Amphion and Dracius, led the Epeians; Podarces and Medon, Little Ajax's bastard-brother from Phylace, led a mixed force of Thessalians and Boeotians.

Great and Little Ajax laboured side by side, like a team of plough-oxen:

> Two hardy oxen dark as wine,
>   A strong and docile pair,
> With equal fortitude combine
>   In dragging the ploughshare.
>
> Nothing divides them but the pole
>   To which their yoke is bound;
> Their brows are wet with beads of sweat
>   That drip upon the ground.

> O labour nobly on, you steers
> That plough the fallow field!
> Until the furrow's end appears
> To sloth you never yield.

But whereas Great Ajax's men-at-arms gave him staunch support, and even carried his enormous shield when its weight oppressed him, Little Ajax's Locrians were unaccustomed to this style of fighting, and possessed no helmets, shields, or spears. They used bows instead, or slings of braided yarn, volleys from which caused the Trojans heavy losses. Thus Great Ajax's Salaminians fought Hector's bronze-corsleted comrades on equal terms, while Little Ajax's Locrians, keeping behind cover, galled them with arrows and sling-stones.

The Trojans might have retreated to Troy at this point, had not Prince Polydamas once more approached Hector. 'Hector,' he said, 'you are difficult to persuade, because your extraordinary talents as a soldier make you claim similar eminence as a strategist. Zeus' studied policy, however, is to let one man excel in battle—or in dancing, or lyre-playing, or singing—but to confer on another the shrewd judgement which saves lives. So pray listen! Though we have crossed the rampart and set the whole battle-front ablaze, some of our troops are standing idle, leaving others to struggle desperately in scattered knots. Why not allow yourself a brief respite from fighting, summon a council-of-war, and decide whether we can expect Zeus to approve a well-organized attack on the fleet; or whether we should retire before anything worse happens? The Greeks, smarting from yesterday's defeat, may perhaps turn the tables on us: particularly since Achilles cannot be trusted to abstain much longer from the sport he loves so dearly.'

Polydamas' apt advice pleased Hector. 'Take charge of these troops,' he said, 'while I see how the battle is progressing elsewhere! I shall return after giving the necessary orders.'

He hurried off, majestic as a snow-capped mountain, and shouted to the Trojans and their allies: 'Polydamas will assume temporary command!' Then he went to search for Deïphobus, Helenus, Adamas, and Adamas' father Asius, son of Hyrtacus; but found none of them in the fighting line. Some lay dead, near the sterns of the Greek ships; some had gone wounded home to Troy. On the Trojan right flank only Prince Paris was boldly pressing the attack. Hector cried in exasperation: 'Still alive, beautiful brother—womanizer, vile seducer? But where are Deïphobus, and brave Helenus, and Adamas, and Asius, and Othryoneus? The Trojan army is melting away disastrously!'

Paris answered: 'If you persist in blaming me unjustly, Hector, I may abandon this war altogether; for, despite your reproaches, I was not born wholly a coward! Since the battle began, my company has been engaged without a pause. Adamas, Asius and Othryoneus lie dead; Deïphobus and Helenus have left the field, both severely wounded in the hand. We survivors are ready to follow courageously wherever you lead, so long as we can stand. But even courage does not do much for a man once he is exhausted.'

These words calmed Hector; he guided Paris and his company through the camp to reinforce Polydamas, Cebriones, Phalces, Orthaeus, and Prince Polyphetes—also a draft of Bithynians who had arrived, on the previous morning, from the fertile shores of the Ascanian Lake: namely Palmys, Ascanius, and Morys, son of Hippotion.

> Loud thunder rolled,
> The wind blew cold
>   And with the sea played pranks:
> Malignly curled,
> The breakers whirled
>   Forward in foaming ranks!

The Trojans advanced, rank upon rank, their helmets shining; Hector led them, under cover of his huge, round, thick, bronze-plated bull's hide shield, and the tall plume nodded as he went. Yet Hector's awesome presence failed to cow the Greeks, and up stalked Great Ajax. 'My lord Hector,' he said, 'you waste your time! Ours is too experienced an army to be scared, and these recent reverses only mean that Zeus has been punishing us for some slight fault. I know what you have in mind, but we are well able to defend the fleet; one day it will be Troy that is taken and burned! What is more, before nightfall I may see your chariot storming across the Scamandrian Plain in a cloud of dust, while you pray Father Zeus and the other Immortals to make the team fly swifter than falcons!'

An eagle soared by on Ajax's right hand, an augury which drew a cheer from the Greeks. Hector, however, replied: 'Ajax, you blundering fool, enough of threats! I should love to be Hera's son by Zeus, and honoured like Apollo or Athene; but as certainly as I am no less human than yourself, so certainly must this battle end in utter disaster for you! Dare challenge my spear, and your lily-white skin will be torn open: a feast to glut the dogs and carrion-birds of Troy.'

Hector charged, his men raised a war-cry, and their enemies stood fast, yelling defiance. The combined roar rose high to Heaven, where Father Zeus holds splendid court.

Book Fourteen:

Hera Outwits Zeus

King Nestor of Pylus, still drinking cheese-flavoured Pramnian wine with Machaon, son of Asclepius, could no longer disregard the battle that raged through the camp. 'What shall we do, noble Machaon?' he cried anxiously. 'The din grows louder. I ought to make a tour of inspection. But you are welcome to stay here and drink until Hecamede has warmed a cauldronful of water and washed the clotted blood from your wound.'

Thrasymedes had borrowed his father Nestor's shield, and left his own highly-polished one lying in the hut. This Nestor took and, after selecting a stout, keen-bladed spear, went outside. A shameful spectacle confronted him. The Trojans were over the rampart and pursuing a mob of Greek fugitives.

> Gloomily labours the great sea,
> But no waves yet appear;
> While all four winds blow fitfully
> In random, brief career
> Instead of choosing a sole source,
> How can the waves decide their course?

Old Nestor felt equally uncertain. Should he enter the battle at once, or should he go in search of Agamemnon and urge him to organize the defence? He chose the latter course only when the clash of weapons against armour, mixed with cries of exultation or despair, sounded even closer, and he saw Diomedes, Odysseus and the High King himself approaching.

Let me explain that since the sandy stretch between the two headlands could not accommodate all the ships of the Greek fleet, later arrivals had been hauled far up the foreshore in rows. The rampart was built behind the highest row. Thus the flotillas of Diomedes, Odysseus and Agamemnon, having landed first, lay farthest from the Trojan attack. These three wounded, dismal kings now hobbled forward to view the battle, leaning heavily on their spears. The sight of Nestor at the door of his hut intensified their gloom. Agamemnon cried: 'Why, Nestor, son of Neleus, Glory of the Greeks, what is this? Are you a deserter? Have you forgotten Hector's boast, that he would not go home before he had breached our fortifications, burned our ships, and massacred the crews? He looks in a fair way to make it good. I fear that many of you princes, like Achilles, are nursing some grievance, and refusing to defend the fleet.'

'King Agamemnon,' answered Nestor, 'Zeus, Lord of Thunder, has declared against us! The rampart is over-run and dismantled; a massacre has begun. Our men scurry about in such disorder and noise that you would find it hard to say from which particular point they were retreating. I suggest therefore that we avoid battle ourselves—for what can wounded men do?—and hold a council instead, to consider possible means of saving the day.'

Agamemnon assented: 'Yes, indeed, friend: Almighty Zeus must have willed our ruin. The fortifications which cost us so much labour, and to which we entrusted the security of our fleet, are over-run and the Trojans have reached the highest row of ships. When Zeus was actively helping the Greeks, I knew it well; but now I know with equal certitude that he has bound our hands, drained our strength, and granted the Trojans as much glory as if they were Immortals. I trust you will agree that we ought at once to embark in our flotillas—namely those on the water's edge—throw out mooring-stones at a safe distance from the shore, and wait there until nightfall. If the Trojans then retire, though even darkness may not check their fury, we will perhaps succeed in launching further ships. Nobody needs to apologize for evading disaster, especially by night. The quicker you run, I say, the longer you live!'

Odysseus glared at Agamemnon. 'Son of Atreus,' he exclaimed, 'what did I hear? Worthless wretch—fit only to command a rabble, not the good soldiers whom Zeus has, worse luck, authorized you to waste in a series of disastrous campaigns until all are killed—do you propose to raise the siege, after these many years of effort and suffering? Pray keep your mouth shut, or someone may catch a remark that no sceptred king handling so huge a force as yours, and supposedly endowed with common sense, has any right to make! I am scandalized by your view that we should launch our flotillas, while the issue of this battle still remains in doubt—thus playing into the Trojans' hands, and increasing our chances of defeat. If the troops yonder get wind of your intention, they will look over their shoulders, break off the fight, and rush panic-stricken towards the shore—a disaster for which, my lord, you alone will be accountable!'

Agamemnon answered: 'Your sharp reproach abashes me, Odysseus; but upon my word, I was not insisting on an evacuation against the army's wishes. By all means let one of you offer more bellicose advice. I should welcome that from any prince, old or young.'

Diomedes of the Loud War-Cry answered: 'You need not go far for advice, son of Atreus, if you will accept it without resentment. True, I am the youngest man present, yet nobody can say that mine is an ignoble lineage. My great-grandfather Portheus had three sons: Agrius, Melas, and Oeneus the Horseman; Oeneus, my grandfather, was the bravest of the trio, who lived in the district of Pleuron and rocky Calydon. However, my glorious father Tydeus, since fallen at Thebes, obeyed the wishes of Zeus and the other Olympians by migrating to Argos. There he married Deipyle, one of King Adrastus' daughters, and had a large, rich mansion, surrounded by wheatlands, fenced orchards, and flocks of sheep at pasture. Tydeus having proved himself the finest spearman in Greece—you all know that I speak the truth—no one must belittle my advice by accusing me of inherited cowardice. Very well, then: I hold that it is our duty to appear on the battlefield where, though we decide to stay out of spear-range and thus avoid being wounded a second time, we can at least spur forward those of our comrades whom some obstinate grudge has hitherto kept in the rear.'

Diomedes' speech was cordially received, and the whole group, headed by Agamemnon, moved on.

*

Poseidon the Earth-Shaker, observing them intently, adopted the disguise of an old, old man and caught Agamemnon by the right hand, exclaiming heartily: 'My lord King, if Achilles loves to watch the rout and slaughter of his fellow-Greeks, he cannot have a grain of sense. Why, he runs a considerable risk of getting killed himself! May Zeus cripple him for his cruel heart! However, the gods are far less angry than they appear. Believe me, my lord, you will yet see Trojan chariots streaming back across the plain in a cloud of white dust.'

Poseidon then ran off, and uttered so tremendous a shout that it altogether restored the Greeks' flagging spirits: the sort of shout that might have issued from the lungs of nine or ten thousand men as they clashed in battle.

Standing on a peak of Mount Olympus, Hera of the Golden Throne gazed down at the naval camp, and was delighted to recognize her brother Poseidon busily rallying the Greeks; though a glance at Mount Ida told her that Zeus was still seated there. Oh, how she loathed him! But, she thought, what about visiting Ida, dressed as attractively as possible, and making him conceive a sudden passionate desire for her? That might be the best way of outwitting him! Once he had been decoyed into bed, Sweet Sleep could be persuaded to settle on his eye-lids and fog his sharp wits.

Hera retired to her boudoir—their lame son Hephaestus had built it, hinging the stout doors to pillars and providing a secret bolt, the management of which she alone understood. In she went, shot the bolt and, taking off all her clothes, used an ambrosial lotion to remove every stain or smutch from her delicious body. Next, she rubbed ambrosial oil into the skin—so penetratingly fragrant did it smell that she had merely to shake the flask anywhere in Zeus' brazen-floored Palace, and the scent would spread through Heaven and the entire earth! Then she poured a little of the same oil on her hair, combed it well in, and plaited the long, shining tresses. After that, she chose a fresh linen robe, tastefully woven by Athene, pinned on a number of handsome jewels, and fastened it across her breast with gold clasps. She added a girdle of a hundred tassels; hooked a lucent three-drop ear-ring into each ear to make herself look even lovelier; and finally draped a splendid new veil, bright as the Sun, over her head and shoulders. Nor did she forget a beautiful pair of sandals.

The result satisfied Hera, who left the boudoir and called Aphrodite the Laughter-Loving aside. 'Will you deny me a favour, dear child,' she whispered, 'just because you support the Trojans in this war, and I am supporting the Greeks?'

Aphrodite whispered back: 'Queen Hera, daughter of great Cronus, tell me your needs and, unless the favour is beyond my competence, I shall be charmed to grant it.'

Hera then asked craftily: 'Could you lend me Love and Love-longing, the two powers you employ for defeating Immortals and mortals? The fact is, I am visiting my ancient uncle and aunt, King Oceanus and Queen Tethys. When Zeus the Far-Sighted imprisoned our father Cronus between earth and barren sea, this kindly couple took me from Mother Rhea's care and brought me up in a palace at the brink of the habitable world. My mind is set on ending that stale old quarrel of theirs; they have not caressed each other or slept in the same bed for ages. If I can reconcile them, and arrange a second honeymoon, they will hold me in affection and esteem.'

Aphrodite unfastened the exquisite embroidered girdle which housed her enchantments—Love, and Love-longing, and Love-talk —powers that fool even the wisest intelligence. Handing the girdle to Hera, she said: 'I could not refuse your plea without the greatest impropriety, Queen Hera; after all, you are the wife of Father Zeus, no less! If you stow this away in the fold of your robe, I hardly think that your mission will fail.'

Hera smiled for answer, and accepted the advice.

No sooner had Aphrodite gone, than Hera flew eastward, touched at Pieria and pleasant Emathia, skimmed the snowy hills where the Thracian horse-breeders roam, and from Mount Athos crossed the rough Aegean Sea. At Lemnos, the home of Prince Thoas, she met Sleep, the twin of Death, and grasped him by the hand. 'Sweet Sleep,' she cried, 'please help me again, and I shall be eternally grateful! I want you to wait until Zeus and I have performed the act of love, then you must settle on his shining eyes and softly close their lids! In return, I will order my son Hephaestus to forge you an imperishable golden throne, complete with a foot-stool, for festival use.'

Sleep replied: 'Divine daughter of Cronus, it is easy enough to make other Immortals drowse off, even Oceanus himself, the senior god still reigning; but I dare not serve Zeus the Shield-Bearer so, unless he gives me his express sanction. I found myself in frightful trouble a couple of generations ago, after doing you this very favour: because, taking advantage of Zeus' comatose state, you let loose a great tempest and drove his son Heracles' ship far from home, to the populous island of Cos. Zeus awoke in anger and began tossing the Olympians out of his Palace; frantically trying to capture me. I would soon have been hurled down from the bright upper air, to perish in the Pit of Hell, had it not been for dear Mother Night, with whom I took hurried refuge; she protected me; and, enraged though he was, Zeus feared to displease that swift-flying subduer of gods and men—so he abandoned the chase. You ask me to risk my life a second time? I regretfully decline.'

'Sweet Sleep,' Hera told him, 'your qualms are foolish! How can Loud-Voiced Zeus feel as strongly about those Trojans as he did about his beloved son Heracles? Grant me this favour and I will marry you to one of the younger Graces: yes, to Pasithea herself, with whom you have always been in love!'

'Agreed,' said Sleep:

'Swear by the waters of the Styx—
    No firmer oath is known—
Which no god dares to take in vain
    Lest Heaven be overthrown;

'But, as you swear, fail not to grasp
    The earth with your right hand,
And with your left the shining sea,
    For all to understand—

'All deathless ones inhabiting
    Earth, sea or upper air,
Even those old gods, by ZEUS bound
    In CRONUS his dark lair—

> 'That to my merry marriage-couch
>   A Grace you'll surely bring,
> Sweet PASITHEA, whom I love
>   Far beyond everything!'

Hera duly swore by the waters of Styx, naming all the Immortal Gods as witnesses, even those Titans who lie banished and bound in a dark lair below the horizon.

Under cover of mist, Hera and Sleep then left Lemnos, passed over Imbros, and continued towards Mount Ida, mother of wild beasts. Leaving the sea behind them at Lecton, they skimmed above the Idaean forest. Here Sleep halted, just out of Zeus' sight and, disguised as the shrill-voiced bird which gods call a *chalcis*, but men a 'night-jar', perched on the tallest pine-tree in the whole district. Hera flew forward alone to Gargarus, the highest peak of the range, where Zeus still sat.

Now, as soon as Zeus saw Hera, a most passionate desire seized him: it was exactly like the delightful occasion, centuries before when, unknown to their kind-hearted parents, these two first committed incest together. He rose to his feet. 'Hera,' he said, 'why have you not brought your chariot and horses with you for the steep return journey?'

Queen Hera answered slily: 'I am visiting our ancient uncle and aunt King Oceanus and Queen Tethys, who live at the brink of the habitable earth. My mind is set on ending that stale, old quarrel of theirs; they have not caressed each other or slept in the same bed for ages. I only wanted to tell you this plan of mine: you might have been annoyed if I had gone away without any explanation to Oceanus' palace beside his deep-flowing, world-girdling river. My chariot-team stands tethered at the foot of this mountain.'

'Darling Hera,' said Zeus, 'surely another day will do as well? Let us make love at once! Never in my entire life have I felt such intense longing for goddess or nymph as I feel for you this afternoon! Why, my interest in Ixion's wife Dia, on whom I begot the wise Peirithous, was nothing by comparison; and this also applies to Danaë, daughter of Acrisius, the girl with the beautiful ankles, on whom I begot the hero Perseus; and to the celebrated Europa, daughter of Phoenix, on whom I begot King Minos and his brother Rhadamanthus. In-

deed, it applies to Semele, on whom I begot the universally adored
Dionysus; and to Alcmene the Theban, on whom I begot bold Hera-
cles; and to our sister Demeter, the goddess with the beautiful hair,
on whom I begot Persephone; and to the famous Leto, on whom I
begot Apollo and Artemis. Why, I would venture to say, dearest
wife, that I have never yet conceived so delirious a passion even
for you yourself!'

Hera's answer was as sly as before: 'Revered Son of Cronus, what
a shocking idea! Do you actually mean us to make love up here,
in full sight of Olympus? Suppose some god were to play spy, and
tell the other Immortals all he had seen? I should not have the face
to go home after that; it certainly would give me a pardonable griev-
ance against you. But if I must humour you in this inconvenient
fashion, pray escort me to your Olympian bed-chamber, with its
stout doors hinged to pillars, built by our son Hephaestus. We can
be private there.'

'No, no, Hera,' replied Zeus. 'You need not fear that any god or
man will witness our marital sport! I shall spread an immense
golden cloud over you, which the brightest eye in existence, the
Sun's, would fail to pierce.'

Zeus then caught hold of Hera, laid her down masterfully, and
took his pleasure of her. The earth beneath them was divinely in-
duced to sprout a soft, thick, vigorous crop of fresh grass, tender
clover, crocuses and hyacinth flowers, that raised the lovers a hand's
breadth into the air. So they embraced, on the crest of Gargarus,
covered by a golden cloud from which cool, sparkling dew dripped
upon their naked bodies; until Zeus dozed off, conquered by the
arts of Love and Sleep, still clasping Hera to his breast.

Sleep hurried towards the naval camp, where he sought out Po-
seidon. 'Earth-Shaker,' he said urgently, 'the coast is clear at last!
Hera has tricked Zeus into pleasuring her, and I have lulled him
asleep. So help the Greeks as much as you wish; let them enjoy
their hour of glory!'

Sleep then passed on, but though he took this message to several
illustrious princes, it was Poseidon whom it cheered the most.
Springing ahead of the front-line, Poseidon shouted: 'Greeks, shall
we allow Hector, son of Priam, a second triumph? Is he to capture

our fleet? That has been his boast ever since Achilles retired in a sulk. But if we encourage one another to fight, there will be no massacre to trouble Achilles' conscience. Do as I say! Collect the toughest, broadest shields, and the tallest spears in camp, put on glittering helmets, and form up behind me! You may be sure that Hector, despite his courage, will not long withstand us. And if a stubborn fighter has only a small shield, he should hand it to a less dependable comrade in exchange for a larger!'

Poseidon's advice was eagerly accepted. Despite their wounds, Agamemnon, Diomedes and Odysseus armed themselves and supervised the distribution of shields and weapons—the best gear went to the better soldiers, the worst to the worse. So the army paraded under Poseidon—he carried that terrible, keen-edged sword of his which resembles a lightning flash, and which nobody dares face in battle. The Trojans had meanwhile been marshalled by glorious Hector. A wave came hissing among the ships and huts, and at that signal the Greeks advanced with a resonant shout behind Poseidon:

> Seas that break against the hill,
>> When winds blow north-easterly;
> Fire that sweeps a wooded hill;
>> Gales that howl in bush or tree—

none of these natural forces ever made so dreadful a noise as the roar of battle that arose when the Trojan and Greek armies met once more!

First Hector threw his spear at Great Ajax's exposed breast, and struck it at the point where shield-baldric and sword-baldric crossed. The blade turned, without piercing the corslet, and Hector retired in vexation. But suddenly something flew over the rim of his shield and caught him below the neck: Ajax had picked up and flung one of the many big boulders—chocks for beached vessels—now rolling among the fighters' feet. It spun Hector around like a peg-top!

> The sudden lightning stroke
> Blasted a forest oak;
>> Mortals who saw
> With what a shock it fell

> Sniffed at the brimstone smell,
> Trembling for awe!

Hector's fall caused the Trojans similar terror. Though dropping his spear, he lost neither helmet nor shield as he clattered to the dust. The exultant Greeks threw a volley of spears and rushed up, trying to drag him off; but the bravest Trojans in the field—Polydamas, Aeneas, Agenor, King Sarpedon of Lycia, and Prince Glaucus—had by now solicitously interposed a barrier of shields, and no enemy could reach Hector. He was carried moaning to where his chariot-team stood ready harnessed beyond the fosse, and driven away towards Troy. Pausing at the ford of the deep River Scamander (whose god can address Zeus as 'father'), his friends took Hector out of the chariot and poured water on his face. He recovered consciousness, looked about him, struggled to his knees, vomited blood, and fell again in a dead faint. Ajax's boulder had tamed that bold spirit!

As soon as Hector left the field, the Greeks began to enjoy themselves. Little Ajax darted ahead of them all and speared Satnius, son of Enops, in the side: Satnius' mother was a Naiad who had taken Enops as her lover while he herded his flocks beside the River Satniöeis. He tumbled lifeless, and a fierce tussle ensued for the possession of his corpse. Polydamas, son of Panthous, advanced to the rescue and drove his stout spear clean through the shoulder of Arëilycus, son of Prothoenor, mortally wounding him. Polydamas yelled: 'Once more I have not struck in vain! Arëilycus can keep my spear as a crutch when he limps down to Hell.'

The taunt grieved Prothoenor's comrades, particularly Great Ajax, who made a quick cast from close range at the retreating Polydamas. He bent aside, but Fate had ordered that the spear should catch Antenor's son Archelochus just above the top-joint of his spine and sever both neck-tendons. Archelochus collapsed, his face striking the ground a little before his knees and legs. Ajax shouted: 'Confess, my lord Polydamas, that I have not done badly to avenge Prothoenor by killing a fighter who can hardly be sprung from mean stock—in fact, his features suggest that he is either a younger brother or a son of Antenor the Horse-Tamer.' Ajax, of course, knew who Archelochus was.

This vexed the Trojans; and when Acamas saw Promachus, son of Alegenor the Boeotian, dragging Archelochus off by the feet, he plunged his spear into him, crying in grisly tones: 'Enough of taunts, you Greek archers who fancy yourselves as spearmen! We are not alone in suffering cruel losses, and I have now exacted rapid payment for my brother's death. A soldier may well pray to be survived by some avenging relative!'

This vexed the Greeks, especially the resourceful Prince Peneleos. He failed to kill Acamas, but attacked Ilioneus, only son of Phorbas, a rich sheep-farmer whom his patron the god Hermes had prospered. The spear shot down into Ilioneus' eye, gouging out the eye-ball, and emerged at the nape. As Ilioneus flung open his arms, Peneleos beheaded him. 'Trojans,' he cried, 'pray warn Phorbas and his wife to mourn their loss; and when we sail home from here, we will take the wife of Promachus a similar message!' With that he lifted his spear. Ilioneus' head, impaled by the blade, made it look like a tall poppy.

The Trojans blanched, consternation seized them, and they broke.

> Now tell me, gentle MUSES,
> Who on Olympus dwell,
> What Greek first slew a Trojan,
> And stripped the corpse as well,
>
> After our great EARTH-SHAKER,
> His brother to annoy,
> Had turned the tide of battle
> And brought defeat on Troy.

Great Ajax was the first: he killed and despoiled Hyrtius, son of Gyrtias, the bold Mysian commander. Next, Nestor's son Antilochus accounted for Phalces and Mermerus; next, Meriones the Cretan for Morys and Hippotion; then Teucrus, for Prothoön and Periphetes. Finally, Menelaus drove his spear into the side of Prince Hyperenor, son of Panthous, whose intestines gushed out and whose spirit escaped through the same wide breach.

But swift-footed Little Ajax killed more Trojans than did any of his comrades. He always pressed the hardest on a fleeing enemy.

Book Fifteen:

The Greeks Rally

Driven back over rampart, palisade and fosse with heavy casualties, the Trojans came to where they had left their chariots and halted in confusion; at which very moment Zeus, the Father of men and gods, awoke on the peak of Gargarus. He disengaged himself from Hera's arms, leaped to his feet and looked towards Troy. There he saw a column of Greek champions, led by Poseidon, driving before them a mob of frightened fugitives, while at the Scamander ford, a group of Trojans crouched around the recumbent figure of Hector. Hector was gasping for breath, vomiting blood, and mumbling in delirium. The boulder that struck him had clearly not been thrown by a nerveless hand.

Zeus burst out:

> 'O HERA, with what crooked arts
>   You meddle in this fight!
> Prince Hector bleeds beside the ford,
>   His men are turned to flight.
>
> 'Beware lest now I take revenge,
>   My lovely queen, on you,
> Thrashing your exquisite soft skin
>   Till it turns black and blue.
>
> 'Once, long ago, I trussed you up,
>   I trussed you up so neat
> With golden gyves about your wrists,
>   And anvils on your feet,

'Hanging you from the cloudy pole,
   For all the world to see;
The Immortal Gods were mad with rage,
   But could not set you free.

'For I would catch the unruly curs
   And whirl them round my head,
And hurl them from Olympus' height,
   To hit the earth, half-dead.

'Yet though you suffered your deserts,
   The sight did not assuage
Either my grief for HERACLES,
   Or my relentless rage!

'Had you not cajoled the wild winds
   My plans to set astray,
Driving his ship so far as Cos
   Three hundred miles away?

'I rescued my exhausted son,
   Leading him by the hand
To Argos where fine horses graze,
   His own delightful land—

'The ugly story I repeat,
   False wife, to rouse your fears
That this new treasonable trick
   May end in floods of tears!'

Hera shuddered and swore by Earth, Heaven, and the tumbling waters of Styx—the greatest and most terrible oath used on Olympus—also by Zeus' own sacred head, and their marriage bed to which she always remained faithful, that Poseidon had not taken the field against the Trojans at her desire. He was acting, she declared, on an impulse of pity for the hard-pressed Greeks, and had he consulted her, she would have advised him to obey his elder brother Zeus implicitly.

Zeus smiled. 'If we are now at last of one heart and mind,' he said, 'my stubborn brother Poseidon will soon come round to our way of thinking. But please prove your sincerity by sending Iris here from Olympus; I shall make her order Poseidon off the field. Also, while you are about it, send me Phoebus Apollo; he can revive Hector, heal his injury, and return him safe and sound to the fighting line. My plans are these: Hector the Bright-Helmed must cause a panic among the Greeks, and pursue them once more, with slaughter, as far as the row of ships commanded by Achilles, son of Peleus; and Achilles must rouse his noble friend Patroclus to defend them; and Patroclus must kill a number of Trojans and Trojan allies, including my own son King Sarpedon; and Hector must kill Patroclus; and, finally, Achilles must avenge Patroclus by killing Hector. That will be a turning-point in this war: I shall then let Agamemnon's troops start a new offensive, which can proceed unchecked until Athene shows them how to capture Troy. Meanwhile, I continue implacable in my anger against the Greeks. All Olympus is warned not to assist them before I have fulfilled the promise I made when the Silver-Footed Goddess Thetis caught hold of my knees and implored me to honour her son Achilles; for I confirmed it with my divine nod.'

Hera flew obediently down the slopes of Ida, heading towards Mount Olympus.

> Safe home the seasoned traveller names
> A foreign town— 'Ah,' he exclaims,
> 'That charming spot! I wish I were
> No longer here, but once more there.'
> Then other towns he calls to mind,
> His thoughts run swifter than the wind
> And, though his body does not move,
> Revisit every scene they love.

In the same way, Hera needed merely to think of Olympus, and there she was: entering the banqueting hall of Zeus' Palace. Her fellow-Immortals rose in welcome, and offered cups of nectar. She took a cup from Themis the Fair-Cheeked, who had run to meet her, inquiring: 'Goddess, what makes you look so thoroughly out of sorts? Has Zeus been uttering more of his threats?'

'Do not question me on so painful a subject, Themis!' replied Hera. 'You know well enough how vain and stubborn he can be.

But now let the divine banquet begin, and I shall announce Zeus' brutal decisions. It is most improbable that you gods will like them, even such few as are unaffected by this crisis and keep a hearty appetite for food and drink. Nor, I believe, will many mortals like them, either.'

Hera mounted her throne amid a hush of foreboding, smiled sardonically, drew her dark eye-brows together in an indignant frown, and said: 'We are fools if we give vent to our rage! None of us can hinder Zeus' schemes, or dissuade him from them. He cares nothing for us, but sits apart and makes light of our feelings, convinced of his own absolute pre-eminence. We must therefore resignedly accept whatever sorrow he chooses to cause. Ares, for instance, has suffered a cruel loss: dear Prince Ascalaphus, whom he claims as his son, fell in battle today!'

Ares slapped his muscular thighs with the flat of both hands, exclaiming bitterly: 'Fellow-Olympians, do not blame me if I go off at once and avenge Ascalaphus; even though Zeus may see fit to throw a thunderbolt at my head and leave me out-stretched among the corpses on that dusty, blood-soaked shore.' He shouted orders for his chariot-team to be yoked.

The quarrel between Zeus and the other Immortals would have flared up again, had not Athene, terrified of what might happen, sprung up suddenly and darted through the door in pursuit of the impetuous Ares. He was already harnessing his horses, Fear and Terror. Athene snatched the helmet from his head, the shield from his shoulder, the spear from his fist and, flinging them away, shrieked: 'You are mad, Ares, that is a fact! You have deaf ears, an addled brain, and no sense of awe! Surely you heard Hera's report on her latest interview? Why cause further mischief and make the rest of us suffer for your foolishness? Forgetting about Trojans and Greeks, Zeus will seethe with rage, pursue you back to Olympus, and man-handle each of us in turn—whether innocent or guilty. Show a little restraint! Sit down, and swallow your anger at Ascalaphus' death; after all, many a tougher champion than he has fallen in this war, and will yet fall. It is no easy matter to preserve the lives of every god's son or grandson.' While Athene was subduing Ares, Hera asked Phoebus Apollo and Iris the Golden-

Winged to step outside. There she told them: 'Zeus demands your immediate attendance on Mount Ida; you are to obey his orders without fail, however unpleasant they may be.'

As soon as she had resumed her seat in the hall, Apollo and Iris flew swiftly to Gargarus, where they found the fragrant golden cloud still arched above Zeus, and awaited his desires.

Pleased by their promptness in acting on Hera's message, Zeus turned to Iris. 'Here is a warning for Prince Poseidon,' he said. 'You must be careful to deliver it correctly.

> "Break off the fight, POSEIDON,
>   And prove your awe of me
> By soaring into Heaven
>   Or plunging into Sea!
>
> "But if this order irks you,
>   Consider well and long
> Whether it can be prudent,
>   Although your limbs are strong,
>
> "To challenge ZEUS your brother,
>   Almighty and First-born,
> Whom no god in Olympus
>   But you dares treat with scorn!" '

Iris immediately took off for Troy.

> North Wind, born in the bright air,
> Hail or snow from clouds you tear . . .

but the speed of whirling snowflakes or pelting hailstones was nothing compared with that of Iris as she swooped to Poseidon's feet. 'Dark-Haired Embracer of the Earth,' said she. 'I carry an urgent warning from Zeus the Shield-Bearer.' Then she repeated her message in Zeus' exact words.

'Damnation take him!' Poseidon answered. 'How presumptuous, to address me so! He forgets that I rank as highly as he does. There were three of us divine brothers: Zeus, myself, and Hades, sons of Rhea by our father Cronus. After Cronus' removal, we divided his kingdom into four parts—Earth, Sky, Sea and Hell. Earth, with

Mount Olympus, was held jointly by all of us, but we drew lots for the remaining three parts. I won the grey Sea; the murky Underworld fell to Hades: which left Zeus the Sky and its clouds. I therefore protest against Zeus' bullying. He should stay quietly in his own domain and not try to scare me into submission by violent threats of violence. Let us keep these for his sons and daughters, who owe him natural obedience.'

'Poseidon, Embracer of the Earth,' pleaded Iris, 'must I really convey this rude, stubborn message to Zeus? Could you not perhaps soften it, like a good fellow? I need hardly remind you that the Furies always support the elder brother in a quarrel about authority.'

Poseidon gave way. 'I thank you, Iris,' he exclaimed. 'What a pleasure it is when a messenger shows common sense! You must pardon my heat: scoldings from Zeus, to whom Fate has assigned an equal inheritance with me, are not easy to bear. Very well, I shall control my temper and do as he desires. None the less, I can assure you of one thing: that if ever he flouts the combined wishes of myself, Athene the Spoil-Winner, Queen Hera, and the gods Hermes and Hephaestus, by saving Troy from utter destruction, we will never forgive him! Make Zeus understand this!'

Poseidon then dived out of sight into the sea, deserting the Greeks —how sadly they missed his support!—and Zeus turned to Apollo. 'Dear Lord of Archers,' he said, 'your uncle Poseidon has, I see, been wise enough to leave the naval camp. Had he stayed, my anger would have flared up so fiercely that the old gods, who share my father's imprisonment deep down below the horizon, would now be witnessing the inevitable sequel. Still, I am glad for both our sakes that he obeyed; his defiance would have forced a pretty hard tussle on me. Here, take my Aegis, shake it at the Greeks, and scare them silly! I entrust glorious Hector to your care: rouse in him such battle-fury that he drives his enemies through their rows of ships and back to the edge of the Hellespont. I will then create a diversion, during which the Greeks can recover their breath.'

Apollo glided from Gargarus like a falcon, the swiftest bird known, and one hated by doves. He found Prince Hector in better spirits: no sooner had Zeus thought about him than he sat up, recognized his comrades, and began to breathe more easily.

Apollo addressed Hector: 'Why so far from the fighting, son of Priam? You look sick and shaken. What happened?'

Hector answered faintly: 'Your questions do me honour, gentle god. As I stood killing Greeks close to the uppermost row of ships, a boulder thrown by Great Ajax struck me high on the breast and checked my advance. Everyone feared that I would gasp out my life and visit Hades' kingdom before the day was over. But who are you, and how did this incident escape your notice?'

'Courage!' cried Apollo. 'Zeus the Son of Cronus, from his seat on Mount Ida sends you a powerful ally, one who has long protected the Citadel of Troy and yourself: me, Phoebus Apollo the Golden-Bladed! So prepare for a chariot charge against Agamemnon's fleet. You can count on me to fly ahead, smoothe your course, and spread panic among the Greek leaders.'

Apollo then gave Hector enormous strength.

> A stallion on pearl-barley fed,
>   A nimble horse of noble breed,
> Has burst the halter-rope and fled
>   From his full manger at full speed.

> He runs in pride with streaming mane,
>   Towards waters that will cool his rage,
> And whinnies at the mares again
>   In their accustomed pasturage . . .

Hector's movements were equally vigorous: he re-joined his chariot-fighters and organized a new attack.

The Greeks were still pursuing the Trojans with swords and spears, bladed at either end of the shaft, when suddenly they became aware that Hector had taken the field again. At once every man's heart sank to his sandals.

> Peasants chase behind their pack
> On a hart's or a goat's track,
> Scrambling up the wooded hill,
> Gay and venturesome until

At a turning of the path,
Hark! a bearded lion's wrath,
Roused by clamour of the chase,
Sounds a threat they will not face.

Hector's appearance proved no less disconcerting to the Greeks. Thoas, son of Andraemon, an Aetolian hero—famous for his spear-throwing, his deadliness in close combat, and a debating skill which few of Agamemnon's younger Councillors could surpass—was the first to remark upon it. 'Alas,' he cried, 'I can hardly believe my eyes! We all thought that Hector had been killed by Great Ajax; but look, he has cheated Fate, and is back at the head of his army again! Some god must have revived him, and I fear that, not content with the damage already done, he hopes to inflict yet more on us. I suspect Zeus himself of working this miracle. Now, take my advice: let the common soldiers retire in good order, while we champions form a barrier and prevent his getting loose among them! Inspired though he seems to be, we may yet fend him off.'

Thoas' suggestion was approved. The common soldiers fell back, while Great Ajax, King Idomeneus, Teucrus, and Meges, each supported by a group of chosen comrades, stood fast.

Hector's free-striding team led the chariot charge, and in front of him flew Apollo, his shoulders wrapped in cloud, carrying the Aegis, a bright, dreadful, shaggy-fringed shield, which Hephaestus had given Zeus as a means of terrorizing mortals.

The Greeks closed their ranks and greeted Hector's chariotry with a roar of defiance. Arrows leaped from bow-strings, and spears from powerful hands. Some found their hoped-for billets in the flesh of Trojans; most of them, however, fell short and struck only barren soil. The exchange of missiles was equal and both sides suffered casualties so long as Apollo held the Aegis steady; but when he shook it, yelling, at the Greeks, they were reduced to impotence.

Lioness and lion leap
    On a herd of cows by night,
Or a numerous flock of sheep
(Where's that shepherd? Fast asleep),
    Scaring them to frantic flight.

That is how the Greeks fled at the approach of Apollo and Hector!
Pressing on the ruck, Hector killed a Boeotian nobleman named
Stichius, also Archesilaus, an intimate friend of King Menestheus
the Athenian. Prince Aeneas accounted for Medon, Little Ajax's
bastard brother who, after killing a kinsman of his step-mother
Eriopis, had taken refuge at Phylace—far from Locri, the home of
his father Oïleus—and now commanded the Methonians. Another
of Aeneas' victims was the Athenian leader Iasus, son of Sphelus and
grandson of Bucolus. Polydamas killed Mecisteus; Polites killed
Echius; Prince Agenor killed Clonius; and Deiochus, fighting in the
front-line, had just turned to run when Paris speared him clean
through the lungs beneath the shoulderblade.

While these Trojans paused to harvest their spoils, the Greeks
dashed into the fosse and scurried hither and thither, searching for a
breach in the palisade which would give them access to the rampart.
Hector's voice rang out: 'Leave those bloody spoils until later! At-
tack the ships! Any man who skulks or dawdles shall die; nor shall
his corpse be honoured with a funeral pyre. Dogs will devour it in full
view of the Citadel!'

He whipped at his team, and sounded the charge. The chariot-
fighters, now lined up on either flank, echoed his shout and galloped
forward; for Apollo had made them a bridge from the broken parapet
of the fosse. Over this bridge, wide as the champion cast in a spear-
throwing contest, rolled the chariots, and Apollo, Zeus' Aegis proudly
flaunted, made their course smooth.

> A little boy, laughing for glee,
> Builds castles by the summer sea,
> Then exercises foot and hand
> To scatter them in clouds of sand . . .

With equal ease and merriment, Apollo kicked down an ample
length of the rampart and drove the Greeks, who had taken such
trouble to construct it, panic-stricken back. They halted at the ships,
jabbering to one another, or addressing Heaven in vehement prayer.
Old Nestor, Guardian of the Greeks, prayed memorably, as follows:

'Great ZEUS, have mercy on us,
      Who never fail to heap
Your altar with the thighbones
      Of oxen and fat sheep!

'Remember your firm promise,
      When once these Greeks and I
Prepared the voyage Troywards
      And bade our homes goodbye,

'That to our lovely cornlands
      We should return in joy—
Keep faith with us, Shield-Bearer,
      And bring defeat on Troy!'

A loud roll of thunder acknowledged the old man's supplication; but the Trojans read this as a sign favourable to themselves, and pressed on more recklessly yet. Their chariots neared the ruined rampart, and swept across it towards the fleet:

      Storm-driven waves wap on a galley's side,
      Swamping both deck and bulwarks in their pride.

They engaged the uppermost row of ships, now manned by Greeks brandishing the huge, jointed pikes which were kept aboard for use in sea-battles.

Meanwhile, Patroclus had been laying a poultice of herbs on Eurypylus' wound, and talking cheerfully to him; but when he heard the Trojans hurtle past, he groaned, pummelled his thighs in exasperation, and cried: 'Eurypylus, despite your urgent need of me I cannot stay; savage fighting has broken out again. Your charioteer must take my place while I hurry off and try to make Achilles change his mind. Perhaps with Heaven's help I shall succeed; there is no persuasion so strong as a friend's!' Patroclus was already through the doorway before he had finished speaking.

The Greeks put up a stout resistance, yet could not drive off the smaller Trojan force; neither could the Trojans dislodge the Greeks:

      ATHENE's cunning hands have made
      New tools for the ship-builder's trade:
      Such as the line, stretched by a weight,
      Which helps them cut their planking straight.

Level as the sides of a plank, taut as a carpenter's line—that was how the battle went. Hector, still inspired by Apollo, sought out Great Ajax, but failed to fire the ship which he held. Thus the contest remained indecisive, though Ajax thrust a spear into the breast of Caletor, son of Clytius, and sent him crashing down, torch in hand. Grieved at his cousin's death, Hector shouted: 'Trojans, Lycians, tough Dardanians, fight on fiercely and prevent the Greeks from seizing Caletor's armour!'

The spear he cast missed Ajax and caught Lycophron, son of Mastor, just above the ear, tumbling him over the stern of his vessel. Ajax shuddered at the sight, for this was the Lycophron who had fled from Cythera, Aphrodite's sacred island, after murdering a neighbour, and found service with him as his squire. 'Teucrus,' cried Ajax, 'Hector has killed our comrade Lycophron, whom at home in Salamis we honoured like a father! Where is the bow that Phoebus Apollo gave you? And where are your death-dealing arrows?'

Ajax's half-brother Teucrus ran forward, displaying his bow, and engaged the Trojans. Cleitus, the noble son of Prince Polydamas' friend Peisenor, had driven up to assist Hector; but none of his loyal henchmen could save him from destruction. As he busied himself with the team, one of Teucrus' arrows pierced the nape of his neck and he fell lifeless to the dust. His horses backed, rattling the empty chariot, which Prince Polydamas at once asked Astynous, son of Protiaon, to mount and hold in readiness for him; then he resumed the fight. Teucrus took careful aim at Hector, and if he had shot, the battle would have ended suddenly. But Zeus, who was guarding Hector, denied Teucrus any such glory by snapping his bow-string. The bronze-headed arrow fled wide, and the bow dropped on deck. 'Alas!' he cried, trembling for disappointment. 'Heaven is against us! Some god tore the bow from my grasp and broke the fresh, well-twisted bow-string with which I fitted it, only this morning, in expectation of a hard day's work.'

Ajax answered: 'Yes, brother! Since the god has put your bow and arrows out of commission, throw them away and show an example to our men by using a spear and shield! The Trojans won the last bout, but it will give me great pleasure to make them pay dearly for these hulls.'

Teucrus hastened to his hut, where he abandoned the bow in favour of a bull's hide shield four layers thick, and a handsome helmet surmounted by a terrifying horsehair plume. Then he chose a huge, well-sharpened spear, hurried aboard Ajax's vessel again, and stood at his side.

Hector, who had seen the bow-string snap, shouted: 'Trojans, Lycians, and tough Dardanians! Fight on, fight on savagely! Zeus has disarmed the finest Greek archer alive. When the Thunderer glorifies his favourites, or confounds their foes, he does so plainly enough. Close your ranks, capture those ships, and if anyone gets wounded, why, that will be his fate . . . And if he falls in defence of Troy, and in defence of his wife, children, house and lands—oh, to rid this shore of Greeks!—that will be a heroic end.' Hector's words made the Trojans redouble their efforts.

'Shame on you, comrades!' yelled Ajax. 'It is all or nothing now—either victory, or utter ruin! Do not think that, if Hector the Bright-Helmed destroys our fleet, we shall simply walk home by dry land! You heard him haranguing his army. He was inviting them not to a dance but to an act of arson. Hold fast, and repel boarders! What other choice have you? It is far better to risk instant death than be slowly and miserably driven into the sea by an inferior force.' Ajax's words made the Greeks redouble their efforts likewise.

Hector killed the Phocian Prince Schedius, son of Perimedes; and Ajax, Antenor's son Laodamas, commander of the Trojan infantry; while Polydamas cut down Otus of Cyllene, a resolute Epeian, brother-in-arms to Meges, son of Phyleus. Meges rushed to take vengeance on Polydamas, whom Apollo was protecting, but he ducked and let the spear hurtle past. It entered Croesmus' breast, and Meges immediately began stripping his corpse. Then along came Dolops, son of Lampus and grandson of Laomedon, the bravest member of a brave family, and breached Meges' shield with a spear-thrust, though not his armour: for Meges wore a weapon-proof mail corslet, which his father Phyleus had once been given by King Euphetes of Elis, during a visit to Ephyra on the River Selleëis. In return, Meges lunged at Dolops' face; but did no more than shear off the new, scarlet-dyed horsehair plume that topped his helmet. As Dolops was about to deal a decisive blow, King Menelaus speared him through the shoulder from behind, thus saving Meges' life.

When Meges and Menelaus coveted the spoils, Hector called on all members of the Trojan royal house—Hicetaon's son Melanippus in particular—to drive them off. This Melanippus had been breeding cattle at tranquil Percote before the war, but news of the Greek invasion brought him straight back to Troy, where he won high praise for his soldierly conduct. He lived next door to King Priam, who honoured him as if he were one of his own sons.

'Melanippus!' Hector cried. 'Two princes are despoiling our cousin Dolops! Does the sight not enrage you? This is no longer a war fought at a distance—the Greeks investing Troy, we shooting casually from the walls—it has become a death struggle, man against man. Follow me!'

Hector ran forward, and burly Melanippus followed at his heels.

Great Ajax cried: 'Hold fast, Greeks! By shaming one another into heroism, you will stand a good chance of survival, and none of disgrace.'

His cheering companions formed a ring of bronze around the ship (which Zeus, nevertheless, encouraged the Trojans to break), and Menelaus begged Antilochus for a display of his gallantry. 'Son of Nestor,' he shouted, 'as the youngest, most agile, and strongest of us champions, make a sortie, and strike down a Trojan if you can!'

Menelaus withdrew as Antilochus sprang out of the Greek ranks, glanced shrewdly in every direction, and cast his glittering spear. The Trojans scattered, but he had taken careful aim: struck near the right nipple, Melanippus fell dying, and Antilochus rushed on, like a hound retrieving a wounded fawn, to capture his armour. Then up strode Hector, and:

> The lion, conscious of his crime—
> Killing a herdsman or a hound—
> Deserts his victim, just in time,
> Before the neighbours gather round.

This was how Antilochus slunk away, escaping a shower of missiles; yet turned and faced about when safely among his comrades again.

Ferociously now the Trojans advanced. Zeus, because of the promise he had given the presumptuous Thetis, wished Hector to burn the fleet. Impatient for the sight of a blazing ship, he goaded on the

Trojans and dispirited the Greeks. Hector needed little enough goading: he raged like Ares in a battle-fury, or like a forest fire that sweeps the hills; foam flecked his lips, his eyes glowed beneath menacing brows, and the helmet he wore rattled to the throbbing of his temples.

Indeed, Zeus awarded Hector immortal fame: one hero challenging so many, and not fated to live long, either—since Athene was already trying to hasten his death at the hand of Achilles. He charged the Greek line wherever he found the strongest concentration of troops and the most resplendent armour, but always without success:

> The embattled headland, steep and wide,
> Howled at by storms from every side
> And roared against by swelling seas,
> Cares not for threats as vain as these!

Then a divine light enveloped Hector, and he leaped upon the Greeks—

> The sky grows black.
> A sudden gale
> Bellies the sail.
> Taken aback,
> The sailors shout:
> 'Put her about!
> Look out, beware!
> Here comes a wave
> To dig our grave!'
>
> It strikes them square.
> In foam they flounder,
> And all but founder.

No less dismayed by Hector's leap, the Greeks panicked:

> Our herdsman has not learned the art
>   Of foiling a fierce beast
> That ventures forth with shameless heart
>   Upon fat cows to feast.

Thick on the meads beside a lake
They browse and have no fear,
Whether his post they see him take
In front or in the rear.

But careful watch he does not keep:
Observe their terror now
When the dread lion leaps his leap
And slaughters a fat cow!

Hector's victim, Periphetes the Mycenaean—a son of the notorious herald Copreus, whom King Eurystheus once employed to take Heracles new orders after each of his twelve tasks—did not favour his father; he was a fine athlete, a sturdy fighter, and the most gifted nobleman in Mycenae. Turning to avoid Hector, Periphetes tripped over the rim of the enormous shield he carried and fell, his helmet striking the ground with a clang. As he struggled to rise, Hector speared him in the breast, nor did his men run to rescue him, despite their grief. Though restrained by shame from scattering wildly, Ajax's troops ceased to defend the uppermost row of ships, and darted through them. Forming up in front of the huts built between this row and the next, they shouted at one another: 'Stand fast! Stand fast!'

Nestor appealed to them all by name. 'Quit you like men,' he cried, 'and fear nothing but the contempt of your fellows! Let every soldier remember his wife, his children, his house, his lands, his parents whether living or dead—oh, my lads, prove yourselves heroes, I beseech you, for the sake of your dear ones far away!'

Nestor's words steadied them, the strange mist that had hitherto clouded their eyes rose at Athene's command, and the sun shone again. Now they could see how the battle went—Hector and his savage comrades opposing them, a mass of Trojan infantry ranked in the rear, loth to enter the mêlée; and Great Ajax, alone, defending the abandoned row of ships. He brandished a thirty-foot sea-pike, ringed securely at the joints. But:

The tawny eagle on his rock
Observes below him a bird flock—

It may be swan or goose or crane—
By a broad river in the plain . . .

That eagle's swoop was no swifter than Hector's! He attacked the nearest ship, which happened to be formerly commanded by Protesilaus, the first Greek to die in the war.

Who would then have thought that both sides had been engaged since morning? They fought like fresh troops: the Greeks desperately, the Trojans exultantly, urged forward by Zeus. No arrows or javelins were used: nothing but axes, hatchets, broadswords, and two-bladed spears. Many was the handsomely-hilted sword that fell from the fingers of a dying man or, still in its dark scabbard, from his shoulder; much blood also stained the earth. Hector seized the ship's stern-ornament and clung to it, shouting: 'Trojans, fetch torches, raise your war-cry! Welcome our crowning hour! The Greeks are here in despite of Heaven, and have plagued us year after year, ever since that cowardly Royal Council would not let me lead you out against them. Yet, if Zeus the Far-Sighted then dimmed our wits, he has made amends at last by directing our attack.'

The Trojans fought so fiercely that Ajax's position on the deck of his vessel became untenable. He retired amidships, pike in hand, to a seven-foot-long oarsman's bench. There he stood, beating off all attempts to fire the ship, and yelling: 'Brothers, heroes, favourites of Ares, keep courage! Why pretend that we have a walled city behind us, or allies to march up in support and turn the tide of battle? We are caught on the Trojan plain, far from Greece, the sea at our backs, a savage enemy at our throats. We can do no more than fight, and fight again!'

He scowled defiance, and would dart his spear down whenever he saw a Trojan with a torch trying to obey Hector's orders. He thus killed or wounded a dozen men in succession.

Book Sixteen:

Hector Kills Patroclus

While this struggle beside the ships was in progress, noble Patroclus visited the hut of Achilles the Swift-Footed, and:

> His tears ran down as mournfully as if
> They were some dark stream oozing from a cliff.

Achilles rallied him: 'Why come weeping to me, Patroclus, like a heart-broken little girl to her mother?

> ' "Mother," sobs the pretty creature,
>   Clutching at her gown,
> "Take me with you, pick me up,
>   Carry me to town!"

> 'And the mother, though molested,
>   Has no other choice:
> She obeys that tearful, shrill,
>   Too insistent voice.

'Have you bad news for the Myrmidons, or for me—some private message from Phthia? Your father Menoetius and my father Peleus are both still alive, I trust—if either were reported dead, all we Myrmidons would go into immediate mourning. Or can it be that this slaughter of Agamemnon's army—the just punishment for his unpardonable conduct towards me—provokes your tears? Out with the truth!'

Patroclus replied, groaning: 'Best and bravest of Greeks, do not be angry because I take their ruin to heart. Most of our leading champions have come back wounded: Diomedes, son of Tydeus, Odysseus, and the High King himself. Eurypylus has an arrow in his thigh. The surgeons are overwhelmed with work. Oh, how can I persuade you to relent? May I never be the victim of so disastrous a grudge! What thanks will future generations give you when your fame rests mainly on a refusal to intervene while their fathers were being massacred? Must we still believe that you are a child of noble Peleus and the gentle Thetis? You seem hard-hearted enough to have been sired by the stony cliffs on the tempestuous sea. Possibly your refusal to fight can be explained by some oracle, or by some promise that Zeus made your mother. If so, why should I not lead the Myrmidons as a forlorn hope against the enemy? Please put them under my orders and, while you are about it, lend me your arms. When the Trojans recognize them they may well withdraw, mistaking me for you, and thus allow our comrades time to catch their breath. Hector's men are equally exhausted, and a charge by fresh troops should drive them out of the camp and home again.'

Patroclus little knew what gift he was begging to have bestowed on him: his own violent death. Achilles sighed heavily. 'Patroclus,' he said at length, 'what a speech! No oracle that I am aware of prevents my fighting, nor has Thetis acquainted me with any promise from Zeus; this black mood is due solely to resentment at being robbed by Agamemnon. After all my labours and perils, how could I forgive him for presuming on his power as Commander-in-Chief, though of no higher rank than myself? In carrying off Briseis, my prize of honour, whom I captured at Thebe, he has treated me like a mere camp-follower! Yet no man can stay angry for ever. So, if it is true that the whole male population of Troy has swarmed over the rampart and confined us to this narrow strip of beach, I shall let bygones be bygones, albeit sworn not to fight until the Trojans threaten my flotilla. Very well: borrow my famous armour and lead out the Myrmidons. It is some days, of course, since the Trojans saw the glitter of my helmet, and had Agamemnon offered me decent respect, they would never have ventured so far, but fled in panic at sight of me and filled the river beds with their corpses. Yes, you are right: Diomedes has evidently been put out of action, nor is Agamemnon raising his hateful war-cry. I hear only Hector's yells of encouragement to his Trojans, and their answering cheers as they force the Greeks back. In fact, Patroclus, you had better lose no time. What if they burn the fleet and cut off our retreat?'

Achilles added: 'Now listen carefully! I want you to win me such fame that the Greeks will gladly restore Briseis, and shower splendid gifts on me besides. But once you have driven the Trojans from our camp, go no farther: though Zeus the Thunderer may crown your arms with glory, it will hurt my honour if you yield to ambition or blood-lust and take too much on yourself. Also I foresee the danger that a single-handed pursuit of the enemy towards the city might bring you up against some Olympian or other—Apollo the Archer, for instance, who favours the Trojans. Therefore return, as soon as your main task is finished, and leave the two armies battling on the plain. Ah, if only Father Zeus and Athene and Apollo would let the Trojans kill every one of the Greek champions, except you and me; and then let us slaughter what remained of the Trojans, and capture their Citadel!'

Zeus had decided that Ajax's stand in the galley should be brought to an end while Achilles and Patroclus were conversing. He was hacked or lunged at ceaselessly, and dazed with blows raining on the cheek-pieces of his helmet; the tower-like shield made his shoulder ache. He laboured for breath, sweat bathed his limbs; and at last he could fight no more.

> Tell me, ye gracious MUSES
> Who on Olympus dwell,
> How fire from Trojan torches
> Into that galley fell.

It happened as follows. Hector swung his broadsword and struck Ajax's sea-pike just below the socket, severing the head, which flew off and left him a mere pole to brandish. Ajax now understood that Zeus had withdrawn his favour and was helping Troy; so he leaped down and rejoined his comrades in their new line of defence. The Trojans could at last send flames coursing along the galley from bow to stern, and Achilles, slapping his thighs for vexation, cried: 'Look, Patroclus! A ship is on fire! You must intervene at once and protect our flotilla, if we are ever to return. Buckle on my armour, and I will parade the Myrmidons.'

Patroclus buckled on a handsome pair of greaves with silver clasps, and Achilles' strong corslet, twinkling like the starry sky. Next, he borrowed his baldric and powerful silver-studded sword; also his huge shield, and bright, tough helmet topped by a menacing horsehair plume. Finally he chose two stout spears of suitable weight and length, rejecting the extravagantly large lance which Achilles alone could wield—this lethal weapon, lopped from an ash-tree growing on a peak of Mount Pelion, had been presented by Cheiron the Centaur to King Peleus.

Then Patroclus asked Automedon, whom he admired and trusted as a fighter, to yoke and harness Achilles' divine team, the wind-swift Xanthus and Balius—out of Podarge the Harpy by West Wind, and both foaled near the Ocean Stream. Automedon harnessed a third horse, using a side-trace; namely Pedasus, a stallion captured at Eëtion's city of Thebe and, although not of divine breed, exceptionally fast.

Achilles went around the Myrmidons' huts, calling them out on parade.

> The wolves dined well today
>   High on the wooded hill,
> An antlered stag their prey:
>   I'll swear they ate their fill!
>
> Their jaws with blood are red
>   As in a pack they go,
> Most sumptuously fed,
>   To where dark waters flow.
>
> Thin-tongued they lie and lap
>   The surface of a pool
> And belching, chap to chap,
>   Their throats at leisure cool.

It was with a similar sense of well-being that, fresh from their long holiday, the Myrmidon chariotry and infantry formed up behind Patroclus. Their flotilla of fifty ships, each manned by a crew of fifty, had five detachments. Menestheus of the Shining Corslet, son of

Achilles' lovely sister Polydora, commanded the leading detachment. His putative father, Borus, son of Perieres, had paid King Peleus lavish bride-gifts for Polydora's hand; but his real father was the tireless River-god Spercheius, a son of Zeus.

Another captain of divine parentage commanded the second detachment: namely Eudorus, son of Phylas' dancing daughter Polymele. Hermes the Gift-Bringer, famous for having killed the hundred-eyed giant Argus, had fallen in love with Polymele, singling her out from the Archer-goddess Artemis' troop of singers, and gone straight up to her bedroom. When Eudorus was born, Echecles, son of Actor, demanded Polymele's hand, offering lavish bride-gifts, and married her; but old Phylas took charge of Eudorus (who proved an outstanding athlete and soldier) and brought him up as tenderly as if he had been his son.

Brave Peisander, son of Maemalus, the best spearman, apart from Patroclus, in the whole force, commanded the third detachment. King Phoenix commanded the fourth detachment; and Alcimedon, son of Laerces, the fifth.

Achilles inspected his parade. 'Myrmidons,' he said firmly, 'do not let me find you repudiating your recent fierce threats against the Trojans, which, by the way, came joined with taunts that my mother must have nursed me on gall, instead of milk—I was so hard-hearted. You agreed that it would even be better to sail home than stay here, shamefully restrained from battle. I cannot forget those impudent words. Now, however, a great task confronts you, such as should warm your hearts: to clear this camp of enemy troops. Face it like men!'

Enthusiastically the Myrmidons closed their ranks. Shield to shield, shoulder to shoulder, plume to plume, they were as tightly wedged as the carefully hewn stones of a storm-proof house-wall. Patroclus and his comrade Automedon posted themselves at their head, in full armour and eager to fight.

Achilles visited his hut and went to a painted chest in which, before he came away from Phthia, his mother Thetis, had stored warm tunics, cloaks for bad weather, and rugs. Here he kept a splendid cup, strictly reserved for libations poured to Zeus—he alone might handle it. Taking out the cup, Achilles used brimstone and

clear water to purify the bowl and, after cleansing his own hands,
filled it with bright wine. Then he stood in the centre of the parade-
ground, poured Zeus a libation, fixed his eyes on Heaven, and prayed:

> 'Pelasgian ZEUS, you live and move
> In chill Dodona's awesome grove,
> Surrounded by your Sellian priests—
> They lie upon the ground like beasts
> With unwashed legs, and from the sound
> Of leaves true oracles expound.
> You are the god who pitied me,
> Who honourably made good my plea
> By humbling Agamemnon's pride;
> O now, once more, be at my side,
> While here I wait unarmed, and send
> Patroclus out, who calls me friend,
> My warlike Myrmidons to lead
> Against the Trojans.
>   Deign to speed
> His victory, O All-Seeing One;
> Vouchsafe that when the fight is done
> Hector will grant that my dear squire
> Burns with his own unaided fire:
> Not waiting for me on the field,
> To help him shine with spear and shield;
> Also, that when from this our fleet
> The routed enemy retreat,
> He shall march back across the plain
> Unwounded to my arms again.'

Zeus, who had been listening attentively, granted no more than
the first part of Achilles' prayer; he allowed Patroclus to drive Hector
from the camp, but not to march back unwounded.

Achilles replaced the cup in its chest, and paused at the doorway of
his hut, anxious to watch the Myrmidons' performance.

> Wasps that build their fragile nest
> By the track can prove a pest:
> If a careless passer-by
> Treads too near it, out they fly,

> Buzzing loud with fortitude
> In defence of their young brood.
> Still more strident are their tones
> When small boys come flinging stones:
> Furiously they attack
> All who venture up the track.

Like wasps, the Myrmidons streamed out in defence of their ships, Patroclus turning to yell: 'Forward, comrades! Show what you can do! Teach the High King how blind he was to dishonour our great commander Achilles, son of Peleus—the finest fighter in this army, as you are its finest contingent!'

The frenzied Myrmidons leaped upon the Trojans, who at once recognized Achilles' well-known armour, chariot, and driver. Feeling certain that he had forgotten his grudge and come to terms with Agamemnon, they wavered, glancing around them to make sure that a line of retreat lay open.

Patroclus drove straight for a group of Trojans massed beside the burning galley, and hurled at Pyraechmes: this bold and capable Paeonian king had brought a large force of chariotry from Amydon on the Macedonian river Axius. The spear transfixed Pyraechmes' right shoulder, and he fell groaning to the dust. With wild shouts of dismay the Paeonians retired behind the uppermost row of ships. Some Myrmidons pursued them, others extinguished the fire before the galley was more than half consumed; and a fearful din went up.

> Raise the gloomy mist that shrouds
> Heaven, O Guardian of the Clouds!
> Sweet it is when, clear displayed,
> Spur and promontory and glade
> (Solace to the wearied eye)
> Edge the infinite blue sky.

The Greeks were glad to suffocate the blaze, which might have shrouded their whole camp in smoke; but did not pause to look about them, for though the Trojan line had been driven a short distance back, it still held. Numerous hand-to-hand combats between champions ensued. First, Patroclus speared Areilycus in the thigh, breaking the bone, and sent him flat on his face. Next, King Menelaus struck Thoas on the right breast past the rim of his shield; he died at once. Then Meges son of Phyleus stopped Amphiclus' rush by a deadly lunge at the bulging muscles of his thigh.

Nestor's sons, Antilochus and Thrasymedes, engaged two brothers named Atymnius and Maris, close friends of Sarpedon, and descendants of the Lycian King Amisodarus, who reared the monstrous Chimaera, later destroyed by Perseus. Antilochus thrust Atymnius in the side, toppling him over; Maris ran forward furiously to defend the corpse; but a sharp blow from Thrasymedes crippled his arm, and he soon caught up with Atymnius on the gloomy road underground.

Cleobolus, knocked down in the mêlée, yet unhurt, was struggling to his feet; Little Ajax swung a sword and warmed the blade in blood from Cleobolus' severed neck. Peneleos and Lycon cast at each other, but both missed their mark. Lycon then broke his sword-blade off at the hilt against the base of Peneleos' crest; Peneleos struck home behind Lycon's ear and left the head dangling by a strip of skin. Meriones of Crete pursued Acamas, wounding him mortally in the shoulder while he tried to remount his chariot. King Idomeneus drove a spear through Erymas' mouth and out at the back of his skull, dislodging the teeth. Blood filled his eye-sockets, nostrils and mouth as the black cloud of death covered him.

> Marauding wolves observe a flock
> That on the hillside feeds;
> Their shepherd, piping on a rock,
> The danger hardly heeds,
> Thus each bold wolf can make his bid
> For hauling off a lamb or kid.

The Trojan rank and file, seeing so many of their champions killed, fled like sheep from wolves. Hector also retired. Great Ajax made several attempts to kill him, but this experienced soldier protected his shoulders with a broad bull's hide shield and let the spears and arrows whistle past. He knew well that the tide of battle had turned and, since the Trojans were streaming away in disorderly flight, like wisps of clouds when a storm blows up, he himself headed slowly back for Troy, across the bridge heaped by Apollo. Many of his comrades, however, reached the fosse at a point where its banks remained steep. Their chariot-poles broke off in the descent, and the horses bolted.

Patroclus went after Hector, shouting encouragement to his Myrmidons, and taunting the Trojans who were now scattered in wild confusion and hidden by a tall dust-cloud. He charged at the largest mass of fugitives, tumbling down chariot-fighters, driving over their dead bodies, and wrecking their chariots. Then he guided Achilles' immortal team in vain pursuit of Hector.

> The expected rains are falling now
>   To enrich the good black soil,
> For thus in autumn ZEUS rewards
>   The honest ploughman's toil.
>
> But hold, enough! without a pause
>   In prodigal downflow
> Rain fills the torrents over-full,
>   And through the vale below
>
> Enormous floods of water pour
>   Cascading to the sea;
> Our orchards from the roots they rend
>   And with our farms make free.
>
> The cause is daylight clear: Great ZEUS
>   Detests the City Hall.
> Our magistrates are godless rogues
>   And ruffians, one and all!

The flight of the Trojan chariotry was no less precipitous; yet Patroclus headed off several squadrons, forcing them into an angle between the rampart and the river. There, in vengeance of his dead comrades, he slaughtered them by the score. First he killed Pronous, spearing his exposed right breast. Next, he lunged at Thestor, son of Enops, who, out of his senses with fear, had let fall the reins and sat crouched on the chariot floor. The spear pierced his jaw, and lodged so fast among the roots of his teeth that, in trying to tug it free, Patroclus pulled him gaping over the rails. It was as when:

> Perched on a rock with glittering hook and line
> The lusty angler gaffs a fish divine.

He then hurled a boulder at Euryalus' helmet, which crushed his skull. One after the other, he dispatched Erymas, Amphoterus, Epaltes, Tlepolemus, son of Damastor, Echius, Pyris, Ipheus, Euippus, and Polymelus, son of Argeas; all of them Lycians, as their loose-woven tunics plainly showed.

King Sarpedon, aghast at Patroclus' progress, cried: 'For shame, men of Lycia, what are you about? Take heart now! I will myself engage this unknown Greek champion who has destroyed so many of our gallant soldiers.' Sarpedon thereupon sprang to the ground, fully armed; and Patroclus did the same. These two heroes flew at each other like ospreys—

> With crooked talons and curved beaks they fight,
> Those ospreys, screaming from a dreadful height!

Zeus watched them pityingly, and observed to Hera: 'Alas, that my beloved son Sarpedon Patroclus must kill! It is his doom. None the less, I have a good mind to defy the Fates by snatching him alive out of this duel, and setting him down safely in his own rich land.'

Hera protested: 'Most revered Son of Cronus, your admission appals me! So you consider snatching a mortal from the death to which the Fates long ago sentenced him? Do as you please, of course; but none of your fellow-Olympians will approve. Indeed, I warn you solemnly that any such intervention would scandalize most members of your household: they have beloved sons by the dozen still battling before Troy, and all want to save their own doomed darlings. You would be a fool, in fact, to whisk Sarpedon away alive, however deeply you may deplore his end. Why not let him succumb, but afterwards send Death and Sweet Sleep to carry the corpse to Lycia, where the royal family and their friends can bury it in a hero's barrow under the customary pillar?'

Father Zeus, taking Hera's advice, foreshadowed King Sarpedon's death by releasing an ominous shower of blood-red rain.

The two champions approached each other, and Patroclus killed

Sarpedon's charioteer Thrasymelus, a famous fighter, with a spear-cast just above the groin. Sarpedon's return cast missed Patroclus, but wounded his trace-horse Pedasus in the right shoulder. Pedasus foundered, and the squeals of agony he raised frightened the two divinely-born team-mates. They reared and baulked, entangling the reins and making their yoke creak. Automedon leaped from the chariot, sword in hand, and cut the side-trace; at once they grew manageable again. As Sarpedon flung another spear, which harmlessly skimmed past Patroclus' shield, he felt himself struck on the midriff, close to the heart.

> Shipwrights with sharp axes go
> Up the hillside, to and fro,
> Seeking timber suitable
> For a merchant-vessel's hull.
> Silver poplar, pine and oak
> Fall beneath their deadly stroke.

So fell Sarpedon, and lay stretched on the plain, clawing the bloody dust in his despair:

> The tawny lion down did pull
> A noble-hearted bull;
> Dying among the cows, he lay
> And roared his life away.

'Dearest Glaucus,' Sarpedon moaned, 'show what a magnificent soldier you are! Collect your comrades, draw swords, and defend my body. If Patroclus is permitted to strip it of armour, you will never escape the disgrace, not even in old age! To work, Glaucus, and restore the day!'

These were the last words he spoke before death glazed his eyes. Patroclus set one foot on his breast, for purchase, and tugged at the spear, bringing out the midriff with it, and giving the soul a convenient egress. Lycian men-at-arms restrained Sarpedon's horses from taking off the now masterless chariot; but Glaucus was in a quandary. Though he longed to protect the royal corpse against despoilment, the arrow-wound inflicted by Teucrus earlier that day had crippled his right arm. Gripping the shoulder to ease its pain, he humbly prayed to Phoebus Apollo:

'Wherever you may be,
    In Lycia's lovely land
    Or on the Trojan strand
Wandering free
APOLLO, turn to me!

'Look where the best of kings,
    My lord Sarpedon, lies!
    (ZEUS closed his anguished eyes.)
Of all dire things
His death my heart most wrings!

'Yet how may I go near
    Who cannot grip my sword
    Nor any help afford?
Physician dear,
Heal me, as I pray here!

'Ay, in this hour of need
    PHOEBUS, I turn to you,
    As all good Lycians do.
Watch how I bleed!
O stanch the flow with speed!'

On hearing Glaucus' prayer, Apollo at once stanched the flow of blood, eased the pain, and restored his courage. Glaucus felt the change and, after urging his Lycians to defend their dead King's corpse, strode joyfully in search of Polydamas, son of Panthous, Prince Agenor, Aeneas and Hector. Finding them at last, he cried: 'Hector, pray remember your allies! They marched far from their homes to fight for Troy, and are now being slaughtered. Would you leave them to their fate? King Sarpedon has been killed by Patroclus! Come, meet anger with anger: protect his corpse from despoilment! These Myrmidons are bent on avenging the Greeks who fell beside the ships.'

This news caused Hector and his companions bitter grief. Sarpedon, although no native of Troy, was the best fighter in the large allied force he led, and regarded as a mainstay of the city's defence. Hector headed an immediate charge to where the dead man lay;

and at the same time Patroclus summoned Great and Little Ajax.

'Friends,' he said, 'I have speared King Sarpedon, the first Lycian to scale the rampart, and would be glad of your help. We must counter all attempts to rescue his corpse, and strip it naked ourselves. Be as brave as ever you were, or even braver!'

Great and Little Ajax needed no encouragement. The struggle for Sarpedon's spoils became a full-scale battle between Glaucus and his Lycians strengthened by Hector's Trojans, and Patroclus' Myrmidons strengthened by the Locrians and Salaminians. Arms clashed, voices roared, and Zeus, to glorify his dead son, drew a cloak of darkness about this cruel combat.

The Trojans killed a leading Myrmidon: Epeigeus, son of Prince Agacles, formerly ruler of Magnesian Budeion. Epeigeus, having murdered a kinsman, had gone as a suppliant to King Peleus and his queen, the Goddess Thetis, who welcomed him at their court and later sent him off to war in the company of their son Achilles. As Epeigeus caught hold of Sarpedon's feet, Hector struck his helmet with a boulder, crushing the skull, and tumbling him over the corpse that he coveted. Patroclus pressed forward to avenge Epeigeus:

> Like a gier-falcon whose sharp beak and claws
> Scatter a flight of starlings or jackdaws . . .

and hurled another boulder, which hit Sthenelaus, son of Ithae-menes, on the neck, killing him at once.

Hector and his Trojans then gave ground for the distance of a spear-cast—a long cast, such as might be made at an athletic contest, or in the desperation of battle. Glaucus, pursued by Bathycles, son of Chalcon, the wealthiest Myrmidon on the field, whirled about and lunged at his breast. Bathycles fell with a crash. The delighted Trojans rallied behind Glaucus and drove the unhappy Greeks back to their starting point. Meriones the Cretan went for Laogonus, whose father Onetor, High Priest to Idaean Zeus, was given semi-divine honours at Troy; his spear pierced Laogonus under the jaw-bone, and killed him instantly. Aeneas cast at Meriones, who was rushing up, but he ducked and the javelin whistled over his shield, to stick quivering in the soil. 'Meriones,' Aeneas cried angrily, 'you may consider yourself lucky that I did not end your dancing days!'

'Yes,' Meriones replied, 'though the son of a goddess, you are none the less human, and can hardly expect to destroy all your opponents. If ever I am granted the good fortune to push a spear into you, no skill nor courage will keep your soul from entering the kingdom of Hades; and your fame will be mine!'

Patroclus scolded Meriones. 'Why bandy words with Trojans?' he cried. 'Insults cannot drive them off. You must first destroy more of their champions! Reserve your verbal thrusts for Council meetings, where they are in order, and try spear-thrusts instead!'

Patroclus charged again, followed by Meriones. The subsequent clash, clatter and roar recalled the noise that drifts down from the mountain when wood-cutters are excitedly felling timber. Soon, not even a keen-eyed man could have distinguished Sarpedon's corpse, drenched in blood from head to foot, covered with dust and the wreckage of war.

> Fierce warriors by the hundred shout
>   And tussle, knee to knee,
> Like flies of spring that buzz about
>   The farmyard busily
> When milk pours foaming into pails:
> To number them no count avails.

That was how the Greeks and Trojans swarmed around the dead king.

Zeus, on Mount Ida, kept his bright eyes fixed on the scene. He wondered whether Patroclus should now be killed by Hector, and stripped of his armour; or whether he should first cause the enemy fresh losses. Deciding on the latter course, he weakened Hector's courage and made him aware that the divine scales were tipped against him. Presently, Hector mounted his chariot, and gave the signal for withdrawal; the Lycians obeyed, abandoning Sarpedon's corpse, by this time hidden beneath a pile of other corpses. Patroclus thereupon possessed himself of the disputed arms, and sent them back for safekeeping.

Zeus turned to Apollo: 'Pray, dear Phoebus,' he said, 'rescue King Sarpedon from the mêlée, wipe off the clotted blood, and carry him to a quiet spot beside the Scamander. When the body has been thoroughly washed in river water, anointed with ambrosia, and clothed in an everlasting pall, let Sleep and his twin-brother Death swiftly convey it to the rich, extensive land of Lycia. The royal family and their friends can then bury Sarpedon in a hero's barrow under the customary pillar.'

Apollo at once flew down to the battlefield; rescued Sarpedon's body from the mêlée and carried it to the Scamander for a thorough washing in river water. Sleep and his twin-brother Death then swiftly conveyed their burden—now anointed with ambrosia, and clothed in an everlasting pall—to the rich, extensive land of Lycia.

Zeus, who can fool anyone, encouraged Patroclus to exploit the victory. Forgetful of Achilles' instructions, which might have saved his life, he remounted the chariot at Automedon's side. Here is a list of Patroclus' new victims in the order of their death: first, Adrestus; next, Autonous, followed by Echeclus, Perimus, son of Megas, Epistor, Melanippus, Elasus, Mulius, and Pylartes. He would indeed have taken Troy single-handed, because the Trojans were impotent against his attacks from front and flank, had it not been that Apollo the Archer harboured most unfriendly feelings against him. Three times Patroclus tried to gain a lodgement on the bastions where Apollo stood; but each time his shield was pressed back by the god's immortal palm. At the fourth attempt, Apollo yelled a warning: 'Away with you, Patroclus! Though descended from Zeus, you are not fated to capture Troy; nor yet is Achilles—a far better soldier than yourself.'

Patroclus withdrew, prudently respecting his divine anger. Meanwhile, Hector halted his team at the Scaean Gate and considered whether to counter-attack once more, or whether to rally his forces in defence of the city walls. Before he could make up his mind, Apollo appeared, disguising himself as young Asius—the brother of Queen Hecuba, and the son of Dymas, who lived by the banks of the Phrygian river Sangarius. 'Hector,' cried Apollo, 'why did you break off the fight? Such caution is shameful! If I were as much stronger than you, as you are stronger than me, I should insist on your re-entering the battle. Come, nephew, face Patroclus! Who knows but that Apollo may grant you the glory of killing him?'

When the god had vanished, Hector told his half-brother Cebriones to wheel the chariot about. Apollo helped them by spreading panic among the Greeks and, disregarding all other champions, Hector made straight for Patroclus. Patroclus leaped to the ground: a spear in his left hand and, in the right, a bright, jagged stone. Planting his feet wide apart, he let fly, and took so true an aim that the stone struck Cebriones on the forehead. As Cebriones toppled from the chariot, with a broken skull and both eyes dripping on his cheeks, Patroclus taunted him: 'What a graceful plunge! If that man were a sailor, his diving would soon be well known. Down he would go, below the vessel's keel, even in stormy weather, and fetch up oysters! These Trojans are past masters at diving!'

> The lion's rage undid him when
> We caught him by our cattle pen:
> Wounded in breast and galled in side,
> He fought it out, for foolish pride.

Although Patroclus had escaped being wounded, his pride undid him: he sprang to despoil Cebriones, as a lion might spring to feast upon a slaughtered heifer. Hector also dismounted, and now there were two lion-like heroes hungrily tussling over a carcase.

Hector seized Cebriones by the head, Patroclus seized him by the foot, each pulling hard. Other Greeks and Trojans joined in the tug-of-war:

> East Wind and South a wager made
> Who first could strip the mountain glade.
> Then loudly did the branches clash
> Of cornel-cherry, beech and ash.
> Lumps of dead wood came tumbling down
> And leafy twigs from the trees' crown.

Dust whirled, spears flew, arrows leaped from bow-strings, and great boulders crashed against shields, above the corpse of Cebriones— nobly born, nobly fallen, and no longer concerned with the arts of chariot-fighting. It was only at sunset, the hour when oxen are unyoked and led to their stalls, that the Greeks gained a larger ad-

vantage than Heaven could allow. They drew Cebriones' body out
of the fight and despoiled it; after which Patroclus again sprang to
the attack. Three times he charged—Ares himself could not have
been fiercer!—and each time he killed nine men.

The fourth charge proved to be the last; he then received a divine
chastisement for presuming on his mortality. Cloaked in mist,
Apollo stepped behind Patroclus and struck him on the neck, using
the edge of his palm. The borrowed helmet flew off and rattled away
—Zeus' destructive gift to Hector, who took it from under the horses'
hooves and set it on his own head. While that helmet framed Achil-
les' handsome face, its horsehair plumes, nodding in their upright
socket, had never touched the ground; but now they were befouled
with blood and dust. Simultaneously, Patroclus' sharp, stout spear
shattered in his grasp, the baldric holding the tasseled shield slipped
off his shoulder, and Apollo unbuckled his corslet. As he stood
dazed, trembling, and at a loss, Euphorbus, son of Panthous—the
finest young spearman, charioteer, and athlete of the whole Dard-
anian contingent—stabbed him between the shoulderblades. Eu-
phorbus, whose first battle this was, could already claim to have
accounted for twenty Greeks; nevertheless, he did not venture to
dispatch Patroclus, though seeing him disarmed and at his mercy.
He recovered the spear and hastily hid among his comrades. Patro-
clus staggered back, trying to avoid death, but Hector darted for-
ward and speared him low in the belly. He crashed down, to the
horror of the Greeks.

> A lion sprang at a wild boar
>   When, crazed with cruel thirst,
> Beside a mountain spring they met
>   And each would drink at first;
> It was the stalwart lion's luck
>   That panting boar to worst!

So Hector the Lion mortally wounded Patroclus the Wild Boar, who
had ripped up many Trojans that afternoon. 'Son of Menoetius,' he
cried, 'why did you threaten to sack Troy, and enslave our women?
You should have reckoned with Prince Hector, the champion and
guardian of our city, standing here, spear in hand, his swift horses

straining at the yoke! Now vultures shall devour your corpse, poor wretch. Achilles betrayed you when he said—of this I am sure—"Patroclus, do not show me your face again until you have carved holes in Prince Hector's bloody corslet!" Only a fool would have listened to him!'

The dying hero replied faintly: 'Boast of your triumph, son of Priam! It was given you by Zeus, Son of Cronus, and by Apollo, who had no difficulty in disarming me—they unbuckled my corslet! Otherwise I could have dealt with a score of champions as strong as yourself. Fate, in the person of Apollo, struck the first blow; Euphorbus struck the second; you, the third! But be warned, you cannot live much longer. I see Death and Fate hovering near; for Achilles the Aeacid will avenge me.'

'Patroclus,' asked Hector, 'why prophesy my destruction? Are you sure that I will not spear Achilles before he spears me?'

Patroclus, however, was already dead, and his ghost descended to the kingdom of Hades, bewailing the cruel shortness of life.

Hector placed one foot on the supine body and drew out his spear. Then he rushed away, hoping to use it against Automedon; but too late: Xanthus and Balius, the Olympians' wedding gift to Peleus, had carried him safely off the battlefield.

Book Seventeen:

Menelaus' Day of Glory

When Menelaus the Fair-Haired heard that Patroclus had been killed, he hurried through the mêlée and straddled over him, with spear and shield held ready for immediate combat.

> The cow that never calved before
> Stands lowing in surprise
> At this new creature on the floor—
> She seems to doubt her eyes!

But what cow was ever so protective of her first-born calf, as Menelaus of that corpse? Euphorbus, son of Panthous, shouted to him: 'My lord Menelaus, though you are joint-commander of the Greeks, pray step back and let me despoil Patroclus! I was the first to drive a spear into him and, rather than forfeit the glory of taking his arms, I shall do the same to you.'

'O Father Zeus!' Menelaus cried indignantly. 'Such rudeness is more than I can abide! Panthous' sons remind me of leopards, or lions, or even wild boars—the most pugnacious of all wild beasts. Yet when this man's brother, the famous Hyperenor, dared call me the feeblest fighter in our whole army, he never got home to his admiring wife and family, though a far younger man than I!' He added: 'My lord Euphorbus, unless you retire at once to the shelter of your comrades' shields, I must kill you as I killed Hyperenor! Fools learn from their mistakes, but sometimes too late.'

Euphorbus brushed aside Menelaus' warning. He answered in scorn: 'Foster-son of Zeus, I will stop your boasts and make you pay dearly for the death of my brother! After widowing Hyperenor's newly married bride, Phrontis, and afflicting our father Panthous with the deepest sorrow, you cannot, I am sure, expect me to refrain from vengeance. Your severed head and blood-stained armour may be a slight consolation to them.'

Euphorbus lunged at Menelaus' shield, but the spear-point turned harmlessly on the metal plate. Breathing a short prayer to Zeus, Menelaus put his full strength behind a counter-stroke, which drove through Euphorbus' neck. Down he clattered, the blood staining his exquisite hair, which was tied with gold and silver ribbons and worthy of the Graces themselves.

> I cut a likely olive-shoot,
>   I planted it in a fine field
> Where hidden water fed its root
>   Till spring the pale white bloom revealed.

> But though my tree stood firm and stout
>   When with all lesser winds at play,
> A fierce north-easter wrenched it out
>   And tossed it scornfully away.

Young Euphorbus lay prone on the ground, like that olive sapling.

> A mountain lion in his might
> Leaps at the herd, which takes to flight.
> A single cow, the unlucky one,
> Will never know tomorrow's sun.
> Her neckbone with his teeth he snaps
> And gluttonously gulps and laps;
> Neither the herdsmen nor their hounds
> Venture to tread within his bounds.

Neither did any Trojan venture to oppose Menelaus, when he began despoiling Euphorbus. Phoebus Apollo, however, grudged him this success and, appearing as Mentis, the Ciconian commander, recalled Hector the Bright-Helmed from his vain pursuit of Automedon.

'Hector,' he cried, 'let those divine horses be! They are not for you. Achilles can master them, because his mother is a goddess; but they obey no other mortal. Meanwhile, Menelaus has killed one of your finest men—Euphorbus, son of Panthous.'

Apollo vanished, and Hector looked anxiously around. He saw

Euphorbus lying dead in a pool of blood, and Menelaus bending over him. With a yell of rage he advanced—

> Like a terrible flame
> When HEPHAESTUS the Lame
> Blows hard at the coals in his furnace . . .

'Alas,' Menelaus muttered in alarm, 'having come here on an errand of vengeance, I ought not to abandon these spoils, nor ought I to desert Patroclus. Some Greek might accuse me of cowardice. Yet if I stand fast and Hector brings the entire Trojan army against me, what then? But enough! Once a man dares challenge a hero favoured by Zeus, he courts destruction. Nobody should blame me for retiring when all the gods support Hector. Still, Great Ajax and I—if I can find him—might risk the anger of Heaven and appease the anger of Achilles by conveying this corpse back to camp. Yes, that is my best course in a fearful predicament!'

> The lion tosses his long mane,
>   Chased from the fold with spears and cries,
> But loathes to leave: once and again
>   He turns, and the whole hunt defies,
> Though there's a chillness at his heart
> That serves him notice to depart.

He withdrew, faced about as soon as he reached safety, and saw Great Ajax on the extreme left flank, rallying the terror-stricken Pylians. Menelaus ran to him and panted: 'This way, dear Ajax! It is too late to save Patroclus' armour, because Hector has despoiled him; but hurry, and we may rescue the corpse. Achilles will want that.'

Ajax followed Menelaus. They found Hector already dragging off the naked corpse for decapitation; he intended to keep the head as a trophy, but dogs would devour the trunk. On recognizing Ajax's tower-like shield, however, he mounted his chariot and drove away hastily—sending the captured armour by messenger to Troy, where it would win him much applause.

> A lion, leading out his cub
> Quietly through the mountain scrub,
> Narrows his eyes in fury when
> He hears the loud approach of men,

> Lashes his tail and dares confront
> The noisy onset of our hunt.

What lion was ever so protective of his cub, as Ajax of Patroclus' corpse? He spread his shield above it; and beside him, in rage and grief, stood Menelaus the Warrior.

Glaucus, son of Hippolochus, now sole commander of the Lycians, frowned contemptuously at Hector. 'You look like a brave man,' he scoffed, 'and claim to be a hero; yet when battle is joined, you turn tail! Tell me, how long could your people hold Troy without our aid? The question will shortly have to be considered, because, upon my word, none of us Lycians enjoy this ungrateful warfare. Can we count on your respecting the corpse of any lesser soldier, when you allow King Sarpedon—your guest, your intimate friend, your loyal ally—to be stripped naked and left for the dogs? Yes, if these men obey me, I shall repudiate our treaty and march home! Why do you Trojans not show gallantry of the sort that brings all honest citizens hurrying out in defence of their homes? Then we should help to drag the corpse behind your walls. Since Patroclus was squire to the Greeks' greatest champion, they would gladly buy it at the price of Sarpedon's armour. But you are frightened of Ajax, and expect us to undertake this task ourselves.'

Hector returned Glaucus' frown. 'Having hitherto thought you the most level-headed of all Lycians,' he said, 'I am astounded that so noble a prince can speak so foolishly! Frightened of Ajax? It is a falsehood! Nothing ever daunts me; only, I dare not oppose the will of Zeus the Shield-Bearer, who often overawes even the bravest veteran, and then suddenly encourages him to draw sword again. Come, stand by me, friend Glaucus! You shall soon see whether I am a coward, or still soldier enough to rid the corpse of Greeks.

'Trojans, Lycians, and hard-fighting Dardanians!' Hector bawled. 'Be men, be heroes! Hold your ground while I briefly absent myself and put on the armour—Achilles' armour—which Patroclus was wearing when I killed him.'

Away hurried Hector, retrieved his famous spoils from the messengers who were taking them to Troy, and made a quick change; so they went off with his own armour instead. The borrowed suit had been the Olympians' wedding gift to King Peleus, who passed it on to Achilles when too old for battle himself—though Fate would not let Achilles grow old in it.

Zeus, watching Hector, shook his head sadly and muttered: 'Poor wretch! Unaware of the doom that follows him so closely, he dares buckle on that armour: a divine suit, and stripped from brave, gentle Patroclus, brother-in-arms to the most formidable of these Greeks! I shall reward his effrontery with another short burst of triumph; but he must not leave the field alive and present those spoils to Andromache.' Zeus nodded emphatically, and nothing could now annul his verdict.

The armour was a perfect fit; a martial spirit again strengthened Hector's limbs and braced his heart. He ran shouting among the allies, who wondered when they saw how closely he resembled Achilles. Mesthles, Glaucus, Medon, Thersilochus, Asteropaeus, Deisenor, Hippothous, Phorcys, Chromius, and Ennomus the Augur—Hector addressed them all. 'Loyal allies!' he cried in urgent tones. 'You were not invited here for a vain parade of numbers; it was to save our wives and children. But the expense of supporting you worthily has strained the city's resources both in treasure and food; so why not fulfil your treaty obligations at once? Charge full butt against these rapacious Greeks, and either conquer or die! Whoever drives Great Ajax from Patroclus' corpse and hauls it back to Troy may share with me half of whatever ransom Achilles may offer; and therefore half the glory of killing Patroclus.'

Hector's allies levelled their spears and went resolutely for Ajax and Menelaus, yet failed to capture the corpse. How few of these unfortunates escaped death! Nevertheless, Ajax confided in Menelaus: 'My dear lord, we can hardly hope to survive such a storm of missiles without reinforcements. In fact, the question is not whether we will save this corpse from decapitation and outrage, but whether we will keep our own heads on our shoulders. Summon help! Some true friends may hear you.'

Menelaus cried at the top of his voice. 'Princes of the Supreme Council, messmates of my brother Agamemnon and myself, you who owe your honour and fame to Zeus! In the murk of battle I cannot distinguish faces sufficiently well to summon you by name; but Patroclus, son of Menoetius, has fallen, and his corpse will glut the dogs of Troy unless you assist me!'

Little Ajax heard the summons and was the first to arrive; after him came Idomeneus the Cretan with his brother-in-arms Meriones —and I refrain from listing the other champions who crowded up.

The Trojans did not succeed in killing any defenders of the corpse, but forced them back; however, Great Ajax, always the bravest and stoutest fighter in the Greek army—Achilles alone excepted—returned to the attack like a wild boar:

> The fierce wild boar at bay
> Evinces no dismay:
> His rush sends hounds and men hurtling away!

A Trojan ally, Hippothous, son of the famous Pelasgian King Lethus of Larissa, had fastened a strap around Patroclus' ankle, and was dragging him off, as Hector wished; but nobody could stand against Ajax when he charged through the mêlée and lunged, piercing Hippothous' bronze cheek-piece. Blood and brains oozed from the wound; he dropped the strap, and tumbled beside the corpse . . . His parents had little to show for the trouble of rearing him, so young he died!

Ajax managed to dodge the spear which Hector flung. It caught Schedius—son of King Iphitus the Phocian, who ruled at famous Panopeus—on his collarbone and emerged under the shoulderblade; he fell with a clang of armour. When Phorcys, the prudent son of Phaenops, bestrode Hippothous' corpse, Ajax speared him in the belly, breaking the corslet-plate. Down he went, clutching at the dust, and his intestines poured out.

Hector and the Lycians did not prevent the Greeks from seizing these bodies, and seemed ready to flee behind their city walls, yielding the Greeks more glory than Zeus intended for them. But Apollo, disguised as Aeneas' friend Periphas, the old herald—his father was the still older herald Epytus—spoke to Aeneas. 'Troy,' he said, 'could never have resisted so long, had the gods disapproved! I find it strange that whereas the Greek princes trust in their own strength and valour, even at the risk of Zeus' displeasure, you Trojans are reluctant to fight even when he offers you victory.'

Aeneas knew Apollo, and shouted to Hector and his companions: 'All is well! A god has just assured me that Almighty Zeus favours our cause. Let us make one decisive charge! We must not allow the

Greeks to rescue Patroclus' corpse too easily, or drive us behind the walls in disgrace.'

He sprang forward and killed Leiocritus, son of Arisbas. This encouraged the Trojans—although, indeed, bold Lycomedes, son of Creon, ran up immediately and avenged Leiocritus, by spearing Prince Apisaon, son of Hippasus, in the liver. Apisaon had come to Troy from fertile Paeonia and, after Asteropaeus, was the most skilful fighter of his contingent. Asteropaeus now tried to take a Greek life in exchange, but found a solid fence of shields and hedge of spears surrounding Patroclus' corpse; for Great Ajax forbade anyone either to retreat or to thrust himself ahead: they must stand shoulder to shoulder, he urged. The earth was red with blood and strewn with corpses. Yet fewer Greeks fell than Trojans—they were more careful to protect one another.

In this fiery combat even strong champions felt choked by the dust, and oppressed by the weight of their armour. So thick was the gloom, that sun and moon might neither have existed—a strange contrast to the rest of the battlefield, where the benign sun shone from a cloudless blue sky, and the two armies fought in desultory fashion, often moving out of spear-range.

Nestor's sons, Antilochus and Thrasymedes, had not heard that Patroclus was dead: and imagined him to be still in the front-line. Obeying their father's instructions, they kept on the flank, ready to enter the main battle only at signs of a Greek retreat.

> When the bull is flayed, our lord
>   Soaks the hide in fat,
> 'Lads,' he tells us, 'form a ring,
>   Take a hold of that!
>
> 'Grip it, stretch it, supple it,
>   Tug from every side,
> Watch it lapping up the grease,
>   Tug until it's dried!'

No bull's hide was ever so roughly handled as Patroclus' corpse; the Trojans hauling it towards Troy, the Greeks towards their camp. Ares himself or Athene, Goddess of Battle, for all their annoyance, could hardly have been indifferent to this furious conflict. Sweat ran down every leg from thigh to foot, down every arm from shoulder to hand, and into all eyes.

Achilles also knew nothing of Patroclus' fate, because the battle had been fought far away, under the walls of Troy. He expected his friend to reach the Scaean Gate, touch it, and return in safety; the notion that he could be either making a single-handed attempt on Troy, or lying dead, had not yet occurred to him.

Relentlessly the struggle proceeded, both sides suffering heavy losses. Sometimes a Greek would exclaim: 'Comrades, we cannot retreat! May the earth open and swallow us, if the Trojans take this corpse to their city!' Or a Trojan would exclaim: 'Comrades, we cannot retreat, even if we are all fated to die for its possession!' The iron clamour ascended through the upper air until it rang against the brazen vault of Heaven.

Meanwhile Achilles' horses, having escaped from the mêlée, stood weeping beside the river—they had wept ever since they saw Hector kill Patroclus. Automedon, son of Diores, tried to rouse them with blows of the whip, shouts, words of endearment; but they would not budge.

> Staunch as a head-stone on the tomb
>   Of man or woman dead,
> Each creature stood oppressed by gloom:
> In anguish at Patroclus' doom,
>   Abasing his proud head.
>
> Large mournful tears from every eye
>   Trickled without a sound;
> Their golden manes, once flaunted high
> Above the yoke, drooped dismally
>   Upon the marshy ground.

Zeus pitied Xanthus and Balius when he observed those tears. Shaking his locks sadly, he muttered: 'Poor immortal team-mates, why did we Olympians present you to King Peleus, in the first place? You were not meant to share Man's sorrows; and, upon my word, I can think of no more miserable creature that draws breath and crawls on the face of this earth! Still, I promise one thing: Hector, son of Priam, shall never mount Achilles' beautiful chariot and become your master! That he should preen himself in Achilles' armour is bad enough! So be it: I will renew your strength and courage, letting you carry Automedon out of the danger which threatens the Greeks; for by sunset, Hector must slaughter so many of them that the rest have no alternative but retreat.'

Zeus comforted Xanthus and Balius: they raised their muzzles, shook the dust from their manes, and galloped off—though towards the battle, rather than the camp. Automedon, despite his grief, amused himself by scaring Trojans: he would swoop at them in the divine chariot, like a griffin-vulture harrying a flock of wild geese, then sheer away and swoop again. Since he lacked a companion, however, he could not handle a spear at the same time as whip and reins. Soon Alcimedon, son of Laerces, son of Haemon, hailed him: 'Automedon, has some god destroyed your wits? Why are you driving aimlessly about, when Hector is flaunting Achilles' armour?'

Automedon answered that the horses would allow no one to fight from their chariot, except Patroclus or Achilles. 'Nevertheless,' he said, 'climb up and take the reins, while I attack the Trojans on foot!'

Alcimedon did so, and Hector remarked to Aeneas, son of Anchises: 'My lord, look yonder at Achilles' team! The men in charge do not greatly impress me. Let us capture their equipage. I hardly think that they will offer much opposition.'

Aeneas and Hector advanced under cover of huge, tough, bronze-plated bull's hide shields. Chromius and Prince Aretus followed, eager to kill the two Greeks and seize their wonderful horses; not foreseeing what the attempt would cost them. Automedon prayed to Zeus, and felt immediate benefit; yet he asked Alcimedon: 'Pray, keep the horses so close behind me that their breaths warm my neck! Hector seems determined either to cause general dismay by killing us both and seizing the chariot, or to fall dead himself.' Then he shouted: 'Help, Great Ajax, Little Ajax! King Menelaus, help! Leave Patroclus' corpse, and defend us instead! We are threatened by Hector and Aeneas. Yet whether you come or stay, I shall fight and commend my soul to Zeus. The issue lies in the lap of Destiny.'

Automedon cast a spear, exerting his full strength; it struck Aretus' shield, and hurtled through belt, corslet and belly:

> The sturdy farmer swung an axe
> That caught the bull on its pax-wax
> Beneath the horns; forward it sprang
> And hit the pavement with a bang!

Aretus made a similar convulsive leap, and the spear quivered in his guts where he lay. Then Hector aimed at Automedon, but he bent his head and the weapon flashed past, to bury itself in the earth beyond. A brisk sword fight would have ensued, had not Little Ajax run up at Menelaus' call and saved Automedon by chasing away his enemies. Automedon stripped the mortally wounded Aretus of his armour, exulting: 'This is some solace for Patroclus' death, though Aretus was nothing like so accomplished a spearman!'

He took the spoils, stowed them in the chariot, and drove off. His feet and hands were as blood-stained as the paws of a lion after it has devoured a bull.

On second thoughts, Zeus sent Athene flying down from Olympus, to save the Greeks who were protecting Patroclus' corpse.

> 'Look, a rainbow in the sky!
>   What can that portend?'
> 'War,' you say; 'Storm,' say I,
>   'Causing work to end
> In the woods, on the farm,
> Threatening flocks and herds with harm!'

Athene's arrival in a rainbow-coloured cloud portended trouble for the Trojans. Disguised as old Phoenix, Achilles' tutor, she said to Menelaus in piping tones: 'My lord King, it will be a lasting stain on your reputation if the body of Achilles' faithful friend is torn by dogs beneath the walls of Troy! Come, exert yourself, and make everyone else do likewise.'

Menelaus answered: 'Ah, Phoenix, veteran of half-forgotten wars! Patroclus' death has affected me deeply; but when Hector plies his fiery spear and Zeus supports him, I need Athene to renew my strength and parry blows.'

Athene, glad that Menelaus had named her first, put new strength into his shoulders and knees, and inspired him with the bold persistence of a horse-fly:

> Greedy fly, stinging fly,
>   Is my blood so sweet?
> Twenty times at least have I
>   Forced you to retreat.
> Back you flit, I know not why,
>   To the self-same seat!

Back went Menelaus to Patroclus' corpse; and once more his spear drank sweet human blood, transfixing Podes, son of Eëtion, Hector's brother-in-law and one of his closest friends, who had turned to run. Menelaus sprang forward and dragged Podes' fallen body from under his comrades' feet.

Then Apollo, disguising himself as Phaenops the Abydian, son of Asius, an even closer friend of Hector's, said: 'If you shrink from Menelaus, Prince Hector, the Greeks will cease to shrink from you! Though he never ranked highly among their champions, he has now killed your loyal brother-in-law Podes—a fine soldier, always on the offensive—and removed his body for despoilment.'

This reproach stung Hector to the quick. He strode about in his suit of flashing armour and, as he did so, Zeus shrouded Mount Ida with sudden cloud, conjured up a violent thunderstorm, and shook his bright, tasselled Aegis at the dismayed Greeks. The Trojans then began to score fresh successes. Polydamas cast at short range, and seriously wounded Peneleos the courageous Boeotian: the spear grazed his shoulder-bone. Hector stabbed Leïtus, son of Prince Alectryon, in the wrist: Leïtus, no longer able to grip a weapon, glanced wildly around him and withdrew, pursued by Hector; whereupon King Idomeneus of Crete hurled a spear which struck Hector's right breast. The Trojans shouted for relief when it broke off at the socket against his mail corslet; and Hector would have dispatched Idomeneus, who had entered the battle on foot, but Coeranus, Meriones' charioteer and friend, from the Cretan fortress of Lyctus, rescued him. This service cost Coeranus his own life, because Hector's spear, aimed at Idomeneus, caught him just below the ear. The blade sliced his tongue and dashed out his teeth; he tumbled dead over the chariot-rail. Meriones was standing near; he stooped, gathered up the fallen reins, and said to Idomeneus: 'Take these, and make for camp! Use the whip! You know as well as I that we are beaten.'

Glad to escape, Idomeneus lashed at the horses and drove off in terror. Great Ajax and Menelaus shared Meriones' forebodings. 'Alas,' complained Ajax, 'not even a fool could deny that Father Zeus has deserted us! Every Trojan spear finds its mark now, however unskilful the spearman, whereas every Greek spear lodges in the ground. We had better decide on some means of getting safely back

with Patroclus' corpse. Our friends are anxiously looking this way,
wondering when Hector will break through and attack the camp
again. If only someone responsible would run and tell Achilles of
Patroclus' death—I am sure the news has not yet reached him! But
this cursed gloom prevents me from recognizing men's faces; and
the teams are equally indistinct.'

Then Ajax prayed, weeping for vexation:

> 'ZEUS, Almighty and All-wise,
> Remove the cloud that cloaks our eyes!
> Grant us at least, if we must fall,
> A sunny sky to be our pall!'

Zeus, pitying him, scattered the dark, misty cloud, so that the whole
battlefield became clearly visible in the sunshine. Ajax then said:
'Pray glance about you, King Menelaus! See whether Antilochus
is still alive. He would be a most suitable messenger.'

Menelaus did as Ajax asked:

> All night long we countrymen,
> Guarding cattle in their pen
> (Aided by our dogs that growl
> Fiercely when marauders prowl),
> At a neighbouring thicket stare.
> Ay, a fulvous lion's there,
> Empty-bellied, watching for
> A chance to leap with sudden roar
> On the neck of a plump cow . . .
> 'Look, my lads, he's coming now!'
> In a volley from strong hands
> Spears are cast and burning brands!
> Be his anger what it may,
> We have baulked him of his prey;
> Off he slinks before the day.

Menelaus quitted his post no less reluctantly, fearing that the
Greeks would give ground while he was absent and allow Hector
to capture the corpse. He enjoined Meriones, Great Ajax and Little
Ajax: 'Hold fast, my friends! Patroclus was always loving and gentle
in his life, and now in death he deserves your gratitude.'

> The eagle has a sharper eye
> Than any bird that haunts the sky—

> An eye no creature can evade.
> The hare finds refuge in a glade
> Under some thick and leafy bush;
> Down swoops the eagle with a rush,
> Five hundred feet or more, to tear
> The guts of that unhappy hare!

Menelaus' eagle-eyes searched the plain, and soon recognized Antilochus on the extreme left flank. Running towards him, he gasped: 'Prince, I bring bad news! The Trojans are being assisted by Zeus, and I deeply regret to announce that our greatest champion has been killed—Patroclus, son of Menoetius—doubtless you guessed what had happened when they counter-attacked? We are all heart-broken. Pray inform Achilles at the camp! He may be prevailed upon to help us rescue his friend's corpse—though Hector is already wearing the spoils.'

Antilochus listened in horror, his eyes filled with tears, and he choked for grief. Wordlessly he undertook the painful task imposed on him: removing his armour and handing it to a noble comrade, named Laodocus, who drove up at that moment, he started sorrowfully off. Menelaus would not stand by Antilochus' weary Pylians, thus left leaderless; but placed Prince Thrasymedes in command of them, and hurried away to straddle Patroclus' corpse again. He told Great and Little Ajax, who were still there: 'Antilochus will take the message; yet I shall be surprised if Achilles appears at once, however angry he may feel—Hector is wearing his armour, and he cannot fight without. As you say, we had better decide on some means of removing this corpse and getting safely back ourselves.'

Ajax answered: 'Very well, my lord Menelaus! Let you and Meriones shoulder the corpse and carry it off the field; Little Ajax and I will act as your rearguard. We are one in heart, as in name, and always fight side by side.'

Menelaus and Meriones stooped; they heaved the corpse on their shoulders.

> The boar was speared, and yelping hounds
> Ran forward with great leaps and bounds
>   To seize their prey.
> But when, too proud a beast for flight,
> He charged them, trusting in his might,
>   They shrank away!

Much the same happened here. The exasperated Trojans saw the corpse carried off, and noisily pressed the attack; but as soon as Great and Little Ajax turned to charge them, blenched and shrank away.

> Our whole town is on fire,
>   Its glare turns night to day,
> The flames leap always higher;
>   Which fills us with dismay.
> So furiously the north wind blows
> That houses crumble in long rows!

No roar of flames, no screams of terrified townsfolk, could have been louder than the din of this battle: chariots rattled, hooves clattered, armour rang, men yelled!

> The mules put out enormous strength
>   When down the mountainside,
> Some massive tree-trunk, or huge length
>   Of timber, they make slide.
> And though their bodies gleam with sweat,
> Their spirit is not broken yet.

No mules ever worked so hard as did Menelaus and Meriones in carrying that corpse!
Behind them strode Great and Little Ajax:

> A wooded ridge defends the plain,
> And in a season of much rain
> Though rivers growl, though torrents roar
> (As often they have done before)
> And high their lurid waters lift,
> Here is a shield they cannot shift!

The shields of Great and Little Ajax resisted the Trojan flood with equal stolidity. Yet when:

> Flocks of starlings and jackdaws
>   Scatter through the sky,
> They themselves announce the cause:
>   'Hawk, 'ware hawk!' they cry.

And when Hector and Aeneas led a charge, the Greeks scattered too. Before regaining their fosse, they were being slaughtered in droves. Hector gave them no respite.

Book Eighteen:

Hephaestus Forges Arms

Achilles the Swift-Footed, with a gloomy presentiment of bad news, asked himself: 'Why are our troops streaming back across the plain?' He thought: 'I pray that the gods have not done what I most feared! Before I die, according to my mother Thetis, the Trojans must kill the best of my Myrmidons. Does she mean Patroclus? Oh, why has he been so reckless? Surely I warned him to rejoin me as soon as the Trojans had been driven across the rampart, and to avoid meeting Hector?'

Achilles' anxiety deepened when Antilochus, son of Nestor, approached at a run, the tears streaming from his eyes. 'Alas, Prince Achilles,' he choked out. 'Here is a message which I loathe delivering. Patroclus, son of Menoetius has been killed, and we are fighting for his corpse—his naked corpse, despoiled by Hector the Bright-Helmed!'

Achilles seized handfuls of black ashes, which he poured over his head, rubbed on his face, and let fall on his tunic. Slave-girls saw him tumble groaning to the ground in an excess of grief. They rushed from the hut and gathered about him, their knees trembling; beat their breasts, and wailed aloud. Antilochus likewise lamented and shed further tears, but was careful to hold the hero's hands for fear he might cut his own throat. Achilles' groans were so deep and dismal that Thetis heard them far off at the bottom of the sea, where she sat next to her old father Nereus, surrounded by numerous sisters— Actaea, Agave, Amathyia, Amphinome, Amphithoe, Apseudes, Callianassa, Callianeira, Clymene, Cymodoce, Cymothoe, Dexamene,

Dynamene, Doris, Doto, Galateia, Glauce, Halie, Iaera, Ianassa, Ianeira, Limnoreia, Maera, Melite, Nemertes, Nesaea, Oreithyia, Panope, Pherusa, Proto, Speio, Thaleia and Thoë—all of whom lived down there in a bright cavern, and who simultaneously began beating their soft breasts.

Thetis led the lament, singing:

> 'Nereids of the dark blue Sea
> Listen to me—
> Listen and sympathize
> With dewy eyes!

> 'It was a glad day when
> I bore the best of men,
> Achilles young and strong,
> The subject of this song.
> It was a joy to see
> Him sprout like a young tree
> Planted in fertile soil,
> Yet FATE had cursed my toil
> Of tender motherhood:
> FATE had decreed he should,
> While yet a beardless boy,
> Sail with his ships to Troy
> And come not home again
> From the Scamandrian Plain
> To Peleus, Phthia's king.
> Now he lies sorrowing,
> And groans without relief,
> Nor can I cure his grief
> Or lighten his distress.
> Poor child! Nevertheless,
> To Troy I must needs go
> And learn why his tears flow.'

Thetis then swam from the cave, and her sisters followed in sympathy through the salt water, until the long procession landed on the shore of the Hellespont, where Achilles' ships lay beached, gunwale to gunwale. Kneeling beside her recumbent son, Thetis clasped his head in both arms, and cried desperately: 'Why do you weep, child? Tell me what ails you! Instead of hiding your sorrow, share it with me! Did not Zeus at last grant your plea, by crowding the Greeks back among their ships and allowing them to be slaughtered in droves?'

Achilles moaned: 'Alas, Almighty Zeus certainly granted my plea, and it has brought me nothing but pain! Patroclus, whom I loved as myself, is dead! Today, Hector killed him and despoiled his corpse of my splendid suit of armour, the Immortals' joint wedding-gift to King Peleus. Ah, Mother, you should have stayed with the Nereids, and let my father marry a mortal bride! New sorrows must now invade your heart by the thousandfold! No, you shall never welcome me home! Rejecting the inglorious old age which the Fates offered me, I have decided to stay and avenge Patroclus.'

'Then, dear son,' Thetis sobbed, 'your death cannot be delayed many days. The Fates rule that it shall immediately succeed Hector's.'

'Whenever Heaven pleases!' stormed Achilles. 'My beloved friend died far from his native land, and I failed him in his hour of need, as I failed my other comrades. Here I sat, a useless encumbrance to the earth, while Hector slaughtered them, though nobody fights better than I! Ah, if I could also claim that nobody is wiser than I! And if anger could cease utterly, both among Immortals and among mortals—even righteous anger! (How delightedly I nursed my grudge against the High King Agamemnon! It smouldered in my heart, and was as sweet to me as trickling honey.) But bygones must be bygones! I will forget my injury and exact vengeance on Hector; then Zeus and his Olympians may destroy me at their pleasure. After all, not Heracles himself, Zeus' favourite son, escaped death; Fate and Hera's persecutions laid him low. Death shall lay me low, too! Yet before he strikes, I am resolved upon great deeds: I will make some lovely, full-breasted Trojan woman weep and lament as I have wept and lamented—vainly trying to stanch the tears that furrow her cheeks. The Trojans must know to their cost that I am fighting once more! Mother, in your deep love, please do not dissuade me, or I shall stop my ears.'

Thetis replied: 'Child, who can blame you for rallying to the aid of your distressed comrades? Hector, however, is flaunting your own fine armour; and, even if his days are numbered, I beg that you will wait until tomorrow before challenging him! At sunrise, I promise to bring you a suit newly forged by none other than the God Hephaestus the Master Smith.'

Turning from Achilles, she addressed the Nereids: 'Be good enough, sisters, to tell our old father what has been decided! Explain that I am visiting Olympus, where Hephaestus will, I hope, forge a glorious suit of armour for my son.'

They nodded and swam off towards their cavern.

Meanwhile, the routed Greeks were unable to carry Patroclus' corpse out of spear-range. Hector and Aeneas overtook the gallant group who had charge of it, and their attack was like a spurt of flame; but though Hector three times caught at the corpse's feet, Great and Little Ajax always drove him away. He persisted in his efforts, urging his comrades forwards, and charged time after time.

> 'Begone, have done!' the shepherds shout
>   As the fierce lion mauls his prey,
> A fine fat cow; yet fail to rout
>   The hungry beast resolved to stay.

Nor could Great and Little Ajax rout Hector, who would have captured the corpse, and thus earned deathless fame, had Hera not sent Iris the Golden-Winged in haste from Olympus, with a private message for Achilles.

Iris appeared beside his ship, crying excitedly: 'Rouse yourself, redoubtable son of Peleus! A fearful combat is in progress around your friend Patroclus' corpse. The Greeks are struggling to carry it back here; whereas Hector wants to fix the decapitated head on the palisade above his city walls. Up with you! Show a decent respect for the dead! You could surely never allow your dead friend's body to be devoured by the dogs of Troy? If his ghost went underground headless and mangled, the disgrace would be yours!'

Achilles asked: 'Goddess, who gave you this message?'

Iris answered: 'Wise Queen Hera gave it me; but neither her husband nor any lesser Olympian knows that she did.'

Achilles asked again: 'How can I fight without armour? Hector is wearing my suit, and I have been forbidden by my mother Thetis to enter the battle until she fetches me a new one from Hephaestus' smithy. And where could I borrow armour? I know nobody of the same height and bulk as myself, except Great Ajax, who seems to be already using his tower-like shield and lance in stubborn defence of Patroclus' corpse.'

And again Iris answered: 'We are fully aware that your divine armour is not available. But visit the fosse just as you are, and show yourself to the Trojans! They may well recoil in terror, thus giving the Greeks a brief respite.'

Iris vanished, and when Achilles rose up, Athene threw her tasselled Aegis over his strong shoulders, and ringed his head with a halo of golden, flame-tipped cloud.

> Smoke signals from an island tell
> Of danger to the citadel,
> Of pirate ships come swooping down
> To raid the wharves and burn the town.
> All day those islanders defend
> Their walls and the same message send,
> But when night supervenes, the glow
> Of urgent beacons in a row
> Calls loyal allies, far and near,
> To man their ships and show no fear.

The warning glow of beacons in the night sky shone no brighter than Achilles' halo, as he scaled the rampart and paused at the brink of the fosse. Though his mother's advice restrained him from fighting, he roared a challenge—shrill and terrible, like trumpets blowing the assault on a city—to which Athene added distant echoes. The Trojan chariot-teams baulked and tried to bolt, while their awe-struck drivers wondered at the fiery blaze above Achilles' head. Three times he repeated his challenge, and each time caused such confusion that, in all, twelve Trojan soldiers were accidentally killed: either run through by one another's spears, or crushed under the wheels of chariots. This interlude enabled the Greeks to fetch Patroclus' corpse clear away at last, and lay it on a litter. His bereaved comrades gathered around. Achilles shed scalding tears when he saw the torn and naked body of his dearest friend—whom he had himself equipped and sent into action.

Hera now made the unwilling Sun plunge into the Ocean Stream beyond the horizon: darkness fell, and the Trojans withdrew. On reaching their former bivouacs and unharnessing their teams, they did not think of supper but called a council-of-war. Achilles' reappearance had scared them so badly that they were even afraid to sit down.

Prince Polydamas son of Panthous, the only nobleman present who could foresee future events by a careful study of the past, spoke first. He might be called Hector's twin, having been born on the same night; and excelled him in debate as much as he was excelled in battle. His honest and wise address went as follows: 'Comrades, pray march home at once! This spot is too near the Greek camp and too far from the city. While Achilles still bore a grudge against King Agamemnon, the Greeks could easily be routed; in fact, yesterday I approved your choice of bivouacs, and hoped that we should seize their fleet. Tonight, however, the situation has altered. Achilles, I fear, is so exceedingly angry that, scorning to fight in the plain, as usual, he will make an attempt on Troy. We must therefore retire behind the walls and guard our women. Pray silence, my lords! Listen attentively!

'Dusk checked Achilles' furious spirit, but let him catch us here tomorrow, and nobody need doubt his identity! Any soldier who has seen that divine chariot approaching will be fortunate if he finds himself safely in Troy again. Unpalatable advice, perhaps, yet the dogs and vultures may turn your refusal to good account. Come, march off, bivouac on the Assembly Ground, and trust in Troy's towers and closely barred gates! At dawn, we must defend the walls; and the bold hero who tries to scale them can feed the dogs. When the Greek charioteers have exhausted their teams by driving this way and that way across the plain, or round and round our walls, back they must go. Troy is impregnable!'

Hector gazed sternly at Polydamas. 'Your change of tone displeases me,' he said. 'Do you really enjoy being penned up behind those walls? In the old days, Troy was renowned for its treasures of gold and bronze; but since Zeus first brought these misfortunes on us, we are constantly stripping our houses of valuables to pay war-debts in Phrygia and Maeonia. Now that he has kindly let us raid the enemy camp and besiege the besiegers, I will not tolerate such foolish advice as yours; nor will any other right-minded Trojan! My lords, be persuaded by me! I suggest that we post sentries and eat supper here, without breaking formation. Whoever feels anxious about the fate of his household goods may distribute them among the common soldiery; better that they, rather than the Greeks, should profit. At dawn, we will attack the naval camp. Achilles has reappeared—what of that? If he ventures against us, so much the worse for him! I undertake to meet his challenge calmly, and we shall see who wins. Impartial Ares does not mind a famous killer being killed in his turn.'

Robbed of their usual sagacity by Athene, the Trojans were foolish enough to applaud Hector's boastful speech and reject Polydamas' prudent one. Thus the council-of-war ended, and they ate supper.

All that night the Greeks bewailed Patroclus. Achilles, as chief mourner, laid his powerful hands on the corpse's breast and howled horribly, like a bereaved lion.

> A hunter, stalking venison,
> By merest chance has lighted on
> The lion's undefended lair:
> Two infant cubs are lying there.
> Each by its furry scruff he catches
> And hauls them off, in spite of scratches.
>
> The father lion coming back,
> Sees red, and bounds along the track.
> Death to that rascal who dared touch
> The whelps on which he dotes so much!

'Alas,' sobbed Achilles, 'for my rash words at Opus: I promised Menoetius to bring his son home in glory from the sack of Troy, first making sure that he received his due share of the spoils! Man proposes, Zeus disposes! Patroclus was doomed to redden this earth with his life blood: and now my parents will never welcome me home, either!'

Then he pleadingly addressed his dead friend: 'Patroclus, since I must soon follow you underground, allow me to delay the funeral until I have taken vengeance on Hector, fetching his armour and his head as a gift for you. In proof of my anger and sincere grief, I swear to cut the throats of twelve noble Trojan prisoners before your pyre. In the meantime, pray lie here patiently among the ships. The young Trojan and Dardanian women captives whom you and I won by hard fighting at the assault of their cities, shall bewail you, day and night.'

Achilles ordered his comrades to make preparations for laying out Patroclus' corpse. They kindled fires beneath a large, three-legged cauldron, full of sweet water. Flames wrapped themselves around the belly of the cauldron, and it presently came to a boil. This hot water served to wash the gory corpse, which the layers-out then rubbed with olive oil. After pouring fresh unguents into the wounds, they placed Patroclus on a bier and threw over him a thin linen sheet and a white cloak. The assembled Myrmidons lamented loudly at Achilles' side throughout the hours of darkness.

✳

In Heaven, Zeus remarked to Queen Hera: 'That is your doing, wife! It was you who finally roused Achilles. Anyone would think that yonder Greeks were your own bastards!'

'Revered Son of Cronus,' Hera protested, 'what a thing to say! Even a man, a mere mortal lacking the divine wisdom which we gods possess, considers how he can best help or injure his fellow-men. Then why should I—the supreme goddess of Olympus, by birth as well as marriage—not punish the Trojans who have earned my anger?'

Their debate continued during Thetis' visit to the palace of Lame Hephaestus. Built all of bronze, it twinkled like a star, and could be readily distinguished from the other palaces on Olympus at a great distance. Thetis had found Hephaestus, bathed in sweat, working on a marvellous array of twenty tripods which were to line the walls of his hall; each tripod stood on three golden wheels, designed to roll it automatically into Zeus' Council Chamber and back again, as required. The task was not quite done when Thetis entered the smithy: he still needed to add elaborate handles, and weld certain necessary chains.

His wife, Charis the Bright-Wreathed, advanced to greet Thetis, exclaiming, as they shook hands: 'This is a pleasant surprise, my dear! We have always loved and esteemed you, but your appearances are rare indeed! Has anything happened? Do please be seated, while I fetch refreshments.'

Charis offered her a silver-studded throne and foot-stool, both of exquisite workmanship, shouting: 'Hephaestus, Thetis is here! Come at once!'

'An honour and a pleasure!' he shouted back. 'I cannot forget how generously she ran to the rescue, long ago, when my shameless mother Hera had taken a dislike to my club-foot, and flung me from the summit of Olympus. Never could I have survived that terrible fall, but for her and Eurynome, daughter of Oceanus! Nine years I spent hidden in their underwater cave, working at my forge: making brooches, torques, cups and necklaces, as the foaming Ocean Stream circled perpetually past. Those two Immortals alone knew where I was. So Thetis has visited us, eh? How could I possibly refuse her any favour? Fetch refreshments, Charis! I must now see to my bellows and tools.'

Hephaestus heaved up his huge bulk, and moved busily about on his shrunken legs. A set of mechanical assistants, whom he had constructed in gold to resemble living women, helped him to snatch his bellows from the furnace and stow his tools in a silver coffer. (They could not only use their limbs and speak, but were endowed with human feelings, and displayed superlative skill.) Then he sponged himself clean—forehead, hands, powerful neck and shaggy chest— put on his tunic, grasped a stout staff and limped forward to greet the visitor.

Struggling into a throne beside Thetis, Hephaestus squeezed her fingers affectionately. 'This is a pleasant surprise, my dear,' he said. 'We have always loved and esteemed you; but your appearances are rare indeed.' He added: 'Tell me what I can do, and I will gladly oblige you—if it is both possible and permissible.'

Thetis wept. 'No goddess on Olympus, dear Hephaestus,' she replied, 'has ever suffered so much sorrow as I! Why did Zeus single me out from all my Nereid sisters for marriage to a mortal—Peleus the Aeacid—though well aware that I detested the idea? Today, of course, he lies bed-ridden, far too old to be my husband in any true sense of the word. Worse, I bore him a son!

> 'It was a joy to see
> Him sprout like a young tree
> Planted in fertile soil,
> Yet FATE had cursed my toil
> Of tender motherhood:
> FATE had decreed he should,
> While still a beardless boy,
> Sail with his ships to Troy
> And come not home again
> From the Scamandrian Plain
> To Peleus, Phthia's king.
> Now he lies sorrowing,
> And groans without relief,
> Nor can I cure his grief:
> Though to his side I go,
> His tears for ever flow!

'Here is the story. King Agamemnon robbed Achilles of Briseis, a captive princess voted him as a prize of honour. He was vexed by that, and refused to fight; so the Trojans raided the naval camp. The Greeks soon thought better of their folly, and a deputation offered him wonderful gifts if he would save the fleet for them. These he rejected, but later lent his armour to Patroclus, who marched against the enemy at the head of a large force and drove them back as far as the Scaean Gate. Patroclus would, in effect, have sacked Troy, had not Phoebus Apollo halted his proud progress, and given Hector the glory of killing him. Look, I clasp your knees in suppliant fashion! Please, oh please forge my short-lived son a strong new shield and helmet, stout greaves fitted with ankle-pieces, and a tough corslet! Patroclus, you see, had borrowed my son's armour, and its capture by the Trojans has made him unhappier than ever. He is rolling on the ground in utter misery.'

'Enough, enough!' replied Hephaestus. 'I shall be delighted to oblige you . . . What a pity I cannot snatch Achilles from his doom, and hide him somewhere safe! But at least I can promise you so beautiful a suit of armour that it will be a universal wonder!'

Impulsively Hephaestus limped away, replaced the bellows beside the furnace—twenty pairs—and told them to blow on the crucibles. They obeyed, puffing wind from every direction, and making flames rise high where the most heat was needed. He put bronze, tin, gold and silver into the crucibles; then, having set a huge anvil on its stand, picked up his tongs and a heavy hammer.

Hephaestus went to work. He forged a broad, strong shield, five layers thick—bronze, tin, gold, tin, bronze, in that order—with a shining triple rim, and a silver baldric. The surface of the shield was elaborately ornamented: he began by engraving a design of earth, sea, sky, the Sun, a full Moon, and such nightly constellations as the Pleiads, the Hyads, Orion the Hunter, and the Great Bear. (This Great Bear—sometimes known as The Wain—turns slowly around the Pole Star, being the only one of these constellations never to dip into the Ocean Stream, and keeps a cautious eye on Orion across the vault of Heaven.)

He then engraved two prosperous towns. The first was mainly devoted to weddings and festivals. Brides were shown, escorted through the streets from their homes, with trains of attendants waving torches and chanting a loud bridal song. Young men, much admired by housewives, each posted at her own front-door, performed an intricate wedding dance to the sound of flutes and lyres. But citizens also thronged the market-place, to witness a bitter legal conflict. A man had been murdered, and though the murderer was volunteering to pay the highest blood-price sanctioned, the next-of-kin demanded his death. The crowd being by no means unanimous in its sympathies, heralds kept order, and provided white rods for the city elders, who sat on smooth marble benches in the holy circle of justice. Both litigants agreed to accept arbitration and would plead their cause alternately before these elders; at whose feet lay two talents of gold destined as a reward for whichever of them spoke most to the point.

The second town on the shield was threatened by a pair of allied armies, and their leaders were arguing whether it should be plundered, or allowed to capitulate—whereupon its treasures could be fairly divided between them. So far from capitulating, however, the obstinate townsfolk—leaving women, boys, and old men to defend their walls—took the offensive. With the help of Ares and Athene, depicted as of more than mortal stature, and wearing golden armour —they laid an ambush near a river ford, which was the common watering-place for that district. Two careless cattlemen who approached the ford, playing on pipes, were enemies, as the townsfolk knew from scouts; they killed them, and drove off their herds and flocks. Meanwhile, the allied leaders, still busily discussing capitulation, heard a distant hubbub, and hurried to the ford. Some of their chariots had already sprung the ambush and become engaged.

On the battlefield, Hephaestus engraved the figures of Strife, Tumult, and Death. Strife, recognizable by her blood-stained tunic, grasped a freshly-wounded man; Tumult, an unwounded one; Death held a corpse by its ankles. The combatants were extraordinarily life-like: they cast spears, lunged, struck, hauled away the dead for despoilment.

A further design showed numerous ox-teams ploughing, cross-ploughing, and re-ploughing a wide, rich fallow. One ploughman who had reached the edge of the field was proffered a goblet of wine when he turned about. His companions, eager to drink themselves, were goading their beasts on. The furrows ran dark behind each plough, just as nature ordains—an artistic triumph, because the scene had been executed entirely in gold!

Hephaestus also portrayed a royal demesne, including cornfields, vineyards, and pastures. Reapers swung sharp sickles and laid down armfuls of cut corn; which three sheaf-binders then secured with ropes of woven straw. The king, staff in hand, complacently supervised their work; a group of courtiers could be seen jointing a sacrificial ox for the harvest feast; and women were preparing to feed the reapers on generous portions of barley porridge.

Hephaestus made the vines of gold, their abundant clusters of obsidian, the vine-poles of silver. A ditch of lapis lazuli, and a fence of pure tin, surrounded the village; its single entrance was now used by many vintagers—girls and boys, carrying wicker baskets full of sweet grapes. A boy thrummed his lyre as he gently sang the Flax Lament; and every foot kept time to the melody.

Long-horned cows, in gold and pure tin, trotted lowing from their byre to graze by a reed-flanked river. Four golden cattlemen and nine hounds followed them; but a pair of terrible lions had dragged down the leader of the herd—a bull that bellowed agonizedly as they tore open its stomach and devoured its intestines. The hounds, though urged to the attack, stood barking at a safe distance. Beyond lay a peaceful valley, where flocks of sheep pastured beside the huts and sheep-cotes of a farm.

There was a dancing-floor, too, recalling the one built by Daedalus at Cnossus for the Princess Ariadne centuries ago. Young men and well-to-do girls formed a long chain, grasping wrists. The girls wore wreaths and fine linen gowns; the young men wore close-woven tunics, faintly stained with olive oil, and golden daggers hung from their silver baldrics. First, these dancers would circle around very prettily, whirling as fast as a potter's wheel when the potter crouches to give it a trial spin; then they would form two lines, advancing towards each other, and retiring. A couple of acrobats tumbled about among them, and spectators grinned delightedly.

On the outermost rim an endless river coursed: the Ocean Stream.

Having finished this tremendous shield, Hephaestus forged Achilles a corslet brighter than flame; a massive, exquisitely engraved, golden-ridged bronze helmet, of the right size for his head; and greaves of pliant tin. All these he laid before Thetis. She gathered them up thankfully, and swooped like a falcon from the peak of Olympus.

Book Nineteen:

The Reconciliation

> Rising from her bed-chamber
> Where Ocean's waters wind,
> DAWN, saffron-robed, brought daylight
> To gods and mankind—

at which early hour Thetis the Silver-Footed reached the Greek camp. Achilles still lay on the ground beside Patroclus' corpse, lamenting hopelessly among a large crowd of Myrmidons. She took his hand in hers and cried: 'Dear child! Leave him for a while, however profound your grief. Remember: the Immortals decided his fate from the very beginning. See what I have here: gifts to make you proud—the most glorious armour man ever wore!'

She laid down her burden with so rich a clank that the Myrmidons averted their awe-stricken eyes; but when Achilles raised his, the fires of pride, delight, and battle-fury shone beneath their lids. He admired every piece in turn, exclaiming: 'Mother, they are worthy of the divine giver; what human smith could dare to forge anything so splendid? I would use them immediately and avenge Patroclus, were it not that flies might settle on his wounds during my absence, breed maggots, and cause decay.'

Thetis reassured him: 'Those are idle fears! No fly shall approach Patroclus; and if he has to lie a twelvemonth, his flesh will, I promise, be as sound then as it is today—or sounder! Now, before fighting, you must summon a General Assembly and renounce your grudge against Agamemnon the High King.' Having thus imbued her son with strength and courage, Thetis poured into the corpse's nostrils a mixture of red nectar and ambrosia, which would preserve the flesh for ever, if need be.

Achilles strode along the shore, summoning all Greeks to the Assembly Ground. Nobody disobeyed his fierce shout, even helmsmen, stewards, and such, who never took part in a battle. Two famous champions, Diomedes, son of Tydeus, and King Odysseus the Crafty, limped painfully out of their huts, each leaning on a spear, and sat in the foremost row of the Assembly. Agamemnon arrived last, nursing his arm—the wound inflicted by Antenor's son Coön troubled him.

When he too was seated, Achilles rose. 'My lord Agamemnon, son of Atreus,' he cried, 'you will agree that neither of us has profited from our recent scandalous quarrel about a girl-captive. I heartily wish that Artemis the Huntress had shot her dead in Lyrnessus! No Greeks would then have been slaughtered because of losing her. Hector's Trojans were the sole gainers, as our army will always recall. So, why not let bygones be bygones, forgiving each other the injuries we suffered and, henceforth, keep a close guard on our tongues? I am ready to forget my anger—a reputation for implacability sullies a prince's honour—if you marshal your army at once and appoint me their leader. I must see whether the Trojans remain anxious to bed down in this camp. My prediction is that any of them fortunate enough to escape from me will be glad to rest their weary legs in whatever shelter offers.'

The Greeks applauded Prince Achilles' change of front.

King Agamemnon's wound prevented his rising. Still seated, he said: 'Heroic comrades, pray show your courtesy by listening in silence, as though I were standing up! Even a practised orator finds it hard to ignore a buzz of interruptions; nor can his audience hear what he is saying. I shall address the son of Peleus, and call upon every man present to witness my words.

'Prince Achilles, others beside yourself have often reproached my ill-considered utterances; yet Zeus, Fate, and the Fury who walks in darkness, are more to blame than I. They fooled me by suggesting that I should demand a possession of yours. Pray show forgiveness: we mortals are at the mercy of the Immortals—the very worst of whom is Mischief, Zeus' eldest daughter. Everyone is beguiled by that goddess:

> 'Delicate are her feet; they do not stalk
> This earth, like yours and mine, but unseen walk
> On air above our heads. It is her way
> To trip us up, or send our wits astray.

'Yes, even Zeus, whom we worship as the greatest and wisest of gods, was once hoodwinked by Queen Hera—at Mischief's instigation! On the day that Alcmene of Thebes should have borne him his magnificent son Heracles, Zeus made a solemn speech before the assembled Immortals:

'"Give ear, all gods and goddesses,
Who dwell in Heaven apart,
And I shall freely broach to you
The counsels of this heart:

'"ARTEMIS, Goddess of Childbed,
Today shall bring to birth
One who shall rule my royal sons
Scattered about the earth!"

'Hera slily interrupted: "But how can we trust you not to cheat us? Come, Lord of Olympus, swear a sure oath that the descendant of yours who is born today will rule Greece as High King!"

'Zeus, unsuspectingly, took the oath. Hera darted off to Argos where, she knew, the wife of King Sthenelus, a descendant of Zeus, was seven months pregnant. She induced the premature birth of this child, while magically prolonging Alcmene's travail, and brought the news to Zeus herself: "God of the Lightning Flash, a future High King of Greece has been born today—Eurystheus, son of Sthenelus. Being descended from your son Perseus, he is most worthy of the distinction."

'Startled into fury, Zeus seized Mischief by her bright locks and vowed that, for deceiving and blinding everyone, she should never again visit either Olympus or the starry Heavens. He whirled her round his head and let fly: Mischief sailed through the air, then crashed to earth. But Zeus still groaned and muttered against her, years later, because Eurystheus was imposing those cruel labours on Heracles.

'I sympathized with Zeus, Prince Achilles, as I watched Hector's slaughter among the ships; that is to say, I cursed Mischief for provoking my outrageous behaviour towards you. Yes, I fully admit the error, though not the responsibility, and am eager to make amends in the form of handsome damages. I ask no return but that you will lead my army; a commission which you have anticipated. If, therefore, you care to wait while the gifts mentioned by Odysseus are placed at your disposal, I will gladly keep my promise and give the necessary orders.'

'My lord King,' replied Achilles, 'whether you keep your promise or not must be your own concern. I have set my heart on immediate battle; and subtle speculations about the divine authorship of our dispute do not interest me. What matters is that I should destroy Trojans, and that my men should remind themselves as they fight: "We have Achilles with us again!"'

Odysseus rose to protest. 'Your courage is unquestionable,' he said, 'but do not take hungry men into the field! Since both Greeks and Trojans will be equally inspired by the gods, this struggle should prove a hard one; and who, however gallant, fights well on an empty belly? A substantial meal remedies such ailments as thirst, hunger, and lassitude; it also prolongs a soldier's resistance until the armies part at dusk. So, pray allow your comrades to breakfast on meat and wine; in the meantime, Agamemnon can produce his gifts for us to admire. I am sure that they will please you. Further, by way of perfect appeasement, the High King must publicly swear that he has never yet slept with, or otherwise enjoyed, this woman Briseis. Afterwards, you should attend the banquet of reconciliation due to you at his headquarters.' Addressing Agamemnon, Odysseus added: 'My lord, although the proposed damages do not detract from your honour, you must try to treat allies more handsomely in future.'

Agamemnon answered: 'I accept these strictures, son of Laertes, and will take that solemn oath—for which I needed no prompting. Let Achilles and his comrades curb their impatience, while the gifts are fetched and I confirm the oath by sacrifice. Here is a task for you, King Odysseus! Choose a group of young princes, lead them to my treasure-hut, and collect everything I promised Achilles: including the female captives. Talthybius must also secure a boar, which I will dedicate to Zeus and the Sun.'

Achilles demurred. 'Most noble son of Atreus,' he said, 'another occasion—some short respite from war—would suit me better. My heart is too restless now. And how can you suggest breakfast, when so many Greek corpses strew the plain—corpses of your friends whom Zeus helped Hector to kill? I would have the army fight dry-throated

and empty-bellied all day, and at nightfall enjoy a huge feast in cele-
bration of vengeance victoriously taken. Myself, I will touch neither
food nor drink before then. Ever since Patroclus' battered body has
lain stretched on that bier, his feet towards the hut-door, I can think
only of warfare, blood, and the groans of the Trojans I intend to
destroy.'

'My lord Achilles,' exclaimed Odysseus. 'I dare not compete as a
fighter with our greatest living champion; yet, since I am older, more
experienced, and wiser than you, pray listen to me! Harvesters weary
when they reap much straw, but little grain; soldiers weary when the
issue of a hard-fought battle hangs in Zeus' balance, and they fore-
see many wounds, but little plunder. It is absurd that these troops
should fast in particular mourning for Patroclus! Hundreds of their
comrades are killed daily. A similar honour paid to every fallen sol-
dier would soon exhaust them. No, we survivors should inter the
dead, lament briefly, then force ourselves to eat and drink as a means
of preserving martial strength. The call to arms has already sounded,
and need not be repeated. But any man who, after breakfast, skulks
behind in the camp, instead of marching out and playing the hero,
must expect no mercy!'

Odysseus duly chose seven noblemen: Nestor's two sons,
Meges son of Phyleus, Thoas, Meriones, Lycomedes son of Creon,
and Melanippus, whom he led towards Agamemnon's treasure-hut.
There they collected his gifts: seven tripods, twenty new cauldrons,
twelve horses, seven captive craftswomen, and the lovely Briseis.

Having weighed the promised ten talents of gold, Odysseus led his
companions back, and they set everything down on the Assembly
Ground. Talthybius, the loud-voiced royal herald, held a struggling
boar, and Agamemnon, who stood beside him, drew his dagger from
where it always hung—next to the sword scabbard—and severed the
victim's fore-lock. Looking up to Heaven, he prayed shrilly:

'Almighty Father, merciful to men,
You too, sweet Mother EARTH, vigilant SUN,
And black Infernal FURIES who avenge
The breach of solemn oaths: be witness now
That I have neither slept with Briseis
Nor carnally possessed her. She has dwelt

Chastely secluded in my treasure-hut.
If these be lies, I grant you liberty
To plague me as a faithless wretch forsworn!'

His dagger slit the boar's throat, and Talthybius, catching the carcase by the trotters, swung it into the sea as food for fishes.

Achilles rose again, and spoke: 'Since this is what you require of me, comrades, I agree that Father Zeus cruelly deranges men's wits, and that, had he not planned to destroy large numbers of Greeks, the High King would never have angered me by shamelessly demanding my prize of honour. So begone to your breakfasts; we will fight as soon as they are eaten.'

The Assembly broke up at once, Achilles' Myrmidons carrying the tripods, cauldrons, and talents to his compound. They were followed by Briseis and his seven new slave-women, while grooms took charge of the twelve horses.

Briseis (who was no less attractive than Aphrodite the Golden) flung herself on Patroclus' corpse and wailed aloud, tearing her breasts and neck and beautiful face. 'Dear protector!' she sobbed. 'When I left this hut you were still alive. Oh, how I am dogged by misfortune! My parents married me in style to a suitable husband; but he and my three brothers died at the capture of Lyrnessus. Now Patroclus' turn has come! After Achilles had widowed me, he would often say: "Dry your eyes, Briseis, daughter of Mynes; I will persuade him to marry you. We three shall sail off together and celebrate your wedding at Phthia." My heart aches for him; no kinder man ever lived!' Briseis' seven fellow-captives wailed too, though they were brooding on their own troubles, not lamenting Patroclus' death.

The Royal Councillors pressed Achilles to take some nourishment. He groaned in answer: 'Can none of you understand that my grief is too great for eating or drinking? I will fast until sunset, whatever it may cost me.'

Defeated by his obduracy, they all walked away, except Agamemnon, Menelaus, Odysseus, Nestor, Idomeneus of Crete, and the venerable Phoenix, who vainly tried to comfort him. He sighed heavily, and addressed Patroclus once more: 'Dearest friend, who used to prepare such savoury breakfasts, and with such speed, too, those mornings when we had to rise at dawn and battle against the Trojans; but this cruel blow has destroyed my appetite . . . King Peleus' death would have affected me far less—poor old father, I can imagine him shedding big tears, longing for my return from what he calls "that foreign war caused by Queen Helen's fatal beauty". He must be very frail and miserable now, in daily fear of news that he has out-lived me. Not even my son Neoptolemus' death in Scyros—where I have had him educated—could cause me so much grief as yours, Patroclus! Though doomed to die at Troy myself, I trusted that you would survive and sail home by way of Scyros, fetching the boy, and showing him his inheritance at Phthia—my lofty palace, my servants, my treasures.'

Achilles' tears were catching: the High King and the five Council-lors remembered their distant homes, and wept in sympathy. At last, Zeus took pity on Achilles, saying to Athene: 'Daughter, why casually abandon your favourite hero? Can he be in disgrace with you? There he sits, broken-hearted and lonesome, and continues to fast when everyone else is feasting comfortably. Fly away, and stave off his pangs of hunger by giving him a little divine food!'

Athene gladly swooped down and, while the Greeks re-armed themselves, let fall on Achilles' breast a subtle distillation of nectar and ambrosia, which penetrated his skin and made him enormously strong; but she vanished before the parade formed up.

> The north wind blows; from realms of sky
> Huge clouds of snowflakes earthward fly!

Bright and numerous as snowflakes, the Greeks poured from their ships, the gay sunlight twinkling on polished helmets, shield-bosses, plated corslets, and sharp spear-blades. The glint was clearly visible in Heaven, and the earth around them laughed. Tramp, tramp, went their feet; and Achilles, with a furious gnashing of teeth, and such intolerable grief for Patroclus that his eyes blazed, buckled on the divine armour.

First the greaves and their silver ankle-pieces—then the corslet, then the baldric, from which hung a great silver-studded broadsword —I forgot to mention this gift—then the famous shield.

> By adverse winds across the sea
>   Borne far out of our course, we stare
> Ahead in doubt and misery;
>   But yonder, see, a distant glare

Of firelight through the gloom, that spills
From some lone farm-house on the hills!

The Greeks gazed at Achilles' shield no less hopefully. It shone like
the full moon. On his head, he placed the new, strong, lucent, bright-
crested helmet—Hephaestus had inserted golden plumes among the
horsehair—and leaped about to prove that the armour allowed his
limbs free play. All was well! The corslet and helmet gave him wings,
so to speak; he felt free as a bird. Finally, returning to the hut, he
snatched from its stand the huge, heavy, tough lance which he alone
could wield. This lethal weapon—the shaft, an ash-tree that grew on
Mount Pelion—had been presented to his father Peleus by Cheiron
the Centaur.

Automedon and Alcimus yoked Xanthus and Balius on either side
of the chariot-pole; adjusted the breast-harness, set bits in their jaws,
saw to the reins. Automedon took his whip and mounted. Achilles,
who might have been mistaken for Hyperion the Sun Titan, fol-
lowed. He now sternly admonished the horses: 'Foals of Podarce,
behave better this time than last! Whatever happens, do not aban-
don me, as you abandoned Patroclus! I expect to be brought safely
back.'

A miracle! Queen Hera the White-Armed opened the mouth of
Xanthus! He bowed submissively, dipping his mane to the ground,
and neighed: 'Most noble Achilles, Balius and I are your loyal steeds
until nightfall. You still have a few days of life, but we will not
accept the blame when death strikes. It was no negligence on our part
that let the Trojans despoil Patroclus. Phoebus Apollo, Leto's glori-
ous son, half-killed him in the mêlée; Hector struck only the final
blow. Understand that, though able to race against our father Zephyr
—reputedly the swiftest of the winds—we cannot outstrip Fate. You
yourself, Master, are doomed to die, like Patroclus, at the hands of
an Immortal—and of a mortal!'

The Furies officiously intervened before Xanthus could finish his
speech, and Achilles cried in anger: 'Xanthus, what ill manners!
How dare you prophesy my death? I was already aware of its immi-
nence; nor will this prevent me from first giving the Trojans a proper
surfeit of war.'

He drove forward with a yell.

Book Twenty:

God Fights God

As Achilles and his fellow-Greeks armed themselves, so also did Hector's Trojans in their bivouacs overlooking the naval camp. At the same time, Zeus the Cloud-Gatherer asked Themis, Goddess of Law and Order, to summon all gods of whatever rank or standing to an immediate council on Olympus' topmost peak. They trooped up by the hundred, among them being every known river-god, with the exception of old Oceanus, and every single forest-nymph, fountain-nymph and meadow-nymph, without exception; then settled down under the polished colonnades which Hephaestus, the ingenious Smith-god, had built at his father Zeus' desire.

Poseidon the Earth-Shaker had obeyed the summons. 'Brother of the Lightning Flash,' he cried, as he emerged from the sea and took his place in the middle of the Assembly, 'why have you called yet another divine council? Can it be to discuss the new fierce battle that seems imminent at Troy?'

'Earth-Shaker,' replied Zeus, 'there was no need for that question. I have the fortunes of both armies very much at heart, even when they engage in mutual slaughter; so I shall post myself between two crags of Olympus and enjoy a quiet view of the battle . . . Listen, all gods and goddesses: you are hereby permitted to take the field on either side, just as you please. This is because Achilles the Swift-Footed will soon break the Trojan ranks unless I concede them divine assistance. They have always been terrified of him and, with his ill-temper now exacerbated by the death of Patroclus, I fear he may transgress the writ of Fate, and try to storm Troy.'

...rds excited such passionate feelings that the Immortals at ...ormed rival factions. The Greeks secured as their patrons Queen Hera, Pallas Athene, Poseidon, Hermes the Helper (the cleverest strategist and tactician on Olympus), also powerful Hephaestus who hobbled busily about on his shrunken legs. The Trojans secured the indefatigable War-god Ares, Phoebus Apollo, his sister and fellow-archer Artemis, their mother Leto, the Trojan River-god Xanthus, and laughter-loving Aphrodite.

So long as these deities avoided battle, the Greeks could do as they would, since Achilles had clearly been invigorated by his rest; but when they at last appeared, Strife towered up among them, cheering on both, and the odds grew shorter. Beside the fosse, Athene screamed her war-cry, then went along the echoing shore and repeated it; whereupon Ares gave a hideous counter-shout, like the noise of a black, rushing storm, first from the Citadel of Troy where he stood, and then in flight down the banks of the Simöeis and over Callicolone.

This time, not content merely to exhort their champions, the Immortals entered the fray themselves, and a dreadful clamour arose; for Apollo confronted Poseidon; and Athene, Ares; and Artemis, Queen Hera; and Hermes, Leto. Hephaestus was challenged by the god of the great, deep-eddying river which the Olympians call Xanthus, but men Scamander. Zeus thundered terribly from the sky, while his brother Poseidon shook plains and high mountains with a heavy earthquake. The spurs of many-fountained Mount Ida quivered, so did the Citadel of Troy; and the Greek fleet rocked, though on dry land. The third brother, King Hades, sprang from his subterranean throne shouting in alarm, lest the ceiling might collapse and leave his vast, grim, loathsome palace exposed to the gaze alike of mortals and Immortals.

Apollo knew that Achilles' heart was set upon meeting Hector, whose blood seemed the most suitable sacrifice he could offer Ares. Disguising himself therefore as Prince Lycaon, Priam's son, he approached Aeneas, and asked in Lycaon's own voice: 'What of the boasts you made, son of Anchises, while drinking wine among the Trojan Royal Councillors? You undertook to fight Achilles.'

Aeneas answered: 'Why urge me to challenge that mad hero? Anyone can see how little I would enjoy the encounter, which would not be our first. Achilles once raided my cattle on Mount Ida, drove me away at the point of his spear, and afterwards sacked the towns of Lyrnessus and Pedasus. Zeus graciously strengthened my legs, and I escaped. I had no alternative, because Athene flew ahead of Achilles, providing light for the slaughter of Trojans and Lelegians. Nobody could stand up to him! Some Olympian is always at hand to parry thrusts; nor does his lance ever miss, but bursts through the strongest armour and drives straight into the flesh. If Zeus would match us two on equal terms, that might be a different tale: although Achilles boasts himself solid bronze, he would find victory harder to achieve.'

'True, my lord,' Apollo agreed. 'Yet, since you are reputedly the son of Aphrodite, why not resort to prayer? Achilles has a less exalted birth than yours. His mother Thetis is a mere Nereid, daughter of the old Sea-god Nereus, whereas Aphrodite's father is none other than Almighty Zeus. Come, hurl your spear at Achilles, despite his taunts and threats!'

Apollo then breathed high courage into Aeneas, whose armour flashed as he strode forward. Hera, observing him, nudged Athene and Poseidon, saying: 'Consider well, dear allies, what will happen if we do not intervene! We must either turn him back without delay, or else one of us must reassure Achilles that he has the pick of the Olympians behind him, and that the patrons in whom the Trojans trust are fickle as the wind. Surely we descended from Heaven on purpose to give Achilles a successful day? Later, of course, he is bound to suffer the doom which Fate's spindle span him at the hour of his birth; but now, unless first emboldened by an immortal voice, he will shrink from any hostile god who opposes him. Remember that, as a rule, mortals avert their eyes in our presence.'

'Hera, you are unreasonably fierce!' replied Poseidon. 'I am opposed, myself, to pitting gods against gods. Why not let us all quit the field, and sit apart, leaving these Trojans and Greeks to fight it out? Only if Ares or Phoebus Apollo join in the battle, or dare hamper Achilles' feats of matchless valour, should we take arms ourselves; and then, no doubt, they will both flee to Olympus before our superior strength.'

Poseidon brought Hera to her senses. They went off together and sat on the high rampart between beach and plain which, many years previously, Athene had helped the Trojans to build as a shelter for Heracles while he was rescuing King Laomedon's daughter Hesione from a sea-beast sent by Poseidon himself to plague Troy. The other gods who favoured the Greeks now joined their seniors, wrapping themselves in cloaks of impenetrable cloud; whereupon Ares, Apollo, and their faction occupied Callicolone's pleasant bluffs. Every god planned stratagems; but though Zeus, far away on Olympus, wanted to see them fight, they were all averse to active warfare.

Infantry and chariotry covered the wide battlefield; arms glittered brightly, and earth echoed when the two armies, each headed by a resolute champion—Aeneas and Achilles—confronted each other on the plain.

Aeneas' plume tossed menacingly, he brandished his spear and displayed his deft management of a shield. Achilles rushed to meet him, like a lion:

> The tribe advancing on a lion chase,
>   Knew well what beast had ravaged their hill farms;
> He did not stop the vengeful horde to face
>   But kept an even pace, scornful of arms.
>
> Confusion! At the lion's tawny side
>   Some youth had flung a javelin, and aimed true.
> Foam flecked his fangs, he opened his jaws wide
>   Roaring in pride against the insolent crew.
>
> With frequent lashings of his tufted tail
>   And noble eyes afire, he crouched to spring—
> Resolved on this: either he must prevail
>   Or gloriously fail, as fits a king.

A short cast from his opponent, Achilles paused. 'Son of Anchises,' he cried, 'what are you at? Trying to gain King Priam's favour and be named as successor to the Trojan throne—is that it? Foolish fellow! Even if you killed me, your claim would fail—Priam still has his wits about him, and sons of his own. Or have the Trojans voted a rich estate of cornlands and orchards to my victor? It will be a hard prize to win. How fast you ran down the slopes of Mount Ida, once, when we met among your herds—never a backward glance! Following your trail to Lyrnessus, I sacked the town—assisted by Athene and Father Zeus—enslaved the women, and butchered all the men. Or all except you: for the Olympians furthered your escape. Yet their protection must not be counted upon again; so take my advice and retire while your skin is whole! Even a fool learns wisdom after the event.'

'Son of Peleus,' answered Aeneas, 'I am no easily scared child. I know well how to bandy threats and insults, if need be. You have heard my lineage blazoned, and I have heard yours; although neither of us has set eyes on the other's parents. People say that you are Thetis the Nereid's son by King Peleus; my father is King Anchises, my mother the great Aphrodite. And since this combat cannot end, as it began, in idle words, one of these goddesses must mourn her son tonight. Let me present my pedigree. Zeus the Cloud-Gatherer had a son, Dardanus by name, who founded the city of Dardania on Mount Ida—long before Troy was built yonder. Dardanus' son Erichthonius, the richest man alive, kept three thousand mares at grass in these water-meadows, foals frisking behind their heels; but Boreas, the North Wind, lusted after the lovely beasts and, assuming the form of a dark-maned stallion, covered twelve of them. They bore him an equal number of fillies, swift-footed enough to scud across the top of a ripe barley-field without crushing the grain, or across the crests of sea waves without wetting their hocks.

'Erichthonius' son Tros, the first King of Troy, begot Ilus, Assaracus and Ganymede. Ganymede being the handsomest boy ever born, the gods caught him up to Heaven, and appointed him Zeus' deathless cup-bearer. Laomedon, son of Ilus, begot Dawn's husband Tithonus; also Lampus, Clytius, and soldierly Hicetaon.

'I am descended from Tros' second son, Assaracus, through Capys and Anchises—Hector, son of Priam, comes of the elder line. This, then, is my pedigree; yet I shall lay no great claim to courage— a virtue that Almighty Zeus augments or decreases in a champion, just as he thinks fit.

'But why do we stand arguing like little boys, when battle has already been joined? Tongues are so glib, words are so many and various, that we could both hurl insults at each other by the wagon-load—a two-hundred-oar galley would not serve to ship our cargo!

> 'Once I saw two housewives meet
> Wrangling fiercely in the street—
> Some words false, and some words true.
> Ah, how red their faces grew!
> Anger's a divinely sent
> Means to make man eloquent.

'No: mere talk will never dissuade me from challenging you; we must fight, blade against blade. Guard your head!'

So saying, Aeneas flung his heavy spear, and Achilles' wonderful new shield rang loudly under the blow. Achilles had held it out to the full extent of his arm, fearing that Aeneas might breach all five layers; which was ungracious—he should have known that divine gifts are not easily destroyed. True, the point penetrated the first layer of bronze, and the second of tin, but stuck fast in the third, golden layer.

Aeneas ducked and protected himself with his own shield, as Achilles made a return cast. The great lance struck the edge where the bull's hide was thinnest and covered only by a single sheet of bronze; cut through two of the rims, flew over Aeneas' back, and buried itself in the earth. Terrified by so close a call, Aeneas gazed dumbly at Achilles but, on seeing him draw his sword and rush forward, picked up a boulder—of a weight that no pair of men today could lift between them, and prepared to hurl it. Had he done so, however, the boulder would have harmlessly rebounded from either the divine helmet or the divine shield—leaving Achilles free to hew him down.

Poseidon at once observed the danger. 'Alas!' he said. 'I pity our courageous Aeneas, foolishly lured by Apollo the Archer into the power of King Hades. Why should this poor innocent, who is always burning splendid sacrifices in our honour, be wickedly sacrificed himself? Friends, rescue Aeneas! My brother Zeus will rage if a man dies whom he wished to spare. He had greater love for Aeneas' ancestor Dardanus than for any other of his mortal sons and, though disliking Priam's House, does not want the royal line to die out. He intends that Aeneas shall rule the surviving Trojan stock, and his children's children after him.'

Hera answered: 'Earth-Shaker, please yourself whether Aeneas lives or dies! Athene and I have sworn frequent and solemn oaths never on any account to aid the Trojans, not even when our brave Greeks burn their city.'

Poseidon darted among the fighters, shrouded Achilles' eyes in a magical mist, disengaged his great lance from the broken shield and laid it at his feet; then seized Aeneas and swung him through the air, high over several battalions of infantry and squadrons of chariotry. Aeneas came to earth by the bivouacs and astonished the Cauconians, who were still mustering. 'Aeneas,' expostulated Poseidon, 'what god gave you such inept advice? It was madness to challenge the furious son of Peleus, who is your master in battle, and also our favourite champion! Be warned! Not to withdraw at his approach is to court a premature death—although, once Achilles has gone, you may fight confidently at the head of your army, assured that no other Greek will take your life.'

Poseidon left Aeneas and hurried back to dispel the mist from Achilles' eyes. Gazing wildly around him, Achilles cried: 'A miracle! Here is my lance, but where is Aeneas, whom I tried to kill? Vanished! So his boasts were less idle than I thought! Evidently the Olympians love him too. Ah, enough of Aeneas: having escaped this second time, he will hardly risk a third combat. I shall call for support, and destroy other Trojans instead.'

He bounded along the front-line, appealing to his comrades by name. 'Forward, noble Greeks!' he shouted. 'Let every man choose his opponent, and fight heart and soul. Strong as I am, do you expect me to brave an entire army? Neither Immortal Ares, nor even Pallas Athene, would dare plunge alone into such jaws of destruction. It is your duty to prevent them from closing behind me as I exert the full power of my arms and legs, pressing on until the Trojans break. Those who stand within reach of this lance will certainly have small cause for rejoicing.'

Hector, on his side, encouraged the Trojans: 'Gallant comrades,' he cried, 'pay no heed to that wordy hero! With words I, too, could match myself against even the Olympians; but weapons are a very different matter! Achilles cannot make good all those boasts. He may achieve part of his design; what remains will shiver in pieces. Meanwhile, I am ready to meet him, though his hands be fire and his spirit flashing steel!' He strode ahead of the line.

The Trojans grasped their spears firmly, and a fierce, ragged cheer arose. Apollo, alighting at Hector's side, exclaimed: 'Back to your comrades at once! Why offer Achilles an easy target? He will either spear you, or rush up and use his sword.'

Hector retired in surprise; but indomitable Achilles leaped among the Trojans, yelling horribly. His first victim was Iphition, son of Otrynteus the City-Sacker, by a Naiad who lived beneath snow-clad Mount Tmolus in the rich land of Hyde. As Iphition charged, Achilles hurled, split his head clean open and sent him crashing down. Achilles exulted: 'There you lie, redoubtable son of Otrynteus! Born by Lake Gyges, between the turbulent Hermus River and Hyllus famous for its fishing; killed at Troy!' Chariot wheels crushed Iphition's corpse.

Next, Achilles lunged at Demoleon, son of Antenor, who faced him courageously. The lance burst through the cheek-piece of Demoleon's helmet, broke open his skull, scattered his brains. Hippodamas, the driver, sprang out of the chariot and scurried off; but Achilles pierced his spine as he ran. Hippodamas died with such a roar of anguish that he might have been a sacrificial bull being dragged to Poseidon's altar at Helice. (He loves nothing better than bull's blood.)

Achilles did not despoil his two victims. He had caught sight of quick-heeled Prince Polydorus, Priam's youngest and favourite son, who despite his father's frequent injunctions to keep away from the battlefield, was sportively dodging about between the front-rank fighters. As he darted by, Achilles threw a javelin and struck the gold belt-buckle where his corslet and taslets overlapped behind. The point emerged from Polydorus' navel; he halted, fell groaning on one knee, pressed back the bowels as they gushed out, then sank in death.

Hector watched the scene. Tears filled his eyes, and he could no longer bear to obey Apollo, but ran up, vengefully brandishing a spear. In savage glee, Achilles shouted: 'Here comes the Trojan who killed my best friend! Here comes the Trojan who hurt me more than I was ever yet hurt! We meet at last!' He growled at Hector: 'The closer you approach, the sooner you die!'

Hector answered calmly: 'Son of Peleus, I am no easily scared child. I know well how to bandy threats and insults, if need be. You are a famous hero and, admittedly, my master in battle. The issue of our combat, however, lies with the gods. They will decide whether this spear, though not so powerful as your lance, is to rob you of life; indeed, its blade has proved sharp enough of late.'

He poised and let fly, but Athene gave a gentle puff that sent the weapon curving back, to fall at his feet. Achilles ran towards him, roaring vengeance, and Apollo intervened by shrouding Hector in a thick mist. Three times Achilles vainly charged his unseen adversary; then, pausing, he exclaimed: 'Dog, once again you escape destruction, and by a narrow margin only! There is no doubt whom you invoke amid the spears: Phoebus Apollo, who now saved your life! Nevertheless, if any god deigns to assist me at a later meeting, I know which of us two will die . . . So be it, whom else can I destroy?' He turned and speared Dryops in the neck, below the chin, tumbling him dead, but left his body undespoiled.

The lance next caught Philetor's son Demuchus on the shin, and halted his charge. Having cut him down, Achilles sprang at Laogonus and Dardanus, the sons of Bias, hurling both of them from their chariot—Laogonus with a spear-cast, Dardanus with a sword-sweep. Tros, son of Alastor, clutched his knees. 'I am young like you. Pity me!' he pleaded, unaware how foolish it was to expect tenderness of that bloodthirsty hero. Achilles struck at the simpleton and sliced his liver; blood spurted on his breast, and he died. Achilles' lance also transfixed Mulius' head, going in at one ear, out at the other; and his sword shattered the skull of Echeclus, Agenor's son—the blade reeked as he withdrew it. Again that long lance darted, piercing the crook of Deucalion's elbow; thus disabled, the Lycian champion knew that he had lost all. Achilles' sword swept off his head and helmet. The trunk fell supine, its severed backbone dripping marrow.

Then Achilles made for Rhigmus the Thracian, son of Peires, casting a javelin that breached his lungs and sent him flying over the chariot-tail. As Rhigmus' driver Areithous wheeled the team about,

he received a mortal lance-thrust between his shoulders. The master-
less horses bolted in terror.

> From the hillside parched with drought
> Flames leap out.
>   Up deep valley-lands they go,
>   Wheresoever the winds blow,
> Burning forests all about,
>   Laying tall trees low.

Achilles raged like a forest fire, killing Trojans wherever he went.

> Goad the noisy ox-team round
> Our well-littered threshing-ground;
> Quickly will their hard hooves tread
> Barley forth to give us bread.

So it was that Achilles circled the battlefield in his chariot drawn by
Xanthus and Balius. They trod upon corpses and shields, until blood
from their hooves and blood from the wheel-rims reddened the whole
conveyance. Achilles' irresistible hands were also stained with blood.

Book Twenty-one:

Achilles at the Ford

The routed Trojans made for the deep River Scamander, whose god Xanthus was Zeus the Thunderer's son. Achilles cut their forces into two parts at the ford, chasing one of these across the plain where his comrades had been routed by Hector on the previous day. The other stumbled into Scamander's silver eddies, their shouts echoing from bank to bank. The current tossed them hither and thither, like a half-drowned swarm of locusts.

> By a scorching fire pursued,
> Locusts make for water:
> There they shiver in the river
> To escape from slaughter!

Achilles, ablaze with anger, leaned his great lance against a thicket of tamarisk, and leaped splendidly into the river after the floundering fugitives, content to use his sword alone. They uttered dismal groans as he struck at them; their blood stained the stream.

> Wide-mouthed the dolphin loves to swim.
> The fishes go in fear of him,
> And when they see this monster rove
> Greedily towards their favourite cove,
> All dart for shelter to rock pools—
> Where he devours the pretty fools.

Many Trojans similarly crouched in shallows all along the steep riverbanks, and Achilles massacred them by the score. He paused

awhile in his grim work to choose twelve young men for sacrifice at
Patroclus' pyre, drag them out of the stream, more like frightened
fawns than soldiers, and pinion them with their own stout leather
belts. Having ordered his Myrmidons to march the victims off, he
rushed away, fiercely intent on further slaughter.

Suddenly he saw Prince Lycaon, a son of King Priam, emerging
from the river—the same Lycaon whom once, during a night raid on
Priam's orchards, he had discovered chopping down wild-fig saplings
to trim for chariot-rails. Captured, and shipped overseas as a slave,
Lycaon became the property of the Lemnian King Euneus, Jason the
Argonaut's son. Later, King Eëtion of Imbros, a former guest of Ly-
caon's, paid Euneus a heavy ransom for him. Since Eëtion dared not
offend the Greeks by letting Lycaon fight again at Troy, he was sent
under guard to the city of Arisbe, but escaped and made his way
home. There he spent eleven days among the Trojan royal family in
joyful celebration of this good fortune, before joining his brothers on
the battlefield. Destiny now threw him back into Achilles' hands.

Watching Lycaon struggle weakly ashore, without helmet, shield
or spear, Achilles thought indignantly: 'Surely I sold him to King
Euneus? Most slaves on Lemnos find the sea an impassable barrier,
but this one seems to have cheated his unkind fate! Soon, no doubt,
even the Trojans I have killed will emerge from Hades' murky king-
dom. My lance shall be the test: whether Lycaon succumbs finally
to a good thrust, or whether Mother Earth (who breeds heroes and
clasps their bodies when they fall) fails to hold him.'

Achilles recovered his lance, and hurled it. The blade would have
pierced Lycaon's breast, had he not dived nimbly forward and caught
his captor by the knees. Then, releasing one hand, he reached behind
him and clutched at Achilles' lance, which stood imbedded in the
soil, but made no attempt to dislodge it.

'Foster-son of Zeus,' babbled Lycaon, 'be merciful to your suppli-
ant—who can claim guest-right, too; for when taken in my father's
orchard, I broke bread at your table. Besides, you benefited greatly:
my purchase price was a hundred head of cattle! King Euneus, by
the way, did not release me himself, but accepted a ransom—charg-
ing Eëtion of Imbros three hundred head—and I returned here just
twelve days ago, after many sufferings.

'So I am your prisoner a second time—how Father Zeus must hate me! I seem doomed to die young. My mother Laothoë, you may know, is a daughter of the venerable Altes, King of Lelegian Pedasus, a city commanding the Satniöeis River, and my father is King Priam. He has begotten children on many wives, but only two on Laothoë. Today you killed my brother, Prince Polydorus, in the front-line, and I despair of escaping the same fate. Yet please take one thing into consideration: that I was not born of the same mother as Prince Hector, the hero who killed your gentle and courageous comrade!'

Achilles answered implacably: 'I reject this childish plea for mercy, and will accept no ransom. Until Patroclus died, I often spared suppliants, and sold them abroad; but now all Trojans whom I catch will die, especially all sons of King Priam! Yes, friend, including you. Why bemoan your lot? Patroclus, a far better fighter, is dead, too. And look at me! Did you ever see so strong or so handsome a man? Yet, though my father was a hero, and my mother a goddess, immediate death threatens me. Some day soon—whether it will be morning, noon, or nightfall, and whether by spear or arrow, nobody can foretell—I am doomed to fall in battle.'

Despair seized Lycaon, who let go Achilles' lance, and crouched with arms outspread, awaiting the sword-sweep. Swiftly it descended, sheering through collarbone and lungs. Lycaon tumbled prostrate, and his lifeblood soaked the earth. Achilles took the corpse by a foot and tossed it downstream, crying exultantly:

> 'Among the fish, Lycaon, lie!
> Their dainty tongues your blood shall try;
> Nor can Laothoë come near
> To stretch your cold corpse on a bier,
> With shrill lament; for there you go,
> Borne on Scamander's rippling flow
> To the salt bosom of the deep
> Where dogfish hungrily shall leap
> Through turbid waters, quick to tear
> Strips from your white flesh floating there.

> 'So perish every man of Troy!
> Whole squadrons now I will destroy,

> Forcing the rest to flee pell-mell
> Until I sack her Citadel.
> Think not, my foes, that sacrifice
> Of bulls, or other rich device—
> Such as to toss a chariot-team
> Alive into Scamander's stream—
> Shall curb my vengeance-hungry blade!
> An ample blood-price must be paid
> For those who with Patroclus died
> When, all too long, I nursed my pride.'

This speech enraged the River-god Xanthus. Already vexed that his waters were reddened by such ruthless butchery, he decided to stop Achilles from carrying out his threats. Meanwhile, Achilles had caught sight of Asteropaeus, son of Pelegon—and therefore grandson of the River-god Axius by Periboea, Acessamenus' eldest daughter. When Xanthus gave Asteropaeus courage to stand in the ford brandishing two spears, Achilles addressed him: 'Who are you? Where do you live? The parents of any man who opposes me deserve my commiseration!'

'Bold son of Peleus,' he replied. 'Why ask these questions? My name is Asteropaeus, son of Pelegon, and eleven days ago I brought a company of spearmen here from the distant, fertile land of Paeonia. Pelegon, a well-known soldier, was son to the great River-god Axius. Now, fight!'

As Achilles poised his lance, Asteropaeus hurled both spears together, for he happened to be ambidextrous. One struck the divine shield and failed to penetrate beyond the central golden layer; the other grazed Achilles' right elbow, drew a spurt of blood, then buried itself greedily in the earth. This scratch confused Achilles' aim; his lance missed Asteropaeus and hit the high riverbank, entering so deep that only its butt protruded. Sword in hand, he leaped at his enemy, who was trying to get possession of the lance. Three times Asteropaeus tugged with all his might but, unable to dislodge it, would have snapped the haft in two, had not Achilles' sword first plunged into his belly. Asteropaeus' bowels gushed out, and he died gasping.

Achilles set a foot on his breast and stripped off the armour, crying: 'Lie there, Paeonian! Even a river-god's grandson should avoid challenging descendants of Almighty Zeus, of whom I am one—my father Peleus was son to Aeacus, King of the Myrmidons, and Aeacus had Zeus for father. Zeus being far stronger than all river-gods whose waters go murmuring seaward, his stock must naturally be far superior to any stock of theirs! Quite a large river flows beside you, but Scamander ranks low in the divine scale—he could never fight the Son of Cronus! Nor could Acheloüs himself, though unmatched in Greece; and even old Oceanus, renowned for his broad, deep, world-girdling stream, the source of every known river, sea, spring, or fountain, lives in terror of Zeus' lightning and his roaring, rattling thunder!'

So saying, Achilles wrenched out the lance, and left Asteropaeus' corpse awash on the sandy verge. Eels and fishes swarmed up, tearing at his exposed kidney-suet, while Achilles slaughtered the Paeonian chariotmen, huddling along Scamander's banks and paralyzed by terror at their leader's death: including Thersilochus, Mydon, Astypylus, Mnesus, Thrasius, Aenius, Ophelestes. He was continuing his savage task when Xanthus assumed human shape and roared angrily from an eddy.

'Son of Peleus, you are the strongest of all living men and, secure in the Olympians' patronage, you do more evil than any. If Zeus indeed sanctions this ruthless massacre of the entire Trojan army, have the courtesy at least to fight on the plain, not in my channel. You so clog this pleasant reach with corpses, that its waters are impeded as they journey to the sea. Leave me alone; your behaviour is outrageous!'

'As you please, Immortal Xanthus,' replied Achilles. 'Yet my sword-play cannot cease before Hector meets me face to face in mortal combat, and all other Trojans are back behind their walls.'

When he set upon the enemy again, evincing divine rage, Xanthus asked Apollo: 'Lord of the Silver Bow, why neglect the commands of your father Zeus? Were not you and I ordered to assist the Trojans and maintain their defence until dusk?'

This question offended Achilles. He sprang into the middle of the river and challenged Xanthus, who thereupon gathered up a great volume of water and, with a loud bellow, swept the corpses across the plain; but he arched protectively over such Trojans as survived, hiding them beneath his bright wave. Achilles' shield proved powerless to stem the River-god's rush; nor could he even keep his feet. A fine elm grew near by; though he braced himself by clutching at it, the current ran so fast that the entire tree came away in his grasp, tearing the bank down, and damming the river with its branches, trunk, and tangled roots. Somehow Achilles escaped the foaming whirlpool, clambered out of the stream, and fled. Xanthus, intent on saving Troy from such cruel vengeance, pursued him in the form of a tall, turbid wave. A spear-cast ahead of his pursuer, Achilles darted forward like a black eagle—no other bird of prey excels the black eagle in strength or swiftness—and his armour clanked terribly as he swerved to avoid the violent, noisy deluge.

> At evening we release the flow
>   From a dark fountain, which
> To fields and orchards far below
>   Is joined by a steep ditch.
>
> Mattock in fist, a lad makes haste
>   To clear the water's path,
> But quickly finds himself outpaced
>   As off it roars in wrath,
>
> Hurling bright gravel down the slope
>   With a huge hissing burst:
> That mattock-lad can hardly hope
>   To reach the orchard first.

Achilles, despite his speed, was similarly outpaced—men have little chance against gods—and whenever he turned to see whether all the Olympians were coming in support of Xanthus, an enormous wave would slap his shoulders. He tried desperately to leap above the current, which tugged at his legs and pulled the soil from underneath his feet. Groaning aloud, and gazing up at the wide sky, he prayed:

> 'O ZEUS Almighty,
>   Quick to show mercy,
> Will no god pity
>   King Peleus' son?

This cruel river,
Divine SCAMANDER,
Pursues me ever,
     Though swift I run.

'Long life I seek not,
Of death I reck not,
And therefore speak not,
     Unless to blame
THETIS, my mother,
Who swore no other
Power could me conquer
     But PHOEBUS' aim.

'If noble Hector
Might be my victor,
Of that poor honour
     I should be fain;
For THETIS taught me
That death must take me
In gallant tourney
     Upon Troy's plain.

'But now in anguish,
Alas, I perish—
Ah, ZEUS, how foolish
     A fate is mine!
Like some imprudent,
Young mountain-peasant
Drowned by a torrent
     While tending swine!'

On hearing this appeal, Poseidon and Athene hurried towards Achilles, disguised as mortals, took his hands in theirs, and pledged their assistance. Poseidon spoke first: 'Courage, son of Peleus! Zeus has permitted Pallas Athene and myself to rescue you—because drowning is not your prescribed fate; and you shall soon enjoy seeing Xanthus retire in discomfiture. While I am about it, let me offer a piece of advice: fight on without fear until you have driven those fugitives back behind the celebrated walls which I once built! Then, after killing Hector—a glory we vouchsafe you—return at once to the naval camp and launch no further attacks on Troy.'

The Olympians vanished and, heartened by Poseidon's words and given new strength by Athene, Achilles continued his difficult journey. The current whirled along valuable weapons, armour, and corpses, but he went skipping through it. Xanthus, still angrier, sent a prodigious crested wave curving against him, and called to his partner, the River-god Simöeis: 'Help, dear brother! We must restrain this champion from routing the Trojans and sacking King Priam's Citadel! Fill up your bed with spring-water, call out your torrents, form a deluge, roll down tree-stumps and boulders to overwhelm Achilles! Since he has challenged a god, he deserves a lesson. I swear that neither his vigour, nor his beauty, nor his glorious new armour shall be of any avail when I catch him in my sands, when I wrap him in slime, when I encase him in so much shingle that the Greeks will neither know where to dig for his bones, nor need to heap a barrow above their hero—already buried alive!'

Xanthus advanced in the form of a mountainous dark flood—thundering, foaming, thick with corpses—and that would have been the end of Achilles, had not Hera uttered a shriek, and summoned her son Hephaestus. 'To the rescue, lame son!' she shouted. 'You were the opponent chosen by Xanthus when this battle began. What I need is a blast of flame to scorch all yonder grass and brushwood; I shall raise a sudden strong wind from the south-west which will fan the flames into a magnificent blaze for consuming the dead Trojans and their armour. Then spread your fire to Xanthus' banks, char his trees and make his very stream boil! But do not be coaxed or threatened into relaxing your efforts until I give the word.'

Hephaestus accordingly kindled a fierce fire on the plain; it soon consumed the thick heaps of corpses left in Achilles' wake, and also checked Xanthus' advancing flood.

> Gardeners love the autumn wind
> For doing what is wanted:
> His cheerful toil dries out the soil,
> Which can at last be planted.

Hephaestus' blast similarly dried up the battlefield, much to Achilles' relief, and then assailed the riverbanks: burning elms, willows, tamarisks, clover, rushes, and aromatic sedge growing there in profusion. Eels and fishes, darting through the water, were distressed by the heat, and Xanthus cried: 'Have done, Hephaestus, your fire is unbearable! I resign all further concern in this battle: let Achilles expel the Trojans from their city as soon as he pleases—I will raise no finger to help him.'

> A log-fire glows beneath the pot
> Where fatted pork is frying,
> And jets of grease supremely hot
> Over the rim come flying!

The Scamander bubbled like that pot, powerless against Hephaestus' scorching blast. Xanthus urgently appealed to Hera: 'Queen, why has your champion singled me out for punishment, when I have hurt the Greeks less than any other god of the Trojan faction? If he calls off his attack, I will surrender, swearing never again to assist Troy, even though the Greeks set her roofs ablaze!'

Hera reproved Hephaestus. 'Quench your fire, my son,' she cried. 'You should not have injured an Immortal so cruelly for the sake of a mere human!'

Hephaestus quenched his fire, and the Scamander once more rolled in peace along its familiar bed; and though Hera still felt bitter towards the Trojans, at least she kept the peace between these two fighters.

✳

Meanwhile, the other gods had come to blows. Earth groaned under the shock of their terrific onset, and the Heavens rang as if with trumpets. Zeus, watching from Olympus, was much entertained by the family battle, which Ares began. Levelling his long spear at Athene, he taunted her: 'Dog-fly, do you dare confront a male god? I wonder at such temerity; nor have I yet forgotten who prompted Diomedes, son of Tydeus, to wound me a few days ago; and who herself took a lance and unabashedly thrust it through my divine skin! Upon my word, I must be well avenged for that!'

The barbarous god lunged ineffectually at Athene's fearful, tasselled Aegis, which Zeus' thunderbolt itself cannot shatter. She stepped back, caught up an enormous black, rugged rock—anciently placed there as a landmark—and hurled it at him. Struck on the neck, Ares collapsed with a crash of armour, soiling his locks in dust and blood.

'Poor fool!' Athene laughed. 'You never seem to learn that I am more than your match. This will cause Queen Hera great satisfaction, since she cursed you for deserting the Greeks in favour of the Trojans.'

Athene turned, and left Ares stretched supine over seven acres of ground; but Aphrodite helped him to his feet and led him off, groaning and half-dead. Hera saw them go. She shouted to Athene: 'Invincible daughter of Zeus, look yonder! That creature Aphrodite is guiding my nasty, pugnacious son Ares out of the mêlée. After her!'

Athene cheerfully attacked Aphrodite, knocking her down with a tremendous slap on the breasts. Ares lost his balance, too; and the pair of them sprawled hand in hand at Athene's feet. 'So may all gods tumble,' she crowed, 'who choose the wrong side—even though they are as courageous as Aphrodite! If I could so humble the rest of them, Troy would soon be sacked.'

Poseidon challenged Apollo. 'Why do you and I not fight each other?' he asked. 'We shall be disgraced by standing aside when everyone else has entered the fray. Imagine my crossing the brazen threshold of Zeus' Palace without having cast a single spear! Still, as the older and more experienced god, I should invite you to begin the combat. But what an imbecile you are to forget how badly we two were treated, long ago, in the reign of Priam's father Laomedon! At Zeus' orders, he employed us for a year as hired labourers. I built a huge, wide, impregnable wall around the city, while you tended his cattle on the woody spurs of Mount Ida; then, at the close of our engagement, he sent us away unpaid! Surely you recall Laomedon's threats that, should we utter a word of protest, he would pinion our wrists, fetter our ankles, lop off our ears, and sell us as slaves overseas? We went home in deep resentment; and now you favour Laomedon's stiff-necked people, instead of helping us to destroy them miserably—women, children, and all.'

Apollo answered: 'Earth-Shaker, I may be an imbecile. I would, however, be a far greater one if I fought you for the sake of a few wretched mortals, who today eat, drink and are merry, but tomorrow fade like the foliage of a tree, drop to earth, and die. Let us break this quarrel short, leaving Greeks and Trojans to end the war themselves!'

As Apollo withdrew, ashamed at the notion of shooting an uncle, he was taunted by his sister Artemis, the Crescent-Crowned Huntress. 'What, surrender without a single shot? Why carry a bow which you fear to use? May I never again hear you boast in our father's Palace of being a match for Poseidon!'

Apollo kept silent, but Hera grew enraged. 'Shameless bitch,' she screamed at Artemis, 'how dare you challenge me? Although empowered by Zeus to shoot down travailing women at your pleasure, you have taken on too strong an adversary this time! Go, climb the mountains and hunt mere lions or stags instead! Not that I mind first teaching you what war means.'

With her left hand Hera seized both of Artemis' wrists, snatched the bow from her shoulders with the right, and then, as she struggled to escape, boxed her ears soundly. The pitiless arrows tumbled out of Artemis' quiver; and she fled weeping.

Hermes, Conductor of Souls, the god who had conquered Hundred-Eyed Argus, stood pitted against the Goddess Leto. 'Queen Leto,' he said, 'it would ill become me to exchange blows with a former wife of Zeus. I decline this combat. You may claim a resounding victory.'

Leto silently picked up her daughter Artemis' curved bow and arrows, which lay scattered on the dusty plain, and disappeared.

Artemis flew back to Olympus, as a dove makes good its escape from a falcon by darting into a rock-cleft, and bounded across the brazen threshold of the divine Palace. There she sprang on Zeus' knees, sobbing so piteously that her tunic shook.

Zeus hugged his daughter, and asked chuckling: 'What? One of the Immortals boxed your ears as though you were guilty of a public misdemeanour? Who was it?'

Artemis replied: 'Father, it was your own wife, Queen Hera, who started these quarrels in Heaven.'

Soon all the other Olympians, except Apollo, trooped into the Palace, some angry, some exultant, and sat down in Zeus' presence;

but Apollo visited Holy Troy, fearing that the Greeks might break in and sack the Citadel before their appointed hour.

✳

Achilles continued his carnage; while he was busy at the ford, Hera had used an impenetrable mist to baffle those Trojans who were already heading for the Scaean Gate.

> The gods have cursed a city
> And set its roofs on fire;
> They glower and show no pity
> But make the smoke rise higher;
> The scorched inhabitants in grief,
> Must fight the flames without relief!

Achilles' massacre of Trojans caused equal misery and confusion. Old King Priam, posted on the watch-tower, saw his terror-stricken people streaming towards him. With a shout of alarm, he descended to the battlements. 'Sentries,' he cried, 'unbar both wings of the Gate, and keep them wide open to admit your hard-pressed comrades! This is a disaster! But when all are safely home and recovering their breaths, shut the Gate again in the face of that bloodthirsty prince!'

As the sentries drew the bars and flung open both wings, Apollo leaped out to organize a rear-guard action which would assist the Trojans' entry. Parched and grimy, they came pelting along, harried by the great lance of triumphant Achilles, Sacker of Cities. Troy would then assuredly have fallen, had Apollo not encouraged Agenor, son of Antenor, a vigorous and noblehearted fighter, to oppose Achilles. The god wrapped himself in thick mist and leaned against Zeus' oak, prepared to intervene should his champion's life be threatened.

When Agenor saw Achilles making for him, he soliloquized: 'If I run from Prince Achilles like the rest of this demoralized horde, he will catch and kill me; and I shall die a coward. But suppose that I abandoned my men, escaped across the Ilian Plain to the foot-hills of Mount Ida, and hid among the bushes there? I could refresh myself by a bathe in the river, then slip back to Troy at dusk. On second thoughts, no! Achilles, the swiftest as well as the strongest hero alive, would soon head me off and kill me. My best course is to stay and challenge him. His skin is not weapon-proof nor, despite Zeus' favouritism, can he have more than a single life, and that presumably a mortal one.'

> A leopardess dares to confront
> The savage leader of a hunt
> Whose hounds about him bay,
> And, though pierced through with thrust or cast,
> She keeps her courage to the last,
> Scorning a break-away!

So Agenor scorned to run before he had tested Achilles' mortality. Brandishing his shield and spear, he shouted: 'My lord, do not expect to sack Troy! More blood must first be shed around its walls. We are bold, proud, and numerous; we also have parents, wives and children to protect. This is where you die, however redoubtable a hero!'

He flung his heavy spear, which flew straight at Achilles' left shin. Yet though the newly-forged tin greave clanged fearfully, a spell laid upon it by Hephaestus made the weapon rebound.

Achilles' cast also proved inconclusive, because Apollo whirled Agenor off in a thick shroud of mist, setting him down safely at a great distance from Troy, there to enjoy a peaceful life for the remainder of the war. The god then impersonated Agenor and drew Achilles away from the main Trojan force, letting himself be chased towards the Scamander, and keeping only a few paces ahead—as a result of which manoeuvre the Trojans regained and held their city. None of these fugitives dared wait outside the Scaean Gate to enquire who had been killed, and who survived; but all poured impetuously through, as fast as their legs would take them.

Book Twenty-two:

Death of Hector

Safe back in Troy, but all a-tremble like frightened fawns, the Trojans leant on the battlements, slaking their thirst and cooling their sweaty limbs. The Greek army advanced with raised shields, but found no opponents still facing them on the plain: except Hector the Bright-Helmed alone, whom Destiny compelled to post himself in front of the Scaean Gate.

Thereupon Phoebus Apollo called over his shoulder to Achilles the Swift-Footed: 'Why blindly neglect your task of harrying the Trojans, to pursue an Immortal? They have now retired behind their walls, while you wander along Xanthus' riverbank. And your exertions are futile: I never die!'

Choking with anger, Achilles replied: 'Archer Apollo, most mischievous of gods, what a mean trick to play! But for this, I should have rolled many Trojans in the dust before they hurtled through that Gate. You have light-heartedly robbed me of renown, safe in the knowledge that I cannot exact vengeance—as I should certainly do, had I the power.'

Achilles darted away at full speed, as if he were a proud, victorious chariot-horse. Old King Priam soon observed him: his armour blazing like Sirius, harbinger of fevers, the evil star (also called Orion's Hound) which dominates the night sky in harvest time. Priam uttered a yell, drubbed on his head, and waved wildly to catch the attention of Hector, who stood below, prepared for stern combat.

'Hector, sweet son,' he cried, gesticulating, 'I beg you not to remain there, alone and unsupported! Achilles is far stronger than you, and knows no mercy; he will cut your life short. Ah, that the gods felt as little love for him as I do! Then he would die on the spot, leaving dogs and vultures to ease my heart of its pain. He has robbed me of a dozen splendid sons, by killing them or selling them into slavery abroad. And now I miss two more among those who have just returned: Lycaon and Polydorus, my sons by Laothoë, pearl of women! They may of course be captured. In that case I could offer as ransom part of her dowry, which Altes paid me in bronze and gold. But if they are dead, she and I will be past consolation. Nevertheless, dear Hector, none of my subjects, whether men or women, will feel their loss deeply, so long as you survive.

'Back, back! Inside! Protect us! Would you let Achilles triumph over your helpless and unfortunate old father, who can yet suffer agonies of grief before Zeus, Son of Cronus, brings him to a miserable end? Fearful horrors must first appal these eyes: sons butchered, daughters dragged into captivity, palace sacked, infant grandchildren dashed against stones, daughters-in-law outraged by the evil Greek soldiery. And last of all they will kill me: someone will hack or thrust me down in yonder palace gateway, and the hounds lying there will greedily tear my flesh—the very hounds that I fed at table and trained as watch-dogs. A young man fallen in battle undergoes no humiliation, even if his body be mangled, and left stark naked; but when a white-headed, white-bearded veteran has his secret parts ripped off by dogs, that is a shocking and pitiable sight indeed!'

Though Priam might pull his hair out by the roots, he could not weaken Hector's resolution. Queen Hecuba also wept, undoing her upper garment and displaying a wrinkled breast. 'Hector, my child,' she wailed, 'I charge you by this breast which once gave you suck, to do as your father orders! Achilles is ruthless, and if he kills you there, Andromache and I will be denied the poor solace of weeping over your dead body—carried off to the Greek camp for dogs to tear.'

The old couple continued their lamentations, imploring Hector to come back and organize the city's resistance; but he calmly awaited Achilles, who was bounding towards him on his powerful legs.

> A serpent, coiled in a dark den,
>   That has on noxious herbage supped
> Conceives a hatred of all men
>   (Such poisons can the soul corrupt),
> And, glowering rage, resolves to lie
> In ambush for a passer-by.

With equal resolution, though less venomous feelings, Hector leaned
his polished shield against a buttress of the tower. He thought un-
happily: 'If I do as my parents ask, Polydamas will blame me for
having disregarded his advice. I should have listened when he begged
me to lead the army home before Achilles could destroy it. But now
that we are ruined by my obstinate folly, I am ashamed to face the
lords and ladies of Troy. And some churl is bound to mutter:
"Hector's vainglory was our downfall." That I could not bear; so I
must either kill Achilles, or else die gloriously. Yet, another alterna-
tive offers: to remove my helmet, lay it on the ground, lean my spear
beside this shield, and meet him with a peace proposal. I might say:
"We will restore Helen and her entire fortune (Paris' theft of which
caused the war) to King Agamemnon and his brother Menelaus;
we will, moreover, divide the city's own treasures into halves, and
give you one of them as a condition of your raising the siege." Then
I should have to make the Royal Council swear that no valuables
would be concealed or withheld from the common stock. Impossible!
If I went forward unarmed, Achilles would doubtless disregard the
overture and fell me ruthlessly, as though I were a woman. This is no
occasion for whispered agreements, such as a girl might exchange
with a gallant from the shelter of a rock or an oak-tree. We must
fight, and let Zeus choose between us.'

Achilles was almost upon Hector, brandishing the dreadful lance.
He resembled the formidable God of War, and his bronze armour
flashed like a bonfire, or a sunrise. Hector, aghast at the sight, turned
and fled.

> The mountain falcon, mighty-winged and swooping from above
> With screams of rage, hotly pursues a terror-smitten dove.

Going at a great speed close under the walls, Hector flashed by
Priam's look-out tower and the wind-blown fig-tree which had taken
root on the western curtain; then along a wagon track towards two
neighbouring sources of the Scamander—one so hot that it smoked,
as if heated by a furnace; the other as cold as snow, hail or ice, even
in summer. Near them stood a pair of massive troughs used by Tro-
jan housewives and girls when they washed their fine linen—in days
of peace.

Hector ran past these troughs, with Achilles in fierce pursuit. A desperate struggle, since the runners were contending not for the carcase of a sacrificial beast, or an ox-hide, or any such ordinary prize; but for Hector's life! Yet it did recall a chariot-race, where a tripod or a woman-slave is the prize and competing teams wheel rapidly at the stadium's goal-posts; because Hector kept his lead and drew Achilles three times round the whole circuit of walls.

All the Olympians sat watching in a rapt silence, finally broken by Zeus himself. 'Alas,' he sighed, 'how sad to see a man whom I love chased around his own city walls! Hector has burned me countless sacrifices on the spurs of Ida and at the Trojan Citadel—beautiful thighbones wrapped in prime fat. Come, friends, your advice! Is this brave fellow to be rescued from Achilles, or shall I let him die?'

'Father Zeus, Lord of the Lightning and the Dark Storm Cloud,' Athene the Owl-Eyed cried. 'What is this? Would you dare rescue a mortal from the fate to which he has long ago been destined? Do as you please, of course, but without our approval.'

'Dear child,' Zeus answered, 'you must not take me too seriously. I am very well disposed to you. There will be no interference with your schemes.'

So Athene flew down from Olympus and found the rival champions once more circling the walls.

> A hound pursues a brocket stag
> Through glen and glade, nor does he flag
>   But onward yelping goes;
> For though his prey may halt beside
> A bramble bush and seek to hide,
>   The hound can trust his nose.

Hector's tactics were to make for the battlements covering the Dardanian Gate, where his comrades would send a volley of spears at Achilles; but whenever he approached it, Achilles always spurted, took the inside berth, and forced him towards the plain.

> Often in dream I chase a fleeing man,
> Eager to catch and kill him if I can;
> Yet there's no finish, struggle how we may:
> I cannot reach him, nor he get away.

Here the case was similar, because Apollo so strengthened Hector's lungs and legs that even the Swift-Footed failed to overhaul him.

Nevertheless, Achilles tossed his head as a sign that no Greek must steal the triumph by aiming at Hector as he rushed past.

When they came to the troughs in their fourth circuit, Zeus grasped his golden balance and laid a lot in each of its pans—one for Achilles, one for Hector—and poised them carefully. Hector's lot sank down; at which token of doom, Apollo abandoned him to his fate.

Athene thereupon revealed herself to Achilles, crying: 'Glorious son of Peleus, Zeus' favourite! Together we will kill Hector, despite his valour, and drag his corpse victoriously to your camp. This time he cannot escape us, even if Apollo should fall grovelling at the knees of Zeus the Shield-Bearer and plead his cause in desperation. So halt and recover your breath; I shall induce Hector to make a stand!'

Grateful for the respite, Achilles paused, leaning on his long lance; while Athene, disguised as Hector's brother Deiphobus, ran on shouting in his familiar loud voice: 'Dear brother, you are being roughly handled! Stop, and let us face Achilles, you and I; then he will be battling against odds.'

'Deiphobus!' exclaimed Hector. 'Always the best of brothers to me —which is natural, because we have the same father and mother— and never more welcome than now! So you alone dared venture to my aid!'

'Yes, brother,' answered Athene, 'although our parents and friends all begged me to remain on the battlements—they are terrified of Achilles—compassion and grief proved too strong, and here I come! We must fight like heroes; it will soon be seen whether Achilles can kill us and carry our blood-stained spoils back to his ship, or whether, contrariwise, you can destroy him.'

Tricked by Athene's ruse, Hector strode towards Achilles. When within casting distance, he announced: 'Son of Peleus, after three circuits of my father's city I have resolved to stand fast, and engage you in mortal combat. Yet first we should swear an oath—solemnly calling on our gods to witness it—that whichever of us, by Zeus' permission, kills and despoils the other, will abstain from maltreating the corpse and convey it to his own people for burial.'

Achilles replied grimly: 'Dare you bargain with me, madman? If man meets lion, or wolf meets sheep, what chance of agreement can there be? We shall never clasp hands in friendship, nor even in ratification of a pledge. The sole feeling we share is pure hatred; and one of us two must surely fall, his lifeblood glutting the implacable God of War. Now summon all your skill to fight and die like a hero, since no escape is left. I am promised victory by Pallas Athene, and I will make you pay in full for the bitter grief that you have caused me and mine!'

Poising his great lance, Achilles hurled at Hector, who crouched low, letting it whizz over his head and plunge into the earth beyond.

'A miss!' Hector cried. 'You are mistaken. Zeus cannot have told you of my doom! Nor will your smooth tongue and crooked speech scare me into turning about and exposing my kidneys. Should Heaven grant you the upper hand, I shall die from a thrust through the lungs as I charge. But beware! May my spear-blade skewer your flesh, and free Troy of the worst terror that this war has brought upon her!'

His hurtling spear struck the centre of Achilles' shield, but rebounded harmlessly. Angered and discouraged by his ill-success, that being the only spear he carried, Hector cried: 'Quick, Deiphobus, lend me yours!' No answer came and, glancing behind him, he found that Deiphobus had vanished. Then he understood. 'Alas,' he thought, 'Heaven has led me to the slaughter! That was Athene's work. She disguised herself as Deiphobus, who is still watching from the battlements. I am trapped. Zeus and his son Apollo, though careful of my life until today, must have staged this scene long ago. Yet I will not die without first performing a feat of arms to stir the hearts of all posterity.'

He drew his huge, sharp, heavy broadsword, brandished it, gathered himself, and ran at Achilles as a soaring eagle swoops at a lamb or cowering hare on the plain beneath. How was he to know that Athene had covertly pulled the famous lance from the ground and restored it to the grasp of his opponent? In an ecstasy of rage, Achilles leaped to the encounter, shield lifted and golden plumes waving.

> Darkly, darkly falls the night.
> One fair star is burning bright:
> HESPERUS his name, and he
> Rivals all the stars that be.

Starlight flashed at Achilles' lance-point, as he planned a mortal thrust against some vulnerable part of Hector's body.

The suit of proof armour, however, won from the corpse of Patroclus, afforded him complete protection, except that it lacked a gorget. Achilles took aim at Hector's bare neck, the most dangerous spot of all, drove the lance clean through, and sent him crashing to the dust.

'Aha, Hector!' Achilles exulted. 'You thought yourself safe when you stole these arms from Patroclus! Did it never cross your mind that his brother-in-arms, a far doughtier antagonist, might be serving in the same camp? At last I am avenged! At last I can give Patroclus a splendid funeral, while leaving you to the dogs and carrion-birds.'

Hector whispered in reply—for the lance had not severed his windpipe: 'Son of Peleus, I beseech you by everything that you hold dearest—your life, your strength, your parents—spare my corpse! King Priam and Queen Hecuba will ransom it at a noble price; grant me decent burial among my people!'

'Scoundrel!' was Achilles' harsh answer. 'I despise these idle appeals to life, strength and parents. If only my stomach did not revolt against such a diet, I would carve your raw flesh into gobbets and swallow them—a fitting punishment for the wrong you did me! Ransom? I should scorn ten or twenty times what your family might tender. Even if King Priam came out here himself, with a pair of scales, eager to pay me the weight of your body in gold, I should laugh at him. No: Queen Hecuba shall never have the solace of lamenting at the bier on which she has laid you! Nothing in the world can keep the carrion-birds from tearing at your belly, or the dogs from crunching your bones!'

Hector spoke his dying words: 'Now I know you; now I see clearly! Fate forbids me to melt a heart of iron, yet beware: my ghost will draw down the wrath of Heaven on your head—when Paris, aided by Phoebus Apollo, destroys you at yonder Gate.'

The shadow of Death touched Hector, life left him, and a ghost fled to the kingdom of Hades, bewailing his lost youth and vigour.

'Die, then!' Achilles stormed. 'And I am ready to meet my own doom as soon as Zeus and his fellow-Immortals give the order.' He freed the lance, and stooped to unbuckle Hector's blood-stained armour.

A crowd of Greeks ran up, noisily admiring the corpse's muscular perfection. None failed to plunge a sword or spear into it, and the jest went round: 'He is much easier to handle today than yesterday, when he fired our fleet!'

Achilles stripped Hector to the buff, rose, and began a speech: 'Princes and Councillors, since by the gods' help we are rid of a champion who did us more harm than all the rest of Priam's brood together, we should probe the city's defences without delay. Perhaps the loss of their commander-in-chief will induce these Trojans to capitulate . . .'

Suddenly Achilles broke off. 'Alas!' he exclaimed. 'What am I saying? Patroclus' corpse still lies stretched unburied on his bier, and so long as I breathe and move, I cannot forget him. No, no! Though every other ghost in Hades' kingdom forgets his fallen comrades, yet I shall always be faithful to my love, even in the grave. Enough, friends! Sing me a paean of victory, while I haul this carrion to the camp. We have won great glory: we have slain Prince Hector, to whom the Trojans paid almost divine honours.'

Achilles set himself to outrage the corpse: having slit the tendon of each foot from heel to ankle, he looped a rawhide throng through the holes and bound both ends to his chariot-tail. Then he mounted, flung the spoils of battle beside him, lashed Xanthus and Balius to a gallop. Away they flew, and Hector's corpse trailed after them, churning up the dust, his dark, flowing locks dishevelled, and his once glorious features begrimed with filth of the battlefield. Such was the fate ordained for him by Zeus: to have his body desecrated in full sight of his fellow-citizens.

Queen Hecuba screamed, tore her hair, and cast away her bright veil: King Priam moaned piteously, and his subjects wept and howled as though Troy were tumbling in blackened ruins about their ears. They could hardly restrain Priam from a mad escape by the Dardanian Gate. Throwing himself in the dirt, abasing himself to his Councillors, whom he called upon by name, he shrieked: 'Friends, stand back, unhand me! If I still have your love, oh, let me pass through the Gate! Let me visit the Greek camp, and beard that accursed savage. I might perhaps shame him into showing me mercy. He has slaughtered many of my splendid young sons; yet this single grief for Hector outweighs all former griefs: it will kill me! Would that he had expired in my arms! Then his wretched mother and I could comfort ourselves by lamenting on and on.'

The entire Court vented their tears in a shower, and Hecuba led the women's dirge:

> 'Dead, Hector, dead? My lovely son!
>   So sharp this pain to me
> That loth I am to linger on
>   Robbed of his company.
>
> 'From dawn to dawn he was my boast
>   In every house of Troy,
> By all I met beloved the most:
>   Their miracle, their joy.
>
> 'Godlike to them his gracious tread,
>   His glories were their own.
> Now cruel FATE has shorn the thread
>   And each must mourn alone!'

Andromache knew nothing of Hector's death; no reliable message, even of his decision to stay outside the city walls had reached the house. She sat at her loom, weaving a floral design into the purple cloth of double width. Presently she ordered the maid-servants to place a huge, three-legged cauldron on the fire: Hector would be glad of a hot bath when he returned. Poor woman: she little guessed that he would never bathe again—that Athene had helped Achilles to murder him. Then, at the sound of distant shrieks and groans, she started—so violently that the shuttle fell from her hands—and called to a couple of servants: 'Follow me! We must hear the worst! My heart leaped into my mouth when I recognized Queen Hecuba's voice. I feel dizzy. Some terrible misfortune has surely overtaken one of Priam's children—I wish I did not need to know whom! What if Achilles has cut Hector off, holding the Gate against him? Or chased him across the plain and finally humbled his stubborn pride? That may well be: Hector will not stay in the ranks, but always charges ahead. He hates to yield the palm of courage to another.'

Frantically Andromache rushed from the house, her breast heaving and the two servants hurrying after her. On arrival at the battlements, now thronged with soldiers, the women looked down; and all went black before Andromache's eyes. A group of princesses caught her as she fainted, distraught by the sight of Hector's corpse dragged behind Achilles' chariot. She had already thrown off the gay head-dress, consisting of a frontlet, a net, a woven band and a veil—Aphrodite's present on the day she married Hector, to whom King Eëtion paid an enormous dowry.

When Andromache regained consciousness, great sobs racked her and she wailed aloud: 'Ah, Hector, I am undone! We were born to share the same wretched fate: you in Troy, I at Thebe, my luckless father Eëtion's city, shaded by the pleasant woods of Mount Placus. I wish he had never begotten me! You, too, my love, have descended to the hidden kingdom of Hades, leaving me a grief-tormented widow, and Scamandrius an orphan. Heir to our ruin, the poor infant cannot ever profit from your love, nor you from his. Though perhaps destined to escape the clutches of those cruel Greeks, ill-luck and penury must always plague him.

'An orphan is an outcast; he hangs his head, his cheeks are wet with tears. Let him approach his dead father's friends, in search of consolation, plucking this man by the cloak, that by the tunic, and one of them may compassionately set a wine-cup to his little lips and moisten them, but will not tilt it for a drink. Then I can see some rough lad, whose father still lives, bustle Scamandrius from the table: "Off you go! Your father is no guest here!" And the boy slinks weeping back to his widowed mother . . .

'Scamandrius would sit on Hector's knee and nibble only beef-marrow or the tenderest morsels of mutton; and, when he felt tired after play, would snuggle in bed clasped by the soft arms of his nurse—no happier child alive! But Hector is gone, and the darkest future awaits Scamandrius—everyone nicknamed him Astyanax, because his father was the champion whom they trusted to defend our gates and walls. Oh, my Hector, you lie far away, stretched out for the dogs to feed upon—and when they have eaten their fill, the wriggling maggots shall devour what remains—stretched out naked, though there are clothes in plenty at home: fine, clean clothes, delicately woven by my servants! Since you cannot wear them, I must burn them all in your honour, as a tribute from the lords and ladies of Troy.'

A crowd of women gathered around Andromache, loudly taking up her lament.

Book
Twenty-three:

Funeral Games for Patroclus

Back in their camp by the Hellespont the Greek army dispersed, every contingent to its own ships, except for the fighting Myrmidons, whom Achilles addressed as follows: 'My lads, do not unharness your teams until we have honoured our dead comrade in proper fashion: he needs a cavalcade of chariots and the chanting of a dirge. Once this rite has been performed, you may fall out and prepare supper.'

A full-throated dirge arose, led by Achilles, as the Myrmidons drove slowly three times around Patroclus' bier. Thetis the Silver-Footed made everybody weep: the sand was wet with tears that dripped from their corslets and seeped through the floor-boards—so tremendous a hero were they mourning! Achilles laid his murderous hands on the corpse's breast and sang a threnody:

> 'Hail, Patroclus, hear my call
> Echoing through King HADES' hall!
> All that I have sworn to do
> Shall be done, I warrant you:
> Hector dragged by his dead feet
> Naked for the dogs to eat,
> And twelve young Trojans at your pyre
> Slaughtered to appease my ire.'

As a further outrage, he stretched Hector's corpse, buttocks upward, in the dust beside the bier. Then the troops disarmed, stabled their whinnying horses, and sat down to a splendid funeral feast near Achilles' ship. A herd of fat oxen, one flock of sheep, and another of goats had been sacrificed; and slices of pork from several large, plump, tusky boars hissed on spits over glowing embers. Blood by the gobletful was spilled about dead Patroclus.

The Greek leaders found difficulty in persuading Achilles, still crazed by his loss, to present himself before King Agamemnon; and when he arrived at headquarters, they asked the royal heralds to heat an immense cauldron of water, so that he might first wash the gore from his face, arms and legs. This he refused to do, pronouncing a solemn oath in Zeus' name:

'I swear by ZEUS, Greatest and Best,
    That water shall not flow
Over these hands until they rest
    From what to love they owe.

'O, I must heap a funeral pyre
    To lay my friend thereon,
And, weeping, cleanse his corpse with fire
    Till all the flesh be gone,

'Then must I shave my head, and heap
    A barrow on the plain;
For never sorrow half so deep
    Shall pierce my heart again!'

Turning to Agamemnon, he said: 'Now I will eat, however mournfully; and at daybreak, my lord King, pray send out axe-men to fetch fuel and make suitable provision for Patroclus' journey below. A huge, swift-burning pyre is needed; the troops can then resume their military duties.'

Agamemnon humoured his wishes. Supper was soon served, nor could any man complain of meagre portions. When they had all eaten and drunk their fill, the Councillors went off to bed. Achilles alone lay awake on the shore among his Myrmidons, groaning and listening to the melancholy hiss of waves. At last, wearied by his previous night's vigil, the struggle with Xanthus, and the pursuit of Hector, he fell asleep.

Patroclus' ghost visited him in a dream, exactly as he had looked while alive: the same tall figure, handsome eyes, gentle voice, fine clothes. He bent over Achilles accusingly: 'Asleep, and careless of my plight? You never used to neglect me, not for a moment. Bury my body without more ado, so that I can win admittance to the Underworld. Infernal demons and ghosts of men long dead are waving me away. Excluded from their ranks, I knock at every gate in Hades' kingdom, but to no avail. Have compassion, dear brother; supply the requisite funeral fire! As soon as it has purified my flesh, I will cease to trouble you.

'Alas: we two shall never again draw apart from our comrades and sit talking quietly together! I was fated to die young. You too, Achilles, despite your prodigious feats, must perish under the walls of Troy. Oh, grant me a final favour: that your own calcined bones shall be buried beside mine, in memory of our boyhood friendship! You remember how Menoetius hurried me to Phthia because, though still a child, I had committed manslaughter at Opöeis—by striking young Clysonomus, son of Amphidamas, in a quarrel about dice, and misjudging my strength. King Peleus, as Menoetius' first cousin, welcomed us at his palace, and treated me generously; so I became your squire. Our bones should lie together in one urn—the two-handled golden urn which your mother Thetis gave you.'

'Brother,' Achilles answered, 'why come and remind me of my obligations? I will do everything according to your wishes. Yet since you are here, let us briefly embrace and weep upon each other's necks.'

He stretched out both arms, but the phantom evaded his clutch, turning to vapour and sinking through the earth with a shriek. Achilles leaped up, horror-stricken: 'Then it is true!' he exclaimed. 'There are spirits of the dead in Hades' kingdom: active minds, though unsubstantial and lifeless! Yet how marvellously Patroclus' ghost resembled his living self when it stood lamenting and pleading with me!'

He roused the weary Myrmidons, who were forced to resume their mournful howling. The red streaks of dawn discovered them still at the bier; and then King Agamemnon ordered all the contingents in camp to detail men for fuel-gathering. Meriones, lieutenant to Idomeneus the Cretan, supervised the task. Carrying axes and stout ropes, they drove a herd of mules before them: up hill, down dale, along winding tracks, across open country, towards the foothills of Mount Ida. There Meriones set them to fell a copse of tall, leafy oaks.

When this had been done, they split the timber with wedges, and presently mules' hooves poached the soft earth as their trailing load flattened shrubs and bushes. Meriones also made everyone drag away lopped branches. Home again, they spread out their spoils in a single row, ready for heaping into a pyre, and sat awaiting Achilles.

His Myrmidons paraded under arms; chariots leading, infantry behind. In the middle, Patroclus' corpse was carried on his comrades' shoulders: feet foremost, and lolling head supported by Achilles himself. Locks of Myrmidon hair, shorn off as tributes of grief, strewed the pall.

Achilles directed the building of the pyre. He had a long, well-combed, golden curl, once dedicated to the Thessalian River-god Spercheius. Gazing over the western sea, he spoke in tones of deep regret:

'To you, SPERCHEIUS, I must make address,
Whose silver ripples lovingly caress
My native fields. Dear god, remember how,
Nine years ago, King Peleus vowed a vow:
That if, by your good graces, I, his son,
Should voyage home, my dangerous duties done,
That same day he would reverently bring
Fifty fat rams to your high sacred spring
Where at a rural altar raised for you
(Smoking with incense of the East), we two
Would sacrifice those champions of our flocks;
Moreover, I should shear my flowing locks
And cast them on the flame. Alas, but now
Your negligence annuls my father's vow.
I am not destined to win home again
And therefore, at a pyre upon Troy's plain,
In dead Patroclus' hand this curl I set—
Proof of a love that never can forget.'

He cut the curl and placed it between the dead fingers, which excited loud sobs from all who stood by. They would have wept until nightfall, had Achilles not addressed Agamemnon: 'My lord King, though the troops do well to mourn, please dismiss them. It is their supper hour. My Myrmidons and I, who feel Patroclus' loss most keenly, will burn the corpse: your Council's attendance at the rite would, however, gratify us.'

Agamemnon accordingly dismissed his troops; but the Myrmidons, assisted by Patroclus' noble friends, built a tall pyre one hundred feet square, upon which, with anguish at their hearts, they reverently placed the bier. Next, they flayed a whole flock of sheep and a herd of cattle. Achilles took the carcases, stripped off the fat, swathed Patroclus in it from head to foot, then spread the flesh about him. He also leaned a row of two-handled jars containing honey and oil against the bier; sacrificed four gallant horses (groaning aloud as he did so), two of Patroclus' nine hounds, and lastly the twelve Trojan prisoners reserved for this occasion, adding their bodies to the holocaust.

This done, he invoked the dead man's ghost:

> 'Hail, Patroclus, hear my call
> Echoing through King HADES' hall!
> True to the promise that I made,
> Twelve Trojans on your pyre are laid;
> Then rest assured I will not pay
> Like honour to mad Hector's clay:
> In vengeance of his impious deed
> No flames, but dogs on him shall feed!'

Nevertheless, despite his threats, all dogs were kept away. The Goddess Aphrodite guarded dead Hector day and night, after anointing him with ambrosia, which smelled as fragrant as roses and would protect his flesh from injury, should Achilles meditate further violence. Apollo helped her by drawing down a dark cloud to cover the corpse and prevent its shrivelling beneath the sun's rays.

Patroclus' pyre did not catch alight when the Myrmidons set torches to the green wood; but Achilles knew what was required. He took a golden cup and invoked Boreas the North Wind, and Zephyr the West Wind, pouring them a libation of wine, at the same time promising them a rich reward if they would puff on the lazy flames. Iris, Messenger of the Gods, overheard his prayer. She flew to Windy Island, and paused on the threshold of Zephyr's house, where the company of winds were feasting. They sprang up, and each begged her to sit beside him. Iris politely declined. 'No seat for me, thank you!' she answered. 'I must be back with my fellow-Immortals on the banks of the Ocean Stream—the Ethiopians are offering us another banquet of hundred-beast sacrifices. But I have brought a message from Achilles. He desires you, Boreas, and you, blustering Zephyr, to puff on the lazy flames under a pyre raised for Patroclus, whom the Greek besiegers of Troy are lamenting. A rich reward is promised.'

As Iris flew off, the boisterous winds rushed out of the house and skimmed the sea, driving clouds along and raising huge waves. At Troy, they not only attacked the pyre so forcefully that the flames raged and roared, but persisted at their game all night. Achilles tramped about the pyre, emptying on the earth a two-handled goblet which he constantly replenished from a golden wine-bowl: moaning, howling, and crying farewell to Patroclus' ghost. He might have been a father at the funeral of his newly-married son, whose death has ruined the family. At last:

> PHOSPHORUS, herald of daylight,
>   Shone clear as clear could be;
> Soon DAWN in saffron robes bedight,
>   Would brighten the broad sea.

By this time, lack of fuel had made the fire burn low. Boreas and Zephyr hurried home across the Thracian Gulf, which they stirred to a lusty swell. When Achilles turned exhausted from his labours, Sweet Sleep leaped upon him; but did not hold him long. The High King and his Councillors approached in a body, their clatter and clash awakening Achilles, who sat bolt upright.

'My lord Agamemnon, princes and Councillors,' he said, 'I have a task to impose on you. Pray quench those glowing embers with wine, then help me recover Patroclus' bones—they are easily found, because I placed him in the middle of the pyre, whereas horses, hounds, Trojans and so forth were flung at random along its edges. Fold two layers of fat around the precious relics and store them in a golden urn until my own may join them; but raise no huge barrow for him yet—a modest one will suffice. When I am dead and the urn can be filled, I expect such of you as survive to heap the earth very broad and high over us both.'

Obediently the Councillors tossed quantities of wine on the hot ashes, quenching the live embers beneath. Next, they laid the foundations of a barrow, gathered earth and heaped it to a decent height.

They would then have dispersed, had not Achilles made the entire army sit down in a vast ring, while he sent to his ships and storehuts for three-legged cauldrons, ordinary cauldrons, horses, mules, plough-oxen, handsome slave-women, and the like. These would be awarded the winners of events in Patroclus' funeral games, which he had resolved to hold on the spot.

Achilles rose and announced prizes for the chariot-race:

'*First Prize*: a woman-slave, well trained in handicrafts. *Item* a three-legged cauldron with handles; capacity sixty gallons.

'*Second Prize*: an unbroken six-year-old mare; in foal of a mule.

'*Third Prize*: a hitherto unused copper cauldron; capacity eleven gallons; perfect condition.

'*Fourth Prize*: two ingots of gold.

'*Fifth Prize*: a new two-handled bronze urn.'

He added: 'My lord Agamemnon, princes and Councillors: the prizes are now on view! If these games honoured anyone but Patroclus, I should myself take part in the chariot-race and, of course, be victorious. It is well known that no team can match my immortal stallions: the Earth-Shaker's wedding gift to King Peleus. However, I shall not run them, since they are still out of sorts. They miss their splendid driver—so kind to the poor beasts, he was!—why, he would wash their manes in spring water and anoint them with olive oil! Yes: you should see how Xanthus and Balius mourn him, muzzles lowered in dejection, manes trailing on the ground! But come, my lords, I invite all of you to race who flatter yourselves on possessing fast teams and strong chariots!'

Five competitors excitedly gathered at the starting-line: first, Eumelus, a skilful charioteer, the son and successor of Admetus, who ruled Thessalian Pherae. Next, Diomedes, son of Tydeus, driving the famous horses of Tros, owned until recently by Aeneas the Dardanian—whom he would have killed but for Apollo's intervention. Then fair-haired King Menelaus, son of Atreus, behind a formidable team consisting of his brother's mare Aethe, who seemed eager to run, and his own stallion Podargus. (Echepolus of Sicyon had bought himself off war-service at Troy by presenting Aethe to Agamemnon; and stayed comfortably at home, in his wide green pastures.)

Fourth came Nestor's son Antilochus, whose stallions were bred at Sandy Pylus. He knew a great deal about chariot-racing, but Nestor could not resist offering him seasonable advice. 'My son,' he said, 'though young, you have enjoyed the favour of Zeus and Poseidon, and learned to drive from them; so I hardly need instruct you myself in the art of wheeling around a post. Yet these nags of ours are pretty slow, and I fear their performance may be disappointing, unless you exploit your superior skill. Chariot-racing is like sailing: a clever helmsman can steer close to the wind, where anyone else would be taken aback or blown off course; a clever charioteer can outwit an inexperienced rival. Never make a wide sweep at the turning-post—as greenhorns do who rely on their team to think for them—and thus lose control! Watch the post, and decide just how far to force your horses down the straight, holding them well in hand; but keep one eye on whatever chariot has gained the lead!

'Now, pay attention: the turning-post will be a stout tree-stump, flanked by two white stones. Whether it is oak or pine, whether a monument raised to some ancient hero, or the turning-post of an abandoned race-track, I neither know nor care. At all events, the ground is smooth there, and you may drive in perfect safety. Let your near-horse hug the post, until the wheel almost grazes it; but check him a little. As you do so, lean to the left, lash the off-horse, give him free rein, then haul him round. Be careful not to foul the flanking stones; otherwise the chariot will be smashed, your horses crippled, and everyone will deride you. Time the race precisely; and if you can gain the lead at the turn, nobody else has a chance, however fast his beasts—though he were driving divine Arion (once the property of Adrestus), or Laomedon's horses, the fastest in Troy.'

Nestor finished talking and resumed his seat.

The fifth competitor who accompanied these champions to the starting-line was Meriones the Cretan. Achilles asked them to mark lots and drop them in his helmet. Then he shook it, and Antilochus' lot leaped out first. Thus he won the innermost lane. Eumelus was placed second; Menelaus, third; Meriones, fourth; and Diomedes, outermost, though easily the best charioteer present.

They formed up, wheel to wheel. Achilles showed them the distant post, where the venerable Phoenix, his former tutor, would act as umpire and report on mishaps or irregularities.

At a given signal, the five drivers lashed their horses, slapped them with the reins, yelled and shouted, each intent on glory. Away they flew—dust rising like a cloud or whirlwind, manes streaming, and the chariots often bouncing high into the air.

All teams negotiated the post successfully, and came thundering back. The field had strung out: the Thessalian mares first, but so closely followed by Diomedes' Dardanians that these seemed about to leap into Eumelus' chariot, and their breath warmed his broad shoulders. Doubtless the race would have ended either in a dead-heat, or a victory for Diomedes, had not Apollo, who bore him a grudge, knocked the whip from his hand. Diomedes wept tears of rage to see the Thessalians scudding along more swiftly than ever, while his own team slowed down. But Apollo's foul play incensed Athene. She picked up the whip, restored it to Diomedes, and gave the Dardanians greater speed. Then, angrily darting at his rival's chariot, she snapped the yoke. His mares bolted in different directions, the pole dropped, the wheels jolted to a standstill, and Eumelus was thrown forward over the rail, barking his elbows, chin and nose as he fell, and severely bruising his forehead.

Diomedes took the inner lane, and kept well ahead; Athene had invigorated his horses and wanted some of the fame for herself.

Next came Menelaus, hotly challenged by Antilochus, who was shouting at his Pylians: 'On you go, fly like the wind! We have no chance against Diomedes and Pallas Athene; but catch Menelaus at all costs! Aethe is only a mare—do you want her to ridicule my two sturdy stallions? Imagine letting that team win! Listen to me— and this is not an idle threat—unless we carry off the second prize, King Nestor will no longer make much of you, but use his sword on your hides instead. After them, at full gallop; and trust me to get the better of Menelaus as soon as the track narrows.'

His angry tones impressed the stallions. They swept forward to where a torrent had eaten away half the track. Menelaus headed for the sunken part and, seeing Antilochus follow suit, expostulated: 'Son of Nestor! What reckless driving! There is not width enough for both of us. Wait until we have some elbow-room, else you will foul my wheel and wreck both chariots!'

Feigning deafness, Antilochus plied his lash more fiercely than before. The teams ran neck and neck for the length of a discus-throw and then, to avoid a certain collision, Menelaus yielded: in his view, a prize could be too dearly won. He yelled as Antilochus went past: 'A plague on you! Despite your reputation as a well-behaved young man I never in my life met anyone so rash, or so malicious. Claim the second prize, and you will be tried for dangerous driving!'

Then he reproved his horses: 'You may feel sore, foolish beasts, but why slacken your speed? Those Pylian stallions cannot keep it up; they are too long in the tooth. Chase them!'

On rushed the four chariots in a thick cloud of dust. King Idomeneus of Crete, seated somewhat higher than his companions, was the first to distinguish a horse—chestnut, with a round white blaze—and at the same time heard Diomedes' distant but familiar shout. Standing up, he cried: 'Friends, Princes, Councillors, does anyone else recognize the leading team? Eumelus' Thessalians, which were ahead at the turn, have apparently come to grief; they are nowhere to be seen. Perhaps he lost control of the reins and fouled the post? If so, he will inevitably have taken a toss and smashed his chariot, leaving the mares to wander off the course. Stand up yourselves, and look! Surely, the driver is King Diomedes of Argos?'

Little Ajax rudely interrupted Idomeneus: 'Why always advance such absurd claims? The chariots are too far away for recognition by even the keenest-sighted of us; let alone so bleary-eyed a fellow as you! Bragging in royal company is the height of ill-manners. Allow me to inform you that Eumelus' mares, driven by Eumelus himself, still keep the lead.'

Idomeneus burst out: 'Son of Oïleus, I object to these spiteful remarks. The sole advantages you have over the rest of us are that your tongue is looser and your mind shallower. What about wagering a tripod or a cauldron on the issue, with the High King as umpire? I should like to make you pay for a lesson in courtesy.'

Little Ajax's rejoinder was even more offensive, but Achilles smothered the dispute. 'Enough of that, my lads!' he shouted. 'Set an example in decent behaviour. You would both hasten to suppress any foul-mouthed quarrel among your comrades. Stay seated, if you please, and watch! The winner's name will soon be common knowledge.'

He had scarcely spoken, when Diomedes came into full view, dust-begrimed, and flogging the Dardanians with blows delivered straight from the shoulder, as they scudded towards the finishing-line. His chariot, decorated in gold and tin, had travelled so fast that it scarcely left wheel-tracks on the soil. He reined in amid general applause, sprang to the ground, and unharnessed the horses, leaning his whipstock against their yoke. Sthenelus at once sent the slave-girl and the three-legged cauldron down to Diomedes' lines.

Antilochus ran second, after snatching a clever victory from Menelaus. It was a close tussle: no greater distance separated them than lies between the rump of a chariot-horse and the wheel-rim—which its tail brushes as it trots. Though Antilochus' manoeuvre had gained him the length of a discus-throw, Aethe and Podargus reduced it to almost nothing—another couple of strides, and they would have won.

Meriones followed a spear-cast in rear of these two, and won the fourth prize. Finally Eumelus appeared, driving his Thessalian mares before him and dragging the car by its pole. Achilles rose to greet Eumelus, exclaiming: 'The best man comes last, and on foot! Diomedes has clearly earned the first prize; you deserve the second.'

This remark was greeted with a roar of assent, but before he could give the brood-mare to Eumelus, Antilochus entered a protest: 'My lord Achilles, if you do that, I will be furious. Granted, he is a good driver; granted, he was unfortunate in breaking his yoke. Yet a timely prayer to an Immortal would have saved him from finishing fifth. Since he stands so high in your esteem, why not award him a worthy consolation prize? Your store-huts are bursting with treasure: gold, bronze, fast horses, attractive women-slaves. The sooner you offer him something valuable, the louder your comrades' applause. But nobody save myself shall lead away that mare; I will fight whoever attempts it.'

Achilles smiled, recognizing a kindred spirit. 'By all means,

Antilochus,' he answered. 'Eumelus shall have his consolation prize. What of the tin-inlaid bronze corslet captured from Asteropaeus? He is sure to appreciate that.' Automedon fetched the corslet, and Eumelus was overjoyed.

Menelaus' complaint had still to be settled, so Talthybius set a gold-studded wand in his hand, and called for silence.

Menelaus spoke: 'You used to be a prudent young man, Prince Antilochus! How dared you publicly humble me by thrusting your slow horses in front of my admirable team? I would ask these kings and Councillors to judge the case, without fear or favour, but that some people might afterwards remark: "Menelaus has brow-beaten the son of Nestor into surrendering his prize. Rank and influence, of course, secured him the verdict; yet, whatever he may say, his horses were no match for those Pylians."

'I shall therefore try the case myself, counting on this Assembly's approval, when it sees how justly I handle it. Bring your equipage here, if you please, Prince Antilochus; then face the horses, touch them with your whip and swear by Poseidon, Earth-Enfolder and Earth-Shaker, that you did not maliciously force my chariot out of the running.'

Antilochus replied: 'I ask pardon, my lord Menelaus! You are far older than I am, higher in rank, and a better man; but, as you must know, it is easy for a youngster to go wrong from hastiness and lack of thought. Pray, therefore, allow me to surrender the mare; and, if you need further proof of my sincere regret, assess the damages to your dignity, and I will pay them on the nail: to avoid either forfeiting your esteem or incurring the displeasure of Heaven.'

He untethered the mare and brought her over to Menelaus. The sequel was a complete reconciliation.

> As ripening corn is softened by the dew,
> So, angry man, let my plea soften you!

Menelaus' anger died. 'Antilochus,' he answered, 'I had never before seen you act irresponsibly, and am sure that this incident will teach you never again to play tricks on your elders. It would have been difficult for another Greek to make me relent, yet your whole family has fought well in support of our cause; and you have my free pardon.

Indeed, since you acknowledge that this mare is rightfully mine, she shall be yours as a gift; and no one henceforth will, I hope, dare call me vainglorious or unreasonable.'

Menelaus handed the mare to Antilochus' charioteer Noëmon; but took the bright new cauldron offered as a third prize. Meriones had won the two gold ingots; and, when Eumelus, content with Asteropaeus' corslet, failed to claim the fifth prize—a bronze urn—Achilles carried it along the ranks until he reached Nestor. 'Take this, venerable hero,' he said, 'and treasure it in memory of Patroclus, whom we shall see no more: a prize for which you need not compete, being already too old to attempt the other events: boxing, wrestling, javelin-throwing and running.'

Nestor gratefully accepted the urn. 'That is true enough, my son,' he agreed. 'I can no longer trust my legs or feet, or swing my arms lightly to and fro. Ah, that I were the man I once was: when King Amarynceus died and his sons held funeral games in his honour at Epeian Buprasion! Neither the Epeians, nor my own Pylians, nor the brave Aetolians could overcome me. I entered for the boxing match and flattened Clytomedes, son of Enops; I entered for the wrestling match and threw Ancaeus of Pleuron; I entered for the foot-race and left Iphiclus, a magnificent performer, far behind; I entered for the javelin-throw and beat Phyleus and Polydorus. I should have finished first in the chariot-race, too; but Actor's sons were so ambitious for victory, because this event carried the most valuable prizes, that they cut across my lane and crowded me out. They were twins, and took turns at the whip and the reins. Yes, that was a lifetime ago, and now I must leave athletic exercises to my juniors; age cripples even famous champions. Well, pray continue to honour the late Prince Patroclus with these games. Meanwhile, accept my gratitude. I am enchanted that you still think warmly enough of your venerable friend—I reciprocate the sentiment—to give him a prize which is no more than his due. May Heaven grant you all happiness!'

*

Achilles went back to his place, where he announced prizes for the boxing match. The winner would get a strong, unbroken, six-year-old mule (here he produced and tethered this almost untameable beast); the loser, a two-handled goblet.

Huge, tough Epeius sprang up. Laying hold of the mule, he shouted: 'Anyone is welcome to that goblet; but the mule must be mine! Though I may rank low as a chariot-fighter—no one man can excel in everything!—I have yet to meet the Greek who will out-box me. My challengers' comrades should stand ready to lug him away when he has been sufficiently battered.'

A deep silence reigned. Gallant Euryalus, son of Mecisteus and grandson of the Argive King Talaus, alone dared face Epeius. Diomedes groomed him for the fight: tightening his boxing-belt; winding rawhide straps across the flat of each hand; securing them at the wrists; and all the while giving him hearty encouragement. He recalled how, when Oedipus, the famous Theban king, died in battle, Euryalus' father Mecisteus had attended his funeral games and won every contest.

Epeius and Euryalus advanced towards each other. Both raised their weighted fists, and the match began. Soon they were sweating hard, grinding their teeth and going at it hammer and tongs until, at last, Epeius rushed in decisively. Euryalus, crouching to block his lead, caught a powerful uppercut on the cheekbone.

> This beach so virginal and bare
> Dark piles of weed now stain;
> The brutal north wind brought it there—
> But look, a fish leaps in the air,
> And then flops back again.

Up went Euryalus, and then down, just like that fish! Epeius amicably heaved him upright and let Diomedes' Argives return their champion to his place: feet trailing, and dizzy head drooping. They fetched him the two-handled goblet, while he spat blood from his torn mouth.

*

Achilles announced prizes for the third event: a wrestling match. The winner would obtain a large, three-legged cauldron, valued at twelve cows; the loser, a highly-skilled slave-woman valued at four. 'Competitors, forward!' he cried.

Great Ajax and Odysseus the Crafty accepted the invitation. Having donned boxing-belts, they came together and grappled; arching their bodies until they might have been a securely locked gable built to baffle the worst storm. Their bones creaked, sweat bathed their flanks, and bloody claw-marks scarred ribs and shoulders. Each had set his heart on the cauldron, yet neither could disturb the other's balance by any amount of tripping or shaking. Ajax, aware that the Greeks were already losing interest, gasped: 'Son of Laertes, no more of this! Throw me, or else I will throw you, and let Zeus choose between us!'

With a tremendous effort he lifted Odysseus from the ground; but, as he did so, received a heavy kick at the hollow of his knee and, to everyone's surprise, tumbled over backwards with Odysseus on top of him. In the next round, failing to swing Ajax clear off his feet, Odysseus crooked a knee behind the leg which withstood him, and heaved. Down they went into the dirt, side by side.

The match was stopped by Achilles. 'Desist, my lords!' he cried. 'Enough punishment has been given and taken, and the spectators have two other events to watch. Since you can both claim a victory, both shall be awarded a cauldron of identical size.'

Ajax and Odysseus were not sorry to wipe themselves clean and resume their tunics, while Achilles announced the following prizes for the foot-race:

'*First Prize*: an engraved silver mixing-bowl of Sidonian workmanship; capacity more than sixteen gallons, the handsomest ever seen, and valued at one hundred oxen. It was the Phoenicians' gift to King Thoas of Lemnos; but Euneus, son of Jason the Argonaut by Thoas' daughter Hypsipyle, bought Prince Lycaon with it from Prince Patroclus, my representative.

'*Second Prize*: an enormously fat ox.

'*Third Prize*: half an ingot of gold.'

Then he shouted: 'Competitors, forward!'

Great Ajax and Odysseus again rose, and Antilochus, the fastest runner of his generation, made the third. They crouched in a row, and Achilles showed them the turning-post.

At his signal they flashed away, each eager to establish a lead. Ajax secured it, but Odysseus pressed him so hard that the distance between them was no more than separates a weaving-rod from a noblewoman's breast as she draws the spool across her loom. Odysseus trod in Ajax's foot-steps before the dust had time to settle in them, and breathed hot against his neck. The Greeks applauded such courage and persistence.

As they rounded the bend, Odysseus prayed silently to Athene: 'Owl-Eyed Goddess, speed my feet!' At once she made them light as air, and his hands too. The rivals were spurting to the finish, when Ajax fell; because Athene tripped him on a patch of slippery dung, where oxen had been slaughtered for Patroclus' pyre; his mouth and nostrils got clogged with the nasty stuff. Odysseus consequently won the race and the mixing-bowl; Ajax, only the fat ox. He grasped one of its horns, spitting out dung and expostulating: 'A scandal! Athene lost me the race. That virgin goddess has always mothered Odysseus!'

A roar of sympathetic laughter greeted Ajax's sally, and then Antilochus crossed the line. He smilingly claimed the last prize. 'Friends,' he said, 'I call you to witness that Heaven favours elder men even in funeral games. Ajax has a few years' advantage of me, but Odysseus might be my father! A green old age surely awaits him, since none of us can yet outstrip him—the Swift-Footed son of Peleus alone excepted.

Achilles thanked Antilochus for his compliment. 'I will raise the prize to a whole ingot,' he said; and, what is more, paid him on the spot.*

*

Lastly, Achilles announced the javelin-throwing contest. His prizes were a long spear and a newly-forged cauldron embossed with flowers.

Two competitors stood up: Agamemnon, and Meriones the Cretan. Achilles therefore said: 'My lord, son of Atreus! We Greeks honour you as our greatest hero—one who can toss javelins so much farther than any man alive that a contest would be idle. Pray deign to accept the embossed cauldron; but, unless you care to take both prizes, let Meriones have the spear—though I do not insist on this.'

Agamemnon kindly gave Talthybius the cauldron, and left the spear to Meriones.

---

* Here follow eighty-five lines containing fanciful and somewhat tedious accounts of spear-fighting, putting the weight, and archery. Since Achilles does not mention any of these in his list of events, nor do they figure in Nestor's record of Amarynceus' funeral games, I omit them as spurious.

Book Twenty-four:

The Trojans Bury Hector

These funeral games being over, the various Greek contingents dispersed: every man eager for supper and sleep, except Achilles, who alone went fasting to bed. There he tossed restlessly on his side, on his back, on his face; and great tears blinded him at the thought of strong, bold, gentle, warm-hearted Patroclus, and their adventures together by land and sea.

Rushing wildly out of his hut, he stumbled along the shore and, as soon as Dawn gilded the Thracian coast, once more dragged Hector's naked corpse three times around the barrow, tied to his chariot-tail; then returned, leaving it prone in the dust; and still could not sleep.

Phoebus Apollo, however, had flung his golden Aegis protectively about the dead hero. Several other Olympians, who shared Apollo's concern, urged sharp-eyed Hermes, God of Thieves, to rescue the corpse from further spiteful mishandling. An inveterate hatred of Troy set only a small group against this plan: Hera, Poseidon and Pallas Athene. Hera and Athene could not pardon a verdict given many years previously by Hector's brother Paris, when they visited his sheep-farm with Aphrodite and asked him to judge which of them was the loveliest. Hera's bribe had been an offer of wide king-ship, Athene's an offer of glorious conquest, but Aphrodite's an offer of the most beautiful woman alive. Paris awarded Aphrodite the prize, and was thus able to seduce Helen; though he violated the laws of hospitality by doing so. Poseidon supported Hera and Athene: in his view Paris' behaviour was atrocious—King Priam should have refused Helen and her treasures admittance into Troy.

Twelve days later, Apollo rose in the Council Hall: 'Stern-hearted and bloody-minded colleagues,' he cried, 'did Hector never burn you any sacrifices—the thickly larded thighbones of choice bulls? Why then withhold the corpse from his unhappy relatives—Queen Hecuba, Princess Andromache, little Scamandrius, King Priam— and from his numerous comrades who long to build him a pyre and celebrate the obsequies in style? Why condone Achilles' unjust and unyielding attitude? He is no more capable of pity or shame than a lion among sheep—a trait which may enrich him, but which also robs him of his good name. Many who suffer worse losses than the son of Peleus—a brother or a son, for example—resolutely dry their tears after the funeral, because the Fates have taught them courage in adversity. Achilles should show the same moderation. He loses a cousin, his friend Patroclus and, not considering that Hector's fall is vengeance enough, must needs tie the corpse to his chariot-tail and drag it around Patroclus' barrow! How can such barbarity benefit him, or redound to his honour? Though a gallant fighter, he offends us by so outrageous a treatment of his dead adversary.'

Hera flared at Apollo: 'Lord of the Silver Bow, what a dishonest speech! Anyone might be deceived into thinking that the two champions were of equal rank! Hector was suckled by an ordinary woman; whereas I myself educated Achilles' mother, the Goddess Thetis, and gave her in marriage to King Peleus, Heaven's favourite hero! We all attended that wedding, did we not? Faithless creature, patron of evil! I well remember your own lyre performance at the banquet.'

Zeus called Hera to order. 'Wife,' he said, 'you should avoid such fierce attacks on fellow-Olympians! I admit the difference in birth, yet Hector was our favourite Trojan—or at any rate mine. He never failed to propitiate me with libations, and his sacrifices always smoked at my altar. I thought for a while of allowing Hermes to rescue Hector's corpse, but dismissed the idea because Silver-Footed Thetis, who has kept watch among the Greek huts night and day, would soon put Achilles on the alert if such an attempt were made. Send her here; I wish King Priam to ransom the corpse for burial, and Thetis can arrange his welcome at the naval camp.'

Iris immediately darted off on Zeus' errand, diving into the sea's green depths with a smack, somewhere between Samothrace and rocky Imbros. The waves closed above her, and she plummeted down like the sinker and baited hook of a fisherman's line.

Thetis sat in her grotto, surrounded by Nereids and lamenting Achilles' imminent death. 'Rise, goddess!' Iris ordered. 'Zeus the Immortal and All-Wise summons you.'

Thetis replied: 'So great a god and yet has need of me? Alas, whatever he says, I must obey; but, as you see, I am in no state to visit Olympus.'

She chose a dark robe, the darkest to be had in the entire length and breadth of the sea; and followed Iris' swift upward leap. They clambered ashore on an island beach, then flew to Olympus, where they found Zeus sitting in Council. Athene politely surrendered her own throne, which stood next to his; and, as Thetis took it, Hera with a pleasant smile brought her a golden goblet of nectar.

She drank, handed back the goblet, and listened to Zeus. 'I know, dear Thetis,' he began, 'what griefs are eating at your heart; but pay attention! For several days a quarrel has raged among us on the subject of Hector's corpse, held by your son, the Sacker of Cities. My family talked of sending sharp-eyed Hermes to steal it; and I paid Achilles a signal honour when I refused consent—though this was done, rather, for the sake of our ancient friendship. Now hurry to your son's hut and give him a personal message from me, with which he will doubtless comply. Announce the gods' displeasure at his denying Prince Hector's parents the privilege of ransom. I shall send Iris to assure Priam that all is well: he can fearlessly visit Achilles and bring home the corpse—provided, of course, that his offer is handsome enough.'

When Thetis reached Achilles' compound he was still moaning and groaning in the hut, while his comrades busily slaughtered a prime sheep for breakfast. She sat close by him and caressed his cheeks, sighing: 'Dear son, this grief will be the death of you! Why not try food and rest? Even sleeping with a slave-girl might be helpful. I cannot bear to watch your gradual decline, especially since I shall soon be left childless. But here is a personal message from Zeus himself. His fellow-gods are angered by your denial of Hector's corpse to the parents, and he shares their anger; so I trust you will not cross him.'

He answered: 'If Father Zeus commands me to surrender the corpse, naturally I obey; though the ransom must be enormous.'

During this conversation, Zeus sent Iris to Priam's palace. 'Down you go,' he ordered, 'and deliver this message:

> 'Out, Priam, out to the Greek camp!
>   Take splendid gifts in hand,
> And seek Achilles where he lurks
>   Beside the salt sea strand!
>
> 'Yet ride alone, poor desolate King,
>   Save for a herald true
> To drive a mule-cart through the night
>   And guide its team for you.
>
> 'Which cart two purposes shall serve:
>   To heap those gifts upon,
> And fetch away the ransomed corpse
>   Of Hector, your great son.
>
> 'But fear no deed of violence
>   When to the camp you go:
> HERMES will guide your chariot well,
>   And guard your life also.
>
> 'Achilles is less infamous
>   Than you presume; for he
> An honest suppliant will treat
>   With grace and courtesy.'

Iris found Priam lamenting in the royal courtyard, surrounded by a tearful group of sons. He had thrown a tattered cloak about him, heaping filth on his head and bowed neck. Daughters and daughters-in-law kept up a loud, steady wail, which the palace walls re-echoed, in lamentation for the many brave princes fallen on the battlefield. Iris' soft address made Priam shiver, but she reassured him: 'Courage, Priam, son of Dardanus! My message, from Almighty Zeus, will gladden your heart:

> 'Out, Priam, out to the Greek camp!
>   Take splendid gifts in hand,
> And seek Achilles where he lurks
>   Beside the salt sea strand!

'Yet ride alone, poor desolate King,
     Save for a herald true
To drive a mule-cart through the night
     And guide its team for you.

'Which cart two purposes shall serve:
     To heap those gifts upon,
And fetch away the ransomed corpse
     Of Hector, your great son.

'But fear no deed of violence
     When to the camp you go:
HERMES will guide your chariot well,
     And guard your life also.

'Achilles is less infamous
     Than you presume; for he
An honest suppliant will treat
     With grace and courtesy.'

Iris vanished, and Priam at once ordered his sons to harness a cart, and tie on its wickerwork tilt. Then he entered the high-ceilinged treasury, redolent of cedar-wood, and summoned Queen Hecuba. 'Wife,' he said, 'a messenger from Olympus has told me to visit the Greek army and ransom Hector's corpse. What do you think of that? I feel bound to obey; besides, there is nothing I desire more!'

Hecuba lamented afresh. 'My lord King,' she cried, 'your wisdom has been famous both at home and abroad; but now you are being downright stupid! Visit that camp all alone? Confront the man who has killed so many of our sons? You must have a heart of iron! To beard the savage and ill-tempered Achilles is to court immediate death; he knows neither mercy nor shame. Stay with me, and let us mourn Hector here; for this was the thread that the Fates spun him at birth: to fall in battle and have his corpse dragged about by a mad-man. Oh, I would gladly use my teeth on Achilles' tripes, like the scampering hounds which make our son their prey! It would be a fit punishment. Hector met no coward's end: he died to save the men and women of Troy, scorning shelter or flight.'

'Croak no more, bird of evil omen!' Priam commanded. 'I am re-solved to go, and you will not change my mind. If the message had

come from a mortal—a soothsayer, say, or an omen-reading priest—
or from any other god except Zeus, then I should mistrust and
slight it. But, having heard the voice and recognized the face of Iris,
Zeus' courier, I must obey. And what though Achilles should mur-
der me? Once my arms have clasped Hector's corpse, and my tears
have wetted it, I too am ready to die.'

Priam opened several carved chests, and chose a dozen women's
robes—very beautiful they were—a dozen women's mantles, finely
woven but not too voluminous, a dozen blankets, a dozen heavy
white cloaks, and a dozen tunics. Next, he weighed gold bullion to
the amount of ten full ingots, and brought out a couple of bright,
three-legged cauldrons, four ordinary ones, and one magnificent gob-
let, a memento of the kindness shown him during his progress
through Thrace—the old King did not grudge Achilles even this, in
his eagerness to ransom Hector's corpse! Finally he drove the noisy
courtiers from the cloisters, shouting: 'Be off, snivelling rascals! Do
you lack fallen kinsmen of your own? Then why disturb us? Is it
nothing to you that Zeus, the Son of Cronus, has crushed me with
the loss of my noblest son? Ah, you will soon learn its significance
when the Greeks renew their attacks, and Hector can no longer de-
fend Troy . . . But may Death claim me before I see my city sacked
and burned!'

He rushed at the courtiers, swinging his staff. They fled, and he
turned his anger on the nine surviving royal princes—Helenus, Paris,
Agathon, Pammon, Antiphonus, Polites of the Loud War-Cry,
Deïphobus, Hippothous, and Dius the Arrogant. 'Make haste, my
sons! I should not have greatly cared had you all been killed in that
raid on the Greek camp, if only Hector were still alive. How Heaven
has cursed me! Your dead brothers were the best soldiers in my
dominions. Mestor, Troilus the Chariot-fighter, and Hector, a very
god among men—yes, his aspect was rather divine than human—
fallen and gone, and mere dregs left me: liars, light-heeled heroes of
the dance-floor, plunderers of poor people's flocks! Harness my mule-
cart, and stow this gear into it, for I am off immediately.'

Priam's rage startled his sons. They fetched a new, stout, smooth-
running mule-cart, to which they bound the wickerwork tilt; and one
of them lifted the heavy box-wood yoke, with guide-rings fixed to its

massive knob; also twelve yards of webbing. Then they engaged the yoke firmly in a crotch on the pole, dropping its slot over an upright peg; passed the webbing three times around the knob, and hooked it underneath. After this they stowed the ransom into the cart, and harnessed a magnificent pair of mules given Priam by the Mysians. Lastly, they wheeled out the royal chariot and yoked the royal team.

When Priam and his sagacious old herald Idaeus were about to drive away, Queen Hecuba blocked her husband's path, offering him a golden goblet. 'Come, my lord,' she said, 'since you wilfully disregard my advice, pour this cup of sweet wine on the ground as a libation to Father Zeus, and pray for a safe return! Address him as the Cloud-Gathering God of Ida—Zeus, who gazes down at the whole Troad—and demand an immediate augury: let him send the swift, strong, Black-Winged Eagle, whom he prefers to all other birds, flying on your right side; and thus convince you of his favour. If no eagle appears, I will repeat my warning: do not trust Achilles, however set on your mission you may be!'

'I shall cheerfully adopt your prudent suggestion,' Priam answered. 'Such a prayer would be most proper.' He dismounted, asked one of the ladies-in-waiting to fetch a basin of water and, when she brought it, rinsed his hands, took Hecuba's goblet, stood in the centre of the courtyard, and prayed:

> 'ZEUS, most glorious and most great,
> On Mount Ida holding state:
> Grant I may accepted be,
> Where we go beside the sea!
> But, my Queen to satisfy
> That fair IRIS told no lie,
> Let your swift, strong messenger
> Whom to all fowls you prefer,
> Black-Winged Eagle, take his flight
> Full in view upon our right,
> Heartening me at last to seek
> Mercy from that ravening Greek.'

Zeus instantly dispatched a Black-Winged Eagle, the bird of prey whose appearance provides the best and surest augury. His wings were wide as those of the closely fitting, heavily locked entrance gate that guards a rich man's mansion; and he soared high on the right above the city, heartening everyone who observed him.

Priam drove his team through the echoing archway, and whipped them down the street behind the cart. A horrified crowd of courtiers, all screaming as though he were bound for execution, ran after him. The Scaean Gate flew open, and both vehicles vanished into the gathering night; but Priam's sons and sons-in-law did not venture to follow.

Zeus saw the teams crossing the plain, and called his son Hermes: 'Helper God, since you enjoy escorting mortals, and are extremely sympathetic, pray guide the hapless King Priam to the Greek camp. I wish nobody to observe him until he gains Achilles' hut.'

Hermes quickly tied on the divine gold sandals that carry him over earth and sea as fast as the wind, grasped his magical wand, which he uses sometimes to enchant men and sometimes to wake them from sleep, then darted off. An instant later he reached the Hellespont and, alighting near the Tomb of Ilus, adopted the disguise of an elegant young prince with a downy beard.

Priam and Idaeus had reined in their teams beside the Scamander, and were watering them. The first to notice Hermes was Idaeus. 'My lord King,' he muttered, 'here comes a prowler! Either drive on at once, or else sue for mercy; otherwise he may hack us in pieces.'

At that, Priam's scalp crawled, and he stood as if paralyzed; but Hermes took him by the hand and asked quietly: 'Father, where are you bound? Why risk your life carting valuables past the Greek camp, even after nightfall? Two such old men have little chance of repelling an attack. But trust me to act as your escort. I could never injure anyone who reminds me so much of my own father.'

'Thank you, lad,' Priam answered. 'This is indeed a dangerous mission; yet Heaven has blessed us by sending a kind-hearted traveller across our path. To judge from your looks, you are the wise son of noble parents and will bring us good luck.'

'That is my desire,' Hermes said smiling. 'Now, pray tell me more! Do you intend these treasures for safe-keeping at some neutral court, or have you fled with them because your heroic son, Troy's greatest soldier, has fallen at last?'

Priam asked in wonder: 'My lord, whom am I addressing? And why speak so highly of my unfortunate son?'

'A shrewd question,' replied Hermes. 'Well, I often saw Hector fighting gloriously on the plain, in particular when he broke through our defences, killing scores of Greeks in his advance. We Myrmidons were forced to stay idle and watch from a distance, since Achilles had a grudge against King Agamemnon and denied us leave to enter the battle. I am one of his squires, and sailed with him in the same ship. My father Polyctor, the rich old prince whom you so closely resemble, has seven sons; we cast lots for service overseas, and I was chosen, though the youngest of them all. Tonight I am out on reconnaissance, because the Greeks plan a dawn assault on your city. Camplife irks them, and they are eager to end this war at a blow.'

'If I can believe your account,' said Priam, 'you may perhaps tell me what I dearly wish to know. Does Hector's corpse still lie in the Myrmidon lines, or has it already been dismembered and fed to the hounds?'

'My lord King,' Hermes replied, 'Hector's corpse lies in our lines untouched by hounds or carrion-birds, as whole as when he fell twelve days ago. What is more, no maggots have corrupted his flesh! I admit that every morning, at sunrise, my master drags him wildly around Patroclus' barrow; but, remarkable though it seems, no harm has yet been done! You would be astonished how clean, sound, and fresh as dew he looks—even the many wounds dealt him by my comrades after death are mysteriously healed. The Immortals must have loved Hector well, to take such care of him.'

'It is certainly prudent,' Priam put in, much relieved, 'to offer them the sacrifices they demand. If ever I had pious sons, Hector was one; and, although his doom could no longer be postponed, the kind gods are evidently showing their gratitude . . . Here is a gold goblet for you! In Heaven's name guide us to Prince Achilles' hut.'

'I am your junior by two generations, my lord,' Hermes answered bashfully, 'but you cannot force me to accept presents behind my master's back—I should feel frightened and ashamed. This goblet is surely part of the ransom? Nevertheless, I will guide you anywhere, by sea or land: as far as famous Argos, if necessary. And, should we be attacked there, it would mean that the Argives had failed to recognize me, not that I was despised by them.'

With these enigmatic words Hermes mounted the chariot, seizing whip and reins and urging the teams forward. At the camp, he cast a magic spell over the sentries, who were preparing supper; drove across the causeway, sprang down, unbarred the massive gates, and admitted both vehicles.

Achilles' hut was large. His Myrmidons had laid pine trunks lengthwise above one another, secured them at the corners, and thatched the roof with soft rushes cut in the water-meadows. A palisade of close-set stakes defended the hut; and three men were required to draw or thrust home the enormous baulk of timber which bolted the gate—though Achilles could manage this feat unaided. So, it proved, could Hermes: he drew the bar and brought the chariot in, followed by Idaeus' cart.

Then he took his leave. 'Venerable Priam,' he announced, 'I am the Immortal God Hermes, whom my Father Zeus sent as your escort! But, because it might annoy certain deities to hear that I have overtly favoured you, let me say farewell . . . Go into this hut alone, clasp Achilles by the knees, and plead your case in the names of his father King Peleus, his mother Thetis the Fair-Tressed, and his young son Neoptolemus. These may perhaps soften his heart.'

As Hermes flew home to Olympus, Priam left Idaeus in charge of the animals, and boldly entered.

He found Achilles at the table, after supper, brooding apart from his attendants—the brave Myrmidons Automedon and Alcimus, second only to Patroclus in his affections. Neither of these noticed Priam as he ran to clasp Achilles' knees and kiss the terrible, murderous hands that had destroyed so many of his sons.

It happens occasionally that a homicide has crossed the city frontier and sought refuge at a neighbouring court—how wildly then the courtiers stare to see this unknown suppliant diving for their master's knees! The Myrmidons felt a similar surprise.

Priam pleaded: 'Magnificent hero, I implore your mercy in the name of King Peleus! Like me, he is old and unfortunate. I fear that his subjects may be ill-treating him while you are absent, and that he has no means of curbing their disloyalty. Yet sometimes news comes that you are alive and well; he grows cheerful again, thinking: "One day Achilles will return!" Alas, no such hopes can sustain King Priam who, when your army landed, had fifty sons: nineteen by Queen Hecuba, the rest by royal concubines quartered at the Palace. They included the finest soldiers in my dominions, all of whom are now dead—the last to fall being the main buttress of our hopes, the acting commander-in-chief. Yes, Hector died at your spear-point in defence of Troy, and I am here with a load of treasure to ransom his body.

'Prince Achilles, honour the Immortals and, for the sake of your father Peleus, show me compassion! My plight is far worse than his, and I have done a braver deed than any man ever did: I have caressed the killer of my splendid sons!'

Achilles gently disengaged Priam's arms, and could not help weeping at this picture of his helpless father. Priam also wept, for Hector; soon loud groans echoed through the hut, because Achilles had once more remembered Patroclus.

Presently, feeling a little better, Achilles rose from his chair and drew the white-headed, white-bearded suppliant upright. 'Alas, my lord King,' he cried, 'how you must have suffered! Only an iron-hearted hero could venture out unescorted into a hostile camp, and there beard the champion who had caused him so much harm. Come, sit down quietly beside me! Let us forget our painful thoughts, if we can . . . After all, these endless lamentations are futile. I wonder why the gods allow us poor humans to lead wretched lives, yet experience no sorrow themselves?

'In the Palace of Zeus, Lord of Lightning, stand two tall urns, one filled with curses, one with blessings. Zeus, as a rule, dips into both of these when he orders a human fate; and should he by chance confer nothing but curses on a man, that will mean a life of scorn and want, of roaming friendless over the face of the earth, hated alike by mortals and Immortals. My father Peleus' nativity was blessed beyond others: he had good fortune, immense treasure, and the Phthian throne. The Olympians even gave him a goddess in marriage. One curse, however, plagued happy Peleus: that of having no male heir, except me alone, a boy destined to die young. Worse, I cannot now comfort him in his decrepitude, but must remain here, kill your sons, and waste your city! Priam, we know that you were once the richest king of this entire coast: from the swarming cities of Lesbos, founded by Macar the Rhodian, northward through Phrygia, and along the Asiatic shore to the Black Sea. Nobody could then surpass you in wealth, or in number of sons. Not until the Olympians sent Agamemnon's ships against Troy, did you learn what it meant to undergo a siege and watch your forces melt away. Yet show a becoming fortitude! No amount of tears and lamentations will revive Hector—or stave off final ruin.'

'Foster-son of Zeus,' Priam complained, 'how can I sit at my ease while his corpse lies unburied in your lines? Accept the huge ransom I carry with me, and let me pore tenderly on those pale features. May you enjoy these treasures to the full and bring them home in safety! Your conduct has been irreproachable.'

Achilles cast him a stern look. 'Venerable King,' he cried, 'do not bait me! I had decided to return Hector's corpse, even before you came, after receiving a personal envoy from Zeus: my own mother, the Goddess Thetis, daughter of Nereus the Old Man of the Sea. I am also convinced that some god has led you to me. Without divine aid nobody, however daring and active, could have escaped the sentries' vigilance or unbarred the gate of my compound. Oh, enough of this! If you provoke my rage, I may not even spare so aged a suppliant as yourself, but offend Zeus by striking you dead.'

Priam being too scared to answer, Achilles sprang like a lion through the doorway, with Automedon and Alcimus at his heels. He asked Idaeus to take a seat in the hut, and the three together unharnessed the teams and emptied the cart of its royal ransom, except a couple of robes and a closely woven tunic. Achilles then told some slave-girls to wash and anoint the corpse—though out of view, lest Priam might be tempted to bitter comments on its filthy condition, and he, for his part, might be tempted to use his sword. So Hector was once more washed and anointed. When the women had clothed him in the tunic and in one of the robes set aside for the purpose, Achilles spread the other robe over the bier and laid him on it. Automedon and Alcimus lent a hand as he lifted the bier into Idaeus' cart.

This done, Achilles addressed the ghost of Patroclus, groaning aloud: 'Do not be vexed, brother, if news reaches you in the kingdom of Hades that I have surrendered Hector's corpse to his old father! He has paid me a royal ransom, of which I shall duly burn your rightful share at the barrow yonder.'

He re-entered his hut and sat on a couch of exquisite workmanship facing the door. 'Venerable King,' he said, 'I have placed your son on a bier, under the tilt of your cart, and in a condition which can call for no complaint. You may drive him away at dawn. Now, what of supper? Remember the case of Niobe, a Theban queen whose six sons Phoebus Apollo riddled with arrows from a silver bow, and whose six daughters Artemis the Huntress destroyed in the same fashion: a prompt revenge for Niobe's boast that she was better than their mother Leto the Golden-Haired, who had borne only two children, as against her twelve. Zeus, at Apollo's request, turned all Niobe's subjects to stone, and the fallen bodies therefore lay nine days weltering in their blood. On the tenth day, the Olympians themselves buried them; and then, unable to weep more, the weary Queen broke her fast. People say that somewhere among the lonely crags of Lydian Sipylus, her father Tantalus' mountain—the supposed haunt of those Naiads who love to dance around Achelöius, God of Fresh Waters—Niobe still broods and weeps, likewise turned to stone. Follow her example, noble father; eat, and gain strength to lament your beloved son as you convey him to Troy. He will there be accorded the many tears that are his due.'

Achilles rose again and sacrificed a pure white sheep. Automedon and Alcimus, after skinning and jointing it, roasted slices of flesh on spits at the fire, and drew them off when done. Automedon then handed around bread in dainty baskets; Achilles served the meat. Priam shared this succulent meal and, when they had eaten and drunk enough, took stock of Achilles for the first time, wondering at his huge, strong frame and radiant good looks. Achilles was equally impressed by Priam's regal bearing and dignified manner. Soon the old king ventured: 'Kindly make up a bed for me, foster-son of Zeus, and let us both enjoy sweet sleep. I have not closed my eyes since you killed Hector twelve days ago—a sight that sent me grovelling in stable muck. Nor had I broken my fast until tonight.'

Slave-women bustled from their apartment at Achilles' orders.

Some held torches, others heavy rugs, coverlets, and cloaks for a double bedstead which Automedon and Alcimus erected on the porch. Priam and Idaeus would lie in comfort that night.

Achilles then said, with a certain rancour: 'My lord King, you would be well advised to spend the night outside the hut. If some councillor came for a midnight conference, as often happens, and were to recognize you, he might inform Agamemnon, who would certainly make trouble about the ransom. But tell me: how many days will Hector's obsequies last? I undertake not to resume the battle while they are in progress, and the other commanders may also abstain.'

'A general armistice, my lord,' answered Priam, 'would be most welcome. Since Troy is closely besieged, we shrink from any distant excursion, such as the felling of timber for Hector's pyre must entail. Mourning will last nine days; on the tenth, we burn his corpse and celebrate a funeral feast; on the eleventh, we raise his barrow; on the twelfth, we do battle—if you attack us.'

'Very well,' Achilles agreed, clasping him reassuringly by the right hand and wrist. 'Count on me to keep the Greek army in camp until the twelfth day.'

So Priam and Idaeus lay down, but outside the hut. Achilles, acting on his mother's advice, took lovely Briseis to bed with him in a recess of the living room.

That night, sound sleep held all other gods and heroes, except Hermes the Helper, who was thinking how to fetch his two charges quietly home. 'Priam,' he whispered, appearing stealthily in the compound, 'are you so simple-minded as to sleep here among enemies? True, Achilles has spared your life in consideration of a huge ransom; but if Agamemnon and his friends got wind of the bargain, they would demand three times as much from your sons for letting you go.'

This alarmed Priam, who woke Idaeus. Hermes helped them to yoke the teams, unbarred the gate, and himself drove Priam's chariot safely across the causeway, unseen by a soul. He left them at the Scamander ford; flying up to Olympus just as Day dawned.

Priam and Idaeus then made speed towards Troy, lamenting the corpse in the cart.

Cassandra, Priam's prophetic daughter whose beauty rivalled Aphrodite's, sighted them first. She had climbed to the Citadel and, recognizing her father, Idaeus, and her brother's corpse, roused the whole city with a piercing cry. 'Trojans, awake!' she shrieked. 'If ever you cheered Hector when he rode in from battle, gather now at the Scaean Gate and bewail his return stretched on a bier!'

Very soon every single man and woman had obeyed her. Andromache and Hecuba led the rush to Idaeus' cart where, hemmed in by a grief-stricken throng, they caressed and wept over Hector. This affecting scene might have lasted until nightfall, but for Priam's loud protest: 'Stand back, good people! Let the mules pass! I must get my son into the city, and then you shall mourn to your hearts' content.'

The crowd parted, and Idaeus drove up the narrow lane. At Hector's house his brothers sadly laid him on a carved bed, and dirge-leaders stood on either side. Andromache embraced her glorious husband's head, and began:

'Ah, Hector, fallen young and strong,
Your widow mourns you in this song:
Despaired because our only son,
This little, ill-starred, prattling one
Can never grow to man's estate
Before old Troy has met her fate.

'Now Hector's gone, who guarded us,
Alas for sweet Scamandrius,
And for all children, and all wives,
Who from sheer doom preserve their lives!
Fearful the horrors I foresee
When, captives, we have crosssd the sea:
My orphaned boy a menial
In some harsh-tempered prince's hall,
Crouched trembling at a slavish stent;
Else, earlier, from a battlement
Tossed by some bloody-minded other,
Avenging father, son or brother—
Truly your hand fell never light,
When out you strode, my love, to fight!

'In every house the Trojans weep,
Your parents' hearts are wounded deep,
But mine is wounded unto death—
I did not hear your last faint breath
Utter a memorable decree,
Nor saw you stretch your arms for me.'

Women took up the doleful melody, and then Queen Hecuba began a new lament:

'Hector of all my children
    Far closest to this heart,
And loved by the Immortals
Who fetched you to these portals
    Laid on a tilted cart.

'My lesser sons, Achilles
    Might sell beyond the sea—
To Samos or to Imbros
Or ever-smoking Lemnos
    In sad captivity.

'Yet with small thought of mercy
    He thrust the bronze in you
And dragged you round the barrow
Of one he could not harrow:
    His friend whom your hand slew.

'Here now in dewy freshness
    You take your ease, as though
To sleep, dear child, reduced by
A gentle arrow loosed by
    Him of the Silver Bow.'

Hecuba's song excited further tears from the women; and lastly Helen ventured on a dirge:

'Of all the princes in this land
    None other so befriended me
As Hector: he could understand
    How much I suffered, only he.

'Paris, my husband, cajoled me
    From lovely Greece, ten years ago—
Like twenty years the ten appear,
    They glide so miserably slow.

'Would I were dead! But not a word
    Harsh or unkind did Hector say,
Such as from all the rest I heard,
    Ay, these that mourn for him today!

'Priam the Venerable, indeed,
    A tender father is to me—
But Hector my ill cause would plead
    And gently chide their obloquies.

'Here, of his generous heart bereft,
    Let me make wail and cry Alas,
Having no kin but Priam left
    Who does not shudder as I pass.'

A chorus of groans greeted Helen's complaint, and then the king was heard shouting: 'Off with you, Trojans, to the hills, and fell trees for my son's pyre! No one need fear a Greek ambush; Achilles has pledged us an eleven-day armistice.'

Priam's subjects accordingly harnessed ox-wagons and mule-carts, flocked to the slopes of Ida, and there spent nine days collecting an enormous store of wood. On the tenth day, they built a tall pyre beneath the walls, and sorrowfully burned Hector's corpse upon it. High blazed that pyre, and when

DAWN, DAY's daughter bright,
Drew back the curtain of NIGHT
With her fingers of rosy light,

the entire population scattered wine on the hot embers. Scouts had been posted to give warning of a possible Greek attack, but none came. Hector's brothers and fellow-commanders gathered his clean white bones, weeping unrestrainedly as they wrapped soft purple tissue about them, and placed them in a golden urn. After digging a shallow grave for the urn, and laying a pavement of flag-stones over it, they heaped his heroic barrow. That done, everybody went off to a memorable banquet at King Priam's Palace.

So ended the funeral rites of Hector the Horse-Tamer.

THE STORY OF PENGUIN CLASSICS

Before 1946 . . . "Classics" are mainly the domain of academics and students; readable editions for everyone else are almost unheard of. This all changes when a little-known classicist, E. V. Rieu, presents Penguin founder Allen Lane with the translation of Homer's *Odyssey* that he has been working on in his spare time.

1946 Penguin Classics debuts with *The Odyssey,* which promptly sells three million copies. Suddenly, classics are no longer for the privileged few.

1950s Rieu, now series editor, turns to professional writers for the best modern, readable translations, including Dorothy L. Sayers's *Inferno* and Robert Graves's unexpurgated *Twelve Caesars.*

1960s The Classics are given the distinctive black covers that have remained a constant throughout the life of the series. Rieu retires in 1964, hailing the Penguin Classics list as "the greatest educative force of the twentieth century."

1970s A new generation of translators swells the Penguin Classics ranks, introducing readers of English to classics of world literature from more than twenty languages. The list grows to encompass more history, philosophy, science, religion, and politics.

1980s The Penguin American Library launches with titles such as *Uncle Tom's Cabin,* and joins forces with Penguin Classics to provide the most comprehensive library of world literature available from any paperback publisher.

1990s The launch of Penguin Audiobooks brings the classics to a listening audience for the first time, and in 1999 the worldwide launch of the Penguin Classics website extends their reach to the global online community.

The 21st Century Penguin Classics are completely redesigned for the first time in nearly twenty years. This world-famous series now consists of more than 1300 titles, making the widest range of the best books ever written available to millions—and constantly redefining what makes a "classic."

The Odyssey continues . . .

The best books ever written

PENGUIN CLASSICS

SINCE 1946

Find out more at www.penguinclassics.com

Visit www.vpbookclub.com

CLICK ON A CLASSIC
www.penguinclassics.com

The world's greatest literature at your fingertips

Constantly updated information on over 1600 titles, from
Icelandic sagas to ancient Indian epics, Russian drama to
Italian romance, American greats to African masterpieces

•

The latest news on recent additions to the list, updated
editions and specially commissioned translations

•

Original scholarly essays by leading writers: Elaine Showalter
on Zola, Laurie R King on Arthur Conan Doyle, Frank
Kermode on Shakespeare, Lisa Appignanesi on Tolstoy

•

A wealth of background material, including biographies
of every classic author from Aristotle to Zamyatin, plot
synopses, readers' and teachers' guides, useful web links

•

Online desk and examination copy assistance for academics

•

Trivia quizzes, competitions, giveaways, news on
forthcoming screen adaptations

•

eBooks available to download